FOREIGN BODIES

FOREIGN BODIES

David Wishart

CRÈME de la CRIME

This first world edition published 2016
in Great Britain and the USA by
Crème de la Crime, an imprint of
SEVERN HOUSE PUBLISHERS LTD of
19 Cedar Road, Sutton, Surrey, England, SM2 5DA.
Trade paperback edition first published
in Great Britain and the USA 2016 by
SEVERN HOUSE PUBLISHERS LTD

British Library Cataloguing in Publication Data
A CIP catalogue record for this title is available from the British Library.

ISBN-13: 978-1-78029-087-4 (cased)
ISBN-13: 978-1-78029-570-1 (trade paper)
ISBN-13: 978-1-78010-793-6 (e-book)

Typeset by Palimpsest Book Production Ltd.,
Falkirk, Stirlingshire, Scotland.

DRAMATIS PERSONAE

(Only those who appear, or are referred to, in different parts of the text are included.)

CORVINUS'S FAMILY
AND HOUSEHOLD

Bathyllus: the major-domo.
Meton: the chef.
Perilla, Rufia: Corvinus's wife.
Phryne: Perilla's maid.

ROMANS

Bassus, Curtius: Catellus's aide.
Caninia: Nerva's wife.
Catellus: governor of Gallia Narbonensis.
Claudius Caesar, Tiberius: the current emperor.
Crinas, Lucius Domitius ('Smarmer'): a doctor.
Gabinius, Quintus: governor of Gallia Lugdunensis.
Hister: governor of Gallia Belgica.
Nerva, Publius Licinius: Gabinius's aide.
Saenius Balbinus, Quintus: Hister's aide.

GAULS/BRITONS
Cabirus's family and household

Cabirus, Tiberius Claudius: the murdered man. Sons **Titus** and **Publius**, daughter **Claudilla**.
Cabirus, Quintus: his brother.
Cotuinda: servant in the Cabirus household.
Diligenta: Cabirus's wife.
Licnus: Diligenta's brother.

Quadrunia: Diligenta's sister.
Silus: Quintus Cabirus's clerk.

OTHERS

Aia: Titus Cabirus's girlfriend.
Anda: Drutus's servant.
Biracus, Julius: co-senior magistrate in Lugdunum.
Drutus, Sextus: a merchant from Durocortorum, dealing in hides.
Florus, Julius: leader of a Gallic revolt against Rome twenty years previously.
Laco, Graecinius: the Belgic procurator.
Oppianus, Julius: Cabirus's political rival.
Optima, Julia: Perilla's companion in Augusta.
Secundus, Julius: member of the Augustan senate, and Optima's husband.
Segomarus/Segus: a Burdigalan wine merchant.
Severa: Drutus's girlfriend.
Sulinus: a silver- and goldware merchant.
Tarbeisus, Trebonius: a jewellery merchant.
Vindus, M Julius: Oppianus's nephew.

ONE

The end of June can be pretty hot in Rome; plus, of course, at that time of year when old Father Tiber is stripped down to his metaphorical vest and underpants and there's more mud to him at the edges than water, the low-lying bits of the city are fairly unpleasant, odour-wise; which is why most people who can manage it up sticks and head for cooler and more salubrious parts. Me, I'm OK with the heat, and so long as you remember to breathe through your mouth when circumstances demand, walking around is just this side of bearable. Perilla, now . . . well, on top of the temperature and the olfactory aspects of big-city life the lady's always been the more outgoing member of the partnership, and between July and September when things begin to settle down again society's thin on the ground. A good time, then, for touching base with the family – adopted daughter Marilla, her husband Clarus and the grand-sprog, young Marcus – at Castrimoenium in the Alban Hills.

So that's where we were off to bright and early the next morning, with all the arrangements made barring the finer details of the packing. That's definitely Perilla's department; me, while it's happening I tend to lounge around on the atrium couch with half a jug of wine and let the lady and Bathyllus, our major-domo, get on with things between them.

Which is what I was doing when Bathyllus himself oozed in to say that a slave had arrived with a message.

'Is that so, now?' I said. 'Who from?'

'The emperor, sir.'

Wine splashed, and I sat up straight. 'You what?'

'A personal request.' Bathyllus's nose had a distinctly elevated tilt to it, and it had nothing to do with the drains: our major-domo is the snob's snob. 'He would be grateful if you could drop by some time today, at your earliest opportunity.'

Uh-oh; this did *not* sound good. Oh, sure, Claudius was a different kettle of fish altogether to his predecessor – at least, unlike Loopy Gaius of not-so-fond memory, he had a full set of tiles on his roof (so far, anyway; give it time) and he was likeable enough in his own right – but impromptu invitations for a cosy imperial tête-à-tête weren't exactly a regular occurrence in the Corvinus household. Not that I was complaining, mind; where mixing with the buggers at the top is concerned, I've always found that keeping your head well and truly below the parapet is the best way to make sure it stays attached to your neck.

I set the now-empty wine-cup down, reached for a napkin, and mopped my wrist. 'He mention what it was about, at all?' I said.

'No, sir. But I imagine, from the wording of the message, that it is a matter of some urgency. I'll fetch your best mantle, shall I?'

'Yeah. Yeah, you do that.' I hate those things, particularly in the summer months when wearing one is like walking through a steam bath wrapped in a sixteen-foot barber's towel, but turning up at the palace in a lounging-tunic wasn't an option.

Bathyllus exited, leaving me frowning: 'a personal request' and 'at your earliest opportunity' definitely boded. In spades. Still, I couldn't very well tell the most powerful guy in the world to take a hike, now, could I?

Damn.

I stood up, just as Perilla came through from the direction of the stairs.

'I'm sorry, dear,' she said, 'but if you were planning to take that old tunic you laid out on the bed with us you can think again. I've already thrown it out twice, and . . .' She paused. 'What's the matter?'

I told her. To give her her due, under the circumstances, the lady was distinctly unfazed; but then like I say Perilla's the social animal in the household, and if she and Tiberius Claudius Caesar weren't exactly long-standing bosom chums they'd at least had a nodding literary acquaintance before his elevation, and a summons to the palace didn't have the effect on her that it would've had when Gaius was running things. Nowhere near. Puzzlement, at best. Plus, given that we were practically en route to the Alban Hills, the barest smidgeon of annoyance.

'But what can he possibly want?' she said.

Bathyllus was back with the mantle. 'Search me,' I said, as he helped me on with it. 'We'll just have to wait and see. How do I look?' I gathered up the last yard or so over my left arm in the obligatory fold. 'Presentable?'

She regarded me critically. 'More or less.'

Grudging as hell. 'Come on!' I said. 'It's the best I've got. You gave me it yourself at the Winter Festival, and it's never been worn.'

'True, Marcus. But then it never ceases to amaze me how even in a new mantle you still manage to appear slightly disreputable.'

I grinned. 'Call it a knack.'

'Then it's one that you should not be particularly proud of. All right; make that "louche", if you prefer. You'll need the litter as well, of course.'

Bugger: swanning around in litters is another activity I can gladly do without. Still, she was absolutely right: turning up at the palace soaked with sweat and the accumulated mud and grime of a walk halfway across Rome wasn't an option. And at least the wine stain on the tunic was now decently hidden. I was just lucky she hadn't spotted that and had me change completely.

'Fair enough,' I said.

She came over and kissed me. 'Have a nice time,' she said. 'And give my regards to Tiberius Claudius.'

I sent Bathyllus to roust out the litter guys.

At least I couldn't complain about being kept waiting. Under the new regime – well, Claudius had been emperor for a year and a half now, so maybe 'new' was pushing it a bit – the imperial admin system had gained an extra layer of unsightly fat, and arranging an appointment involved filling out forms in triplicate and smarming your way past an endless succession of snooty freedman clerks. OK if you've got a few days to spare for twiddling your thumbs in antechambers, but frustrating as hell otherwise. However, right from the point when I gave my name to the hefty Praetorian on the door it was obvious that I was being given the full five-star VIP fast-lane treatment. The clerk detailed to look after me led me straight through the public offices, up the staircase to the private living quarters above and to the same richly panelled door I'd been through eighteen months before, when I'd had my little chat with that bitch Messalina. I just hoped that she wasn't in evidence this time around: cousin or not, emperor's wife or not, that was a lady I wanted nothing whatsoever to do with that didn't involve a ten-foot barge pole and an insulated pair of gloves.

The clerk knocked, opened the door, and stepped aside. I went in.

The room had been refurnished since Gaius's day. Cozy enough, sure, if your idea of coziness is a functioning office with a no-nonsense desk and wall-to-wall book cubbies. Nice collection of bronzes, mind, and considering where I was they'd all be originals.

The man himself was sitting behind the desk, writing. The desk was piled with book-rolls, plus a wine jug and cups that looked like they were permanent fixtures. He looked up.

'Ah, C-Corvinus! Delighted you could come so promptly,' he said. 'Have a seat, my dear fellow. I'll be with you in just a moment.' Uh-huh; well, at least he sounded fairly affable, which was a good sign. Not that I felt particularly reassured, mind. The clerk who'd brought me bowed and went out, closing the door behind him. I pulled up a chair that was as old as the bronzes and probably just as expensive and sat down while he finished what he was doing and laid the pen aside. 'You and your wife Rufia Perilla are well?'

'Yes, Caesar,' I said cautiously. 'We're both fine. Perilla sends her regards.'

'That's excellent. A cup of wine? It's not too early for you?'

'No. Not at all. That'd be great, thank you.' Damn right it would; I wasn't going to pass up what would no doubt be the best imperial Caecuban. One of Claudius's good points – or good in my view anyway – was that he liked a cup or three of wine as much as I did. Besides, I suspected that I was going to need it. 'Thank you.'

He poured and filled his own cup to the brim. I took a sip. Nectar, pure nectar!

'Now. To business. You're w-wondering, no doubt, why I asked you to come and see me.'

'Uh . . . yeah. Yes, sir, I am.'

'Perfectly natural. I want you to look into a murder for me.'

Oh, bugger. Bugger, bugger, bugger!

'Really?' I said faintly.

'You do still handle them, don't you? As a hobby, I mean.

Only I recall our mutual friend Marcus Vinicius mentioning it. The evening of my late nephew's dinner party when you and Perilla shared our table, if you remember.'

Uh-huh; the one just before Gaius got himself chopped. I wasn't likely to forget that little bean-feast in a hurry, was I?

'Ah . . . yes,' I said. 'Yes, I do. Handle them, I mean.' If that was the proper word for it. 'On and off, as it were.'

'That's m-marvellous. Vinicius told me you did when I asked him, but it's just as well to check up on these things.'

I took another mouthful of the Caecuban, said nothing, and tried to look eager.

'It happened just under a month ago, in Lugdunum. The victim was a Gallic chappie by the name of Cabirus. Tiberius Claudius Cabirus.' He took another large swallow of wine and topped up the cup. 'His father had the citizenship from mine when he was governor there shortly before the D-Divine Augustus passed over.'

Maybe I'd misheard. At least, I hoped I had. 'I'm sorry, Caesar,' I said carefully. 'You said "Lugdunum", right?'

'You know it? Charming place, quite delightful. Of course, I was born there, so I'm b-bound to be a little biased.'

'That'd be, ah, Lugdunum in Gaul, yes?'

'Naturally; where else would it be? Cabirus was one of the town's leading citizens.'

Oh, hell.

'So this would, like, involve me in actually going there?' I said carefully. 'To Lugdunum. Over in, ah, Gaul.'

'Well, Corvinus, it might be a little difficult m-managing things otherwise, mightn't it?' He must've noticed the look on my face. 'Oh, my dear fellow, do forgive me! I'm not a tyrant! If you're b-busy at present with other things then you only have to say. I'll understand completely.'

Yeah. Right. And I was Cleopatra's grandmother.

Fuck.

'Only it would be a great pity. A very great pity. Vinicius said you'd had p-plenty of experience in this sort of thing, and that you'd be absolutely perfect for the job.'

Did he, indeed? Fuck again. Double fuck; I was screwed. Thank you, Marcus bloody Vinicius. With knobs on.

'Ah . . . no, Caesar,' I said. 'I'm not busy as such. We had been planning to go through to the Alban Hills tomorrow, but under the circumstances I expect that can wait.' It would sodding well have to, wouldn't it? Perilla would be absolutely thrilled when I told her. Even so, it served her right: Vinicius was her literary pal, not mine, and if he'd put Claudius on to me then it was only because Big Mouth had given him the information in the first place.

Claudius beamed. 'Excellent! I'm m-most relieved that I can leave things in your capable hands. And if you're already p-packed for travelling then it's even more fortunate. You can leave right away. Don't worry about travel arrangements; they're already taken care of.'

'I beg your pardon?'

'My dear chap, do credit me with a little consideration! I am the emperor, after all, and I do have some clout. There's a g-government yacht berthed at Ostia, ready to leave whenever suits you. This time of year, you can be in Massilia inside of three days. And I'm giving you – wait a m-moment, it's here somewhere.' He rummaged about among the papers on his desk and came up with a small, tightly fastened scroll. 'Ah. Here we are. I'm giving you imperial procurator status for the duration, as my p-personal representative.' He handed me the scroll. 'All properly sealed and signed. I've already written to Gabinius, so he'll be expecting you and he'll p-probably already have done the needful at his end, but it's as well to be sure. In any case, show that to any official in the three provinces, Roman or local, of any rank, and he'll fall over himself to be helpful.'

'Gabinius?'

'Quintus Gabinius. The Lugdunensis governor. Solid chap, first rate at his job. You'll like him.'

Gods, we were moving in high society here, right enough: personal use of a government yacht and imperial procurator status, no less. Pressured into it or not, I couldn't complain that I was being short-changed. Which raised an interesting question. I tucked the scroll into my mantle-fold.

'Ah . . . if you don't mind me asking, Caesar,' I said, 'why should you involve yourself here?'

'I beg your pardon?'

'Well, OK, presumably, given his name, this Claudius Cabirus was a client of your family, yes? A current one, I mean?'

'Naturally.'

'Still, for you to go to all this trouble just for a client he must've been special in some other kind of way, right?'

'No.' Claudius picked up a book-roll that had fallen off the desk. 'No, not at all. As I said he was an important man locally – in fact, I understand he was to be officiating priest at the opening ceremony for this year's Gallic Assembly – but he was of no great importance in the grand scheme of things. Certainly not political importance, if that's what you mean. In fact he was a p-perfectly ordinary middle-class merchant. A wine-shipper. Quite prosperous in Gallic terms, but not what we'd call particularly rich.'

'Then I'm sorry, but I don't understand your interest.'

'Oh, the answer's simple enough, my dear fellow. Call it a personal debt, if you like. A very long-standing one, in fact.'

'"Debt"?'

'Two years before I was born, his father saved mine from a very unpleasant death in what is now Treveran Augusta; which, incidentally, is where the family is from, originally. P-pulled him in the nick of time from in front of the horns of a dozen bulls that had escaped from the local slaughterhouse. Hence the personal debt aspect of things.' He smiled. 'If it hadn't been for the Cabiri, Rome would not now be experiencing the inestimable p-pleasure of having me for emperor. We – my mother, while she was alive, and I – have kept a grateful eye on the family ever since.'

'Fair enough.' Well, it made a change to have an emperor who took his debts seriously. Inherited ones, what was more. 'So. What can you tell me, sir? About the murder itself, I mean.'

'Very little, I'm afraid. Only what Gabinius put in his report, which wasn't much. He was killed at his home, as I said just short of a month ago. Stabbed through the heart while he was taking his after-lunch nap.'

'He have a family?'

'A wife – Diligenta, her name is; two grown-up sons and a daughter.'

'Any particular enemies?'

'Not that I know of. Certainly Gabinius didn't say, but then I w-wouldn't have expected him to, not in an everyday official report. Nor indeed to go into things to that length, particularly just now with all the preparations for the British campaign. His mention of the death was more in the nature of a postscript than anything else.'

Yeah, fair enough. Provincial governors were busy men at the best of times, and although the guy probably wouldn't be directly involved militarily with Claudius's upcoming plans to expand the empire, he'd have his share of the bread-and-butter side of things to see to. Major military campaigns involve a lot in the way of extra-to-the-norm supplies and equipment; it all has to come from somewhere, and finding that 'somewhere' is a governor's job. Gabinius just wouldn't have the time to spend on a simple murder, of an imperial protégé or not, nor would he have the staff to delegate, and Claudius would know it.

Hence, presumably, me. Ah, well. It made a change, anyway, and I'd never been west of Ostia. Plus if I was travelling as an emperor's personal rep at least we'd be doing things in style; Perilla would enjoy the novelty. Which reminded me . . .

'I can take my wife along, yes?' I said.

'Oh, my dear fellow, but of course you can! Take whoever you like, within reason. In fact, I was going to suggest it myself. Rufia Perilla will enjoy the trip immensely. Not a p-particularly interesting place, Gaul, outside the old Province, a bit rough and ready, but as I said Lugdunum is charming. Make sure you sample the local wine, too. Very respectable indeed, on its home ground, and I speak from experience.'

'Yeah,' I said. 'Yes, I'll definitely do that.'

'Jolly good.' Claudius beamed and picked up his pen. 'Oh, I almost forgot. Nothing to do with your mission, but you'll have a travelling companion. I thought that since everything will be laid on transport-wise as far as Lugdunum I might as well kill two birds with one stone.'

'Oh?' I said. 'And who's that?'

'One of my own people, a doctor by the name of Lucius Domitius Crinas. I'm sending him to make a survey of the medicinal hot springs near the German border, with a view to developing them for the use of the legions stationed there. After

you reach Lugdunum he'll be carrying on to Moguntiacum, where
the Fourteenth Gemina and Fourteenth Gallica are based.'

Bugger! My son-in-law Clarus aside, doctors I can do without,
particularly on long journeys like this would be. Still, the person
making the arrangements being a ruling emperor, there wasn't a
lot I could do about it. And you never knew; like Clarus, the guy
might buck the trend and turn out to be OK company. We'd have
to wait and see.

It'd only be as far as Lugdunum, anyway.

Claudius reached for his writing tablet. 'Well, that's about it,'
he said. 'There's n-nothing more to be said, really. Certainly no
more information I can give you. So unless you have any questions
yourself . . .'

I could recognize a polite dismissal when I heard one. I stood up.

'Not at the moment,' I said. 'Thank you, Caesar.'

'Oh, tush, tush! What for? You're the one doing the favour, my
dear chap. Thank *you*, and good luck to you. And of course you'll
tell me how things went when you get back. We'll have you round
to dinner, you and Perilla. A quiet family dinner, not one of those
silly big affairs like the last time. Messalina will be delighted.'

Yeah, I'd just bet she would; skeleton at the feast wouldn't be
the half of it. And it wasn't something I was particularly looking
forward to, either. I said nothing.

He stretched out his hand, and I shook it.

'Thank you again, Valerius Corvinus,' he said. 'Do give Perilla
my very best regards. And have a p-pleasant and successful journey.'

I left.

So much for that. Now all I had to do was break the glad news
to the lady that her holiday arrangements were shot to hell.

TWO

Actually, it wasn't quite as bad as I'd thought it'd be; quite
the reverse in fact. Which was fair enough, really:
Castrimoenium wasn't exactly just down the road, but
the trip only took a few hours even travelling by coach, and we

saw the kids often enough one way or the other during the rest of the year to make missing one visit no great deal. Besides, there was the novelty of the thing: like I say, we'd never been anywhere that side of the Pond before, and the lady is always ready to broaden her touristic horizons. The fact that we'd be travelling first class at government expense could've had something to do with it as well, mind.

So I sent a skivvy down to Clarus's and Marilla's to explain, and just before dawn the next morning we set off in the coach and luggage-cart for Ostia; the 'we' being the two of us, Perilla's maid Phryne, and Bathyllus. Oh, sure, no doubt everything would be laid on where we were going, bought help included, but I couldn't do him out of the chance to brag that he was buttling for an imperial procurator, however temporary the job happened to be. Besides, it'd give the little guy a well-deserved break and let him see a bit of the world. Meton, though, was another matter; shit-hot chef though he might be, the joys of sharing that surly anarchic bugger's company all the way to Lugdunum and back was a pleasure I could do without. Besides, it'd probably only lead to trouble: wherever we'd be putting up, the chances were the catering side of things would be well up to scratch, and given Meton's contempt for his culinary colleagues in general he was an international incident waiting to happen.

Like Claudius had said, the government yacht was waiting for us, which was par for the course: these things have to be ready to sail at a moment's notice, and because they're equipped with a full set of oars and oarsmen for use at need they're independent of wind. Fast as hell, too, given the right conditions. Which, according to the captain who met us on the quayside, we had.

'Wind's strong and steady from the east, sir,' the captain said, handing Perilla across the gang-plank as the luggage was unloaded from the cart. 'You couldn't't've asked for better. If it keeps up, which I think it will, we'll have you in Massilia well inside of three days.'

'That's great.' I edged cautiously after her; Italy, in the form of the quayside, was solid enough, but that was where reliability stopped. The captain put out a hand to steady me.

'You haven't had much to do with ships in the past, Valerius Corvinus, have you?' he said.

I grinned. 'Is it obvious?'

'Don't worry, sir, I haven't lost a passenger overboard yet. Particularly while we're still in dock.' Yeah, well, that was a relief. Even so, I wasn't taking any chances. 'You and the Lady Rufia have the aft deckhouse to yourselves, of course.' He paused and pointed. 'That's at the, ah, back, over there. You should find it very comfortable.'

'Your other passenger arrived yet?' I said. 'The doctor. Domitius Crinas, wasn't it?'

'That's right. No, not yet, but we're expecting him at any moment.'

I nodded. 'Good. Good.' It wasn't, but there was no point in being churlish. At least, evidently, we weren't being expected to share the deckhouse with him. Be grateful for small mercies.

The lady was already heading aft, and I followed her. She pushed open the door and went inside.

'But this is lovely, Marcus!' she said. 'A proper room!'

Yeah; I had to admit that it was a lot more swish than I'd expected, and that was putting it mildly: despite what I'd said to the captain, we'd done our share of travelling by sea, and although we'd bunked down in deckhouses before – you could get them, or a share of them, usually, if you paid a whopping surcharge on top of your passage money, which was essentially a bribe for the captain to move out – this one had them all beat, hands down. Which again, I suppose, was par for the course given that this was a yacht purpose-built for transporting VIPs, and you couldn't expect these guys and girls to slum it like ordinary mortals, let alone bed down under an awning in the scuppers as usually happened when you shipped on a merchantman. The room was much bigger, for a start, big enough for two bunks, a small table with a couple of couches and a dressing table to be squeezed into the floor space without looking too embarrassed about it, plus shelves for storage fixed to the walls. I was impressed.

'Look, dear.' Perilla reached up to the sliding panel above and between the two bunks. 'We even have a window.'

She slid it aside. Sure enough, you could see the line of the quay through the space it left. Very handy, although a bit too small and far above the ground to throw up through when the time came. Which, personally and from grim experience, I'd say was the prime purpose of a window on board ship. Me, I was more interested in what was on the table: a silver wine decanter with matching cups and some cold nibbles and fruit. Yet further proof that your ordinary bog-standard merchantman this definitely wasn't.

I lay down on one of the couches, poured a cupful and sipped. Not imperial Caecuban, sure, but a very passable Falernian. Claudius was doing us proud.

Bathyllus and Perilla's Phryne had just finished stowing the gear that we'd need for the trip and left to make their own bunk-down arrangements when there was a tap on the door and the captain put his head round it.

'That's Domitius Crinas come aboard now, sir,' he said. 'He says he'd like to introduce himself, if you and the lady are willing.'

'Sure,' I said. 'In here's fine. Wheel him in.'

And a moment or two later, he did. Lucius Domitius Crinas was mid-thirties, max, and he could have modelled for a statue of Apollo. Done it better than the original, what's more. I saw Perilla's eyes widen.

'Valerius Corvinus,' he said. 'Lady Rufia Perilla. I'm delighted to meet you.'

'Ah . . . likewise.' I held out a hand and we shook. It was like having your fingers caught in a vice. 'You want some wine?'

'Thank you, no. I don't, as a rule, or just the occasional cup, very well watered and taken with a meal.'

Oh, gods! This did *not* sound promising. 'You mind if I do?' I said, reaching for the decanter.

'Personally, no, not at all. But then it's not my liver.'

Delivered with the most disarming of smiles. Yeah, I could just come to love this guy, I could see that already.

'Rhetorical question, pal,' I said, filling the cup.

'Indeed, and I apologize. However, if you did want a professional opinion based on my first impressions of you as a physical type then I'd advise you for your own good to go just a little easier on the sauce.'

Perilla gave a muffled grunt. I set the decanter down.

'*What?*' I said.

'Oh, dear. Now I've really offended you. I spoke with the best of intentions, believe me. Forget that I did so.'

Yeah, well, if he was running for Best Travelling Companion of the Year he'd blown his chances all over the shop right from the outset. 'And what might those impressions be, exactly?' I said. 'Just out of interest, you understand.'

'You really want to know?'

'I really want to know. Humour me. No pun intended.'

'Then from your colour and general condition I'd diagnose an excess of yellow bile produced by a derangement of the liver, which excessive consumption of wine can only aggravate. Your behaviour, from what I've seen of it so far, confirms this. You find yourself prone to bouts of anger. You tend to be peevish and irritable with very little provocation. You—'

'Now listen, friend!'

'You are, in fact, a classic bilious subject. You have problems with excess wind, don't you?'

'The only excess wind around here is—'

Which was when the captain put his head round the door again.

'We're about to cast off, lady and gentlemen,' he said. 'If you'd like to come on deck.'

'I think that's an excellent idea,' Perilla said brightly. 'Don't you, Marcus?'

'Uh . . . yeah. Yeah, all right.' I glared at our co-passenger, who gave me a sunny smile back. 'We may as well.'

Evidently this trip was going to be fun, fun, fun. If some god had made me the offer, I'd even have been willing to swap the bastard for Meton.

They untied the yacht and we left in style. At a fair rate of knots, too. Even when she's well up to speed, with the wind at her back, your average merchantman will roll like a pig in muck; the *Leucothea* – that was the yacht's name – most emphatically didn't; forget the pig, think greyhound, and one after a hare, at that. Like the captain had said, it was a perfect day for sailing: a brisk breeze from behind us, with the result that we creamed along at a rate that would've left even your well-above-average merchantman standing. It was like being perched on top of a racehorse, with the difference that you didn't have to hold on for dear life to the bloody thing's mane. Me, I'm no sailor, not even the fair-weather sort; the first pitch, and I'm heaving my guts out. With the *Leucothea*, I didn't feel so much as a twinge.

Magic. Barring the downside of having to share the boat with our master of tact Domitius sodding Crinas I could even get to like this.

A few hours out, we picked up the dolphins.

If you're looking for just one thing that makes travelling by sea a pleasure – and otherwise your options are limited, to say the least – you can't do better than dolphins. Those things are brilliant; it's the grins that get me, like the whole world's a joke and they're the ones who are playing it. This time, there were at least a dozen of the buggers, half each side of the boat. They were keeping pace with us, slipping through the water like they'd been greased. I watched, fascinated.

Perilla came and stood beside me.

'You know, dear,' she said when after we'd been watching them in silence for a good five minutes, 'so far, for a change, as cases go, this one's turning out to be quite pleasant.'

'Don't get too used to it, lady. It hasn't properly started yet.'

'Pessimist.'

She was right, though, even so: again leaving Crinas aside, I'd had worse starts to a case than a cruise on a luxury yacht with a set of dolphins for company.

. . . at which the lad himself joined us at the rail.

'Marvellous creatures, aren't they?' he said.

'They're OK.' I gasped as one of them leaped clear of the water scant yards from us, shook itself in a shower of rainbow droplets, and plunged back beneath the surface slick as a knife. 'Beautiful!'

Crinas nodded. 'Did you know, Corvinus, that dolphins are the only animals, land or sea, that feed on their backs?'

'Actually, that's not true,' I said.

He frowned. 'Really?'

'You haven't been to many senatorial dinner parties, have you?'

Perilla choked. Not that it fazed Smarty-pants for a moment, mind.

'They're also,' he said, 'the most helpful of wild creatures where humans are concerned.' He turned to Perilla and flashed her a twenty-candelabra smile. 'You've heard, perhaps, Lady Rufia, how the fishermen of Latera go about catching mullet?'

'No. No, I haven't.' Gods! Was that the faintest smidgeon of a blush? And the lady had actually patted her hair! 'Where is Latera?'

'Some hundred miles west of Massilia, on the other side of the bay. Well out of our way to Lugdunum, of course, which is a pity since it would have been interesting to see the process in action, or failing that to talk to the locals concerned.'

'Yeah, well, you could always make the detour yourself,' I said. 'We'd be sorry to lose you, of course, but—'

'*Marcus!*' Perilla snapped.

'Oh, it's quite the wrong season.' I was favoured with the white-toothed smile in all its glory. 'Besides, like you, I'm not a free agent. I have a job to do.'

'Going the round of the local mud-holes testing the water. Yeah, I know.'

'Quite,' he said equably. 'Although I wouldn't exactly call the hot springs of Northern Gaul "mud-holes". Most have been developed as sacred sites by the locals for centuries, and a systematic assessment and cataloguing of their various healing powers will be of tremendous use where keeping our border forces fit and healthy goes. Not only the men, either; there is, to my certain knowledge, a spring near Moguntiacum itself where the waters are of sovereign use in the treatment of sprains and muscular problems in horses.'

'Is that so, now?'

'Marcus, behave yourself,' Perilla said. She gave Crinas one of her best smiles, and her hair another pat. 'You were saying, about the fishermen?'

He turned his back on me. 'The Lateran salt-marsh is a prime breeding ground for mullet,' he said. 'At the close of the breeding season the young fish pour in shoals down the channel which connects with the open sea, but unfortunately this only happens at high tide, which means that the local fishermen can't stretch their nets across it. Accordingly, when the rush begins, they go down to the seashore and call for the dolphins, who gather in a line beyond the shallows between the open water itself and the mouth of the channel and drive the fish back to where the men are waiting with their hand-nets and fish spears. Amazing, really, but as far as I know absolutely true.'

'Bollocks,' I said.

'*Marcus!*'

'Yeah, well, it is.'

Crinas turned, and shrugged. 'As I said, Valerius Corvinus, I haven't seen it happen myself, so I can't give the story my personal imprimatur. But it's well attested, and quite consistent with the creatures' nature. You're at liberty to believe it or not, as you please. Now if you'll excuse me I must leave you for the present. I have my meal to prepare.'

'Oh, don't be silly!' Perilla said. Gushed. 'We've plenty of food, and you're more than welcome to eat with us. Isn't he, dear?'

'Ah . . .' She was right about the food, certainly: Meton had packed enough pre-cooked stuff and sundries in the picnic hamper to feed a dozen people for a month. All the same, if I had to put up with this smarmy bugger's company for the fore-seeable future I'd rather it wasn't at mealtimes as well, if it could be avoided. Besides—

'Thank you for the offer, but no.' Crinas gave her another winning smile. 'I limit myself to a very strict diet, principally spelt porridge, raw vegetables and fruit, and I won't embarrass you by sharing your table.' He bowed slightly. 'Until later, then.'

Perilla watched him go to where, presumably, he was bunking down with his sack of monkey food under one of the awnings near the front of the boat.

'Well, I thought he was charming,' she said.

'So I noticed.'

She coloured. 'And just what is that supposed to mean?'

'You know perfectly well.' I took her arm and steered her back towards our cabin. 'You should be thoroughly ashamed of yourself.'

'*What?*' She stopped.

'As an exhibition of sheer, blatant flirting that took some beating.'

'Marcus, that is complete nonsense, and you know it! If anyone's behaviour was reprehensible it was yours. You were confrontational and boorish from the very start, simply because when you challenged him to give a professional assessment of you he had it right to a T. On extremely short acquaintance, what's more.'

'Oh, come on, Perilla! I've heard this Hippocratean guff before, and—'

'He was absolutely correct about the wine, too. You drink far too much.'

'Now just a minute!'

'In fact, I think that for the duration of this trip you should put yourself in Domitius Crinas's hands. It isn't often that you have someone of his obvious abilities in such close proximity, and you must admit he's a splendid advertisement for his own beliefs.'

Oh, shit; things were taking a seriously worrying turn here, and I needed to nip them in the bud right now. I took her by the arm again. This time we made the cabin, and I closed the door behind us.

'Look, lady,' I said. 'Read my lips. I have no intention of living for the next half-month or however long it takes to get to Lugdunum on spelt porridge and fucking raw carrots just so that you can suck up to Mister Perfectly Proportioned Bloody Smartass. Understand?'

'Yes, of course I do.' She smiled. 'Leaving aside your ridiculous aspersions, naturally. But there's no need to go to extremes. Cutting down on your wine intake would be quite sufficient.'

Bugger. 'Perilla . . .'

'We'll see what Crinas recommends. Meanwhile' – she opened the door again – 'I'm hungry. I'm going to fetch Bathyllus and get him to see to dinner. All right?'

'I don't see why just because you fancy the smoothie bastard I should have to—'

She leaned forward and kissed me.

'Jealousy, Corvinus,' she said, 'is a terrible thing. Especially when there's no reason for it. Now make yourself comfortable on the couch until I get back. Have a cup of wine. The regime doesn't start until tomorrow.'

Well, that was fair enough. After she'd gone I poured myself a belter of the Falernian and settled down on the couch with it.

Fuck.

I was up bright and early the next morning. We'd got another glorious day, with hardly a ripple in the water apart from what

the *Leucothea*, under her full spread of sails, was making herself.
There wasn't a smidgeon of land in sight, which surprised and
unnerved me a bit; most shipping, certainly the commercial stuff,
will hug the coasts as far as possible, or island-hop where the
trip necessitates crossing the open sea, even if that means, as it
usually does, that they take a much longer route to where they're
going. Imperial yachts, though, are laws unto themselves, which
is fair enough when you reckon that there's usually a good reason
for getting their passengers, cargo or documents to where they're
going in double-quick time. And the captains and crews are
naturally the best in the business: when the job description
contains points like, *May be responsible for the safety, well-being
and rapid conveyance of the most important and powerful men
in the Empire*, guys who'd lose themselves on a rowing boat
crossing the Tiber don't get very far in the selection process.

Not that I was the first one awake of the non-crew members,
mind. I noticed that Crinas was up on the half-deck, doing what
I assumed were his normal morning exercises.

Me, like most Romans, I've never understood the Greek passion
for physical exercise. Gently tossing a ball around in the palaestra
before a bath, sure, I can get that, although I'm not one for it
much myself, but sit-ups like our doctor pal was currently doing
– plural, and very much so – are completely beyond the pale.

He looked good on it, mind, I'll give him that. Not an ounce
of flab on his gleaming, tightly muscled torso or even the hint
of a pot belly. Bastard.

He gave me a friendly wave. Yeah, well, maybe Perilla was
right, and I had been a bit crotchety the day before. Plus, after
all, we'd be in his company for some time yet. Time for building
bridges. I went over.

'Good morning, Corvinus,' he said, standing up and mopping
the sweat off with a towel. 'Did you sleep well?'

'Yeah, not bad,' I said. 'You?'

'Oh, I sleep like a log. Always have done, wherever I am.
Besides, it was a wonderful night. Very peaceful, once I got used
to the creaking and movement of the ship.'

'You done much sailing?'

'Almost none. I spent most of my life in Alexandria, where I
did my training, and I only came to Rome four years ago. That

was the longest sea voyage I'd ever made, in fact the only one of any consequence until now. You've been to Alexandria?'

'Yeah, a few years back. It's a lovely place.'

'It is indeed.' He looked past my shoulder. 'Ah, Lady Rufia. You're an early bird by nature too, it appears.'

I turned; she was coming towards us from the deckhouse, dressed in her wrap. Gods alive! *Early bird by nature*, my foot. I hadn't seen the lady up and around at this hour out of choice for a long time. If ever.

Hmm.

'Good morning, Domitius Crinas,' she said. 'How are you this morning?'

'Very well, thank you.'

'I assume Marcus has been asking your advice as to how much he should limit his wine consumption?'

I glared at her. The lady didn't put off time, did she? Even so, raising the subject with the guy almost before we were within shouting distance of breakfast was a whammy well below the belt.

'Ah . . . no, he hasn't.' Crinas had the decency to look embarrassed. 'At least, not yet.'

'I'm sure he was working up to it.' Viper! 'So, what's your opinion? Medically speaking?'

'Hippocrates recommends no more than three cups of wine a day. That's Greek cups, of course, *kylikes*. Let's say the equivalent of four of ours.'

Shit! Only four cups? A *day*?

Bacchus in spangles!

'That, naturally, is the top limit, and well watered. I myself, as I said, prefer to allow myself only one. A cup of wine a day, taken with food, will certainly do no harm, absolutely the reverse. Hippocrates was no champion of total abstinence, and nor am I.'

'There, now, dear!' Perilla turned to me with a dazzling smile. 'Limiting yourself to four cups of wine a day won't be too much of a hardship, will it?'

'Jupiter, lady . . .!'

'Besides, I'm sure you'll feel all the better for it by the time we get to Lugdunum.' She turned back to Crinas. 'Have you been there before, Domitius Crinas?'

'No. Not even to Massilia. As I was just saying to your husband, I've never been west of Italy at all.' He smiled. 'To tell the truth, barring Alexandria where I grew up, I haven't been much to the east, either. Have you been to Gaul before yourself?'

'No. Neither Marcus nor I. We lived in Athens for a while, and we've travelled round the east a little, including Alexandria, but we've never been to the western provinces. I'm quite looking forward to seeing Massilia and Lugdunum. Massilia, of course, is bound to be worth seeing, but Marcus was saying that the emperor told him Lugdunum has its points, too.'

'Then if you don't mind I'll tag along on your expeditions. Assuming we're given the time, of course. And assuming that your husband doesn't object.' The smile was transferred to me.

'Oh, Marcus won't mind, will you, dear? He isn't one for sightseeing in any case. He prefers to lounge about in the local wineshops.'

I unclenched my teeth. 'Yeah, well, I'm not going to have the chance of doing that this time round, am I?' I said. 'Not on four sodding cups of wine a day.'

'Marcus!'

'Besides, once we get to Lugdunum I'll be working, and Chummie here will be en route to his mud baths.'

'I did say if we're given the time, Valerius Corvinus,' Crinas said reproachfully. 'It will naturally all depend on the travel arrangements the governor has made for us.'

'Right. Right.'

Gods!

THREE

We got to Massilia on schedule just shy of noon on the third day.

Since it's in Gaul you forget just how old and respectable, city-wise, the place is. It predates the province that surrounds it by a good four hundred years, and it isn't a Gallic city at all: Massilia is pure Greek, and has been ever since Phocis founded it over six hundred years back, making it just a tad younger than Rome herself. In fact, the reason we Romans got our greedy little hands on it in the first place was because the Massilians asked the Senate for help against their hairy-in-the-hoof Gallic neighbours, only to find that they'd swapped one lot of pushy barbarians for another. Who needs enemies when you can have friends?

So we are talking civilization here, with all that entails. Which unfortunately, unless I could put the kybosh on it pretty smartly, now not only meant my being dragged round a serious number of Places of Local Interest by Perilla but also having to keep a watchful eye on her squeaky-clean co-sightseer and possible would-be toyboy.

Bugger.

'We simply *must* see the temples of Artemis and Apollo, dear,' she said as the *Leucothea* entered the long inlet that formed the town's underbelly and led to the inner harbour, while the three of us watched her progress from the rail. 'Isn't that so, Domitius Crinas?'

'Oh, absolutely.'

'And then there's the statue of Pytheas, of course. That's supposed to have been done from life, by a sculptor who actually knew him.'

'Really?' Crinas said. 'Now that I did *not* know.'

'Who's Pytheas when he's at home?' I said.

They both gave me a Look.

'Oh, Marcus!' Perilla said. 'The famous explorer, of course!'

'Uh-uh. Sorry, no bells.'

'I distinctly remember telling you about him yesterday. He sailed as far as Thule, where the sun never sets and there are floating cliffs of ice.' Yeah, well, no doubt she had told me, but selective deafness is a trait that I've cultivated pretty assiduously over the years where the lady's more arcane interests are concerned. 'Honestly, you really are impossible at times.'

Not half as impossible as sodding midnight suns and floating ice cliffs, that was sure; me, I'd bet the old guy was either lying through his teeth or when he'd made the trip he'd been stewed to the gills first to last. Or maybe somehow he'd got his hands

on a stash of that *qef* the Parthians are so fond of sniffing
and was stoned out of his skull. But then sometimes Perilla and
rationality part company completely, and there's no sense in
arguing with her.

'Look,' I said. 'We're not on holiday; we're on a job here, or
on two jobs, rather. Massilia's no more than a stopover.' I turned
to Crinas. 'You'd agree, wouldn't you, pal?'

'Of course, in principle. But—'

'Really, dear!' Perilla frowned. 'Pushing on to Lugdunum
straight away can't be all that important if this Cabirus man has
already been dead for a month. And Domitius Crinas's hot springs
aren't going to dry up overnight, now, are they? I'm certain that
Tiberius Claudius wouldn't begrudge us a little sightseeing.
Particularly since it's our first visit.'

True enough, all of it. Particularly the bit about Claudius, who
was a fellow sightseeing, box-ticking nut if ever I'd met one.
Hell's teeth. Still, unless whoever was in charge here was
super-super-efficient, there was bound to be a little hiatus before
we headed off into the sticks.

I temporized. 'We'll just take things as they come, OK?' I
said. 'We aren't even ashore yet.'

Not that there was far to go. We nosed our way past the bar
of the inner harbour and docked at an empty stretch of quay. By
pre-arrangement, obviously: I could see what had to be a reception party of slaves with a young guy in a sharp purple-striped
mantle heading it.

The lads tied us fast to the bollards back and front and set the
gang-plank in place. I gave the captain a goodbye-and-thanks
wave, and stepped ashore . . .

Jupiter!

Yeah, well, I'd been expecting it, but after three days on a
boat it still felt like we'd landed in the middle of a full-scale
earthquake. I grabbed the nearest sailor's shoulder for support.

The young guy came up, hand outstretched.

'Valerius Corvinus?' he said. 'Delighted to meet you. I'm
Curtius Bassus, Governor Catellus's aide. Welcome to Massilia,
sir. You had a pleasant trip?'

'Yeah. Yeah, it was fine.' I shook, and glanced back at Perilla,
just in time to see Crinas, who'd followed me down and seemed

completely at ease, put his hand under her elbow to steady her as her foot touched the quay. Bastard. 'Very enjoyable, in fact.'

'That's excellent.' He beamed. 'The governor sends his apologies, or would have done if he'd known you were coming, but he's away on walkabout at present.'

'"Walkabout"?'

'Oh, I'm sorry. The judicial circuit. It's that time of year, I'm afraid.' He turned to Crinas, and the smile slipped down a notch. 'Domitius Crinas, isn't it? The doctor fellow.'

'Indeed,' Crinas said drily. 'The doctor fellow.'

'Jolly good. I'm glad to meet you as well. Now. Not to worry, gentlemen, we have everything in hand. You won't be leaving for Lugdunum until the day after tomorrow, and of course we have apartments prepared for you at the governor's residence. I've a carriage waiting, if you'd like to follow me. Don't worry about your slaves and luggage.' He snapped his fingers at the leader of the bought help standing behind him and pointed him to the gang-plank. 'Those will follow on.'

He turned to go.

'Ah . . . and this is my wife, pal,' I said. 'Rufia Perilla.'

'Mmm?' He turned back. 'Oh, I do apologize. I'm very pleased to meet you, madam.'

So; not one of Rome's foremost egalitarians, evidently, either where women or freedmen doctors were concerned. Not surprising, mind, because if he was one of *the* Curtii – which, as the governor's aide, he probably was – then he was from one of the oldest aristocratic families in Rome. And you don't get anyone more poker-arsed double-dyed, antediluvian conservative than that shower.

Perilla gave him a brittle smile. Yeah, well; fortunately, we'd only be here a couple of days, because any longer and I could see Curtius all-teeth-and-hair-oil Bassus taking the first-mentioned commodities home in a bag.

Crinas wasn't looking too chuffed either, which didn't come as any surprise. Much as I disliked the guy, my sympathies were all on his side.

By the time we reached the carriage – it was parked at the edge of the harbour area itself – I had my land-legs back, more or less. I handed Perilla in and clambered aboard, then with Bassus and Crinas in and facing us we were off.

The governor's residence, it seemed, was in the centre of town behind the market square, so we had a chance to see a bit of the place on the way. Not bad; not bad at all: broad streets in the Greek fashion with tidy-looking buildings, and although it was on the warm side the breeze from the sea meant it was cooler than in Rome. Quieter, too, and more laid back. Yeah; temples and statues aside – and it looked, unfortunately, as if there were plenty of those on offer – I reckoned I could spend a very pleasant couple of days here. I hadn't forgotten what Claudius had said about the wine, either; that I was looking forward to trying. Or at least to the extent that Domitius sodding Crinas's sadistic four-cups-a-day allowance enforced by the threat of being seriously Perilla'd if I didn't keep to it would let me.

The residence was in its own grounds, probably originally the private house of one of the leading families. The gatekeeper opened the wrought-iron gates, and we drove through, up a gravelled drive past clumps of boxwood shaped like animals and birds, trees that looked like they'd been there for centuries, which they probably had, a stretch of eye-hurtingly-green lawn, ditto, over which five or six peacocks dragged their tails, and a riot of bronze and marble statuary that I'd bet was half as old as Massilia itself.

So we were still getting the five-star treatment, then. Not that I was complaining.

'Here we are,' Bassus said brightly.

There was an oldish guy with a slave's haircut and natty yellow tunic standing outside the open door, obviously waiting for us. Bassus and Crinas got out, and Perilla and I followed.

'This is Bion,' Bassus said. 'The major-domo. He'll be looking after you while you're here.'

The guy bowed. 'Welcome, sirs. Madam.'

'Hi, Bion,' I said, making a mental note to warn Bathyllus that I'd dock the touchy bugger's perquisites at the first sniff of a demarcation dispute with the locals. We were guests, after all.

'And now I'm sorry, but I must get back to work.' Bassus gave us another smile. 'Things do pile up, you know, especially with the governor away. We'll meet up again for dinner, naturally; I'm sure the governor would want me to see that you're kept fully entertained during the short time you're with us, and I've arranged things accordingly.'

'Thank you,' I said. Hell's teeth; I didn't entirely relish the thought of what would obviously turn out to be an all-stops-pulled-out formal dinner party, but then if you're a travelling VIP, however temporary, you have to take the rough with the smooth. 'That'll be great.'

'At sunset, then. I'll leave you to get settled in. Now if you'll excuse me.'

He got back into the coach and closed the door. The coach moved away.

'If you'd like to follow me, sirs and madam,' Bion said, 'I'll show you to your apartments.'

The dinner was as bad as I'd thought it would be. Worse. Not the food, mind: Governor Catellus's chef would've given even Meton a run for his money. If Massilia is famous for anything it's seafood, and the huge platter of assorted lobsters, crabs, prawns and shellfish with its selection of dipping sauces that formed the centre-point of the main course would've had Meton crying his little eyes out. Still, when your fellow dinner guests are a pukkah snob like Bassus, a pair of middle-aged local worthies whose main topics of conversation are, respectively, commercial snail-breeding and collecting unusual cloak pins, partnered by their vulture-faced, over-jewelleried, fashion-fixated wives, an Apollo look-alike who picks at his food when he isn't chatting up your wife or giving you disapproving looks when you call the wine slave over for a top-up, and a nondescript little guy sporting what I was sure was a ginger wig, who eats like a horse and doesn't say a word all evening barring 'Pass me the fish sauce, please', by dessert time you're about ready to slit your wrists.

'Well, that was quite nice, wasn't it, Marcus?' Perilla said after we'd finally said our goodnights and retreated back upstairs to our room. Suite of rooms; this was the governorate, after all, and the Roman admin system doesn't stint itself.

'Maybe for you, lady, with Smarmer there all over you from start to finish.' I stripped off the party mantle. 'Personally, given the choice of a rerun or having my back molars removed I'd go for the teeth every time.'

'Come on, dear! It wasn't nearly that unpleasant! And Crinas was only being polite. He's very knowledgeable about Massilia, too, despite the fact that he's never been here before. Did you know that the original founder was given the land by the local king as a wedding present because at a banquet to choose a husband for the king's daughter she took a fancy to him and rejected all the official suitors?'

'No, actually that little gem has slipped past me, somehow. And I'm not altogether sure that under the circumstances it's the sort of story a young unmarried man should be telling a respectable married woman in private at dinner.'

'Listen to yourself! You prig! You complete prig!'

'Even so.'

'Just be grateful that he was distracting me from counting how many refills you had.'

Bugger. 'Two. It was two.'

'Four. I lied; I was counting, after all. That's one cup over our agreed limit.'

'"Agreed"?'

'Tacitly agreed, then.' She reached up and kissed me. 'It's for your own good, dear, honestly. And it's only until Lugdunum. For the present, at least. Truce?'

'I suppose so.' Shit! That *for the present* sounded ominous! 'But—'

'Fine. Now, we have a lot of sightseeing to cram into two days. Phryne should be in shortly to unpin my hair, and then I think we should get straight off to bed.'

Uh-huh. Well, I'd heard worse suggestions.

I wasn't looking forward to the sightseeing, mind.

That was scheduled for right after breakfast. We'd arranged to meet Crinas in the entrance lobby at the beginning of the second hour; I suspected that by that time he'd not only have wolfed down his spelt porridge but done a couple of hundred press-ups, jogged the circuit of the city's walls, and finished the thing off with a bracing half-mile swim in Massilia Bay. Sickening.

He was already there and waiting for us. Sure enough, he looked bright-eyed, bushy-tailed, glowing with health and just *bursting* with enthusiasm to get to grips with those temples.

Like I say, sickening.

'Good morning, Valerius Corvinus. Lady Rufia.' He smiled.
'Did you sleep well?'

'Very well, thank you, Domitius Crinas.' Perilla dimpled. 'And
you must call me Perilla, please. I insist.'

'Then I'm simply Crinas.'

Oh, gods! I suppressed the urge to put a finger down my throat
and bring up my breakfast all over the guy's size-twelve sandals.
'OK, pal,' I said. 'We'd best be off, then. What's the plan?'

Perilla turned to me. 'Now you're absolutely sure you want
to come, dear? You really don't have to if you'd rather not.'

'No, I'm fine. Wouldn't miss it for worlds.'

'I thought the Temple of Apollo and Artemis first, naturally,'
Crinas said. 'It's on the high ground overlooking the Lacydon.'
That was the long inlet that we'd come in by on the way to the
harbour the day before. 'Then down to the market square to
see the Pytheas statue, and if we have time carry on to the theatre,
which I'm told is a particularly fine one. If you're up for the
walk, of course, Perilla. It's a lovely day outside, and not too
hot.'

'That sounds perfect,' Perilla said.

'You're all right with that as well, Corvinus? Not too strenuous
for you? It might be quite a climb up to the temple.'

'I think I can manage it.' I gritted my teeth. 'You may have
to stop a few times on the way, mind, while I get my breath back
and adjust my hernia support.'

'Marcus . . .' Perilla murmured.

'We'll take it slowly. No real hurry.'

'Thanks. Much appreciated.'

We set off.

He hadn't been kidding about the climb, although Massilia
being the city it was we had paved streets most of the way. It
wasn't exactly cool, either, now the sun was properly up; when
we finally got to the temple the tunic was sticking to my back,
and Perilla, who while she's a decent enough hoofer when the
need arises doesn't do a lot of walking, was distinctly puffed.
Not that the lady would lose face in front of Pheidippides here
by admitting it, mind.

'Impressive,' she said, looking up at the pediment with its
Battle of the Lapiths and Centaurs.

'Isn't it just?' Crinas was doing the same; I noticed that the bastard was as cool and relaxed as he'd been when we'd started out. 'Primitive, of course, it's more than six hundred years old, but it does have a certain raw power. I'm not sure who the architect was, but the sculptures are by Dipoenus of Crete. They say he was taught by Daedalus himself, although I can't believe that, personally. I suspect that the choice of subject matter involved a bit of pawky humour on the part of the Massilians at the expense of their less civilized neighbours. Those centaurs do have a certain Gaulish cast to their faces, don't they?'

'Mmm,' Perilla said.

'And of course the matching pediment on the western side shows the Cyclops forging Artemis's bow and arrows. I'd say that strengthened the theory, wouldn't you?'

'Now *that* is extremely interesting. Yes, I would.'

The lady was positively purring. Shit.

'Yeah, well, it also strengthens the theory that most Greeks are smug supercilious bastards who can't resist showing themselves how clever they are, doesn't it?' I said. 'Present company excepted, of course.'

Crinas turned to me. 'You think so, Corvinus?' he said. 'Well, you may have a point.'

Not a blink; water off a duck's back. You can add 'thick-skinned and impervious to sarcasm' to that list.

'Shall we go round and see it now?' Perilla said. 'The west pediment, I mean.'

'Perhaps best to have a look inside first. Pay our respects to the gods.'

'Very well.'

Like there always is in those places, there was the usual gaggle of assorted purveyors of small domestic animals and birds destined for the ecclesiastical chop, incense-sellers, amulet-hawkers and food-and-drink vendors camped out on the temple steps. Crinas went up to one of the incense guys and bought a few pinches wrapped in a twist of parchment.

'The cult statues are supposed to be something else,' he said to Perilla, handing her the package. 'But I'd be glad to have your expert opinion on that score.'

Simper, simper, pat, pat.

'Something else other than what, pal?' I said.

Perilla turned on me. 'Marcus, will you *behave*, please!' she snapped. 'I told you, you didn't have to come with us. If all you can do is grizzle and snipe then—'

I held up my hands, palm out. 'OK,' I said. 'OK! But you two carry on. I'll just stay out here and commune with nature. Go ahead and enjoy. Take as long as you like.' Yeah, well, if Smarty-pants had attempted seduction on his mind – which he very well might – then Massilia's most-frequented temple at its busiest time probably wasn't the ideal place for it. She should be safe enough.

They went up the steps, and I settled down next to a cage of white doves to watch the scenery.

It was certainly something. We were high enough up to see right across the city to the countryside beyond. Which, of course, was the reason why the Massilians had built their patron gods' temple there in the first place, so it could be seen clearly from all directions. Mind you, if it'd been me I'd've factored in a decent-sized wineshop, preferably one with an arboured terrace attached; my tongue was practically scraping the marble, and my throat was as dry as a camel's scrotum. Not that I even thought about buying a cup of wine from one of the booths, mark you: I've got certain standards, and the rot-gut those places sell would take the lining off your stomach. Besides, there was this four-cups-a-day deal. I wasn't going to waste one of those on rot-gut.

They rolled back some half-hour later, in great good humour. Evidently the cult statues had been Something Else indeed.

'Ready to push on, Marcus?' Perilla said.

'As ever was.' I stood up.

'We'll just walk all the way round the peristyle, have a look at the Artemis pediment on the way, and then go on down to the market square and the Pytheas statue,' Crinas said.

Which we did. I glazed over while the pair of them discussed the relative sizes of triglyphs and metopes, the possible reasons for the lack of a frieze, and the proportional relationship of side- to front-and-rear column numbers in comparison with that of later Doric and Ionic temples. Believe me, you do *not* want to know.

We got to the market square at last; busy, but not heaving. The statue was on a large plinth to one side, decorated with dolphins, tritons blowing their conch-shells, and a band of frolicking Nereids. Yeah, well: if Perilla was right, and he'd done his exploring in seas with floating cliffs of ice, then given what little they were wearing it was surprising the whole gang of them weren't down with frostbite.

'There he is,' Crinas said. 'Pytheas the explorer.' He didn't look much to me, and if the sculptor had known his subject personally it wasn't surprising that his wife, given that he had one, had been glad to get shot of him for a couple of years, or however long the exploring took. 'You've read his book, *Concerning Ocean*, Perilla?'

'Of course I have. Fascinating.'

'And extremely relevant, currently.'

'Yeah?' I said. 'And why would that be, now?'

'Oh, Marcus!' Perilla groaned.

'What?'

'But naturally it is, Corvinus.' Crinas smiled. 'Pytheas was the first and only man to sail round Britain. Admittedly, that was almost four hundred years ago, but the topography and geography of the island won't have changed, and since the emperor is planning to add it to the empire, the material contained in the work will be invaluable.'

Fair enough. Maybe the old guy deserved a statue after all. If you could believe what he wrote, given the aforementioned midnight sun and ice-cliffs guff.

'So.' Crinas looked up at the sun; it was a smidgeon past noon. 'Are you up for the theatre, Perilla? We have plenty of time, assuming you're not tired.'

'Oh, yes, I'm fine. Marcus?'

'No, actually,' I said. 'I'm just about sightseeinged out for the day. You go ahead. We'll meet up back at the Residence.'

Perilla gave me a suspicious look. 'You're not planning to slope off to a wineshop, dear, are you?' she said. 'Because if you are—'

'Come on, lady! Give me a break, OK? It'll only be for the one cup.'

'You're sure? That's a promise?'

'Absolutely. Word of honour. I'll spin it out. Sit there, watch the world go by, like I usually do.'

'Hmm.' She was torn, and the suspicious look was still there, but finally the prospect of furthering her culture binge with Mister Perfect Know-it-all squiring her around devoid of grizzling and sniping won out. 'Very well. We'll see you later.'

I glanced up at the sun: still well shy of the seventh hour. We'd passed a very promising little wineshop on the way to the temple with a vine-trellised yard open on the street side, fitted out with tables and comfortable-looking Gallic-style wickerwork chairs. A good few wines on the board, as well, and mostly, from their names, local vintages. Perfect. And, as I'd promised Perilla, I'd only have the one cup, and spin it out while I watched the world go by.

Maybe life wasn't all that bad after all.

FOUR

I n the event, it was another two days before we started out for Lugdunum; a hitch, it transpired, with our transport, which turned out to be one of these big, well-cushioned travelling carriages that at a pinch you can bed down in if nothing better offers. Which, Bassus assured us when he turned up the next day to give us the news and apologize, almost certainly wouldn't happen: the road between Massilia and Lugdunum is a main artery linking the former with the German frontier forts, and there are regular government rest houses for official travellers, plus a number of fair-sized towns en route where no doubt the local gentry would be delighted to feed us and put us up for the night. Or at least would be in serious schtuck with the Roman authorities if they tried to weasel out of it.

So off we duly went, fast as an arthritic tortoise. Lugdunum is over two hundred miles from Massilia as the sleeping carriage trundles, which meant seven or eight days' travel, even allowing for good roads and a regular change of horses at the posting stations because these monsters, last word in comfort though they are, are the slowest things on wheels.

Me, I've never been one for travelling in carriages, even with a wine flask to keep me company, which naturally this time there wasn't. Oh, sure, the countryside we were passing through was pleasant enough – a bit boskier and less intensely cultivated than Italy – but you can get pretty tired of constant bosk, especially moving at a pace where you're being overtaken by everything going including the snails. And I wasn't going to get out and walk on occasion, either, which is what I usually do on long road journeys by coach, because it would've meant leaving Smarmer alone with the lady to work his wicked way. There's always Robbers to while away the hours, of course, but playing board games with Perilla is no fun, because the lady is shit-hot, and you're on to a hiding to nothing before you start. Taking on Crinas, I discovered, was just as bad: he'd creamed me in three straight games before I decided enough was enough and jacked it in in favour of thumb-twiddling.

I won't bore you with the blow-by-blow account, but in note form the journey went something like this.

Day One, to Aquae Sextiae. Veteran colony, hot springs, so Crinas happy as a pig in muck; ditto Perilla (ancient temple to the local goddess Dexsia. Don't ask). Put up for the night with stone-deaf ex-legionary First Spear who looked old enough to have fought at Cannae.

Day Two, to Arelate. Veteran colony again. Serious monuments, but Perilla banned from sightseeing on pain of instant divorce. Crinas went swimming in the Rhone River but unfortunately failed to drown.

Day Three, to Arausio, P. grizzling re missed sightseeing all the way. Yet another colony; Jupiter, how many of those things are there? Time out for hot bath; v. welcome because smelled like monkey's armpit. Hosted this time by sententious hypochondriac; C. prescribed powerful purgative to be taken with next day's breakfast and which (he told us later) should kick in an hour or two after we'd gone. Perhaps he has sense of humour after all.

Day Four, to Acunum (no, I'd never heard of it either). Government rest-house, at river crossing out in the sticks. Food terrible (cook possibly serial poisoner related to Mother's chef Phormio, or just incompetent bastard) so broke into Meton's picnic hamper – too late, in event, because harm already done; P. up and down all night, and not a happy bunny by morning. See next entry.

Day Five, to Valentia. Sudden and frequent stops in order for P. to disappear into undergrowth; possibly some evil-minded deity's cheap revenge for C's parting prescription. Luckily, Valentia major town so C. able to get wherewithal for anti-runs mixture. Lady unwilling to move outside sprinting distance from privy, so stayed an extra day with OK host who knew his wines. Wineshop – unmonitored! Bliss!

Day Seven, to Vienne; another colony, major crossing of the Rhone, and biggest city in the province. C's mixture pretty effective, because P. now bright-eyed and bouncy. Extra day's guilt-driven stopover for further recuperation, sightseeing (temples to Mother Goddesses, Sucellus, Epona, Mars, Juno, etc., etc. ad infinitum, ad nauseam), plus serious shopping binge; personally, glad to get shot of the place.

Day nine, mid-afternoon; Lugdunum at last, and about bloody time, in my view.

Thumb-twiddling over. Now for the easy part.

We wouldn't be slumming it, mind, because again, like in Massilia, we were staying at the governor's residence. Sans, it fortunately transpired, Domitius Crinas: one of the reception committee standing waiting for us was a doctor who was more than happy to put him up for the duration and talk enemas while they shared a convivial raw turnip dinner. Goodbye, Crinas; let's hear it for the medical fraternity's Old Boy network. While Bathyllus superintended the transfer of luggage to our private suite on the first floor, Perilla and I went for a relaxing steam in the bath-house before changing into our best togs – it wasn't every day you ate with a provincial governor – and setting off downstairs to tie on the nose-bag.

'You will remember to go easy on the wine, Marcus,' Perilla murmured. 'You've already had two cups since we arrived. I was watching.'

I stopped dead. 'Come on, lady! The agreement was only until Lugdunum. This is Lugdunum. Ipso facto—'

'Yes, I know, dear. But even so, I do think you've been a lot better for it these last few days.'

'Jupiter! Just because you're missing your doctor pal—'

'That has nothing whatever to do with it, and is sheer nonsense into the bargain.'

'Right. Right.'

'Besides, he'll be here for several days yet, until arrangements can be made for his onward journey to Moguntiacum. And if you're busy, which you will be, it'll be nice to have someone to visit the sites with, and who is genuinely interested.' Hell! 'I won't tell you again; you're just being silly. Now I'm hungry. Carry on down, please, and we'll go in to dinner.'

It was a big place, the residence, which was only to be expected because it doubled for the palace when there were any imperials in town. Fortunately, as we reached the foot of our staircase, one of the bought help was just coming along the corridor.

'Excuse me, pal,' I said, 'but where's the dining room?'

'Along here, sir,' he said. 'They've just gone through. If you'd like to follow me?'

We did. As we went in four pairs of eyes turned towards us.

'Valerius Corvinus! Delighted to see you!' Gabinius – obviously Gabinius, because he was in the host's place – patted the couch to his right. 'Down here, my dear chap. Make yourself comfortable. And Rufia Perilla. Pleased to meet you. You're next to Caninia, if you would.'

'I'm sorry we're late, governor,' I said, lying down and holding out my hands for the slave with the basin and towel.

'Nonsense, we're only just here ourselves. And you'll have needed the time to settle in after your journey. How was it? Reasonably painless, I hope?'

'Yeah, it wasn't bad.'

'That's excellent.'

The wine slave bent forwards to fill my wine-cup. Perilla gave a meaningful cough.

Fuck.

'Uh . . . just make it a half, pal,' I said. 'And top it up with water.'

Gabinius gave me a curious glance. 'Not a drinker, Corvinus? Well, good for you! I could do with cutting down myself.' He tapped his own wine-cup, and the wine slave filled it to the brim. Double fuck. 'Now. Introductions. We're a small party, as you see, but I thought we'd keep things informal. I'll be away on tour myself from tomorrow, unfortunately, but the young shaver next to you is my aide, Licinius Nerva. He'll be looking after you in my absence.' I half-turned and nodded to the guy: competent-looking, early twenties, purple stripe on his mantle. Top Five Hundred high-flyer written all over him. Ah, well, that was par for the course; you couldn't expect anything else, really, in the Diplomatic. 'Caninia there's his wife. She's been in post for all of six months, so if you're agreeable, my dear' – to Perilla – 'she can show you around the place, introduce you to a few people.'

'Thank you,' Perilla said; not that she looked too grateful, mind. Yeah, well, that should cramp Smarmer's style a bit. I gave the girl my best smile.

'My pleasure,' Caninia said. Not a beauty by any means, young Caninia, with a nose like the prow of a trireme and a build that wouldn't't've disgraced a professional wrestler, but anyone who'd be chaperoning our brace of culture-vultures around town and so inadvertently making sure that their conversation didn't stray down the primrose path of dalliance was on a winner with me from the start.

'Last but not least,' Gabinius said, 'our procurator, Graecinius Laco.'

Interesting; judging by the colour of his hair and eyes, the other narrow-striper was a local. Or a Gaul, at any rate. And the imperial procurator, no less; a real one, which meant that he was in charge of the province's financial side. High-powered company was right.

'Valerius Corvinus.' He nodded: stick-thin and dry accountant's voice, like it'd been pickled in vinegar for a year.

'So tell me,' Gabinius said while the slaves set out the starters. 'How are things in Rome?'

'OK,' I said, reaching for a pickled quail's egg. 'At least, the place was still standing when I left. Going pretty well, in fact.'

Gabinius grunted. 'I'm relieved to hear it. Makes a pleasant change. Not that I'm surprised, mind, not in the slightest; he's a good man, Claudius Caesar, and he'll do a good job. Plus of course, being an honorary local, as it were, he's popular here,

which makes our own jobs that much easier.' Turning to the
procurator: 'You'd agree, Laco?'

'I would, governor. Absolutely. Certainly much better than his
predecessor managed.' Laco frowned at a plate of chickpea
rissoles as if he suspected they might contain henbane, before
picking one up and dipping it in the fish sauce. 'If you'll forgive
me saying so, Gaius was a monster, a disgrace to the family. And
where money was concerned he'd no more sense than a flea.'

He made the second charge sound far more serious than the
first, which I supposed was to be expected in a guy for whom
money and its correct management were the be-all and end-all
of life.

'He was here in person, wasn't he?' I dipped the egg in the
sauce. 'A couple of years back.'

'He was indeed, on his way north.' Gabinius took one of
the little vegetable pastries. 'Setting things up with the Rhine
legions for his own British campaign. That came to nothing in
the end, of course, although it was sound enough in principle.
But I didn't meet him myself; that was before my time.'

'The man was a complete mountebank,' Laco said.

Gabinius chuckled. 'Now there, Corvinus, is your typical Gaul
speaking,' he said. 'Unlike the average Roman, they don't mince
their words in company. But I quite agree with you, Laco; we're
well rid of the beggar.'

'Actually, I thought he sounded rather fun,' Caninia said.

'Fun, my dear?' Laco stared at her, rissole poised. 'In what
way?'

'That auction, for a start. I mean, it did have its amusing side,
didn't it?'

'What auction was this?' Perilla asked.

'You didn't hear about it back in Rome?' Gabinius said. 'Yes,
well, perhaps you wouldn't; it hardly showed Gaius in a very
favourable light, and it was an absolute disgrace from beginning
to end. Fellow put together a load of old tat, worn-out sandals,
cracked wine-cups, that sort of thing, and auctioned it off in the
town square. *He* did, in person, I mean, if you can damn well
believe it. Forced the more well-to-do locals to pay through the
nose, what's more. That caused a lot of bad feeling, you can be
sure.'

I had to stop myself from grinning; yeah, that was our Gaius, all right, to a T. And I could see Caninia's point: Gaius might've been a monster – gods, I knew that from personal experience, didn't I just! – but he'd had a quirky, tongue-in-cheek style about him that made up for a lot. Me, I don't have much time for po-faced, social-climbing fat-cats, and I'd bet the great and good of Lugdunum fitted the bill just as well as their equivalents in Rome would've done. Bent over backwards to outbid each other, what's more, even if they did grizzle about it later. Gaius would've enjoyed himself no end.

'The money didn't even go towards the campaign.' Laco re-dipped the rissole. 'For which, of course, they'd already paid extra in tax. "Bad feeling" is putting it mildly. As far as the local community was concerned, it set relations with the imperial family back fifty years.'

'Oh, come on!' I said. 'It can't've been as bad as that, surely? Back in Rome, Gaius was pulling stunts like that all the time.'

Laco set the rissole down again, carefully. 'Gaul is not Italy, Corvinus,' he said. 'Let alone Rome. However Romanized we Gauls seem on the surface, we're a completely different people, even to your own Italians. Money – actual money, specie – is in comparatively short supply here, and almost unknown in the country districts, where people use barter. On the other hand, Rome insists that her taxes are paid in cash. For the ordinary Gaul, this is difficult; where do the coins come from? And the situation isn't much better for what you'd call the upper classes, particularly when, as they do, they try to match themselves with their Roman equivalents. They may be rich enough in land and produce, yes, but by Roman standards they have very little actual money, as such.'

Gabinius held his cup up to the wine slave, who was still standing behind him. Hell, that hadn't lasted him long! Although maybe presently I was just hypersensitive to those little details. 'Laco's right,' he said. 'The thing's a perennial problem, especially when there's something big going on and taxes have to be increased. Like the emperor's British campaign. Oh, we can keep the Gauls happy most of the time by pointing out that a large slice of what they pay in taxes is spent on improving things – more and better roads, amenities, services and so on – but they don't always see it that way. Even after almost a century, a lot of them view taxes as a levy on a defeated people. And, as Laco says, the margin's very narrow, even for what you'd call the rich. Especially for them, sometimes. If you have to find the extra cash at short notice all you can do is go to a Roman moneylender, and these bastards' – he glanced at Perilla and Caninia – 'forgive me, ladies, charge a fortune in interest. So you're in an even deeper hole than before, possibly one you can't get out of. Multiply that on a province-wide scale – three provinces, in Gaul's case – and you're dealing with a lot of unhappy people.'

'You're saying there's a chance of rebellion?' I said.

'Great gods, no!' Gabinius frowned. 'Oh, no, I wouldn't put it nearly as strongly as that. As far as taxes are concerned, at least, the Gauls are no different from any other provincials; they'll moan like hell about having to pay them, but when it comes down to it all they want is to get on with their lives in peace, so fortunately for us when push comes to shove then pay them they do, however hard that is. What you have to remember is that unlike some native peoples they've stayed tribesmen at heart, and that affects things considerably. Which works largely in our favour. I'm correct, Laco, am I not?'

The procurator nodded. 'Certainly you are.'

'How do you mean, governor?' Perilla selected a baton of celery and dipped it in the bean purée.

'He's no urbanite by nature, your average Gaul. Towns – never mind cities like Lugdunum, ordinary towns – are a Roman idea. For most locals the town may be their tribal centre, but that's all it is, a market-place or somewhere to meet for festivals. Not many of them actually live there, comparatively speaking; the bulk of the tribe is scattered throughout its territory, in farms or small villages. Which is why I and the other governors have to go on regular walkabout. The tribes each have their tribal leaders, descendants of the families who held the actual power before old Julius took it from them, and they still wield a huge amount of influence. Although naturally by now most are completely Romanized and part of the establishment: local magistrates, auxiliary commanders, even top imperial officials like Laco here.' He raised his wine-cup to the procurator, who grunted agreement.

'Conscious policy on our part, of course: because they're on our side, as it were, it means they make sure that their dependants – the tribe, in other words – toe the party line.'

'So what happens when they don't?'

'Then, my dear lady, we have trouble. Oh, nothing we can't handle, but sometimes it goes very close to the wire. Usually, as I say, when we have to lean rather more heavily on them financially.' He reached forward and took an olive from the dish. 'You'll recall twenty or so years back in Belgica, perhaps, Corvinus? The Florus and Sacrovir affair?'

Uh-huh; I did, at that: Julius Florus and Julius Sacrovir, both upper-class Gauls serving in the Roman army, had tried to start a revolt in their respective tribes. It'd been put down pretty smartly, sure, but while it lasted it had scared the wollocks off imperial admin.

'Indeed. And the cause was exactly that. Germanicus Caesar needed money and supplies for his German campaign, so he raised the local taxes. Then the money-lenders moved in, and the result for a lot of people was bankruptcy. It took the tribes involved years to recover.' He took a swallow of wine. 'Not the happiest of situations, as you can imagine. So now we're being just a little more careful over mounting the British business. As I said, unlike Gaius the emperor can command a great deal of goodwill in Gaul, and he has a lot more sense than his brother had, thank goodness. I always thought Germanicus was over-rated, myself, though it's heresy to say so.' Yeah, I'd agree, although 'overrated' was putting it mildly: if he hadn't been a full-blown traitor in himself, the bastard had been the next thing to it. 'Still, I expect my Belgic colleague is keeping a watching brief, as I am.'

'To change the subject, Governor,' Caninia said, 'what about this murder that Valerius Corvinus is here to solve?'

'Caninia!' Nerva snapped.

'Come, now, young lady,' Laco said drily. 'I hardly think that that's a matter for the dinner table, is it? Now isn't the time. You'd agree with me, governor?'

'But please!' Caninia said. 'It's the one exciting thing that's happened ever since I got here. I've been looking forward to hearing the details all day, and I'm sure Valerius Corvinus would like them straight away too. After all, it's why he's come, isn't it?'

I noticed that Perilla, lying next to her, had stiffened: Nerva's wife couldn't've been any older than our adopted daughter Marilla, probably not even that, and the two of them were evidently a pair. Up for the gory details every time, whatever the circumstances. Not an attitude that the lady approved of. Nor, by the look on his face, did Licinius Nerva.

I grinned to myself: young Caninia might be fun, after all. She was certainly no shrinking violet, and I suspected that, like our Clarus, Nerva had his hands full.

'In any case,' Laco went on, 'surely your husband has told you all about it already?'

'No, Publius claimed it was *sub judice*, or some such nonsense,' Caninia said. 'I only know what I've heard from other people, and that's probably all wrong. Governor, *please!*'

Gabinius hesitated, then shrugged. 'I've no particular objections,' he said, 'if Corvinus has none.' I shook my head. 'Or, of course, Rufia Perilla?'

'Oh, that's OK,' I said quickly. 'My wife's used to discussing murders over dinner.' That got me a glare, which I ignored.

'Very well, then. Just this once.' The governor smiled. 'At least, I hope it's just this once. Unlike in Rome, murders aren't too common in Lugdunum. Publius, my dear fellow, I think this is your department. And if we're all finished with the starters?' He signalled to the hovering major-domo. 'Trupho. The main course, if you would.'

'As you like, sir.' Nerva cleared his throat, and glanced at his wife: no doubt there would be Words later, in private. I knew the feeling. 'To put you in the picture, then, Corvinus. Claudius Cabirus was one of our most prominent locals, senior magistrate twice, leading member of the city council. He was going to represent Lugdunum as officiating priest at the Condate Altar ceremony on the first of next month.'

'So the emperor told me,' I said. 'That's a big deal, is it?'

'It certainly is.' Gabinius dabbed at his lips with his napkin. 'The summit of any local man's political career, in fact. The annual Gallic Assembly is the single most important event in all three provinces' calendars.'

'Anyway,' Nerva said. 'He was stabbed to death at his home a month and a half ago, the twenty-eighth of May, to be exact, while he was taking his afternoon nap.'

'Inside the house itself, you mean?'

'No. It happened in the garden. There's a small summer house that he used as a sort of private den.'

Uh-huh. 'He was married with two grown-up sons and a daughter, right?'

'Yes. His widow's Diligenta. The sons are both in their teens. Elder Titus, younger Publius. They're still living at home, as is the daughter, although she's off on a visit at present, I think. That's Claudilla; she's a year or so younger than Publius. Diligenta was the one who found the body.'

I took a sip of my wine: we had most of the meal to go, and with Perilla already crotchety I'd have to spin it out. It was good stuff, too, even watered to within an inch of its life.

'This garden,' I said. 'You could get into it from outside?'

'Oh, yes, easily. This isn't Rome. We – or the locals, rather – don't worry too much about security. There's a wall, of course, with a gate at the bottom, but that was never locked.'

'And no one saw anything suspicious?'

'No. There is a gardener – only one, not a slave; you won't find as many actual slaves as you're used to here when you're dealing with the locals, that's another thing that's different from Rome – but he was at lunch himself. He didn't get back until late afternoon. By which time the body had been discovered.'

'Did Cabirus have any enemies? Obvious ones, I mean?'

Nerva hesitated. 'Not really. Like I said, he was well-respected. And well-liked. He was a wine-shipper in private life, but that's not a particularly cut-throat business around here.' He frowned. 'No pun intended.'

I hadn't missed the momentary hesitation. 'People he didn't quite get on with, then,' I said.

'Well' – he glanced at the governor – 'there was Julius Oppianus. But I'm sure he wouldn't commit murder.'

'Who's Oppianus?' I said.

'One of the old aristocracy I mentioned,' Gabinius said. 'Family's been around here for donkey's years, since before Deucalion's flood. He was in the running for Condate priest, as it happens, but Cabirus pipped him at the post and it obviously rankled. But Nerva's right: Oppianus wouldn't have done it. He's not the type.'

Even so, I made a mental note of the name. 'Anyone else?'

'Not that I know of,' Nerva said. 'But then, I haven't really looked into it. Certainly not conducted anything approaching an investigation. You'd have to ask Diligenta.'

Fair enough; and I'd rather start from scratch anyway. 'What about the family?' I said. 'Anything there?'

'Absolutely not. Cabirus and Diligenta were a very close couple, and the sons got on very well with their father, as far as I'm aware. They're good lads.'

'Titus is one of my best junior officers,' Laco said. Oh, yeah: Laco being procurator, with all that entailed re having large amounts of tax-money in his charge, there'd be a force of militia assigned to him, particularly since the job would involve him and his reps travelling around the province much of the time. 'He's always been perfectly reliable.'

'And Publius?'

'He's being trained up by his father to take over the business when Cabirus and his brother retire,' Nerva said. 'Was being, now, I suppose I should say.'

'"Brother"?'

'Oh, that's Quintus. He's the younger of the two. They ran the firm together. He's not your man either, Corvinus; the two brothers got on very well, as far as I know, and Quintus is no killer.'

Maybe not, but I added him to my mental list all the same. 'Anything else you can tell me?' I said. 'Where the house is, for a start.'

'It's not far from here, one of the properties on Ocean Road, just before the Gate. I can arrange for someone to take you, if you like.'

'No, that's OK, I'll find it. I'll go over there first thing tomorrow morning.' I glanced at Gabinius. 'If that's all right with you, governor?'

'My dear fellow, of course it's all right! And you certainly don't need my permission; in fact, as far as this business is concerned as the emperor's personal representative you outrank me.' He smiled. 'Only as far as this business is concerned, naturally; I wouldn't try interfering with the running of the province, if I were you. Don't worry about authorization where anyone else is concerned, either. I know you have your letter from the emperor, but you won't need it. Despite being the provincial capital, Lugdunum's rather insular, more of a very large village, really, and you'll find that anyone you talk to already knows perfectly well who you are and why you're here. Now,' – the slaves had come in with loaded trays – 'that's enough of the shop talk for the present, because you must both be starving.'

True, certainly in my case; and from the look of what was on the plates they didn't do themselves at all badly out here in the sticks. I had plenty to think about, what's more, and a few names and ideas to be going on with. Plus there was my second cup of wine to look forward to. Ah, the joys.

We'd have to see what tomorrow brought.

FIVE

I set out for the Cabirus house after breakfast the next morning.
Getting myself orientated wasn't too difficult. Lugdunum might be the provincial capital, singled out for special treatment by Rome's imperial family, who've always been its particular patrons, but compared with Rome it's no size at all. Technically, sure, it's a city, but basically it's only a large walled town, occupying the ground immediately to the west of where the Arar River joins the Rhone. Most of the centre – what you'd call the town proper, with all the government properties including the mint, the governor's and procurator's residences, the admin offices and the theatre – is fairly new and very Roman, built over the past fifty years or so and grouped around the usual arrangement of two main streets, the Hinge and Boundary Marker Street, where they meet just south of the Market Square. Because we'd come in the day before from the south, through the Narbonensian Gate, and travelled all the way up the Hinge to the Market Square at its end, we'd more or less gone its whole length. Oh, there

were major bits we hadn't seen yet, of course, particularly on
the other side of the two rivers: Condate across the Arar to the
north-east, the big religious complex in honour of the god Lug,
with its pan-Gallic altar, and the main commercial sector, the
Canabae – the name means 'small huts' – across the Rhone itself,
but these could wait.

Outside the formal centre it isn't all that built up either, quite
the reverse, unlike Rome, which is bursting at the seams. The
part of town I was walking through now, west of the Market
Square in the direction of what Nerva had said was the Ocean
Gate, was mainly residential, sure, but it wasn't what I was used
to back home at all. Most of the houses were villa, rather than
town-house style, two-storey, max, often with wooden or even
wattle-and-daub upper floors, and pretty much scattered, with a
bit of ground between or even in front of them enclosed by a
low wall or thorn-bush fencing, which as far as the less up-market
ones were concerned was home to a cow or a few goats, with
maybe a flock of chickens where the little buggers hadn't got
loose and were pecking around on the street itself. I remembered
what the governor had said, about the locals being country-
dwellers at heart, even the townies. That fitted: provincial capital
and Gaul's chief city or not, the place had a village feel to it that
you just wouldn't get in Italy, even in a town half the size. It
was quiet, too. This time of day, when most of the work gets
done, Rome would be heaving, whichever part you were in.
Beyond the centre, I was practically on my own.

So. On the whole, by and large, pretty bucolic. Not that it was
any the worse for that, mind: city boy to my bones or not, I was
getting to quite like Lugdunum.

I asked an old woman feeding her hens for directions, and
was pointed to a walled villa, slightly off the main drag and fifty
or so yards short of the Gate itself.

There was no slave on duty outside, which again by Roman
standards was unusual; but then I was beginning to get the
measure of the place, and I wasn't unduly surprised. I pushed
open the gate – no livestock, although there were a few chickens,
and the area inside was a proper garden, with ornamental bushes,
flower beds, and even a couple of statues – and went in.

The house was the same two-storey variety as the ones I'd

passed, although a tad up-market from the average: stone-built at bottom with a wooden-frameworked upper level and an open porch running its length. Halfway up the gravel path that led to it, to one side, was a small summer house with the shutters up. Yeah, that would be where the guy had been killed. I stopped and looked around me. A good dozen yards to the gate I'd come through, and about the same to the house itself. Twice that, either side, to the boundary walls. No real cover anywhere, barring a few low bushes and the occasional fruit tree, and although the boundary wall was just too high to see over from the road it'd be virtually impossible, once you were inside the gate, to make your way to the summer house and back without being seen. If anyone had happened to glance down from one of the second-storey windows above the porch, then—

'Can I help you?'

I turned. A woman was coming round the side of the house, carrying a basket of roses: mid-forties, small, dumpy, by her fairish-ginger hair done up in braids and her general colouring obviously a Gaul. Smart, good-quality over-tunic and light cloak fastened with an expensive-looking cloak-pin, though, so despite the basket not one of the help.

'Ah . . . yeah,' I said. 'My name's Corvinus. Valerius Corvinus. I'm here to—'

'I know why you're here. You'd best come inside.'

She led the way towards the porch without another word, and I followed, through a small vestibule and into the living room. There was a youngish girl there, obviously from her rough woollen tunic a servant this time. The woman gave her the basket.

'Put these in a vase with water, Cotuinda,' she said. 'They go in the dining room.'

'Yes, madam.' The girl, with a quick, curious glance at me, took the roses and left.

'Diligenta?' I said.

'That's right.' The woman unpinned her cloak. 'Have a seat, Valerius Corvinus. We've been expecting you. The emperor's well?'

'Hale and hearty, when I left,' I said. Interesting; she'd asked after him like he was an old friend, or an acquaintance, at least. But I suppose that was fair enough: Claudius was no stranger to

Lugdunum, and before he'd been made emperor, member of the imperial family or not, he'd been nothing particularly special.

'I'm glad.' She hung the cloak on the back of one of the wicker chairs – there were no couches in the room, just chairs – and sat down. I took the chair opposite. 'So. You're investigating Tiberius's death. What can I tell you?'

Straight in, matter-of-fact; clearly a no-nonsense lady, Cabirus's widow.

'More or less everything,' I said.

'Fair enough. You'll want a clear, orderly account. Give me a moment, then, to organize the facts in my head.' She closed her eyes for a moment, then opened them again. 'It happened about a month and a half ago. We'd just eaten, the family, I mean, and we all went for a lie-down; I don't know about in Rome, but a short rest after lunch is customary here. Tiberius went out to his den as usual – that's what he called the summer house in the garden, by the way. You saw it?'

'Yeah,' I said.

'I went upstairs to our bedroom, Publius did the same, to his.'

'Publius is your son, right?'

'My younger son, yes. He's sixteen. The elder is Titus. He lives with us as well, but he'd had lunch out as he usually does. He's an officer in the procurator's guard, and he generally has duties in the morning and afternoon.'

'Your bedrooms would be where, exactly?'

She frowned. 'I beg your pardon?'

'Overlooking the garden, or at the back of the house?'

'Oh, I see. Ours – Tiberius's and mine – is at the back; Titus's and Publius's are above the porch, either side of the front door.'

'You have a daughter, too living at home, I understand? Claudilla?'

'Yes, indeed. But Claudilla was away at the time, as she still is. An extended stay with an older childhood friend of hers in Arausio who was married last year and is about to have a baby.'

Yeah, I'd forgotten; Nerva had said she was away. 'And your son Publius didn't happen to see anything suspicious?'

'No. Hardly surprising, because there would have been no

reason for him to look out of the window. But you can ask him that for yourself, naturally. He's upstairs at present. I can have him called, if you like.'

Well, it had been worth checking, although I hadn't really expected any other answer: spot someone creeping around the garden the afternoon your father gets himself murdered and you tend to remember it. Besides, if he had seen anything he'd've said so at the time, and Nerva would've told me. 'No, that's OK,' I said. 'Later, sure, if he's at home; I'd appreciate it. So. There was no one up and around who might've seen something? House or garden slaves, that sort of thing?'

'No one at all. We have very few servants, inside the house or out of it; you'll find that's quite normal here. There's the kitchen staff, the cook and two helpers. They would be clearing up, then having their own meal in the kitchen, which again is at the back of the house. Cotuinda you saw; her father Quadrus is our major-domo and his wife Potita is the housekeeper. We have another maid-of-all-work, Escenga. Rather a simple girl, I'm afraid. All of them would be busy with their duties, or resting if they'd finished them. The gardener is Nantonus. He's getting on a bit now, poor man, and he goes home for lunch and a sleep in the afternoons. He lives quite locally, just on the other side of the Gate.'

Uh-huh. Bugger; I'd have to get used to these Gallic names. What was wrong with the good old bought-help tags like Felix and Tertia? 'So what happened then?' I said.

'I came down as usual about the ninth hour; Tiberius normally put in an appearance shortly afterwards, when he went to his study to deal with business matters. You know he was a wine-shipper?'

'Yeah,' I said. 'Yes, I knew that.'

'On this occasion, though, he'd arranged to meet a business associate in the centre of town, so he needed to be up and around earlier. Certainly before mid-afternoon. When I came down there was no sign of him. I assumed, of course, that he'd overslept. I went straight to the den and . . .' She stopped. 'I'm sorry. I thought I was well over this, but it seems I'm not, after all.'

'That's OK,' I said. 'In your own time.'

'Thank you.' She took a deep breath. 'I went to the den and

found him lying on the couch, stabbed through the heart. That's all I can tell you, I'm afraid.'

'Did he have any enemies? Anyone who'd want him dead?'

'Absolutely not, as far as I know. Why should he? Tiberius was no one special, just an ordinary person, and he was well liked locally.'

'The governor's aide mentioned a Julius Oppianus.'

She shook her head decisively. 'Oppianus would never have murdered Tiberius. They didn't get on, of course, they never had done, but Julius Oppianus is no murderer.'

'Yeah, that's what the governor said. None the less. You care to tell me about him?'

'His family's one of the oldest in Lugdunum. They were chieftains of the Segusiavi – that's the local tribe – long before the Romans came, perhaps even before the Greeks settled Massilia. He's rather come down in the world these past twenty years. More or less since the time Tiberius and I moved down here.'

'You're not from Lugdunum originally?' I said.

'No. From Augusta, up north near the border.' Yes, of course; Claudius had mentioned something of the kind when he'd told me the story about his father and the bulls. 'Tiberius's family were wine-merchants there, mine, too, as it happens. Four generations in both cases. Only he decided that he'd do better further south, between Massilia and the big northern markets, especially the military bases on the Rhine. Control things from first to last, production to point of sale. Lugdunum was the obvious choice.'

'You go back often?'

'To Augusta? No, there's no point now. Both sets of parents are long dead.'

'You've no other family? Either of you?'

'I have a sister and a brother, but we lost touch after my marriage, and they've gone their own ways long since. We – the company, I should say – still have a warehouse outlet in the town that used to belong to Tiberius's father, and Quintus is up and down regularly on business, so the family connection still holds.'

'Quintus is your husband's business partner, isn't he?' I said.

'That's right. And only surviving brother. There was a third, but he died. They split responsibility for the route between them.

Tiberius managed things at the Massilia end, the buying and so on, and arranged delivery to Lugdunum, Quintus organized transportation from here to Augusta and beyond. Plus, of course, he handled the incoming cash side of things in the shape of customer deposits and final payments. It worked out quite well.' She half-smiled, for the first time. It changed her expression completely, and I realized that this dumpy, middle-aged Gallic matron must have been quite a looker twenty years back. 'But we've become side-tracked. You were asking about Julius Oppianus.'

'He was a business rival?'

'Oh, no; I don't think he has any business interests, or indeed any interest in business, whatsoever. In fact, he rather despises businessmen like my husband. That was the root of the problem, really.'

'How do you mean?'

She straightened a fold in her over-tunic. 'I said: Oppianus belongs to one of the oldest families in Gaul. A hundred years ago they owned half the countryside for twenty miles around, and naturally they provided most of the tribal leaders. Then, of course, when you Romans came the world changed completely, and unfortunately they – Oppianus's grandfather and father – didn't change with it. Land had to be sold, and by the time Oppianus came into the estate when his father died twenty-odd years ago there was very little left. Enough for him to live on, certainly, but only a shadow of what there was before. And things haven't become any easier in the interim. Quite the reverse.'

'So where did the bad feeling between him and your husband come in? Specifically, I mean?'

'It didn't, not at all, not on Tiberius's side. But Oppianus can be very . . . How to put this?' She thought for a moment, and I waited. 'You must have the same situation in Rome, particularly nowadays when the old order of things is changing, and it's even more common here, where things have happened so much faster. Some members of the old aristocracy feel that they've been bypassed. Supplanted. They find that men whose fathers and grandfathers used to be their fathers' or grandfathers' clients or dependants have moved up the financial and social ladder and consequently expect to be treated as equals, even superiors. People like Tiberius, who've made their money by trade, are the worst of all, particularly since the new system positively encourages them to become involved in the civic government side of things, which the old families consider their personal preserve. In Tiberius's case the situation was made even worse by the fact that, as I said, we were comparative newcomers to Lugdunum, and privileged clients of the imperial family, at that. When Tiberius was first elected on to the board of local magistrates ten years ago, Oppianus found it very hard to accept; and, of course, the fact that he was chosen to represent Lugdunum at this year's Pan-Gallic Assembly was the last straw.'

Yeah; that was another thing that Claudius had mentioned; the governor, too. 'That's quite an important event, isn't it?' I said.

'Oh, goodness, yes! Being Roman, you wouldn't appreciate just how much, but being elected as the representative is the greatest honour the city can give. And what made matters worse was that Oppianus's grandfather had been the officiating priest at the original ceremony, when the emperor's father dedicated the altar sixty years ago.'

Uh-huh. 'So with your husband dead there'll have to be a new appointment made, yes?'

'Naturally, and under the circumstances it may well be Oppianus. But that's no reason to think he's a murderer.'

'You know where I'd find him?'

'He owns one of the properties on the Hinge, opposite the theatre.' She gave me a straight look. 'I'll tell you once more, Valerius Corvinus, just so that it's clear: the gods know that Julius Oppianus was no friend to my husband, or to our family, but he did *not* kill Tiberius. That I will not believe. The man hasn't got it in him.'

Fair enough; me, I'd suspend judgement, at least until I'd met him myself. Even so, in my book he had sufficient motive to be at least one of the front runners, if not the only option going. 'And your brother-in-law? Where does he live?'

She frowned. 'Quintus? Why would you want to talk to Quintus? He wasn't here at the time.'

'No specific reason. I'm just putting information together at present, getting different angles.'

'Well, you might find him at home – his house is outside the walls, on the Rhone Road just beyond the Arar Gate – but during the day he'll more likely be at the office over in the Canabae.'

'Across the Rhone?'

'That's right. The other side of Rhone Gate Bridge. His – our – office is in the south part, by the river itself and facing the port. I'm afraid I can't give you more detailed directions, because it's mostly warehouses around there, but anyone you ask should be able to point it out to you.'

'Fine,' I said. 'Now I wonder if I could have a look at—'

'Who's this, Mother?'

I turned. A youngster – from his adult tunic he must've been in his mid-teens, at least, although he looked about twelve – had come into the room from the inner part of the house.

'Ah, Publius.' Diligenta smiled. 'This is Valerius Corvinus, the gentleman we were expecting from Rome.'

'Hi,' I said.

The kid didn't answer, just gave a brief nod, and the look I was getting was . . . wary? Suspicious? I couldn't place it, exactly, but it certainly wasn't friendly. Diligenta turned back to me.

'I'm sorry,' she said. 'You were saying. You wanted to see . . .?'

'Oh. Yeah. Just the inside of the summer house, briefly, if that's possible.'

'Of course it's possible.' She hesitated. 'But perhaps . . . if you don't mind going down there by yourself? I'm still a little—'

'Yeah, sure,' I said quickly. 'No problem. Or perhaps Publius here could show me?' It'd give me a chance to talk to him, at least.

'Of course,' she said again. 'Publius? If you wouldn't mind, dear?'

He shrugged. 'Sure.'

Without another word, he went out into the lobby, heading for the front door. I stood up. Before I could follow, Diligenta said quietly: 'You must forgive him, Corvinus. He's at an awkward age, and very sensitive. He found Tiberius's death very upsetting, perhaps even more so than any of us.'

'No, that's OK,' I said. 'Thanks for your help.'

'You're welcome. Such as it was. And naturally anything else I – we – can do, please don't hesitate to ask.'

'I'll do that,' I said, and followed the kid outside.

He was waiting for me in the porch. Still no smile.

'It's down here,' he said, and set off down the path, with me a step or two behind.

'So you were upstairs in your room when it happened?' I said.

'That's right.' He didn't turn round, or slow down.

'You didn't see or hear anything?'

'I was asleep.'

'Yeah, so your mother said. Fair question though. Your window overlooks the garden, doesn't it?'

'Yes.' We'd reached the summer house. He stopped shy of the open door and turned back to face the house. 'Here you are. Help yourself.'

I went past him. There wasn't much inside, although the place was fitted out more like a small study than a summer house: reading couch, small table, a single book-cubby against one wall with two or three books in the pigeonholes. I pulled one out at random: Columella's *Treatise on Agriculture*, or part of it, the section on vine-growing and wines. From the wear on the lace fastenings and the general shabbiness of the book itself, it looked well-used.

There was a dark patch of what could have been blood on the upholstery of the couch. Or it could've been just an old stain: if the guy had been stabbed through the heart there probably wouldn't't've been much actual blood. Certainly there wasn't much else to show the place had been the scene of a murder. Which was fair enough, given that it had happened over a month ago.

I came back out. Publius hadn't moved, his back to the open door and his eyes still on the house.

'Your father spent a lot of time here?' I said.

Another shrug. 'No. He did most of his business work in his study. He only used this for his afternoon naps in good weather.'

'You involved on the business side of things yourself?'

'Dad would've liked me to be.'

'But you wouldn't?'

'Don't have all that much choice, do I?' He still hadn't looked at me.

'You got on well together?'

'He was OK.'

Jupiter, this was heavy going! 'Look, son,' I said, 'all I want to do is to find out who killed your father, right? That's not a particularly pleasant job, but it's what I'm here for. You want that too, don't you?' Silence. 'Come on, give me a break. I'm no ogre, and I don't ask trick questions.'

He turned round, slowly and reluctantly. 'What do you want to know?'

'Anything that'll help. Only I don't know what that is yet. You'll have to tell me.' More silence, and still no eye contact; I'd have to back off here if I wanted any sort of cooperation at all, because the kid obviously had issues somewhere along the line. 'So if you're not keen on the wine trade, then what do you want to do?'

His shoulders lifted. 'I don't know. Not many options around here.'

'You got any hobbies? Anything you're interested in?'

'I make models.'

Yeah, well, not much mileage there, right enough. Even so, for the first time he was volunteering.

'What kind of models?'

'Ships. Temples. That sort of thing. I'm making one of the local theatre, to scale. With all the backdrops and so on. I've got a—' He stopped.

'You're interested in the theatre? Acting?'

'No. Production. Masks, costumes, stage machinery. The technical side of things.'

'Uh-huh. Are your friends—?'

'I don't have any friends.'

Delivered absolutely dead-pan. I sighed, mentally; this was like pulling teeth. 'OK. So tell me about your brother.'

That did get me a quick, sideways look. 'Titus? What's to tell? He's my brother, that's all.'

'He's older than you, isn't he?'

'Yes. Three years older.'

'So I'd've expected him to be involved in the family business before you. Is he?'

'No. Titus is even less interested in business than I am. Soldiering, that's his bag. That and—' He stopped again. 'He's with the procurator's guard, but he wants to move on to the proper auxiliaries, maybe even the legions. Dad doesn't – didn't

– mind that. It's respectable.' That came out flat, with a twist to the word. 'So it had to be me, didn't it?'

'You don't get on, you and Titus?'

That brought his head round sharply, and for the first time he looked me straight in the eye. Defiantly, if that wasn't too strong a word.

'Titus is OK,' he said. 'And like I say, he's my brother. Why shouldn't we get on?' He turned away again. 'Now if you've seen all you want to see and asked all your questions I've things to do, and you'll want to be going.'

Yeah, I might as well, at that; I certainly wasn't making much headway here.

Gods!

'Fair enough,' I said. 'Nice to talk to you.' No answer. 'Titus is still living at home, isn't he?'

He turned back. 'Yes.'

'He's on duty now?'

'Until sunset.'

'Where would I find him?'

'Depends what he's doing, doesn't it?'

I held on to my patience. With difficulty. 'You like to give me a possibility or two to work on, maybe?' I said.

'He could be at the procurator's headquarters on the Hinge, or he could be at the barracks. Or there again the procurator might've sent him off on an errand somewhere.'

'And the barracks are where?'

'Further down the Hinge, just before the Narbonensian Gate. Now, like I said, I've things to do. I'll see you around.' Without another word, he turned again and walked away towards the house.

I watched his retreating back. Shit, kids! Well, I supposed I'd been like that myself, once, and Diligenta had warned me. Still, it didn't make it less exasperating.

So; what now? I'd got the names of three people I'd have to talk to, for a start, at least, and it didn't particularly matter which order I took them in. Assuming he was at home, though, Julius Oppianus, with more than a smidgeon of form and a house on the Hinge, was the most sensible option. I set off in the direction of the city centre.

*　*　*

The house wasn't difficult to find, with a bit of asking. Like
Diligenta had said, it was one of the older properties, a two-storey
building in its own grounds set back from the road opposite the
theatre: neat enough in its way, but definitely run-down compared
with the Cabirus place, especially the garden, which had more
or less been left to do as it liked. I went through the gate and
up past beds of unpruned roses and scabby-looking fruit trees to
the front door. This time, there was no one around, but the door
itself was ajar. Peeling paint, and the handle hadn't been polished
for months. Bathyllus would've had a fit. I knocked a few times.
No answer, so I went inside.

Whatever Oppianus's priorities were, impressing visitors didn't
seem very high on the list: the front porch was obviously used
as a sort of storeroom, with boxes and crates piled up one on
top of another along the inside wall, nets of root vegetables and
onions hanging from pegs, and a general air of shabbiness, damp
and mould. A chicken came strutting towards me, stopped, fixed
me accusingly with a beady-eyed stare, and then carried on out
through the open door.

'Anyone at home?' I shouted.

There was the sound of movement from inside the house
proper, and an old woman came out. Plainly a slave or a servant,
in a shabby tunic that matched the condition of the porch.

'Who are you?' she said.

'Valerius Corvinus.' I closed the door behind me. 'The master
at home? Julius Oppianus?'

'He's in his study.'

'You think I could talk to him? I'm—'

'I know who you are. Or I can guess. Wait here and I'll see.'

She shuffled off back the way she'd come. Another chicken
appeared. I opened the front door and got rid of that one, too.
Scion of one of the oldest families in Gaul or not, Oppianus
didn't believe in living in style, that was clear. A mansion on the
Caelian, this wasn't. Not even close.

Five minutes later, the woman reappeared.

'He'll see you,' she said. 'Follow me.'

I did. The room was a bit more upmarket, with some nice
furniture – or rather, I'd guess it had been nice at one time, about
fifty years back – but again everything was pretty shabby, and

the fine layer of dust and general lack of shine suggested that what should've been the house's principal room wasn't used all that much. The old woman didn't pause. She led me through and along a short corridor to a panelled wooden door beyond, knocked, and opened it.

'Valerius Corvinus,' she said.

The study looked a lot more lived-in than the actual living room had; at least it was clean and tidy, although the guy sitting in the wickerwork chair next to the desk wasn't dressed any better than his housekeeper was, in a lounging-tunic that'd seen far better days. He hadn't shaved, either. He set the book he'd been reading – or at least holding – down on the desktop.

'Come in,' he said. 'Pull up a chair.'

There was one beside me, against the wall. The cushions on its seat and back had been plush velvet at one time, but it was so worn in places that the lamb's-wool stuffing showed through the holes. I pulled it over and sat down while he watched me closely and in silence. Mid-fifties at a guess, but he gave the impression of being at least ten years older, and he put me in mind of a moulting cockerel: scrawny neck, nose like a beak, not much meat on his bones.

Sharp pair of eyes, though, and I had their full attention.

'So,' he said, 'this will be about Claudius Cabirus.'

'That's right. I've—'

'No need for explanations. The family have pulled a few strings and had you brought out from Rome to look into his death, yes?'

'Actually—'

'And, wonder of wonders, they've got me put down as the prime suspect.' His lips twisted. 'No surprises there.'

Less than a minute in, and the guy was seriously getting up my nose. I shifted in my chair. To hell with the niceties.

'Look, pal,' I said, 'let's get a few things clear before we start, right? First off, as far as I know, bringing me out from Rome had nothing to do with the family per se; it was the emperor's own idea, and he had it because the governor happened to mention Cabirus's death in a routine report. Secondly, I've just talked to the widow, and she is personally convinced you had nothing to do with it; in fact, she went out of her way to make sure there were absolutely no misunderstandings on that score. Thirdly, I give you my solemn word that, whatever I'm told by any third party, be they who they may, I will make up my own fucking mind as to who was fucking responsible, and then only after due careful investigation and a proper objective weighing-up of the consequently discovered facts. Now is that understood, or would you like me to repeat or rephrase any of it?'

The eyes had widened. He cleared his throat.

'Very well, Valerius Corvinus,' he said stiffly, after a pause. 'Perhaps I spoke out of turn. Not that it's an excuse for bad language on your part, but I'll let it pass. My apologies. Let's start afresh, shall we?'

'Fine with me.'

'So. What do you want to know?'

'You didn't like the man. You care to tell me why, exactly?'

'He was a jumped-up parvenu. A tradesman.' There was enough venom packed into the final word to have kitted out a dozen self-respecting asps.

'Is that all?'

'*All?* Isn't it enough?'

'I wouldn't've thought so, personally, no.'

'Indeed?' He grunted. 'Well, then, it's more than enough for me. Claudius Cabirus came from a nothing of a family, and his wife was the same. Merchants and shopkeepers, the lot of them. He wasn't even local; he only moved here twenty years ago, while my family have been pre-eminent in the region for centuries. If he'd kept to his proper place I'd have had no quarrel with him, but as it was he began trespassing on what should have been the preserve of his betters almost as soon as he arrived, and that I bitterly resented. Does that answer your question?'

Gods! Diligenta had said, or at least implied, that the guy was an arch-snob, and on present showing he could've given even the most right-wing of Rome's starchy top Five Hundred lessons.

'Yeah,' I said. 'Yeah, it does. To a degree.'

'Good. I'm glad. His being elected to the magistracy was bad enough – money will buy you anything these days, wherever sewer it comes from, and the good citizens of Lugdunum are toadies to a man – but getting himself appointed as officiating priest at this year's Assembly was a step too far, even for him.

A pure disgrace. And you ask me why I didn't *like* the man? I'd have thought that was self-evident.'

'Right. Right.' I had to go careful here: the guy was practically spitting, and I was beginning to wonder if there wasn't a bit more than simple, ordinary jealousy and snobbery involved. In fact, I was getting the distinct impression that Julius Oppianus was more than a few tiles short of a watertight roof. 'That mattered to you a lot, did it?'

He looked at me like I'd just sprouted an extra head. 'For a man from Cabirus's background to hold the highest position the city could offer was nothing short of a desecration. A blasphemy. You know that my own grandfather officiated at the original assembly?'

'Yeah. Yeah, I did, as a matter of fact.'

'Well, then! To have that . . . *tradesman* . . . stand in my grandfather's place at the Altar and conduct the ceremony was an insufferable insult, and one not to be borne.'

'So. *Did* you kill him?' I asked quietly.

He blinked. 'I beg your pardon?'

'It's a simple question. Someone did.'

'Evidently. But whoever it was, and for whatever reason, I'll tell you this, Valerius Corvinus: Claudius Cabirus's death was a judgement, one richly deserved. The proper order of things isn't mocked, and dross like Cabirus try it at their peril.' He picked up the book he'd set down on the desk. 'Now. I can't wish you success in your investigations. Good day, sir.'

I didn't move. 'You care to tell me where you were at the time?' I said. 'When the murder was committed, I mean?'

That got me a positive glare. 'No, I would not,' he snapped. 'I expect you can find your own way out. Good day to you!'

He unrolled the book and started reading, without giving me another glance. I stood up and left the room.

Short and a long way from sweet. Yeah, well: obviously totally out of his tree and no mistake, that one, at least where Cabirus was concerned. Whether it made him a killer, though, motive and inclination in spades or not, was another thing entirely.

Onwards and upwards. So: where to next? The procurator's offices, where according to Publius young Titus might or might not be, were back up the Hinge towards Market Square and home;

familiar territory, in other words, and besides, Titus would still be on duty. I might as well see a bit more of Lugdunum while I was at it.

Brother Quintus it would be, then.

I was beginning to get my bearings now. The quickest way to the Canabae was east along Traders' Street, where it crossed the Hinge, to the Rhone Gate, then down Rhone Road to the South Bridge. So that was the way I went.

Like its name suggests, Traders' Street was mostly shops; but where the ones on the two main drags, particularly on Boundary Marker Street, tended to feature luxury goods and be pretty pricey these catered for the everyday needs and wants of what in Rome would be the tunic and plain-mantle clientele. Which meant at that time of day it got as close as Lugdunum evidently did to heaving. Oh, sure, the local version of the bag lady we got back home was a lot more polite and a lot less bloody-minded – you don't get in the way of an incoming Suburban housewife loaded down with shopping if you're wise – but what with the comparative narrowness of the street and the fact that the shopkeepers' wares tended to spill over on to the pavement the going was pretty slow. I made it to the gate at the end eventually and turned right on to Rhone Road. This was pretty busy, too, but it was a different kind of busyness: linking the two ports as it did, it was used mostly by heavy carts, and there were comparatively few pedestrians. Still, the original engineers had laid it out pretty wide, so as long as you listened out for waggons coming from behind it was OK.

Much pleasanter to walk along than its equivalent in Rome would've been, what's more: summer, when the river's low and there's more mud in it than water, is no time for a stroll along the Tiber unless you've as much sense of smell as a radish or don't mind having your sinuses cauterized. Oh, sure, what we'd got here was just a side branch that cut off the wooded central island from the bank, and like riverside dwellers everywhere the locals evidently took the opportunity to use it as a largely self-clearing garbage-disposal system, but since compared with Rome the population density wasn't all that high the smell wasn't, either: what buildings there were – and they were a mixture of commercial properties, small-scale industrial yards, and down-market private houses – weren't exactly packed cheek-by-jowl, and there was plenty of open space for the breeze to blow around.

I crossed the South Bridge into the Canabae and turned down the first road leading off to the right: Diligenta had said that the family's offices were near the river, opposite the port on the mainland side, so they couldn't be all that far away. Sure enough, when I stopped off at a brick-maker's yard to ask I was pointed to a set of warehouses a hundred yards or so further on.

Outside the first one I came to, four or five men were loading amphoras on to a cart. Promising.

'Excuse me,' I said, going up to them. 'This the Cabirus place?'

They paused, and I saw their eyes going to the stripe on my tunic.

'That's right, sir,' one of them said. 'Looking for the boss, are you?'

'Yeah. Quintus Cabirus, yes? He around at present?'

'Sure. Just go straight up.' He turned back to his work.

There was an external stair leading to the first floor, above the warehouse proper. I went up it and through the door at the top, and found myself in an office with the usual complement of clerks, desks and document-cubbies. A chunky middle-aged guy in a smart tunic was standing by one of the desks talking to the clerk behind it. He looked up as I came in, and his eyes, like those of the workmen below, went to the purple stripe.

'Yes,' he said. 'Can I help you?'

'Quintus Cabirus?' I said.

'That's me.'

'Valerius Corvinus. Sorry to disturb you when you're busy, but your sister-in-law said I might catch you here. It's about—'

'My brother's death. Word has got around. Yes. And no, you're not disturbing me.' He turned to the clerk. 'That's fine, Silus, just send these off at once, will you?' He turned back to me. 'We'll go into my private office, if that's all right.'

'Sure.' I followed him past the suddenly attentive clerks to a door at the back of the room. He opened it and stood aside. I went in.

Obviously the place where he took prospective clients: there was a desk, sure, and more document-cubbies against the wall, but there were also a couple of wickerwork chairs – I was getting more used to those things as standard: in Rome, they're mostly used for portable garden furniture – and a low table with a wine jug and cups on it.

He came in behind me and closed the door. 'Have a seat, please,' he said. 'Some wine?'

Here we went again. Conscience won out, and I steeled myself. 'Sure,' I said. 'Half a cup will do fine.' There was no water jug on the table, but I reckoned I could stretch a point for once and have it as it was without breaking my promise to Perilla. I sat down in the nearest chair – the cushions were newer and in far better nick than Oppianus's – while he poured the wine into two cups and handed me one.

'Now.' He settled himself in the other chair. 'How can I help you? If you've talked to Diligenta then you'll already have the basic facts. I'm afraid where those are concerned I can't add anything, because I was elsewhere at the time.'

'You were away altogether? Your sister-in-law said you travel a lot on business.'

'No, I was here in Lugdunum. I just wasn't at the house, that's all. Naturally not.'

'Yeah, well, it would've been a working day, wouldn't it?' I took a sip of the wine. Nice stuff; very nice, and all the better for not being drowned. I held up the cup. 'Massilian?'

'Yes, that's right. It's the top of our range. Single vineyard, only ten acres. Aminnean vines. The annual yield is very small indeed, as you can imagine, and the price is correspondingly high. But we sell all we produce, and we could easily sell five times the amount.'

'You own the vineyard?'

'No. But we have a standing arrangement with the owner to buy the entire vintage, barring what he keeps for his own use.'

'Diligenta told me that you and your brother looked after two separate halves of the business.'

'Indeed. Tiberius did the buying and arranged transport as far as Lugdunum. Most of our customers, though, are north of here, in the smaller towns between us and the Rhine. Plus, of course, we have our share of the army contract. That side of things was my concern.'

'You're from that part of Gaul yourself, aren't you?'

'Yes. From Augusta. The family – or our bit of it, anyway – moved here twenty years ago. Tiberius decided that Lugdunum made a more sensible base.'

'Yeah, that's what Diligenta said.'

'It works – worked – out very well, because it played to both our strengths. I'm the better salesman as such, but Tiberius was the one who could judge what would really sell. Not only that, but pick the wines with mileage.'

'"Mileage"?'

'However good a wine is on its own ground, if it can't travel without deteriorating you won't get its proper price at the other end. Tiberius was a marvel at singling out the wines with mileage. He'd a first-rate palate, too. Not like me.' He held up his cup. 'Oh, I know this is a first-rate wine, but that's only because he spotted it as such to begin with and told me it was. Me, I can't tell the difference between a wine that's just very good and one that's outstanding, and in our business that's not enough. The gods know how the family will cope now he's gone.'

'What about young Publius? I thought his father was training him up?'

'Publius?' He hesitated. 'He's my nephew, Corvinus, so I shouldn't say this, but nice enough boy as he is Publius will never make a wine merchant. You've met him?'

'Yeah. Briefly.'

'Well, then, even on those terms you can probably form a fairly accurate opinion. His mind works the wrong way. And he's not good with people, which you have to be in this line. Prefers sitting in his room all day working on his precious models, or walking around by himself the best part of the night for the gods know what reasons.' He shot me a look, and smiled. 'No, nothing dubious or anything he shouldn't be doing, that I am sure of. It might be better for him if it were, but it's just not in his character.'

'Your other nephew – Titus – isn't interested?'

'No. He never has been. You've met him too?'

'Not yet.'

'Well, then. Titus has only two interests, the army and hunting; oh, girls, too, at his age, but he's pretty secretive where they're concerned, and I don't know much about that side of him. He joined the procurator's guard as soon as he was old enough to be accepted – you know the procurator has a unit under his personal command, independent of the detachment from Rome's Urban Cohort guarding the mint?'

'Yeah. I do.'

'For a provincial family like ours, the army's a good way of getting on. First the auxiliaries, then the legions, and if you can prove yourself then after that the world's your oyster. Look at our current procurator, Laco.'

'He's from Lugdunum?'

'Massilia, I think, although I may be wrong; I don't have much to do with a high-flyer like Graecinius Laco. But it's the same difference; he's a pure-bred Gaul and the second most important man in the province, he's got his equestrian stripe, and with that he's eligible for any top imperial post in the empire. Even the Egyptian governorship. No, I can see why Titus isn't interested in joining the firm. To give him his due, Tiberius could see it too, elder son or not.' He took a mouthful of his wine. 'So you see as far as direct family goes unfortunately the future is largely scuppered. Oh, we're doing all right at present, much better than all right, in fact. But with Tiberius dead we're like a plant that's damaged in its roots.'

'So. Did he have any enemies that you know of? Anyone who'd want him out of the way?'

'None. Absolutely none. Barring . . .' He hesitated again.

'Barring Julius Oppianus?'

A grunt, and a frown. 'You know about him?'

'Yeah. That's one guy I have met. This morning, in fact.'

'Then again you can form your own opinion. He certainly had his knife into Tiberius, but—' He stopped. 'I'm sorry. That was tactless.'

'It's OK.'

'I was going to say that Oppianus had no time for my brother. To put it mildly. But I wouldn't have said he'd take things as far as murder.'

'Yeah. Your sister-in-law said the same.'

'There you are, then. Naturally, I'm not trying to tell you your business, but let's just say that if Oppianus was responsible then I'd be very surprised indeed.'

'Fair enough.' I was noncommittal: me, if Julius Oppianus did turn out to be the perp, I wouldn't exactly put it in the flying-pigs bracket. And at present he was streets ahead the best on offer. 'No one else?'

'I said: absolutely no one. To my knowledge, at least. Oppianus apart, Tiberius was very popular in the city, and highly respected; the Council wouldn't have chosen him to represent us at the cere-mony in Condate if he wasn't. Ex-city judge twice, ex-co-mayor three years running. Tipped for censor in two years' time. And he's done it cleanly, too: no underhand skulduggery, like you often get in local politics.'

'Oppianus would be a front contender now for his replace-ment? For the Condate ceremony?'

'I don't know. Unlike Tiberius, I'm not involved in that side of things at all. Never been able to muster up the interest. But I'd imagine, being who he is, he'd have a very fair chance.'

Uh-huh; that was my feeling, too. And something like that would weigh with a guy like Oppianus, out of all proportion to how much perhaps it should. Still, I knew from experience it was better to keep an open mind.

'So,' I said, 'assuming Oppianus didn't do it for the obvious reasons, and barring any other specific contenders, why do you think he was killed?'

'That's the question that's puzzled me – all of us, in the family – for the past month, Corvinus. And I'm afraid I've not the slightest idea as to what the answer could be.'

Right. Me, neither; at least on present showing. We'd just have to keep on digging.

I swallowed the rest of my wine, what there was of it – that, I wasn't going to waste – and stood up. Quintus did, too.

'Well, thanks anyway,' I said. 'I'll let you get back to things. You busy just now?'

'No more than usual. Which means, with Tiberius gone, I'm practically run off my feet. We've a good man at the Massilia end who's handling purchase and shipping the best he can, so that part of the business is jogging along as normal, but I'll have to travel to Augusta in the next few days and I still have all the arrangements to make.'

'That usual? For you to go in person?'

'Pretty much, yes. Certainly at least one time in three, often more. We've always prided ourselves on the personal touch where customers are concerned, and there're always matters to be handled, decisions to be made, that can't be delegated. It's time-consuming, but I don't mind that. I've no family myself – wife and children, I mean – so it's no great wrench.'

'Fine,' I said. 'I'll leave you to it. Oh – one more thing.'

'Yes?'

'You said you were "elsewhere" the day of the murder. You weren't here, then? In the office?'

'No. No, as a matter of fact I wasn't.'

'So where exactly were you?'

'At home. I'd a chest cold that day, as it happened. Something I'm prone to, before the summer proper. I decided to stay in and give work a miss.' He smiled. 'Boss's prerogative.'

'Right. Right.' I turned to go. 'Thanks again.'

'You're welcome. I only wish I could be of more help. And naturally if you've any other questions before I leave—'

'I'll get in touch,' I said.

I was making my way out between the clerks when I noticed the oldish guy Quintus had been talking to glance in my direction, put down his pen, and half-rise; then, as if he'd thought twice about whatever he was going to do, sit down again, retrieve the pen, and carry on writing like his life depended on it. I slowed, but he didn't look up, just beavered away until I was past his desk.

I continued to the front door, opened it, and went down the steps.

Interesting.

So; back to the residence. The procurator's offices were on my way home anyway, so it wouldn't hurt to call in in passing to check whether young Titus Cabirus was around. Not that I was too bothered, mind: it was only the first day, and I reckoned I'd done pretty well as far as my duty to the emperor was concerned.

I retraced my steps; it was past midday by now, and the streets were a bit quieter, possibly because lunch was a more important meal here than it would've been in Rome. The procurator's offices were part of the city's admin sector, at the top of the Hinge, next

to the mint and just shy of Market Square itself, with a couple
of squaddies on guard outside. I went up to them.

'Excuse me,' I said. 'I'm looking for Titus Cabirus. He on
duty here at present?'

'He is, sir,' one of them said. 'But you won't find him inside.
He's on his lunch break.'

Jupiter; a *lunch break*? Things were certainly more laid back
in the provinces than they would be at home. Still. 'You know
where I'd find him?' I said.

'Sure. He'll be in the cookshop round the corner.'

Yeah, well; that was a bit of good news, anyway. After a
morning spent traipsing around Lugdunum I could do with something to eat myself. Even if I did have to pass up on the wine
accompaniment. I nodded my thanks and went in the direction
he pointed.

The cookshop was halfway down the side street. I went in.
Obviously a popular place, which was fair enough given that
it was bang in the administrative centre of town. What few
tables there were were pretty full, and most of the clientele
looked like they were clerks from the nearby government offices.
There was one guy, though, twenty max, dressed in a military
uniform, sitting on his own at a table in the corner. I made my
way to the counter, ordered up a plate of bean stew, and carried
it over.

'Titus Cabirus?' I said.

'Yes.' He looked up in surprise. 'What can I do for you?'

'The name's Corvinus. Marcus Corvinus. You mind if I join
you?'

Like most people I'd talked to that day, his eyes had gone to
the stripe on my tunic.

'Not at all,' he said. 'You're the one from Rome, aren't you?
Looking into my father's death?'

'Yeah, that's right. I only wanted to introduce myself and have
a quick word, that's all. If you don't mind.'

'Of course not. Pull up a stool.' I put my bowl of stew down
on the table and sat. There were the remains of a plateful of
sliced sausage in front of him. He took a piece and chewed. 'So.
When did you arrive?'

'Yesterday. But I went round to your mother's this morning. And I've talked to your Uncle Quintus.'

He frowned. 'You haven't wasted much time, have you?'

'True.' I scooped up some of the beans with my spoon. They weren't bad; cooked in a good stock, with sage, carrots and onion. No wonder the place was popular. 'Still, it's let me see a bit of the city. And I like to get things clear in my head as quickly as I can.'

'If you've already talked to Mother then there's not much I can tell you. I wasn't home at the time. Not until sunset.'

'So your mother said. You were on duty?'

He hesitated. 'Yes. Yes, I was.'

'And you've no theories of your own?'

Another frown. 'Theories?'

'About why your father was murdered. Who might've done it, even.'

'No. It's a complete mystery.' He picked up another piece of the sausage. 'There's a man called Julius Oppianus who—'

'Yeah, I know. I've seen him this morning too.' Well, where the perp was concerned, as far as the *vox pop.* went Oppianus seemed to be up there on his own. Or at least his was the only name everyone had mentioned.

'Gods, you have been busy.'

'Actually, the interview didn't take all that long. He practically threw me out after five minutes.'

He grinned. 'That's Oppianus, all right.'

'So.' I lowered my eyes to my plate and took another spoonful of the stew. 'What sort of man was he, in himself? Your father?'

The barest smidgeon of hesitation. 'He was OK.'

'You got on well together?'

'How do you mean?' There was a definite edge to the question. 'Why shouldn't we get on?'

'It'd be natural enough for there to be a bit of friction. You're the elder son. He might've expected you to follow him in the business.'

'Maybe he did, at first. But when I told him two years back I wanted an army career he didn't make an issue of it. Besides, he had my Uncle Quintus. They were managing it pretty well between them. They didn't need me.'

'He told me you wanted to move to a legion eventually.'

'Nothing secret about that. Or surprising.' There it was again; I had the distinct impression that, as far as young Titus was concerned, his uncle wasn't exactly flavour of the month and he'd prefer that I dropped the subject. Odd; Quintus Cabirus had seemed perfectly OK when I'd talked to him, and there hadn't been any hint of friction with his nephew on his part. Quite the reverse. 'I don't want to spend the rest of my life here in Lugdunum. The army's the best option.'

'Fair enough.' I spooned up more of the stew. 'There's nothing to keep you? Barring family?'

'Such as what?' A definite note of suspicion there.

'I don't know. Girlfriend, maybe?'

'No. No one special.' He was scowling now. 'Look. What the hell does all this have to do with my father's death?'

'Nothing. Just making conversation.'

'Then mind your own bloody business, OK?'

Gods! 'Fine,' I said. 'I'm sorry. Maybe I was a bit out of turn.'

He took a deep breath and shrugged. 'Forget it; I'm sorry, too. No harm done.' He stood up. 'Now, I'm afraid I have to be getting back. I'll see you around, Corvinus.'

'Yeah. No doubt. Nice to talk to you.'

He left.

Parts of that had been curious. Very curious indeed. Whether or not they had anything to do with the case, mind, was another thing entirely.

I finished up the bean stew and set off for home.

SIX

Evidently, with the governor away on walkabout, we had the residence to ourselves. Which sounds better than it was, because as I say the place had been built on, or adapted to, an imperial scale – or at least a provincial imperial scale, which wasn't quite so grand – and I had the distinctly uncomfortable feeling that we were rattling around like two dried peas in an empty bucket. A gold-plated bucket, mind, but still. Not that the place was empty, of course: even with the staff Gabinius had taken with him on tour and the local conventions re the employment of skivvies there was more bought help around than you could shake a stick at. As I mounted the steps at the front, the door-slave in his natty green tunic almost bounded off the stool he was sitting on and yanked the door open for me.

'Thanks, pal,' I said to him, and went inside.

Bathyllus was waiting in the seriously large frescoed and mosaic-floored vestibule: evidently the move to foreign parts hadn't adversely affected his skills in precognition any. No welcome-home cup of wine, mind; Bathyllus had had firm instructions from Perilla where that side of things was concerned, and no one – but *no* one – bucks the lady when she's really set her mind on something.

'Good afternoon, sir,' he said. 'Did you have a productive morning?'

Smarm, smarm; the amount of oil in his voice would've kept a decent-sized bath-house going for a month. Bathyllus was vicariously enjoying this upgrade to a five-star lifestyle to the full, that much was obvious. Not that I hadn't expected it: Bathyllus was to snobbery what fish sauce was to braised sturgeon, and my promotion to personal imperial rep, however temporary, put the cap on it. If that isn't an unfortunate mixture of metaphors. He'd probably been waiting for an opportunity like this all his life.

'Oh, hi, little guy,' I said. 'What happened to the local staff?'

'The governor's major-domo has accompanied him on his tour of the province, sir. We came to an arrangement before he left.'

'"Arrangement"?'

'I pointed out to him that, since you currently hold the rank of imperial procurator, your own major-domo should outrank his deputy. He appreciated my point of view at once.'

I was grinning. I'd met the guy – his name was Euthymius – briefly the previous day, when we'd first arrived, and he'd definitely been the unassuming, inoffensive type. No match, in other words, for our Bathyllus on the make. If there had been a skirmish over roles and proper protocol – which I'd guess was likely as tomorrow's sunrise – then Bathyllus wouldn't even have had to break sweat. It was just lucky for Euthymius that he'd escaped when he did. Otherwise we might be cleaning blood off the walls.

'So,' I said, 'you're in charge, right? Downstairs, I mean. For the duration.'

'That is the case, sir.' Smug as hell.

'Fine.' I handed him my cloak. 'Congratulations. The mistress at home?'

'No, sir. She went out just after you did. With the Lady Caninia and Domitius Crinas. I understand that they are making a tour of the local sights, plus a number of the better emporia.'

I winced; Smarmer hadn't wasted any time, had he? Still, you had to keep up appearances in front of the domestics. And at least, as I said, the lady would be chaperoned.

'Great,' I said.

'Licinius Nerva, however, is waiting for you in the conservatory.'

'Yeah? Where's that?'

'I'll show you, sir. If you'd care to follow me.'

I did, marvelling: set Bathyllus down in King Minos's labyrinth and he'd know his way around it in ten minutes flat. He'd probably have the skivvies shovel up the Minotaur dung, hose down the floors, polish them till they shone, and make the brute wipe its hooves – or whatever – before he let it in again, into the bargain.

The conservatory was at the back of the residence, forming a good half stretch of the northern end of the peristyle garden. Nerva was sitting in one of the wicker chairs under a potted palm, with a jug and assorted wine-cups on the small table beside him.

'Ah, Corvinus,' he said. 'How did things go this morning?'

'OK.' I pulled up another chair, sat down, reached for the jug, and then remembered. Damn! 'I made a start, anyway.'

'You talked to Diligenta?'

'Oh, yes. And to her sons. Quintus and Oppianus, too.'

He laughed. 'My, you have made a start! Any ideas?'

'Not a lot, so far. We're not at that stage yet. Mind you, I'm not as sure as you and the governor seem to be – or anyone else, for that matter – that Oppianus is in the clear. Far from it.'

'Yes, well, if you've talked to him yourself I can see why

you'd get that impression. Not an easy man to get along with, Julius Oppianus. If he wasn't who he is he wouldn't figure at all in the local community. But the Gauls are a very status-conscious race, family status-conscious, I mean, and where someone from Oppianus's background is concerned they're prepared to make allowances.'

'Yeah. I can see that they'd have to,' I said drily. 'Incidentally, on that score I was wondering if you could give me the name of someone on the local side I could talk to. A colleague of Cabirus's. Someone currently on the Council, for preference.'

'No problems there. Your best bet's Julius Biracus. He's one of the two chief magistrates, house on Boundary Marker Street halfway to the Western Gate. He's known the Cabiri ever since they came to Lugdunum.'

I made a mental note. 'So,' I said, 'what are Oppianus's chances, actually? Of replacing Cabirus as officiating priest at the Assembly?'

'Pretty good, especially with it being less than a month away. I don't know if a formal decision's been made – you can check with Biracus about that – but I'd say it's pretty much certain. His grandfather having done the same job for the emperor's father at the original dedication would weigh pretty heavily, too, particularly since it's more than likely that Claudius will come over for the ceremony himself.'

'Will he?'

'I'd be surprised if he didn't, what with the British campaign coming up, probably early next year. He's a smart man, Claudius, and he knows how important the Assembly is to the Gauls. Not just here in Lugdunum, but all over. Plus, unlike his predecessor, he knows how to work a crowd when he wants something from them, and being a Lugdunan by birth, as it were, he's off to a good start. Like the governor told you, we need all the goodwill we can get when it comes to screwing extra money and supplies out of the local population, which like it or not he'll have to do if the thing's going to happen. When he took over a year and a half ago the public treasury was looking pretty empty.'

'You know that for a fact?'

'Given that my father's in charge of it, yes, I do.'

Spoken off-handedly, and without a trace of side; top Five

Hundred high-flyer was right. Yeah, well, he'd have to have some considerable clout, to be allowed to bring his wife out on what was presumably his first overseas posting, and a daddy who was top man at the Treasury would fit the bill nicely. Still, he wasn't a bad guy, Licinius Nerva.

'Besides.' He picked up his wine-cup and took a sip. 'There's something funny going on at the moment, up nearer the Rhineland.'

'"Funny"?'

'Odd. Or there might be, rather, it's that uncertain. Nothing serious, touch wood, but definitely something to keep an eye on, particularly since things might get a little sticky public relations-wise in the next few months.'

'Namely?' I said.

'I'm sorry, Corvinus.' He set the cup down again. 'I'm telling tales out of school. No offence, but it's none of your business, or your concern. To tell you the truth, it's not properly mine, either. Forget that I spoke.'

'Come on, pal! Spit it out or clam up, one or the other.'

He hesitated, then shrugged. 'Fair enough. You're the emperor's personal rep, and I'm sure the governor wouldn't mind. In any case, how do I know what's relevant or what isn't where your job here's concerned?'

'True. If it's any consolation, I have the same trouble deciding that myself.'

'Very well, then. Someone may be – *may* be – trying to stir up trouble among the local tribes.'

'*What?*'

'I said: it's not definite, no more than a rumour so far, and a faint one at that. And it's not my – or even my governor's – direct concern, because it only affects Belgica, and that's Governor Hister's patch. But it would make good political and strategic sense. If there were trouble of that kind before the British campaign got underway then troops would have to be deployed from the Rhine garrisons to deal with it. Which might well affect the emperor's plans. You see?'

Yeah, I did. Shit; it was Florus and Sacrovir all over again.

'The thing is, we had a curious incident ourselves two months ago. Oh, just the one, there's been nothing since. But the Belgic business put me in mind of it. And the governor, of course; Gabinius is no fool, and he's careful. He has to be, in his job.'

'What kind of incident?'

'A dead wolf dumped overnight in the middle of Market Square.'

'A *wolf*?'

'You get them in the woods around here. They're pretty common, particularly in the winter and early spring, when the game's thin on the ground in the wilder parts and they come down from the mountains after the farm stock. But you see the implication; what *could* be the implication.'

I nodded. Yeah; that much was obvious; it would be to any Roman. The wolf is Rome's animal, as the eagle is Rome's bird. A dead wolf, left in the middle of a Gallo-Roman town . . . well, work the metaphor out for yourself.

'Of course,' Nerva went on, 'it could just have been a prank, and probably was. Gauls are really into practical jokes and cocking a snook at authority, and their sense of humour can be pretty gross. Anyway, we – the governor, I mean – decided to ignore it at the time; no point in stirring things by over-reacting, and after Gaius's little PR exercise here two years back we've enough ruffled feathers locally to be going on with for a while. As you'll have gathered from Laco, Gallic wounds take a while to heal.'

'But now there's the Belgic business, right?'

'Yes. Which, like I say, might be nothing but a mare's nest in itself. Like I say, forget I mentioned it. You've got your own problem to solve, and I'm probably jumping at shadows in any case.'

'So what's Gabinius—?'

'Hello, Marcus. Did you have a successful morning?'

I turned: Perilla was back, with Caninia in tow. 'Oh, hi, lady,' I said. 'Not too bad, thanks. How was yours?'

'Very enjoyable. We didn't do much, just pottered around the shops in the centre. Caninia took me to a little jeweller's on the Hinge, and they had some lovely silver brooches. I got one for myself and another for Marilla, beautiful workmanship, and so cheap. Plus a few other bits and pieces.'

Yeah, I'd bet: we'd probably need an extra luggage cart when the time came to go back home; when Perilla shops, she doesn't pull any punches. Ah, well; at least I wasn't directly involved.

'That's nice,' I said. 'How about Crinas? I understand he tagged on as well.'

She coloured. 'Not for the whole time. But yes, he did join us in the early stages.'

Bathyllus was hovering, doing his perfect butler act. Perilla pulled up a chair.

'Hello, Nerva,' she said. 'Bathyllus, a barley water and honey, if you would. Caninia, the same for you?'

'Lovely.' Caninia sat down in the chair next to Nerva's while Bathyllus shimmered out. 'So how is the murder investigation going, Valerius Corvinus?' she said. 'Do tell.'

'Caninia, I thought we agreed—' Nerva murmured.

'No, that's OK,' I said. 'Anyway, like I told you it's very early days yet. I've seen Julius Oppianus and the family, just to talk to, but that's about it.'

'Oppianus is a real old snob, isn't he?' Caninia said. 'Not to mention a complete crashing bore. I met him at one of those formal drinks-and-nibbles do's just after Publius and I arrived, and all he wanted to talk about was how important his family had been before the Romans came, and how things have gone downhill in the district ever since. Not exactly Lugdunum's most prepossessing citizen, is he, and he didn't like poor Claudius Cabirus at all. Do you think he did it?'

'*Caninia!*' That was Nerva again, of course.

'It's a simple question, dear.' She gave him a dazzling smile. 'He is the most obvious suspect, after all.'

'I'm sure Valerius Corvinus doesn't need your opinion.'

'I wasn't giving an opinion. I was only asking.'

'Even so, I hardly think—'

Time for a little tact. 'Actually, pal,' I said, 'I wanted to ask you about the elder son. Titus.'

Nerva frowned. 'Titus? Why on earth should you be asking about Titus?'

'No reason. Or not much of one, anyway, just a niggle. He didn't seem to have much time for his uncle. You know why that could be?'

'I've absolutely no idea. Certainly, it comes as a surprise;

Quintus seems a perfectly decent sort, he's been a good uncle to the boy, from what I'm told, and they've always got on perfectly well together. Probably some temporary family spat that's put the lad's nose out of joint. You know youngsters of his age; they can take the smallest thing so seriously and let it rankle.'

I had to hide a smile: Nerva wasn't that much older than young Cabirus himself, early to mid-twenties as opposed to Titus's nineteen. Hardly enough of a gap to justify this indulgent elder-man-of-the-world attitude. But then he was a political, and a potential high-flyer at that. 'Fair enough,' I said. 'But I noticed another odd thing. You told me at dinner yesterday evening that he and his brother got on well with their father, too.'

'Yes, I did. And they do, again as far as I know. The Cabiri are a very close family. They always have been.'

'Then that's not the impression I got when I talked to him. Oh, there was nothing obvious, certainly not anything I could put my finger on, but I had the distinct impression that young Titus had issues where his father was concerned.'

'Issues?' Nerva's eyebrows lifted. 'Really? Again, I'm surprised. They certainly wouldn't be connected with his choice of career; Cabirus might have been disappointed that he didn't choose to go into the family business, but he accepted the decision without a murmur. In fact, he was quite proud in a way. If you're right then it's due to something that I know nothing about. You're certain you weren't mistaken?'

'Maybe I was, at that,' I said. 'In any case, it's not all that important. Forget it.' Uh-huh. Interesting; and I wasn't wrong, that I was sure of. Even so, we'd let it ride for the present.

Bathyllus came back in with the drinks.

'You really should try this, Marcus,' Perilla said, picking up her barley water concoction. 'You might like it.'

I winced. 'No thanks, lady,' I said. 'I'll stick to seriously watered wine.'

'Actually, sir, I took the liberty of mixing you up some specially myself.' Bathyllus offered the tray to me. I lifted the cup and took a cautious sip. Watered, sure, but no more than half and half, twice as strong as it should've been. Nectar; comparatively speaking. I glanced at Bathyllus, and got the ghost of a wink.

Not a bad lad, at base, our major-domo. And Perilla couldn't claim I'd put him up to it, either. I took a hefty swallow. Beautiful!

'So,' I said to Perilla as he went out with the empty tray. 'What's next on the agenda?'

'Caninia suggested going across the river to Condate tomorrow.' Perilla set her cup on the table beside her. 'The complex around the Altar itself is very impressive, seemingly. Historically interesting, too: it's been a sanctuary of Lug – he's the Gallic Mercury, seemingly – time out of mind. There was a sacred grove there where the druids used to meet before they were eradicated, but of course that's disappeared – been dug up – long since. You should come, Marcus. I'm sure you can spare a few hours.'

'No, I'll pass. You two go ahead. Enjoy. Will, ah, Crinas be joining you for that?'

'He might, if he has the time.'

I was damned sure he would. Bugger.

'Actually, "eradicated" is too strong a term, Lady Rufia,' Nerva said. 'The druids haven't been rooted out of Gaul altogether, certainly not. Unfortunate, but true; we've been trying ever since the Divine Augustus's day, but they're persistent beggars, and they still crop up on occasion. Particularly among the central and western tribes and in the country districts, where civilization's spread thin. And, of course, any hint of trouble and they're straight in, egging things on. That's another reason for welcoming the upcoming British campaign.'

'I've always thought that they were rather maligned as a sect,' Perilla said. 'Caesar spoke well of them, didn't he? And didn't one spend some time in Rome later on as a guest of Tullius Cicero?'

Nerva laughed. 'Oh, don't get me wrong,' he said. 'We'd have no quarrel with them at all if they stuck to religion and philosophy. Barring the human sacrifice side of things, naturally. But they're political animals by nature, always have been, that's their role, and we can't have that. Particularly if their politics takes an anti-Roman turn, which it always does. They're rife all over in Britain, so I'm told. If the emperor really wants to dig them out root and branch, he needs to do it from the British end.'

'I'd've thought—' I said, and looked up: Bathyllus had just oiled back in. 'Yeah, little guy? What is it?'

'A message from the front gate, sir,' Bathyllus said. 'There's
someone to see you. A Gaul by the name of Silus.'

I frowned; who the hell was Silus? Then I remembered: the
clerk in Quintus's office, who'd looked like he wanted a word
with me as I was leaving. 'Fine,' I said. 'Show him in.'

Bathyllus hesitated. 'The man said he'd prefer to talk to you
in private, sir.'

Was that so, now? 'OK by me,' I said, getting up. 'Excuse
me, everyone.' I followed Bathyllus out. 'Where can I go,
sunshine?'

'There's a small sitting room in the east wing, sir. I think that
would be suitable. If you'd care to wait there I'll have him
brought.'

Jupiter, this place was a real rabbit warren! 'Fair enough,' I
said. 'Lead on, Bathyllus.'

'Small' was a slight over-statement, but in a place like the
residence that was understandable. There was a couch and a
couple of chairs, and the walls had frescos on them that wouldn't
have been out of place in a formal dining room. A bust of the
Wart eyeballed me from a pedestal; the Wart in his younger days,
and with the blemishes tactfully edited out: I doubted that the
Emperor Tiberius *propria persona* had been a sculptor's ideal
model even in his twenties. I'd brought my wine-cup with me,
and I took another sip or two while I was waiting: I might have
Bathyllus on my side, clandestinely, anyway, but the little guy
wouldn't get off with slipping me an extra ration all that often.
Goodness knows how the lady latches on to those things, but she
does, and it doesn't do to push your luck.

I waited. Finally, there was a polite knock, the door opened,
and Bathyllus came in with the clerk from the office.

'Silus, sir,' he said.

'That's fine, Bathyllus,' I said. 'Leave us alone, OK?' He went
out, closing the door behind him. 'Now, pal. Sit yourself down
and tell me what this is about.'

Not exactly prepossessing, this Silus: pushing sixty, small and
podgy, with a few strands of thin hair carefully arranged across
his bald scalp.

'I'll stand if you don't mind, sir,' he said. Add 'nervous as
hell' to the above.

'Suit yourself.' I waited. Nothing. 'Look, you came to see me. If I'm handling the conversation it's going to be pretty short.'

'I'm sorry,' he said. 'This is difficult. Very difficult.'

'Take your time, sunshine. Take a deep breath, then start wherever you like.'

'Quintus Cabirus is embezzling the company funds.'

'*What?*'

'It's true, sir. I don't know how long it's been going on, and it's not done on a regular basis, but I've known for fully six months now.'

Jupiter! Yeah, well, it was plausible, all right; Diligenta had told me that her brother-in-law managed the sales side of things. Even so—

'Why tell me?' I said.

'Because the master's dead, sir, and you're . . . well, you're an outsider, and you're official. I had to tell someone.'

'Six months is a long time to keep something like that to yourself, friend. And the question still stands: why me, not his widow Diligenta? She'd be the logical one to approach first off.'

'Sir, I'd already told the master himself, when I was certain, when I'd plucked up the courage, Master Tiberius, just a few days before he died. He told me . . . he said that he'd take care of it. I don't know if he did or not; it's possible, because there've been no . . . irregularities since that I can see. But then of course . . .' He stopped, and swallowed.

Right. But then of course someone had stiffed him, and there might well be a connection. No wonder the poor guy was chewing his fingernails down to the knuckle.

Gods!

'I've worried about it ever since. My responsibility is to the family as a whole, it always has been. I couldn't, in all conscience, continue to keep silent. But I thought that if I took it any further, told the mistress . . . Well, you must know what I thought.'

Yeah; that if Quintus had murdered his brother to cover things up, and his chief clerk had gone and blabbed to the widow, he might be next on the list. Particularly if he could provide chapter and verse.

'So you decided you'd tell me instead?' I said. 'To be on the safe side?'

'Yes, sir.'

'You're absolutely cast-iron sure about this?'

'Oh, yes. I deal with the customer invoices and receipts. There's sometimes been a discrepancy between them and the final record of takings that Master Quintus enters into the monthly books; not a huge amount each time, and as I say not on any sort of regular basis, but it's mounted up to quite a sum since the beginning of the financial year.'

'So how much are we talking about, in total?'

'Since January, sir, when I first began to check, about five thousand sesterces.'

I whistled: five thousand in six months doubled up made ten thousand a year. Multiplied by however many years the scam had been operating and Silus didn't know about. Brother Quintus had built himself up quite a nest-egg. And as a motive for murder, it'd run, easy. Sure it would.

'You can prove it?' I said.

'Oh, yes. I made copies of the relevant documents. Two sets. I gave one to Master Tiberius and kept the other. That, I still have.'

'Fair enough. You hang on to them for the present, pal, and leave things with me.' I stood up. 'Thanks for coming.'

'You're welcome, sir. It's a great relief to know that someone else knows.' He hesitated. 'You won't tell Master Quintus, will you? That I told you?'

'Absolutely not. You're out of it, as far as I can manage, I promise you that.' How I was going to keep the promise, mind, was another matter; but we'd cross that bridge when we came to it. 'Thanks for coming.'

He left. Shit, what did I do now?

Go back to the conservatory, for a start.

Nerva and Caninia had left, and Perilla was there on her own. 'Well, Marcus?' she said. 'What was that about?'

'*That* was Brother Quintus's chief clerk,' I said. 'To say Quintus has had his hand in the till for an indefinite period.'

She stared at me. '*What?*'

'Yeah, that was my reaction, too. Interesting development, right? And it turns out that Cabirus knew. As of a few days before his death, that is.'

'Ah.'

'"Ah" is right.' I sat down. 'So we have a new principal suspect.'

'What are you going to do?'

I shrugged. 'I'm not sure. I could face him with it, of course, but then I'd have to say where the information came from, and I don't want to do that at present. Or I could go to Diligenta. Technically, it's her business, not mine; with her husband dead, she's the other half of the company. And although it's motive for murder, embezzlement isn't actual proof, as such. So that's what I'll probably do: it's her shout, after all, hers and her sons'. The guy may be a crook, but he's still family.'

'Is it possible that Quintus could've done it? In practical terms, I mean.'

'Sure. No problem. He'd know Cabirus's routine, and where he'd be that afternoon, plus that it wasn't likely that anyone would be around to see him come and go. And if he has an alibi it's the one he gave me himself when I asked him, that he'd stayed at home with a cold that day. Very convenient, in retrospect. I could go to his house, check with the bought or hired help, but there'd be no guarantee that I'd get a truthful answer. Probably not, if he's primed them, like he probably has if he's telling porkies.' I was frowning. 'I wonder if Titus knew? Or suspected?'

'That he was the killer? Why should he?'

'No, not that. Just that he was a wrong 'un. In himself, I mean. Young Titus has a head on his shoulders. And it might explain the coolness latterly between him and both his uncle and his father. If he'd found out somehow, and tried to convince Cabirus—'

'But you said Titus had nothing to do with the wine business. How could he possibly know?'

'Yeah, fair point. It was just an idea. Besides, Nerva gave me the name of another source of information on the family. One of the current chief magistrates, Julius Biracus. I'll go and see him as well tomorrow.' I'd been nursing what little wine was left in my wine-cup. I swallowed it at a gulp. 'See what he has to say.'

Perilla smiled. 'By the way, you're doing very well on the wine front, dear. Keep it up.'

'Yeah, right,' I said sourly.

Mind you, if I was to solve this case there'd have to be a bit of judicious back-sliding at some stage, and the lady would just have to lump it. Gathering evidence was one thing, but when it came to the theorizing, wine was an essential.

SEVEN

I started out next day with Julius Biracus. He wasn't at home, but his housekeeper told me I'd find him in the council chambers back on the Hinge, near the market square, and I managed to nail him coming out of a meeting. I explained what I wanted.

'Delighted to help in any way I can, Valerius Corvinus,' he said. Wheezed: he was a big man, Biracus, and most of it was gut. 'Tiberius was a tragic loss to the city. Tragic. Would you like to go to my office, or should we go elsewhere?'

'Up to you, sir,' I said. 'I don't mind.'

'We'll make it Celer's, then. I find I need something to sustain me mid-morning after a council meeting, and that's where I usually go. He has a back room which is very private, so we won't be disturbed.'

'Fine by me,' I said.

I followed him down an alleyway off the Hinge to a small cookshop at the end, and we went inside. The place wasn't full, but there were two or three punters perched on high stools at the counter. They turned, and one of them gave Biracus a nod. Their eyes had gone straight to my purple stripe, but I was getting used to that by this time.

'Morning, Celer,' Biracus said to the guy behind the counter. 'All right to use your back room? Valerius Corvinus and I have business to discuss.'

'Of course.' Celer raised the wooden flap that barred the way between us and him. 'The usual, is it, sir?'

'Indeed, if you would.' He turned to me. 'Corvinus? Something to eat?'

'No thanks,' I said. 'I had breakfast.'

'So did I. What has that to do with anything? Some wine, then?'

Bugger. 'No. No, I'm OK.'

'Fair enough.' He squeezed through the gap – there wasn't much clearance – and I followed. 'I'm a bit of a traditionalist myself, mind, I prefer beer. Have you tried our Gaulish beer?'

'Uh . . . no.' And I wouldn't be doing it, either: I still had nasty memories of having a quart of the German variety forced on me years back, and I'd no wish to repeat the experience.

'Like some? Celer brews it himself, and it's the best in Lugdunum.'

'No, thanks. I'll pass.'

'Suit yourself.' He pulled back the curtain. Behind it was a small room with a table and three or four stools. 'Have a seat.' I sat. He perched. Overflowed. Whatever. 'Now. Ask away.'

'Licinius Nerva tells me you've known the Cabiri – the family as a whole, I mean – ever since they came here, yes?'

'That's right. They moved down from Treveran Augusta twenty years back, just after that bad business with Florus.'

'You say that as if there was a connection.'

Biracus frowned. 'Do I?' he said. 'Then it wasn't intentional. Even so, it isn't important. You're not a Gaul, Corvinus; you wouldn't understand these things.'

'What things?'

'It was a bad business, like I say, and water under the bridge. Oh, not here, we kept our heads down like most of the Gallic tribes. But the Treveri – they were Florus's own folk, of course – well, some of them supported him, some didn't, and that was that. After the revolt was put down and the main ringleaders were dealt with, the authorities drew a line. Very wisely, in my opinion, because taking things too far would just have led to more trouble. What was done was done, and there was an end of it.' The curtain parted, and the cookshop owner came in with a laden tray. 'Ah, good. Thank you, Celer. Most welcome.'

I waited while the contents of the tray were unloaded: a large bowl of bean stew, the best part of a loaf, a plate of sliced sausage and a wooden mug of beer the size of a small keg. No wonder the guy was the size he was, if this was a mid-morning snack.

'You're sure you won't join me, Corvinus?' he said.

'No. No, that's OK.' Celer went out again. 'So. Are you saying the Cabiri supported the revolt?'

'Oh, now, that I can't tell you. It wasn't the sort of thing you asked, at the time, and besides, it doesn't matter now. Water under the bridge and best forgotten, like I said.' He took a long swallow of the beer. 'Ah, that's better. Mind you, Diligenta's brother was certainly involved on the Florus side.'

'Her brother?'

'That's right. Licnus. I don't know what happened to him, don't know much about the man barring his name.' He tore off a bit of bread and scooped up some of the beans. 'Except that he and Diligenta were very close. Titus idolized him.'

'Titus? The son? He wasn't even born then.'

'No. But she was always talking about him. And Titus picked up on that. He's a strange boy, Titus. Both the sons are, in their different ways.'

Gods! 'I got the impression that he wasn't too enamoured of his Uncle Quintus,' I said. 'Speaking currently, at least. You any idea why that should be?'

'Really?' He scooped up some more of the beans, followed them with a couple of slices of sausage, and then took another long pull at the beer keg. 'No, none at all, or for no reason that I know of, certainly. But he has his moods, young Titus Cabirus, and he's a secretive cove. Take that girlfriend of his, now. Aia.' He chuckled. 'I don't know if Tiberius knew about her, but I'm damned sure he wouldn't have approved if he did. And I wasn't going to be the one to tell him, that was for sure. It was none of my business.'

Interesting; I was certain that, when I'd talked to Titus and brought the subject up, he'd told me categorically that he didn't have a steady girlfriend.

'Why would that be, now?' I said. 'That Cabirus wouldn't have approved, that is?'

'Oh, the girl's family. Father's a man called Doirus. Local farmer, has a place out beyond the Western Gate. He got into a bit of trouble a couple of years back, when Tiberius had my job and sat on the local bench. Tiberius had him flogged, quite rightly so, he thoroughly deserved it. But you try telling him that.'

Jupiter Best and Greatest! 'How come Nerva didn't know any of this?' I said.

'Why should he? As far as the earlier part goes, the revolt side of things, it's ancient history. Young Nerva's only been here five minutes. Governor Gabinius, too.' Biracus finished off the beans and wiped the bowl with the last hunk of bread. 'Where the rest's concerned, Aia and her father – well, no offence, but Nerva's a Roman, isn't he? Romans go around blinkered half the time, can't see their nose before their face.'

Yeah, well, I'd agree with him there. Gods!

'You know anything about a dead wolf that was left in Market Square two or three months back, by the way?' I said.

'No, can't help you there at all, I'm afraid.' Biracus chewed on the bread and reached for the last of the sausage. 'Oh, I know what you're talking about, but that's as far as it goes. The governor asked me the same question at the time, and I'll give you the same answer I gave him: it was just a prank, no more. Some of the local youngsters messing around.' He gave me a direct look. 'Listen, Corvinus. We Lugdunans – Segusiavi, whatever – we've always supported Rome, through thick and thin. We aren't troublemakers, any of us. It was just a bit of thoughtless silliness, with nothing serious behind it, you can take that from me.'

Yeah, well, I wasn't altogether sure that he was being completely open on that score, at least as far as knowing nothing about the matter went – Julius Biracus struck me as a pretty smart and switched-on guy, despite his resemblance to a pregnant hippo – but I was willing to take him at his word. Besides, I reckoned I'd got my sesterce's-worth for this particular meeting. More than. I stood up.

'Thanks for your help, sir,' I said.

'You're welcome.' Then, as I was turning to go, 'Incidentally, Corvinus, did you happen to bump into young Claudilla when you were at Tiberius's house? That's the daughter, of course.'

'No, I didn't,' I said. 'Her mother told me she was on a visit to a friend in Arausio.'

He made a *tssk!* of annoyance. 'Oh, yes,' he said. 'Silly of me. I'd forgotten. The new baby. What was the friend's name again?'

'Diligenta didn't say.' I was frowning. 'Why should I have needed to—?'

'Can't recall who the girl was myself, either. I've a mind like a sieve, you know, and it gets worse as I grow older. Take my advice, boy, and stick at the age you are.' He chuckled. 'Oh, one more name, off the top of my head, before it slips my memory altogether. Julius Vindus.'

'Who?'

'He's an officer in the procurator's guard. Also, Julius Oppianus's nephew and ward, and a good friend of Titus Cabirus's. In fact, they go hunting together quite often, up in the mountains.'

'Is that so, now? What does he—?'

'That's right. Just a suggestion, naturally.' He took another long pull at his beer. 'Good to have met you, Corvinus. It's nice to see a new face, even under these unpleasant circumstances.'

'Ah . . . right. Right.' I was feeling sorely puzzled. 'Thanks again, sir.'

'Don't mention it. My pleasure, any time. As I said, Tiberius was a good friend, both to me and the city. If you can catch the man who killed him then good luck to you.'

'Oh, incidentally,' I said. 'One last question on my side.'

'Yes?'

'Julius Oppianus. He liable to be chosen as Cabirus's replacement for the Altar ceremony?'

'I'd imagine so. Certainly he's by far the most likely possibility.'

Bland as hell.

'Thanks again,' I said, and left.

After that little interview, I needed time to think, badly. Not immediately, though; I had to talk to Diligenta first. That was something I wasn't looking forward to, but it couldn't be put off.

The servant-girl – Cotuinda, wasn't it? – was sweeping the porch when I arrived.

'The mistress in?' I said.

'Yes, sir.' She leaned the brush against the wall and flicked a stray lock of hair out of her eyes. 'She's in the kitchen having a word with the cook about lunch. If you'll wait in the living room I'll go and fetch her.'

I followed her inside.

'Have a seat. She shouldn't be long.' The girl carried on through to the back part of the house. I sat down in one of the wicker chairs.

Sure enough, it was only a minute or so before Diligenta herself came through.

'Valerius Corvinus,' she said. 'I didn't expect to see you back so soon. Was there something you forgot to ask?'

'Uh . . . no, not exactly.' Hell; this was going to be tricky. Still, there was no sense in faffing around, and none in covering up the details, either. 'There've been certain developments. I had a visit from your chief clerk Silus yesterday.'

'Silus? What on earth would he want to see you about?'

'He, ah, told me that your brother-in-law has been fiddling the accounts. Helping himself to the company money.'

She sat down opposite me. 'You're joking!' she said.

'Not at all.'

She was quiet for a long time. 'You're sure?' she said at last. 'I mean, Silus is sure?'

'Absolutely. He has documentary proof. Or so he said.'

'And how long has this been going on for?'

'Silus didn't know. At least six months, but possibly – probably – a lot longer.'

'I see.' She looked down at her hands. 'Why didn't he come to me directly? Or, if it was that long ago when he found out, to Tiberius? That would have been the sensible thing.'

This was the really difficult bit, and there was no way of getting round it.

'Actually, he did,' I said. 'Tell your husband, I mean. Just before he died.'

Silence; *long* silence. Diligenta hadn't looked up.

Then: 'Quintus is not a killer,' she said. I didn't answer. She raised her eyes and looked at me directly. 'I'm telling you, Corvinus. I'm totally sure of that. Quintus did *not* murder Tiberius; he hasn't got it in him. Besides, why should he? They were a good partnership, they each had their separate role to play and they complemented each other. The business was doing well, and it was for that very reason. Quintus would have been a fool to spoil things.'

'Yeah, well, maybe he had no choice. If his brother had found out, which he had—'

'Tiberius wouldn't have done anything drastic. Oh, he would have been shocked, certainly, and gravely disappointed. There would have been words, probably strong words, but they were brothers, after all. The matter would've been resolved amicably in the end, somehow or other; Quintus would know that. How much money are we actually talking about?'

'Silus said a total of five thousand sesterces. That's only since January, mind.'

'Not an absolute fortune, then. Oh, it's a lot, I don't deny that. But as I said the business was doing well, even so. It's not as if he was bleeding us dry.'

I didn't believe this; it sounded like she was actually defending him.

'Look, Diligenta,' I said. 'I'm sorry, but I'd've thought you'd be more—'

'Outraged? Censorious?' She smiled weakly. 'I'm angry, yes; of course I am. Angry, surprised, and, as Tiberius would have been, shocked and very, very disappointed. But as I said – as Tiberius himself would have said – Quintus is family, and that makes all the difference in the world. Thank you for telling me, Valerius Corvinus. Leave it with me, I'll take care of it.' Yeah; more or less what Silus said Cabirus had told him, two months back. Well, I supposed it was fair enough; like I'd told Perilla, it was the lady's business, not mine, and I'd faithfully passed the message on.

I'd keep an open mind where embezzlement as a motive for murder was concerned, mark you.

Diligenta stood up. 'Now, if that's all for the present—' she said.

'Actually, no. Although the other thing's curiosity more than anything else.'

'Curiosity?' She sat down again.

'I've just been talking to Julius Biracus.'

'Yes?'

'About . . . well, about various things. But he talked about when you and your husband – and Quintus, of course – came down from Augusta twenty years back.'

She smiled. 'Forgive me, but there's nothing to be curious

about in that. You knew we were from there to begin with. In fact, we talked about it.'

'Yeah, I know, but according to you it was purely a business move on your husband's part. Biracus seemed to think it had more to do with the troubles following the Florus revolt.' Not exactly true, in fact verging on a complete porky, but I thought a little embroidery might well be justified here. 'He also told me something more about that brother of yours who I think you mentioned; Licnus, was that his name?'

The smile had disappeared, and her lips were set in a straight line. 'Licnus. That's right.'

'He gave me the distinct impression that he'd been involved on the wrong side. Florus's side. And that you and he had been pretty close.'

There was a long pause. Finally:

'Biracus,' she said quietly, 'is an old busybody. That's all in the past; we're Lugdunans now, and life has moved on. As far as Licnus goes, yes, we were close – we were sister and brother, after all – but I haven't seen him since we moved. In fact, I seem to remember telling you that after my marriage I lost touch with both my brother and my sister. Or am I wrong?'

'No. But—'

'There are no buts; I simply did not feel the need at the time to provide full details. Since you seem interested, I will now. Quadrunia, my elder sister, is married to a wholesale draper, an obnoxious man whom I cordially loathed. They make an excellent match. She still lives in Augusta; Licnus does not, and for all I know might be dead. Now is your curiosity satisfied?'

'Ah . . . yeah. Yes, it is,' I said. 'Look, I'm sorry if I caused any offence. It wasn't deliberate. And it isn't Biracus's fault; he told me that what happened during and after the Florus revolt was dead and buried. I just—'

'That is so. And I'd prefer if it stayed that way. What's past is past.' She took a deep breath. 'Now. I'm sorry in my turn that I lost my temper: you're a Roman, Corvinus, not a Gaul, and some things – depths of feeling – you don't understand. You can't be expected to, and I forgot that for a moment. Forgive me?'

'Sure. Forgiven and forgotten.'

'Good. It's reciprocal. Well, if that's all this time—'

'Actually, I was wondering if I could have another word with your son Publius.'

She frowned. 'Publius? Of course. What about?'

'Just a couple of things I wanted to ask him. Is he at home?'

'Yes, he's upstairs in his room. He usually is, unfortunately; it's difficult to get him out of there. Shall I call him?'

'No, I'll go up, if I may.' I hadn't planned, when I arrived, to talk to the kid – sixteen, and so technically an adult, he might be, but I thought of him as such. In the light of events, it might be better to do things in private. 'If it's all right with you, naturally.'

'Of course it is. His room's at the top of the stairs, immediately to your right when you reach the landing. I can have Cotuinda take you, if you like.'

'No, that's OK,' I said. 'I can find my own way. Thank you, Diligenta.'

'You're welcome.'

The stairs were at the far end of the entrance corridor. I went up, found the door, and knocked. No answer.

'Publius?' I said. 'It's me. Marcus Corvinus.'

'What do you want?'

'Just a chat.'

There was a pause. Then he said: 'OK. You can come in, if you have to.'

Grudging as hell. Still. I went inside.

The room was big, and very light, with the sun streaming through the open window facing me. The kid was sitting at a large desk – a table, really – under the window itself. It was covered with a jumble of models: temples, ships, chariots. Pride of place in the centre was one I recognized as Lugdunum's theatre, complete and beautifully made of wood and painted canvas. There was another, smaller table to one side with wood-working tools, a small vice and paint pots and brushes. Rolls of canvas and thin wooden spars were stacked beneath it. The place looked more like a workshop than a bedroom; the only evidence of that was the bed itself, a clothes chest, a few shelves and a couple of cloaks hanging from pegs set in the wall.

'I'm busy,' Publius said. 'What do you want?'

'I told you. Just a chat.' I closed the door behind me. 'It won't take long. I need the answers to a couple of questions, that's all.'

'Questions about what?' He had a tiny paintbrush in his hand, and he was working on what I recognized as a scale model of one of those three-piece bits of theatre scenery that you get in the wings of a stage, with stylized representations of the three main settings for scenes in a comedy: town, country and seashore. He laid it down carefully and turned to face me.

'That's a pretty impressive hobby you've got there.' I indicated the contents of the table. 'Must be skilled work.'

'It is. I'll ask you again: questions about what?'

'Detailed, too. And hard on the eyes. It's a good job you've got so much light here. The window overlooks the garden, doesn't it?'

'You know it does; you can see for yourself. And you asked me that before, didn't you?'

'And whether you'd seen anything, the day of the murder. Yes.' There were a couple of theatrical masks hanging on the wall: a comic slave's and a tragic heroine's. They looked home-made, but they were pretty good, all the same. 'All the same, I'll ask you again, because it's important. Did you? See anything or anyone?'

'No. I said I was asleep.'

'With the shutters open? That must've been difficult, this room facing south and all and it being the early afternoon.'

He hesitated. 'The shutters were closed. I closed them when I came up.'

'Is that so, now? And you didn't happen to look out at all while you were doing it?'

'I may've done. So? It'd only be for a moment. What could I have seen?'

'I don't know. But you'd have a good view. Someone in the garden, perhaps. Someone you knew.'

'Like who?'

'Your Uncle Quintus?'

He stared at me. '*No!* Why should I have seen him?'

'Just an idea.'

'Then it's nonsense. I told you: I didn't see anyone. No one at all. Clear?'

I shrugged; he seemed genuine enough, but it had been worth a try.

'OK,' I said. 'What about Titus?'

He went very still. 'What about Titus?'

'The impression I got when I talked to him was that before your father died Titus had . . . well, maybe "had a disagreement with him" is putting things too strongly. But there was a coolness. Am I right?'

He hesitated again. Odd, though: I had the feeling that the tenseness had gone out of him. Then he said, grudgingly: 'Maybe.'

'You happen to know why?'

'No.'

'Could it have had anything to do with his girlfriend? Aia?'

'How do you know about Aia?'

'So you do? Know about her, I mean?'

'Just that she exists. I've never met her.'

'Your father didn't know. Or maybe he did, that's the point, at least latterly. Did your mother?'

'No. Titus was keeping her a secret. I only know about her myself because he let it slip one day. But he made me promise to keep my mouth shut. Which I did, because she was Titus's business, no one else's.'

'So you didn't tell your father about her? Or Titus didn't?'

'*No!*'

'And your father didn't find out about her some other way?'

'How should I know? Probably not; it was never mentioned, at any rate, and it would've been.'

We were back to the sulky, sideways looks. Ah, well; that was a point or two cleared up. Or at least clarified. On the other hand, there'd been that hesitation over the shutters, and the odd reaction when I'd first brought up the subject of Titus . . .

'Fair enough,' I said, turning towards the door.

'That's all?' Surprise.

'Yeah,' I said. 'Shouldn't it be? Unless there's anything else you want to tell me.'

'No. No, nothing.'

'Right, then. I'll see you.'

But he didn't answer. He was already reaching for the bit of stage scenery he'd been working on and the paintbrush.

I went back downstairs. No sign, now, of Diligenta, but Cotuinda was waiting, and she saw me out.

Right; where to now? There was still a slice of the morning left, and under normal circumstances I'd be reckoning I was due a cup of wine somewhere. However, a promise was a promise, so I was stymied. I still had my doubts about abstinence doing me any good, mind: far from feeling more chirpy and alert, I was going around half the time with my tongue hanging out.

So. Perhaps a call on one of the also-mentioned: this phantom girlfriend of Titus's, or at least on her father. Maybe a waste of time, but my gut feeling was telling me that the change in relationship between Titus and Cabirus was important in some way. Besides, he'd've had to have some reason apart from congenital secretiveness for deliberately lying to me about his love life. And the discovery on Cabirus's part that his elder son was seeing – presumably, from the cover-up, with serious intentions – the daughter of a felon that he'd had publicly flogged would fit the bill pretty neatly.

Doirus it was, then. With his farm, according to Biracus, out beyond the Western Gate. At least, starting from Diligenta's, I was on the right side of town: the Gate lay at the west end of Boundary Marker Street, just down the road, in other words. I'd have to find the farm itself, of course, but there'd be enough locals around to direct me.

There were plenty of farms on offer, mostly growing a selection of vegetables or grain: neither grapes nor olives were a viable crop here, as they would be as a matter of course on farms around a town in Italy, although I suspected that that might be more a result of cultural differences than of weather. Maybe things would change in the future. What you did get a lot of, and wouldn't to the same extent back home, was livestock, particularly sheep and cows. Which was fair enough: wool is a major industry in Gaul, and they use far more dairy products than we do.

I'd covered a scant quarter-mile when I spotted a guy hoeing a field of beans next to the road. I went over.

'Good morning,' I said. 'I wonder if you can help me? I'm looking for Doirus's place.' He just looked at me blankly. Shit, of course; the language barrier. 'Uh . . . I don't speak Gallic. You speak Latin?' Not a flicker. Hell. 'Doirus? Farm?' I put my hand palm down under my brows and mimed searching.

He pointed further down the road. 'Bridge. After—' He tapped his right arm.

'Got you.' Well, evidently we'd reached the limits of his linguistic abilities; not that I could sneer, mind, because my command of Gallic was zilch. 'Thanks, friend.'

'Welcome.'

I carried on. Bugger; now that was something I hadn't thought of. So far, I hadn't had anything to do with the local population, at least the ones outside the towns. Oh, sure, we'd passed through a fair stretch of rural Gaul on our way here, but that had been in a government-owned coach, with government-owned bought help to do the talking where talking had been needed, and stopping, between towns, at government-owned posting stations. We'd been effectively screened, all the way. I was assuming this Doirus guy – and, indeed, his daughter – spoke good Latin. Good enough to communicate in, anyway. If I was wrong then I was in complete schtuck.

There was a bridge ahead, a small wooden one over a rush of stream-water, and, sure enough, a track leading off immediately to the right. I took it.

The track ended in a farmyard: a wattle-and-daub cottage with outbuildings either side, a fenced-off area of tussocky grass with a few goats and a tethered cow, five or six geese, and a small flock of chickens running free about the yard. There was an oldish guy in a short tunic and trousers plus serious Gallic moustache and braids, forking dung-heavy straw out of one of the outbuildings into a wheelbarrow. He laid down the fork, wiped his forehead on his sleeve, and watched me in silence as I came closer.

'Uh . . . you speak Latin, pal?' I said.

'Sure. Why shouldn't I?' A long way from friendly – I was getting a look that was suspicious, at best – but at least we were communicating. That was a relief, at any rate.

'No offence,' I said. 'It's just that the guy hoeing beans that I asked directions from half a mile up the road hardly had a word.'

He snorted. 'That'd be Iccavus. He was putting you on. A real joker, is Iccavus.'

'Right. Right.' Oh, ha! Well, Nerva had said that Gallic humour could be pretty gross. And no doubt the locals viewed any likely Roman as fair game. 'You Doirus?'

'I am.' Still no smile, and the suspicion was there in spades. 'What can I do for you?'

'The name's Corvinus. I'm looking into the death of Claudius Cabirus.'

He spat to one side. 'So?'

'Your daughter Aia's friendly with his son. Titus.'

That got me a long, slow look. 'Is she, indeed? That's news to me.'

Damn; now *there* was a complication I hadn't thought of! 'You mean you didn't know?'

'Too right I didn't. I'd've had words with the little trollop otherwise. And I will, too, now that I do, the next time I see her.'

Oh, hell; I'd really screwed that one up, hadn't I? That was twice in one day I'd put someone's back up. And Titus wasn't going to be a very happy bunny when he found out, either; him and the lady both. Nice going, Corvinus.

'You mean she doesn't live here?' I said.

'No. She's in service in town, has been for the past year. She lives in, naturally.'

'Whereabouts? Just out of interest?'

'"Just out of interest", eh?' He picked up the fork again. 'What's your game?'

'Nothing, pal, nothing.' I held up my hands. 'I said: I'm looking into Claudius Cabirus's murder. On behalf of the emperor.'

'The emperor, is it? Fancy!' But he'd lowered the fork. 'All right. She works for the Valentus family. They've a house near the Ocean Gate.' Interesting; not far from the Cabirus place itself. The two families would be practically neighbours. Maybe that's how the two had met. 'Now if that's all you came for you can push off. I've work to do.'

'I understand you had a brush with Cabirus yourself some time back.'

Another long, slow look. 'Who told you that?'

'The joint senior magistrate. Julius Biracus.'

'Uh-huh.' He sucked on a tooth. 'Well, then.' He laid the fork aside, pulled the tunic over his head and turned round. His back was a mass of healed scars. 'There you are. That was my "brush" with Cabirus. Satisfied?' He turned to face me again and put the tunic back on. 'I'd've thought the girl would've had more pride than to take up with any relation of that bastard. She's a good lass, Aia, at root, always has been. It hit her hard enough at the time, and with her mother dead of the fever when she was five, and her being the only one we had living, we were pretty close.'

'So what was it for? The flogging? You mind telling me?'

'We were behind with our taxes. The procurator sent his men to take most of the season's grain in their place. We'd had a piss-poor harvest that year, and it would've meant either that there was damn all seed corn left for the next season or that we'd have a slim winter of it. I tried to stop them and one got hit. I broke the bastard's nose for him.' He shrugged. 'I should've saved myself the effort. They took the corn anyway, and I got twenty lashes at the next assize. Courtesy of Claudius fucking Cabirus. So don't ask me to be sorry someone stuck a knife into him, because you won't get any tears from me.'

Yeah, well; I supposed that that was understandable, under the circumstances. 'OK,' I said. 'I'll be getting back. Thanks for your help.'

'What help?' He picked up the fork again. 'You see Aia, you tell her from me to drop that sod like a hot brick, find someone decent, or she'll have me to reckon with. She'll listen; like I say, she isn't a bad girl at heart. But you know kids that age, they've no sense, particularly the girls. Think they know best, and to hell with everything else.'

'Yeah. Way of the world, pal. Way of the world.'

'It certainly is.' He turned back to his work, and I started walking back up the track.

Food for thought.

EIGHT

I got back to the residence in the middle of the afternoon. No sign of Perilla yet – she'd still be out on her culture jag with Caninia and, doubtless, Domitius bloody Crinas, over in Condate – so I settled down for a much-needed think in the conservatory with a cup of Bathyllus's doctored-but-don't-ask-too-many-questions wine.

She rolled in – alone, this time – just short of the dinner hour.

'Have a nice time?' I said sourly.

'Oh, yes. It was fascinating.' She sat. Bathyllus materialized behind me. 'The usual, please, Bathyllus. Marcus, the complex is *huge*. You should've come with us.'

'Yeah, well, I was working, wasn't I? And I had a pretty interesting day of my own.'

'Did you?'

'Oh, yes. Profitable, instructive, and in places surprising. Who could ask for more? Except that it was a tad lacking in alcoholic content.'

'Marcus . . .'

'OK.' I shrugged. 'Even so.'

'Did you tell Diligenta about Quintus?'

'Yeah. Actually, she didn't seem too concerned. Still, I can see her point: he is family, and every family has their black sheep. Or at least a seriously-off-white one. She evidently thinks she can sort things out for herself.'

'That's very generous of her. And very forgiving.'

'Maybe. But I wouldn't like to be in Brother Quintus's shoes when that lady gets him on the mat and faces him with it. She's no pushover, Diligenta. The problem is, it knocks the theory that Quintus is our killer into a cocked hat.'

'How so?'

'Well, she seemed to think that, even if he did know, her husband would've taken the same line. There would've been no reason for Quintus to kill him to cover up his tracks.'

'Quintus might not have known that.'

'No. All the same, she said that he would've done, she's known him for a long time, and naturally it goes the other way as well. Plus, of course, the two men were brothers. If she says she doesn't think Quintus is capable of murder – which she does – then her opinion carries weight; while on his part Quintus would've been able to lay a pretty safe bet that, even if he had been rumbled, he'd get away with no more than a smacked wrist. So yes, the guy could very well have been our perp in theory, but in practice there're too many objections. Unless he had some other motive, of course. Bugger.'

Bathyllus shimmered in with the lady's barley water on a tray. 'Dinner will be served shortly, sir. Madam,' he said. 'If that's convenient.'

'Fine, little guy,' I said. 'By the way, we don't need the grand butler act when we're by ourselves with no company, right? So tone it down a little, will you?'

He sniffed, and exited.

'Spoilsport,' Perilla said.

'Yeah, well, we don't, and he should.'

'What other motive could he have? Quintus, I mean?'

'None that I know of. But crooked is as crooked does. I don't altogether trust Brother Quintus any more. Besides, there's something out of kilter about his past. About the whole family's past, for that matter.'

'Oh, yes? What's that?'

'I don't know. Maybe – probably – nothing that's relevant. But that was the second thing I found out today, from my talk with the senior magistrate, Julius Biracus. You know old Cornelius Lentulus? Lives up the road from us, on the Caelian?'

'Yes, Marcus, of course I do. What has Lentulus got to do with anything?'

'They've got a lot in common, those two, besides their size. Ask Lentulus anything about goings-on in the Senate and the murky back corridors of power any time these fifty-odd years and he'll have the details at his fingertips. I reckon Biracus is the same where Lugdunum's concerned. And like Lentulus he knows far more than he's telling. Or in this case hinting; at least, reading between the lines, I think he was.'

'So what, specifically, was he hinting about the Cabirus family?'

'That it was no coincidence that they moved from Augusta to Lugdunum just after the Florus revolt.'

'Perhaps not. And?'

'What do you mean, "and"?'

'Marcus, it would have been perfectly understandable, under the circumstances. Life couldn't have been too easy there at the time. To begin with, in the aftermath there would probably be reparations to pay, so money would be tight in general. And because of the revolt, relations with their former customers outwith the region, Roman and otherwise, would have been soured, or at least tinged with suspicion.'

'Only if they'd supported the wrong side.'

'Did they?'

I frowned. 'That's what I'm not clear on; not as far as the family as a whole is concerned. Biracus fudged it. Oh, he admitted he'd done as much, on the perfectly reasonable grounds that it didn't matter any more, that the world had moved on these past twenty years. But he did say that Diligenta's brother had gone in with Florus, and that the two of them – Diligenta and Licnus, that was the brother's name – had been pretty close. The implication was there.'

'Come on, Marcus!' Perilla sipped her barley water. 'Biracus is absolutely right: the revolt was a generation ago, it's long over and done with, and who supported whom at the time is completely academic. Certainly it has no current relevance.'

'Yeah.' I was still frowning. 'Even so, Diligenta didn't at all like me bringing up the subject. She got quite heated, in fact.'

'Wouldn't you? Some Roman who only arrived two days ago goes poking his nose into a part of her private life that she's long since left behind, then practically accuses a member of her family to her face of being a traitor. How would you feel yourself?'

'I didn't exactly—'

'That's what it sounded like to me, dear. And my sympathies are all with Diligenta.'

'Well, maybe. And as you say it's irrelevant now. Forget it.' I shifted in my chair. 'Anyway, there's a lot more to report. Like I say, Biracus was a gold mine. First of all, young Titus Cabirus has a girlfriend called Aia.'

'So?'

'Only that that's curious in itself. When I talked to him yesterday about his plans for the future he said he was thinking of a career in the army, and that there was nothing barring his family to keep him here. I asked about girlfriends and he said no, he hadn't got one.'

Perilla laughed. 'Marcus, be realistic! He's – what – nineteen years old? For a start, she may be a casual attachment, and for another thing, again, it was no business of yours.'

'Admitted. But you weren't there at the time. It was a straight denial to a straight question. Why should he lie, which is exactly what he did, if it wasn't important in some way? It was no skin off his nose, or it shouldn't have been.'

'There could be several reasons, all perfectly innocent. Is the girl from the same social class as he is? Because if not then he might consider that the fewer people who know about her the better, particularly since the information might get back to his family. Does Diligenta know she exists?'

'No. Actually, she doesn't. I know that for sure. But—'

'There you are, then. Didn't you have any dubious girlfriends yourself at that age?'

'Uh, yeah, as it happens, now you come to mention it, off and on, but—'

'And you kept them quiet from your parents too, yes?'

Bugger. 'Look, lady,' I said. 'Just cut it out and listen, will you? I know what I'm talking about. This is a different ball game altogether.'

'Very well, dear. I'm sorry. You have the floor.'

'I followed the girl up. Her father has a farm out in the sticks, and he was flogged on Cabirus's orders a few years back for punching one of the procurator's men's lights out when they tried to take his grain for unpaid taxes; that's the *procurator*'s men, note, the same outfit that her current boyfriend works for. Aia's an only child, the mother's long dead, and she and her father are very close. Given all that, what would be your conclusion?'

She was twisting a lock of her hair. 'Ah.'

'Right. Ah. Chances are, the relationship is a set-up, and was from the start; she engineered it for reasons of her own. Which means that she's a prime candidate for our perp.'

'Oh, Marcus! That's going just a bit too far, surely.'

'Not at all. At least, not in my book. It makes sense, anyway, particularly if Titus knows nothing about the flogging part of things, which I'll bet you he doesn't. He's never met the father himself, that's for sure, so he'd have no reason to unless she told him off her own bat.'

'Have you talked to her yet?'

'No. But her father says she's a maid or some such with a family by the name of Volentus, who're practically neighbours to the Cabiri. I was planning on going round there tomorrow.'

'My, you have had a busy day.'

I grinned. 'I'm not finished yet, lady. Take it in order. When I was at Diligenta's I had another talk, if you can call it that, with young Publius. Upstairs in his room, which is where he spends most of his time.'

'Yes?'

'Point is, he has a big work-table right under the window overlooking the garden, and when he's working on his models that's where he sits, facing the window itself. OK; so say on the afternoon of the murder Publius wasn't asleep like he and his mother claimed. Say he decided to stay awake and work on the models instead.'

'Then he couldn't possibly have missed anyone going into or coming out of the garden.'

'Right. Oh, sure, it's not hundred per cent certain: the kid's a complete geek where his hobby's concerned, and that type tend to ignore the rest of the world when they're absorbed in whatever they're doing. But when I asked him if he'd gone to bed with the window-shutters open it fazed him for a moment before he told me he'd closed them; so my bet is that he wasn't asleep at all, that he saw someone or something, and that he's covering.'

'Who could he have seen?'

'Yeah, well, that's the interesting part. I mentioned Titus straight after, and he froze up.'

'*Titus?*'

'Like I say: interesting, yes? Only then when I went on to ask him whether he knew of any difference of opinion recently between Titus and his father that might've soured their relationship he seemed to relax.'

'So.' Perilla was still twisting the lock of hair. 'You think Publius might have seen his brother. In the garden. At the time when their father was killed.'

'Yeah. That's about the sum of it.'

'Oh, Marcus!'

I shrugged. 'It's only a theory, sure. What possible reason Titus might have for killing his father – and I admit that it'd have to be a real biggie – I've no idea. But it fits the facts as we know them, or at least one interpretation of them. He was on duty that day, or so he claimed. That much I can check, which I will, tomorrow.'

'Things seem to be revolving round Titus at the moment, don't they?'

'So I've noticed. Still—'

'What else did you get?'

'Ah. That was Biracus again. Right at the end of the conversation he did a Lentulus.'

'How do you mean, dear?'

'You know how the old bugger suddenly comes out with an irrelevance that he knows damn well isn't irrelevant at all, quite the reverse, but doesn't want to tell you as much in so many words?'

'No, Marcus, I don't, not from personal experience. I've hardly ever spoken to Cornelius Lentulus, and when I have the conversation has revolved round dinner parties he's attended and the various forms of entertainment thereat. Usually embarrassingly so.'

I grinned; that was Lentulus, all right. And I'd always had a sneaking suspicion that, on the few occasions he and Perilla had met, he'd gone out of his way to wind the lady up. Nubian contortionist dancing girls with tame pythons came to mind. 'Yeah, well, he does,' I said. 'Which is what Biracus did. For a start, he asked me out of the blue if I'd met Claudilla when I was at the Cabirus place.'

'Who's Claudilla?'

'Exactly. She's the daughter, the youngest of the three, and she shouldn't figure at all, because she's been away in Arausio since before the murder, staying with a friend there who's due to have a baby.'

'And?'

'That's the puzzling thing. Biracus claimed that he'd forgotten. What's more, that he couldn't remember the friend's name. He made a point of it, too.'

'You've lost me. What possible bearing could that have on—?'

'I told you. It was a classic Lentulus ploy. Lentulus doesn't forget things; you know they call him the Elephant down at the Senate House?'

'I thought that was because of his size.'

'Yeah, that as well, but still. And I'd bet Biracus is the same. It was quite deliberate.'

'To what end?'

'I've been thinking about that, and the way he said it. My guess is the story was a fabrication on the family's part to avoid a scandal; that the girl had got herself pregnant and they'd sent her to Arausio for the duration.'

'Oh, Marcus! That is pure wild speculation, and you know it!'

'Of course it is. No argument. But it fits, and it's standard procedure in these circumstances, right?'

'Perhaps it is. Even so, true or not, it's no concern of yours. Or it shouldn't be.'

'Hang on, lady. I'm not finished. Biracus went on to drop another name. A guy called Julius Vindus. He's a friend of the family's, specifically of young Titus's, and like him he's one of Procurator Laco's men. Furthermore, he's Julius Oppianus's nephew.'

'Ah.' She took a contemplative sip of her barley water. 'And you think this Vindus might be the child's father?'

'It's a fair bet.'

'So what does this have to do with Cabirus's murder?'

'Come on, Perilla! Use your head! I haven't worked out the whys and wherefores yet, but it's another link, isn't it? Oppianus has enough of a down on the Cabirus family already; how do you think he'd feel if he found out that not only was a nephew of his interested in the daughter but that the relationship had gone the length of a pregnancy?'

'Hmm.' She twisted a lock of her hair. 'Yes, I see. It still wouldn't explain why he would stick a knife into her father, though, does it?'

'It would if Cabirus had found out who was responsible and was forcing a marriage. That'd do it, in spades.'

'Maybe. But he'd approach Vindus's father, surely, not his uncle.'

'Vindus doesn't have one, or at least that was Biracus's implication. He said that the guy was Oppianus's ward.'

'Ah,' she said again. 'In that case perhaps he would have a motive.'

'Sweet holy Jupiter, lady! How much more do you want?'

'Yes, I'm sorry, Marcus. You're quite right, of course; it's a perfectly valid theory.'

'Thank you.'

'So what are you going to do now?'

'Find Vindus and face him with it. That should be easy enough; like I say, he'll be stationed at the procurator's office, and I was meaning to go down there tomorrow anyway. Then have another word with Julius Oppianus. If I can—'

Bathyllus buttled in. 'Dinner, sir,' he said. He buttled out again. Short and sweet. Perilla and I exchanged glances.

'He seems to have taken your instructions to heart,' Perilla said.

'So it would appear.' I grinned. Ah, well, I doubted if the miff would last all that long; it took a lot to cramp Bathyllus's style.

Tomorrow was another day. We went through to dinner.

NINE

I was off straight after breakfast the next morning. First stop the procurator's offices down the Hinge.

'Me again, lads,' I said to the two squaddies on the door: they were the same guys who'd been on duty before and had pointed me towards the cookshop where I'd talked to Titus. 'Another question for you. You happen to know where I can find a Julius Vindus?'

'Out of town today, sir, I'm afraid,' one of them said. 'On an assignment. He should be back this evening.'

Damn! Still, it couldn't be helped; he wasn't going to disappear altogether, and tomorrow would do just as well. 'Thanks a lot,' I said, and carried on inside.

The lobby was impressive: large, with a coloured-marble floor, decorated walls and a statue of Claudius – idealized again, but what would you expect? – taking pride of place. The sculptor had shown him in the usual pose, dressed in a mantle, left arm gathering up the folds, right hand stretched out in front of him, palm up. Personally, I've often wondered whether the guys who commission those things, or who are responsible for putting them in place, have any concept of irony: for anyone coming into a public building the main purpose of whose occupants is to screw money out of the local population in taxes to be greeted by a representation of the head of the Roman state with his hand out seems pretty ironic to me. Still, we Romans have always been insensitive pragmatists, so maybe it was deliberate.

'Valerius Corvinus! What brings you here?'

I looked to my right: the procurator himself, Laco, in conversation with a couple of clerks next to a very nice bronze of the goddess Artemis. He came over.

'Good morning, Procurator,' I said. 'Just checking up on a technicality.'

'How is the investigation going?'

'Not bad. It's still early days yet.'

'I hope you're not working too hard. After all, it is your first visit to Lugdunum, and you owe it to yourself to relax a little bit, see the sights.'

'No, that's OK,' I said. 'I'm not much one for sightseeing. Perilla's doing the rounds, though. Getting Nerva's wife Caninia to take her in hand was a good move on the governor's part.'

'Yes, well, I'd at least have liked to have you round to dinner, for a real Gaulish meal. But I'm afraid that, like the governor, I'll be away on tour very shortly; it's that time of year, you understand. Up north, into Belgica; my remit covers both provinces. A great pity. I enjoyed our conversation, and of course meeting your lady wife.'

'Maybe another time,' I said diplomatically. A real Gaulish meal, eh? Now that was something I wasn't in any hurry to try. The day Gallic cuisine hits the dinner tables of the empire the sky will be full of flying pigs. Rumour had it that the bastards even used butter to cook their snails in. Meton would have a fit.

'So,' Laco said. 'What's this technicality you're checking up on?'

I couldn't very well not tell him, though I'd've preferred not to. 'Just an entry in the duty roster. For Titus Cabirus.'

That got me a very sharp look. '*Titus*?'

'Yeah. Like I say, it's just a routine check.'

'You surely don't suspect Titus of killing his own father, do you?' He was frowning. 'Besides, I told you at the governor's dinner, the lad's one of my most promising young officers. If I'm any judge – which I am – he has a brilliant career ahead of him.'

'No, not at all,' I lied. 'Just being thorough. Dotting the i's and crossing the t's.'

'Hmm. You know your business best, of course, but I think one can be too painstaking.' He turned towards the two clerks he'd been talking to when I came in and raised his voice. 'Largus! Over here a moment, please.' One of the clerks came over. 'This is Valerius Corvinus, the emperor's personal representative from Rome. He wants to see one of the past duty rosters. Take care of it, will you?'

'Certainly, Procurator.' The man looked at me curiously. 'If you'd care to follow me, sir?'

'If I don't see you again before I go, Corvinus, good luck with the enquiry. A pleasure to have met you, and do give my best regards to the emperor when next you see him.' He held out his hand, and we shook. 'Off you go, Largus.'

'Yes, sir.'

The guy took me along one of the corridors at the back of the lobby, stopped at an office door, opened it and stood aside for me to pass. The place was lined with wall-to-wall document-cubbies.

'Now, sir,' he said, following me in. 'What exactly was the date you were interested in?'

'The twenty-eighth of March this year,' I said. 'I'm looking for a particular officer. A Titus Cabirus.'

That got me a sideways glance as sharp as Laco's had been – yeah, well, there couldn't be many people in Lugdunum who didn't know about the murder, or when it had happened – but the clerk didn't comment. He ran his finger along the line of tags below one set of cubbies, stopped, reached in, pulled out a sheaf of beechwood flimsies and leafed through them.

'March the twenty-eighth, wasn't it, sir?' he said.

'Yeah. Was Titus Cabirus on duty that day?'

The clerk ran his finger down the page. The finger stopped.

'Yes, sir,' he said. 'He was.' Bugger! 'Only he reported sick
and went home at noon.'

'*What?*'

'See for yourself, sir.' He handed the flimsy over. Sure enough,
against his name and rank someone had written *aegr. h. VI.*

Shit. Titus Cabirus had been lying through his teeth.

I passed the flimsy back to the clerk. 'Thanks,' I said. 'You've
been really, really helpful.'

'My pleasure, sir. Was there anything else you needed?'

'No, that'll just about do it.' By the gods it would!

'Then I'll see you out.'

OK; so I had another talk with Titus Cabirus coming up. But
that I'd postpone for the present.

First I had to talk to his girlfriend.

The Volentus house, when I found it, was practically next door
to the Cabirus place. Same sort of arrangement: walled garden
leading up to the house itself, two storeys and a porch. I went
through the gate.

There was an old guy in a rough woollen tunic and wide-
brimmed sun hat busy lashing the stray tendrils of a vine to the
trellis of an arbour.

'Morning, Gramps,' I said. 'You got a girl working here by
the name of Aia, by any chance?'

He tied a slow double knot before answering. I waited patiently.

'Might have,' he said at last. 'Who wants to know?'

'Name's Valerius Corvinus. I'm looking into the death of one
of your neighbours. Claudius Cabirus.'

He grunted and shot me a quick sideways look, then reached
for another tendril and began tying it slowly and methodically
into place.

'So you're that Roman?' he said. 'Yes, Aia's one of ours.
Kitchen maid.'

'Do you think I could talk to her, if she's around? Not for
long, and with your mistress's permission, of course.'

'I reckon you could, at that. You'll find her in by; kitchen's
round the back.' He finished tying the knot and tugged it tight.
'And you won't need any other permission than mine. I'm master
in my own house. Julius Volentus.'

Bugger; I still hadn't got used to the differences in staffing arrangements between Gaul and back home. Or the different social standards. 'I'm sorry, sir,' I said. 'I thought you were the gardener.'

'No bones broken. Easy mistake to make. What does Aia have to do with Tiberius Cabirus?'

'Nothing, as far as I know,' I said cautiously. 'I just wanted a quick word with her to clear something up, is all.'

'Well, you'll know your own business best.' He stooped and picked up another scrap of leather lacing from the ground at his feet. 'Aia's a good girl, and a good worker, that's all I can say and all that interests me. Past the pear tree there and round the corner of the house. Don't be long, because she's the lunch vegetables to do. We eat early.'

'Thanks,' I said, but he was already dealing with another vine tendril.

I went round the side of the house to the back. That was laid out as a kitchen garden, with beds of carrots, cabbage, leeks, kale and beans bordered with thorn-bush hurdles. Half a dozen plump-looking chickens were pecking about the place, and the kitchen itself was a small building only partially roofed over, separate from the house itself, with a cloud of charcoal-smoke above the unroofed section. A girl with red hair bound up in braids was sitting on a stool outside the door, scraping carrots. She glanced up at me, and the knife paused momentarily. Then she lowered her eyes again and the scraping restarted.

If this was Titus's girlfriend then he liked them big: standing, she would be six feet, easy, and built to match. Mind you, I remembered that Doirus over at the farm hadn't exactly been a midget, either.

She was a looker, though.

'Aia?' I said.

'Yes.' She cut the carrot up into chunks, letting them fall into the stew-pot beside her, then picked up another from the basket and started in on that. Big hands, coarse and red, with nails that looked chewed.

'My name's Valerius Corvinus. I'm—'

'I know who you are.'

There was another stool against the wall. I pulled it over and sat. 'Fine,' I said. 'Then you'll know why I'm here.'

'That, no.'

'You're Titus Cabirus's girlfriend, yes?'

'What if I am?'

'You been going out with him for long?'

'About three months, give or take.' She still hadn't looked at me; nothing since that first glance. All her attention was on the carrot, and the knife in her hand.

'You haven't told your father.'

'No. Why should I?' The implication sank in. She stopped scraping, laid the carrot aside, and faced me directly. 'Here! You been talking to him?'

'I went over there yesterday.'

'You got no right! It's not your business!'

'Yeah, well, the jury's out on that at present,' I said. She scowled. 'So why didn't you? Tell him, I mean? According to him, you'd always been close.'

'Work that out for yourself. You know about him, you say you've seen him, talked to him. It shouldn't be all that hard.'

'I might've got it wrong. You care to tell me yourself? Just so it's clear?'

'All right. Three years ago the procurator's men took most of our corn for non-payment of taxes. Dad hit one of them and old Cabirus had him flogged. You think I could tell him that I'd taken up with the son and expect everything to be all sweetness and light? Of course I couldn't. No more than Titus could tell his family.'

'He knows, then?'

'Titus? 'Course he knows. Told him myself, didn't I?'

Hmm. 'So how did you meet?'

'Old Ma Banona – that's our cook – she has trouble with her leg, so I do whatever shopping's needed. Titus lives just up the road, and we used to see each other regular between here and town. He'd always say hello in passing, then one day he offered to carry my basket for a bit and we got talking properly.' She shrugged. 'It started from there. I didn't know who he was at the beginning – he just called himself Titus – and by the time I did it didn't matter.'

Uh-huh. OK; now we came to the tricky bit. 'The afternoon of the murder. You see him then at all?'

A quick sideways glance. 'Yes. He was with me.'

'Here?'

''Course not! The mistress'd have a fit!'

'So where?'

She hesitated. 'We went for a walk in the country, beyond the Gate. The family eat early, at noon. I'd done the washing up and I was free until an hour or two before sundown when I'd to help with the dinner, so Titus arranged to meet me at the Gate itself.'

She was lying, that I'd bet good money on. Still, I couldn't very well face her with it. 'He was on duty that day,' I said. 'But he called off sick halfway through. I checked.'

Her shoulders lifted and she looked away. 'News to me,' she said. 'He never talks about his work. You asked me and I've told you.' She picked up the discarded carrot and started scraping it again. 'Now if that's all you came for I got things to be getting on with.'

I didn't move. 'Did Titus's father know you two were an item?' I said.

The knife stopped. 'No. I said: Titus didn't tell him, no more nor I told mine.'

'He might've found out another way.'

'Another way such as what?'

It was my turn to shrug. 'I don't know. But it's possible.'

'Anything's possible. Doesn't mean it has to happen, though, does it?'

'True. Even so, the chances are that Titus and he had a . . . well, let's call it a difference of opinion just before the old man died. You know anything about that?'

'No. If he did then he never mentioned it. But then we keep off the subject of each other's families. It's better that way.'

Yeah, I supposed it would be, under the circumstances. Still, I only had the lady's word for it, and I didn't trust Aia more than half.

'He was himself that day?' I said. 'The day of the murder? Just as usual, I mean?'

''Course he was. Why should he be any different?'

'You've got long-term plans, you and him? As an item, that is.'

'Look.' She set the carrot down, but she was still holding the knife. 'I've no more to say to you and I've got the lunch to see to. I don't know nothing, or no more than I've already said. So just push off, all right?'

'Fair enough.' I stood up. 'Thanks for talking to me.'

She didn't answer. I left her to her scraping.

Well, we were within a stone's throw of the Cabirus place, so I might as well call in and see if Titus was around: I hadn't asked, when I was at the procurator's office, whether he was on duty that day, but then Aia had been the priority in any case. Now, though, would be a good time: when I faced him with the porky about where he'd been the day of the murder, I could check that their stories matched before they got together and made sure that they did.

He wasn't at home, but he wasn't on duty, either: Diligenta was out, which was fine with me because it avoided awkward questions, but the maid Cotuinda told me I'd find him at the baths down by the Narbonensian Gate. So that's where I went.

I paid my copper piece to the guy on the door, collected my towel and rented oil-flask and scraper, deposited my purse in one of the lockers they had for hire – you don't leave money lying around in those places, whether you're in Gaul or Rome – and went inside. We were still too early for the usual busy time – most punters who can manage it have their bath in the afternoon, when work, at least for the lucky few, is over for the day and they can relax with a hot steam and a chat with friends before dinner – but it was pretty busy all the same, mostly with off-duty squaddies from the auxiliary barracks next door. There was no sign of Titus in the changing room, but I hadn't expected it; Cotuinda had said that he'd been gone for a good half-hour before I arrived, so he'd already be in full bathing mode. I stripped off, leaving the rest of my gear in one of the few vacant cubbies, and went straight through to the sweat room.

Most of the benches were full. I looked around: no Titus as yet. Well, we'd give it a few minutes and then move on. I sat down beside two punters who obligingly shifted up to give me room – auxiliaries, evidently, because they were chatting away in a language that I didn't recognize, but wasn't Latin, or even close – and communed with nature.

So. What was I to make of the girlfriend? She'd seemed straight enough at base, barring the all-important detail of Titus's – and her own – movements the afternoon of the murder, and even there I could've been mistaken. Not telling their respective parents about their relationship was fair enough too; I'd already seen Papa Doirus's reaction when I told him about it, and no doubt if it transpired that their son was showing an interest in the daughter of a farmer with the scars of the council's lash on his back Cabirus Senior – and probably Diligenta, too – would've hit the roof in the same way. Even the bit about keeping off the subject of family altogether made sense: if Aia were genuinely smitten with Titus then given the events of three years before it was an area she might not want to let herself think about. The same went for Titus's job.

OK; that was the case for the defence. The prosecution, now . . .

The bottom line was that she'd consciously taken up with a guy whose father had had her father flogged, solely for the crime of trying to protect the family's future. Worse, that he might not have been personally involved – he couldn't have been that; he'd've been too young at the time to join the proconsul's troop – but he was sure as hell part of the same set-up now, with all that entailed. Also, she'd told me that she hadn't known who Titus was until the relationship was well established, and that I just found too hard to swallow: according to her father, she'd been working for the Volentus family for nine months before she took up with Titus Cabirus seriously, they were practically neighbours, and in any case Lugdunum was small enough and insular enough for the possibility to be a faint one, at best. While on his side I'd be interested to know if he'd known anything at all about the flogging episode to begin with, before Aia had chosen to tell him . . .

So where did that leave us? With the original proposition, that was where: that she'd set him up for reasons of her own. And *that* meant she was still very firmly in the frame. Nothing that I'd seen, or that she'd said, went against that. To what extent Titus himself was involved, mind, was another matter, and that was worrying: slice it how you liked, if Aia was the perp then Titus had to be in on it. Otherwise why the too-coincidental coincidence that he'd bunked off from duty the afternoon of the murder by pretending to be ill? That he certainly hadn't been, because Diligenta had told me right at the start that he hadn't been around because he was on duty. And now it transpired that he was with Aia. *Where* he'd been, of course, was a moot point entirely . . .

The guy next to me nudged me in the ribs. I turned towards him. 'Yeah?' I said. 'What is it?'

He indicated the scraper at my feet. 'You want?' he said.

'Hmm?' He pointed to my back. 'Oh. Oh, right. Thanks, pal.' That's the thing about going to the baths on your own; some bits you can't do for yourself. Still, there's usually a good-natured punter like Smiling George here who'll lend a hand. I gave him the scraper and he set to work, hissing through his teeth as he did it, like he was grooming a horse. Cavalryman, obviously.

His mate said something in whatever language they'd been using, and they both laughed.

'What's funny?' I said.

'My mate say, "Romans no hair. Like baby's bottom."'

I grinned. That certainly didn't apply to those two; I reckoned that they had enough hair on their chests and backs between them for half a dozen cavalry ponies.

'True,' I said. 'Mind you, it saves all that faffing around with curling-tongs.'

That got translated, and they both creased up; yeah, well, auxiliary humour is pretty basic. The guy handed the scraper back to me, and I finished the job on the parts that I could reach.

OK, that was me for the present. Cut it short; best be moving on, or I might miss Titus altogether.

'Thanks again,' I said to the horse-groomer. 'Enjoy the rest of your bath.'

'Welcome.'

I nodded to the rest of the punters steaming quietly on their benches and went back out into the corridor to check the other rooms. He wasn't in the dry heat room, nor among the guys hanging around the cold plunge. I took a quick dip to cool off, came out shivering – July it might be, but 'cold plunge' was right – and carried on through the portico into the exercise yard.

There he was, sitting on a bench on the other side of the yard talking to a big middle-aged man with an impressive moustache and braided hair; common enough features in Lugdunum, sure, although the Romanized part of the citizenry favoured clean-shaven and short back and sides, but this guy stripped to the buff and with his rippling muscles could've modelled for old Vercingetorix himself. When he saw me, Titus broke off the conversation and gave me a wave. The big Gaul glanced in my direction, scowled, got to his feet, and stalked off as I came over. Obviously the outgoing, friendly type.

'Hello again, Corvinus.' Titus grinned. 'Were you looking for me, or did you just fancy slumming it in the public baths with the plebs?'

'The first, actually.' I sat next to him. 'Why did you lie about being on duty the day of your father's death?'

The grin vanished. 'I didn't,' he said. 'I was.'

'Not in the afternoon, you weren't. I checked the roster. You reported sick.'

Long silence. 'So?' he said at last; no friendliness now.

'So where were you? Not at home, or at least not officially, because your mother was under the impression – she still is – that you were at the procurator's offices until sundown.'

'That's none of your business.'

'Yes, it is. Mind you, it's a rhetorical question, because I know damn well you were with your girlfriend Aia.'

He turned to stare at me. 'How the hell do you know about Aia?'

'I know. Where did you go together?'

Another long silence. 'Over to Condate, as it happens.'

Uh-huh. 'You do this often? Bunk off duty so you can be with your girlfriend?'

'No!'

'Why this time, then?'

'She sent me a message to say that she had the day off. Unexpectedly. The family she works for were eating out. That hardly ever happens, so we took advantage of it. Maybe I was out of line shamming sick, but there wasn't much on at the time so it was no big deal.'

'You know about her father? That your father had him flogged a few years back?'

He was getting angry now, and obviously trying to keep it in check. 'For resisting a sequestration order. Yes. Aia told me. The whole story. What does it matter?'

Well, at least she'd been that much up front. 'Not to you, maybe,' I said. 'But I'd say it gave her a pretty valid reason for holding a grudge against your father, wouldn't you?'

Titus's hands clenched into fists.

'Look, Corvinus,' he snapped. 'I've had just about enough of this! I told you; it's none of your business!'

'And I told you it was,' I said equably, keeping half an eye on his hands. 'Which it is, because we're talking about the time of the murder and you're lying through your teeth again. I saw Aia earlier this morning. According to her, that day you met her by prearrangement at the Ocean Gate and you went for a walk in the country. The other side of town, in other words, nowhere near Condate. And the Volentus family hadn't made any alternative dinner arrangements; that afternoon, all she had was a couple of hours free. So one of you is telling porkies, or rather it's my bet that both of you are. You care to tell me the truth now?'

I thought he'd hit me, and I was ready to block the punch, but he just stood up, his hands clenching and unclenching.

'Fuck off,' he said. 'You just fuck right off and leave me alone, OK?'

I stood up too. 'Fair enough,' I said. 'When you've cooled down, you think about it. Have a word with the girl, talk things over. If you change your mind you know where to find me.'

I left him glaring and went back inside to get changed.

When I reached the residence, it was to find Quintus Cabirus in the conservatory waiting for me. I'd been right about Diligenta tearing a serious strip off him; she'd evidently done it with a vengeance, and the guy looked not so much subdued as walked on all over with hobnailed boots.

'Afternoon, Corvinus,' he said. 'Diligenta thinks I owe you an explanation.'

'Yeah, well, more of an elucidation, really.' I sat down opposite him. 'You were skimming off some of the profits, yes?'

He swallowed. 'Nothing major, not enough to damage the company, but yes, I'm afraid I was.'

'You like to tell me why?'

'I like gambling and I'm not very good at it. Sometimes I had to' – he hesitated – 'borrow from the firm to settle an urgent debt.'

'Did your brother know?'

'Latterly he did. Right at the end, in fact. Silus told him. Oh, I don't blame Silus; he's a company man first and foremost, always has been, and I'd got complacent and careless. It wasn't difficult for him to spot what was happening.'

'So how did he react? Your brother, I mean?'

'How do you think?' Quintus gave a weak smile. 'He was furious, of course, called me every name he could lay his tongue to. I promised I'd pay the money back – which I will, over time; I meant it when I said "borrow" earlier – and eventually he calmed down. It wouldn't've been in either of our interests to have made a big thing of it. I told you: we worked well together, we each had our own strengths. If there'd been a rift the company would've suffered.'

'He didn't tell your sister-in-law?'

'No. He said he wouldn't. What would've been the point? When push came to shove it was between the two of us, and as far as he was concerned the matter was closed.' He gave me a straight look. 'I didn't kill him, Corvinus, that I swear to. I wouldn't, whatever he'd decided.'

'OK.' Not that I was totally convinced; like I'd told Perilla, I didn't trust Brother Quintus as far as I could throw him. 'So what happens now? Where you and the company are concerned?'

'Nothing. Or nothing drastic, anyway; it's business as usual, except that I'm on probation, as it were. And as I say I've promised Diligenta that over time I'll repay every copper piece.'

'Just out of curiosity. Your nephew Titus. Did he know as well?'

'Gods, you have been thinking!'

'Yeah, I do that sometimes. So?'

'As a matter of fact he did, yes. He's no fool, young Titus; he worked it out from the other end.'

'How do you mean?'

'Titus isn't a gambler, or not much of one. But he has friends who are, and they talk. I'd been losing heavily over the previous months, but every time I'd managed to pay up on the nail.' He shrugged. 'Titus just got to wondering how, and the answer was pretty obvious. He came to me shortly before Tiberius died and asked me straight out.'

'You admitted it?'

'There wasn't anything else I could do. I told him that it was all over and done with, there'd be no repetition, and that his father already knew. He accepted that; with a very bad grace, mind, and we'll never be close again, but he's family, like Diligenta. We'll all come through to the other side, eventually.'

Uh-huh; well, that explained the sudden coolness, anyway. And Biracus was right, Titus was a secretive cove. Score another for Gallic family solidarity in hiding the dirty linen.

Which reminded me.

'Why did you leave Augusta twenty years ago?' I said.

'What?' Quintus frowned; fazed for a moment, like I'd expected him to be. 'What has that got to do with anything?'

'It's a simple question, pal.'

'But I told you already, when we talked last: it was a business decision, a sensible one as things have proved.'

'Nothing to do with the Florus revolt, then?'

'Absolutely nothing. Why should it have been?'

He was lying, that I'd bet a year's income on. And the question had rattled him; I'd place a hefty bet on that, as well. Interesting.

'When I talked to him Julius Biracus seemed to think it had,' I said. 'Or implied it, rather. And he said for definite that your brother-in-law – Licnus, wasn't it? – had been involved on the losing side.'

'I don't . . . I . . .' He stopped. 'Corvinus, I'm sorry, but you're prying into what doesn't concern you. All that's in the past, some of it is painful – certainly too painful to talk to you about just to satisfy your curiosity – and I promise you it has absolutely no connection whatever with my brother's death.'

'You're up there often enough on business. Do you have anything to do with the remaining family?'

'That'd be Quadrunia – Diligenta's sister – and her husband; Licnus is long gone, where to I don't know and don't care. In any case, your answer's no. Quadrunia still lives in the town, as far as I know, unless she's moved, or unless she's dead, both of which are possible. I've had no contact with her or her husband – none of us have – since the day we left.'

Jupiter, there was real venom there; venom, and something else. What it was, I wasn't sure, but there was no mistaking it. Even so, there was no point in pursuing things any further.

'Fine,' I said. 'We'll leave it at that.'

He stood up; he was looking relieved, and a lot more relaxed than he had been when I'd arrived.

'Very well,' he said. 'By the way, how is the investigation going?'

'Not bad,' I said. 'I'm making some progress, anyway.'

'In any particular direction?'

'There are one or two leads,' I said cautiously. 'You're off up north soon?'

'Yes. First thing tomorrow morning, in fact. We've a consignment due for shipment upriver, but I'll be going by road and travelling light, which means I'll already be in Augusta when it arrives.'

'Fair enough. Have a good journey. Thanks for coming.'

'Yes, well, I hope it's cleared the air. Good luck, in case I don't see you again before you leave.'

He held out his hand. I shook it.

Hmm.

TEN

Perilla got back just before dinnertime.

'Did you have another good day, dear?' she said, kissing me.

'Not bad. Tell you later. How was yours?'

'Excellent. Oh, thank you, Bathyllus.' The little guy had
followed her in with her usual barley-water-and-honey concoction on a tray. 'We did a tour of the local temples. Really local
ones, I mean: Sucellus, Taranis and the Mothers. Most interesting.' Yeah, I'd bet. 'And then Caninia took me on a visit to
a friend of hers, so we spent the afternoon there. Mostly
discussing this year's fashions in Rome. You would've been
bored stiff.'

Never a truer word was spoken. No mention of Crinas, either,
but I didn't feel inclined to push things in that direction. Bathyllus
came round to me and offered the tray with a single cup of wine
on it. I took it and sipped. Bugger! We were back to the watered-
to-within-an-inch-of-its-life stuff; obviously our major-domo was
still in profoundly miffed mode, or – equally likely – he wasn't
risking being found out by Perilla and roasted over a slow fire.
Ah, well.

Now for the bad news. This I was not looking forward to.

'We're going to have to go to Augusta,' I said.

'*What?*' She was staring at me.

'Yeah, I know. There are still avenues to explore here, no
arguments. But the real answer to all this is up north; I can feel
it in my water.'

'Marcus, that is almost four hundred miles!'

'That far, eh?'

'Of course that far!'

Hell; another half-month of thumb-twiddling; still, it couldn't
be helped, unless I did it alone and on horseback, and just the
thought of what would be involved in that made me queasy.
'There's something screwy going on re whatever happened there
involving the family twenty years ago,' I said. 'I've brought the
subject up twice now, first with Diligenta and then with Brother
Quintus, and they both reacted like a cat on hot bricks. I'm not
going to find out any other way, so Augusta it has to be.' I took
a swallow of the wine. What there was of it, versus the water.
'Look on the bright side, lady. At least it'll let us see a bit more
of the country.'

'Quite a bit more. Four hundred miles' worth; double that,
counting the return trip. You're sure the journey's necessary?'

'No.'

'Well, then! For goodness' sake!'

'The main thing is that I don't know for sure that it *isn't* necessary. And if that sounds crazy, then tough. You don't have to come if you don't want to.'

'Really, dear. Be serious.'

'At least we'll be travelling in style again, Nerva will see to that. I'll talk to him first thing tomorrow morning.'

'And you're absolutely certain that everything else can wait?'

'No, just that going to Augusta's more important at present, and it has to be done in any case. Oh, sure, we've got the Vindus side of things to look into, for a start, I'm perfectly well aware of that. And there's some unfinished business with young Titus.' I told her about the interview with Aia and the subsequent one with the lad himself. 'He's covering up for something, or trying to, that's pretty obvious; whether it's direct involvement in the murder or not, I don't know, although I doubt it. On the other hand, I can still easily see the girlfriend as the killer, and he seems pretty stuck on her, so perhaps I'm wrong.'

'He wouldn't help her to kill his own father, surely? Not even if he was completely infatuated with the girl.'

'Perilla, we don't know all the circumstances, OK? Maybe she didn't tell him what she was planning, and he only found out after the event. Maybe she suckered him into helping without him knowing what he was getting into until it was too late, and now he's caught with nowhere else to go. There could be half a dozen explanations.'

'So what do you expect to find out in Augusta?'

'If I could tell you that, we wouldn't need to go. But it's got something to do with the Florus revolt. And I think Diligenta's brother is mixed up in it somewhere, too.'

'I didn't know she had a brother.'

'She doesn't, in effect. Not any more. But she did, twenty years ago.'

'Marcus, dear, you're not making sense.'

'Yeah, I know. My brain's not working properly.' I held up the wine-cup. 'Could be something to do with the lack of fuel.'

'I'm sure abstinence is doing you the world of good.'

'Hah. Anyway, she also has a sister; that's "has", present tense. Name of Quadrunia. She still lives in Augusta, apparently, although the two of them haven't had any contact since Diligenta left, and there seems to be bad blood between the two parts of the family. Which is basically the reason I need to go, because six gets you ten that whatever caused it is important. Neither Diligenta nor Quintus is likely to tell me, so Augusta and Quadrunia it is.'

'Can't you leave it for the present? We've only just arrived, for heaven's sake, and you said yourself there's this Vindus aspect of things to explore.'

'We'll be back, maybe inside of a month if we're lucky—'

'*What?* Marcus, if you think I'm going to—'

'—and neither Vindus nor his uncle are going anywhere in the meantime. In any case, Nerva will want some time to make the travel arrangements. You can't expect him to do that at five minutes' notice, so we'll have some slack, at least.' I looked round: Bathyllus had slid in and was standing waiting. Obviously a Communication. 'Yes, sunshine, what is it?'

'You have a visitor, sir. Titus Cabirus.'

Hey! Speak of the devil! 'Bring him in.'

He exited, reappeared with the lad himself, bowed, and made himself scarce.

'Corvinus,' Titus said stiffly, and nodded to Perilla, who was still looking frosty as hell. 'Madam.'

'Pull up a chair,' I said.

'No, this won't take long.' He cleared his throat. 'I've talked it over with Aia, as you suggested, and we decided it would be best for me to apologize and explain. On the clear understanding that what I say goes no further.'

'Fair enough,' I said. 'Agreed.'

He glanced at Perilla again. 'It's . . . rather personal and private. Perhaps your wife would like to leave us alone?'

'That's OK,' I said. 'I think the lady's pretty much unshockable.'

'Not as of five minutes ago, I'm not.' Perilla shot me a look straight off a glacier. I winced. 'None the less. Do carry on, Titus Cabirus.'

'Well, then.' Another nervous glance and throat-clearing. 'We were—' He stopped, took a deep breath and started again. 'Aia has a friend in town called Vesca; she's a lady's maid with a

family near the Western Gate. Vesca had told her that the family
– all of them, including her – were going away for a few days,
and the house would be empty.'

Uh-huh; I was there ahead of him. 'So you thought you'd
make use of it?' I said.

'With Vesca's knowledge.' He was blushing.

'But not the family's.'

'No.' He swallowed. 'It was the first time, you see. For both
of us. We wanted it to be special. Vesca would leave the back
door unlocked, and of course we promised we'd leave everything
as we found it. Which we did.'

I was grinning. 'That's not so very terrible, pal,' I said. 'Why
not tell me in the first place?'

'But I couldn't do that! Of course I couldn't! There was Vesca,
for a start. If her mistress found out she'd be in dreadful trouble;
she'd certainly lose her job. And you know already that we hadn't
even told our parents that we were friends, let alone—' He
stopped again. 'So it had to be a secret. A complete secret. It
still does.'

'I'll have to check with this Vesca,' I said. 'You do realize
that, don't you? It's important.'

'We've thought of that, Aia and me. She could get her to come
here, confirm the arrangement, on oath if you like. I'd rather that
than have you go round to the house.'

'Yeah, well, it still wouldn't be proof that you actually took
up the offer, would it? After all, you said yourself that she wasn't
there at the time and you didn't leave any traces.'

'Corvinus, please! It's the absolute truth! I'll swear to it myself,
if you want, but that's all I can do.'

I shrugged: the kid had a point, and he was clearly desperate.
'Fair enough,' I said. 'Get the girl to call round, tell me her side
of the story in person, and we'll take it from there.'

'Thank you.' He took another deep breath. 'That's all I wanted
to say. And you're right; I should've told you before.'

He left.

'Well, Marcus?' Perilla said. 'Do you believe him?'

At least the frostiness had gone, for the time being, anyway.
'He seemed genuine enough,' I said. 'Certainly the explanation
was plausible. Even so, as an alibi it's got more holes than a

sieve. Oh, sure, no doubt this Vesca will swear that the arrangement was made all right, but that's all she can do because it's all she knows. The two of them might even have set the whole thing up beforehand so that if they were rumbled – as they have been – they'd have some sort of comeback. If so, then it's pretty clever. I'd put it down to Aia, myself. She's obviously the brains of the partnership.'

'You have a very suspicious mind, dear.'

'Granted. But then there's what Publius said. Or didn't say, rather.'

'I beg your pardon?'

'That he hadn't seen anyone in the garden, when the chances were that he had. And he definitely got twitchy when he thought I was implying he might've seen his brother. Like it or not, lady, that's a sticking point.'

'You haven't considered that he might simply be telling the truth? Even if he was awake and sitting at the work-table?'

'Of course I have. I said at the time: the kid's an obsessive geek. Half the town could've been in and out of that summer house and he still might not have noticed. Even so.' I downed the last of the water–wine mix. 'Ah, hell. Leave it. It'll work itself out sooner or later.'

Bathyllus buttled in.

'Dinner, sir. Madam. If you'd care to come through.'

We did. Tomorrow could wait, and I still had to break the glad news to Nerva. Which wasn't, I had to admit, something I was particularly looking forward to.

I was round at the provincial governor's offices first thing the next morning.

'You want to go to *Augusta*?' Nerva said when I told him. 'Why on earth would you want to do that?'

'Just covering the angles,' I said. 'Is it possible?'

'Of course it's possible.' He frowned; however much he was trying to hide it, the guy was well and truly pissed off, which in the circumstances was understandable. 'Anything is *possible.*'

'Yeah, well, I'm sorry, pal, but I need to talk to someone else in Cabirus's family. His sister-in-law, to be exact. A woman called Quadrunia.'

'Oh, I'm sure where that part of it's concerned Governor Hister will give you every facility. Or rather his aide will. I've met him a couple of times, a man by the name of Saenius Balbinus. He's a nice enough chap, and very efficient. Caninia will be disappointed, though; she's really enjoyed showing your wife around, and a little excitement goes a long way here. How long were you planning to stay?'

'Not long, provided everything goes according to plan. Possibly only a day or so.'

He just looked at me. 'You're joking,' he said.

'No. A day or so should just about cover it.'

I could see him mentally counting to ten, gritting his teeth while he did it.

'Corvinus, you do realize just how far away from here Augusta is, don't you?' he said at last.

'Uh . . . yeah. Or rather, Perilla does. About four hundred miles, right?'

'More or less, yes.'

'There you go, then.'

He sighed. 'Very well. You have the emperor's personal authorization, so if you really want to go there and then come right back then that's your privilege, and I'm duty bound to facilitate things. Leave it with me. I'll send a rider straight away to make sure you're expected, in Augusta itself and at the points en route.'

'Hey, that's no problem,' I said. 'We can take pot luck. I'm sure everything'll be fine.'

He closed his eyes, briefly. 'Read my lips, Corvinus,' he said. 'You are a ranking imperial procurator, appointed directly by the emperor. If my governor discovered that I'd simply waved you off on a four-hundred-mile trip without making thorough arrangements beforehand he would quite rightly have my guts for garters. And when you arrived at the other end – *if* you arrived at the other end – unlooked for and unannounced, Balbinus – let alone Governor Hister – would have an apoplexy. I'd be very lucky if my next posting, effective immediately, wasn't to Mauretania. There's such a thing as protocol, and it's not a discardable option. You understand?'

'Ah . . . yeah. Look, I'm sorry, Nerva.'

'Not as sorry as I am, considering what's involved.'

'That tricky, eh?'

'More than you can possibly know. Still, Procurator Laco is going up there himself in a few days' time. Maybe I can patch you in with him. For the outward journey, at least. Fortunately, getting you back isn't my concern.'

Oh, hell; spending half of a month travelling in the company of that dried fish wasn't exactly a pleasant prospect. Even so, I wasn't about to raise any objections at this point.

'Fine by me,' I said. 'Whatever.'

'It'd certainly simplify things a lot.' Actually, he was looking a bit brighter: problem, evidently, if not solved then at least mitigated. 'And you'd have company on the road. Besides Laco's, I mean.'

'Yeah? How's that?'

'It's clear you're no traveller, Corvinus. Gaul's pretty safe where bandits are concerned, on the main roads, anyway, but it's still best to travel in a group when you can. Laco has his guard – that's what they're there for – so there'll be one or two other people, individuals who happen to be going the same way. In any case' – he stood up – 'leave things with me. I'll let you know for definite tomorrow at the latest, but plan for four days' time. Fair enough?'

'Absolutely,' I said.

Yeah, well, it would have to be, wouldn't it? Still, I only had myself to blame this time round.

ELEVEN

Nerva was as good as his word, and got back to us early the next morning: with Laco's party, leaving in another three days' time, it was. Which meant I had a chance to follow up the Julius Vindus side of things. If my squaddie pal on the gate had had it right, he should be back from his assignment by now.

After Nerva had been and gone, I went down to the procurator's offices. There were a couple of new lads on duty this time, and they didn't know anything about Vindus's whereabouts, but I went inside and found the clerk who'd helped me out with the duty roster the day before.

'Uh . . . Largus, wasn't it?' I said.

'Yes indeed, sir.' He beamed. 'How can I help you?'

'I was looking for a Julius Vindus. You happen to know where I can find him?'

'Of course, sir. He's the duty officer this morning. You wanted to talk to him?'

'Yeah, if that's possible.'

'No problem. I'll have him temporarily relieved and send him to you. If you'd care to use the procurator's private office? Procurator Laco is out at the moment, and I'm sure he wouldn't mind.'

'That'd be great. Thanks.'

'You're very welcome. Follow me, please.'

We went upstairs and he showed me into a very plush office with cedar-panelled walls, a desk you could've sat a dozen people round, easy, and a bust of Claudius staring at me disapprovingly from a pedestal. Luckily, there was also a small table to one side with a set of Gallic wickerwork chairs. I pulled up one of these and sat down to wait.

The guy arrived ten minutes later. Mid- to late-twenties, good-looking in an all-teeth-and-hair-oil way, impeccably uniformed and cocky as hell. There are some people you just *know* are going to get up your nose before they've even opened their mouths. For me, Julius Vindus was there with the best of them.

'Valerius Corvinus?' he said. 'You wanted to see me?'

'Yeah.' I indicated one of the other chairs. 'Take a seat, pal.'

He did. 'What's this about? Oh, I know who you are, of course, but I can't see how I can be any help to you.'

'Tell me about Claudilla.'

He blinked. 'What?'

'Claudius Cabirus's daughter. You got her pregnant, didn't you?'

He half-rose. 'Now look here . . .'

'Just sit down and answer the question. Mind you, to be fair, it was rhetorical because I know damn well that you did.'

He sat again, slowly. 'And just how the hell *do* you know?' he said.

'Never mind that. Just give me the story.'

'You want the sordid details?' He grinned. 'Come on, Corvinus! You're a married man, so surely you can work the mechanics of it out for yourself. Or is it prurient interest?'

'She's what, fourteen? She can't be any older. Half your age, or thereabouts.'

'Old enough to marry, legally. Both here and in Rome. Or am I wrong?'

'Yeah, well, that's the point, isn't it?' I crossed my legs and folded my arms to stop myself reaching over and flattening the bastard. 'I don't think you have marriage in mind. Do you?'

'That's my business.'

I shook my head. 'Uh-uh. It would be, if her father hadn't been murdered a couple of months back. But he was, and that makes it mine, too.'

For the first time, the cockiness slipped. 'What's that supposed to mean?' he said.

'Let me give you a scenario. Correct me if I go adrift, OK?' I shifted in the chair. 'You're a friend of the family through the girl's brother, so you have the entrée. You butter her up, speak sweet nothings in her ear and seduce her. She finds herself pregnant and confesses the whole thing to her mother, who in turn tells her father. Like you said, fourteen's a legal marriageable age for a girl, at least technically, so he buttonholes you, or maybe your uncle, who's also your guardian, and tells you or him he expects you to do the honest thing. Only that's not on, is it? Certainly not with your Uncle Oppianus, who views the family socially as just one step up from pond life. So at the earliest opportunity he, or more probably you, solves the problem by shoving a knife into the guy while he's taking his afternoon nap. What do you think? Possible?'

He was staring at me. 'That,' he said, 'is the biggest load of crap I have ever heard.'

'Yeah? Not from where I'm sitting, sunshine.'

'You say Diligenta knew all about this?'

'Uh-huh. She must've done.'

'OK. So why hasn't she fingered me, or my uncle, for her

husband's murder? Or at least given it as a strong possibility, to you or anyone else? She hasn't, has she?'

Bugger; he was right. Quite the reverse, in fact, in Oppianus's case. And she hadn't even hinted at Vindus; hadn't so much as mentioned him. 'Fine,' I said. 'Then maybe she didn't. Know, I mean.'

'Know about the pregnancy? Or know that I was responsible? If it's the first, then how could she have sent Claudilla away before it showed to cover things up? If the second, then why should Cabirus try to force a marriage on me at all? And if he didn't then what possible reason would either I or my uncle have for killing him? Not to mention the fact that just killing Cabirus wouldn't solve the problem, because given that Claudilla could point the finger at me Diligenta would be able to force the marriage herself, if she wanted to: one step higher than pond life in my uncle's opinion they may be, but the Cabiri are highly respected in Lugdunum, as well as being imperial protégés, so they'd be believed, no question. In fact, if anything it would make things far worse. Admit it, Corvinus; your scenario is pure and utter balls from start to finish.'

Hell; put like that I was inclined to agree.

Fuck.

'It still doesn't get round the fact that you've just confirmed that the girl is actually pregnant and that you're the baby's father,' I said.

'Really?' He looked round the room. 'I don't see any witnesses, myself. Do you?'

My fists knotted, but I said nothing. He gave me a disarming smile.

'Look,' he said, 'I want to be reasonable here. So long as it's off the record, which it is, you're right about the pregnancy, and that I've got no intention whatsoever of marrying the girl. But as far as I know she hasn't told her mother who was responsible. Why that should be I've no idea, but there you go. That's women for you, and she always was a silly little bitch.' He stood up. 'Now if that's all you want with me I have my duties to attend to.'

I was counting slowly to ten in my head while I forced myself to unball my fists. 'Not quite all, pal,' I said. 'You go hunting with Titus Cabirus, yes? Up in the mountains?'

'Occasionally.' He frowned. 'So?'

'I was just wondering. Licinius Nerva told me a story two or three days ago. About a dead wolf that was dumped in the market square a while back.'

'I'd heard about that.' He was guarded. 'What does it have to do with me?'

'Yeah, well, you know best, of course. But so long as we're speaking off the record I thought you might fill me in about how it got there. The consensus of opinion seems to be that it was just a prank, but I'm not altogether sure about that because, and Nerva agrees, it might well have much more sinister implications. In fact, I was thinking about going into the matter more deeply while I'm here. In my capacity as the emperor's personal representative, of course. Naturally, if I did as a result discover anything, whatever form it took, I'd have to put in an official report to the governor.' I waited. 'No hassle, no comeback, I guarantee. Not if the information is freely offered, and there's an innocent explanation after all. Is there, do you know?'

I'd rocked him, that was obvious. He licked his lips nervously.

'Off the record, right?' he said.

'As ever is.'

'Very well. You know what a frat is?'

'Yeah. A bloody stupid all-lads-together society where over-bred young bastards like you play childish games, have jolly midnight romps in their secret clubhouse, and think they're being ever so modern and daring despite actually being a bunch of total prats. That do for a working definition?'

He coloured. 'You're entitled to your opinion, of course. But there's more to it than that.'

'You don't say? Well, well; you learn something new every day.'

'We – most of the guards officers and some of the younger set from the best families – have a frat called the Sons of Lug.' I tried to keep a straight face and didn't quite manage it. He shot me a venomous look and cleared his throat. 'It's pretty exclusive. Prospective members have to be nominated, and before they can join they have to pass a test involving some personal risk, physical or otherwise.'

I was beginning to see the light here; no pun – the god Lug being who he was – intended. 'And dumping the wolf was Titus Cabirus's, right?'

'Yes. We'd killed it a couple of days before and left it in the clubhouse over in the Canabae. It was Cabirus's task to get it from there to the market square without being seen by the Town Watch.'

'My goodness, what a ripping wheeze. Absolutely super.'

That got me another look. 'You can be as sarcastic as you like, Corvinus,' he said, 'but frats have their purpose. They foster comradeship, discipline, resourcefulness—'

'Infantile behaviour, schoolboy humour, and intelligence at an operational level that would disgrace a chicken. Yeah. Fine. With you.' I'd had enough of this; I stood up as well. 'Thank you, Julius Vindus. You've been very helpful. Now bugger off.'

His fists clenched and unclenched, and I was hoping he'd take a swing at me so I could reciprocate. But he didn't. He marched out, slamming the door behind him.

So much for that, then. They were a pair, him and his uncle, but I didn't think they were our murderers.

Damn.

TWELVE

We set off for Augusta just after breakfast, three days later. Accompanied, to my surprise and horror, by Domitius Crinas.

'A very good morning to you, Valerius Corvinus,' he said, giving us his best smile. 'And of course to you too, Perilla. I see that we're to be travelling companions yet again. What a fortunate and unexpected coincidence.'

'What the hell are you doing here, pal?' I said. 'I thought you'd gone north already.'

'*Marcus!*' Perilla hissed.

'Oh, that's perfectly all right, Perilla.' The smile hadn't so much as wavered. 'Actually, the hot springs at the Sanctuary of

Lug deserved more of my attention than I'd thought they would,
and now is really my earliest opportunity to move on. I have my
own mule, of course, so I won't inflict my company on you if
you don't wish it. I wouldn't want to—'

'Nonsense!' Perilla said. 'Licinius Nerva has given us a coach
to ourselves, so we've plenty of room.' She turned to me. 'Isn't
that so, dear?'

Pointed as hell.

'Yeah, I suppose so,' I said between gritted teeth.

'That's settled, then.' The lady beamed. 'You can hitch your
mule to the back and sit inside with us.'

Fuck.

When imperial procurators, real ones, take to the road they
don't do things by halves; which meant that given Laco's entou-
rage – not only his personal household and a guard of a dozen
mounted troops but a gaggle of admin clerks – we were a pretty
big party already. Add in self, Perilla, Bathyllus, Phryne and
Smarmer, plus a sprinkling of merchants who were tagging
along for safety – main arterial route or not, *pax Romana* or
not, we'd be travelling through some rough country where
banditry was part of the local economy – and you got smaller
mass migrations. At least we'd be travelling faster this time
round: because the journey was a regular thing, accommodation
arrangements for the official party were all in place, meaning
we could use ordinary carriages, not the slow-as-a-snail sleeping
variety. The merchants, of course, would have to fend for themselves, but since most of them were regulars on the route in
any case and had their own networks in place that wasn't a
problem. Smarmer . . . well, as far as I was concerned the
bastard could roll himself in his cloak and doss down under
the carriage, but I'd bet anything you liked that with Perilla
fighting his corner he'd end up on the VIP strength. Which, in
the event, was what happened.

One other surprise, although not so unpleasant, was that
the officer in charge of Laco's squaddies was young Titus. He
drifted over while we were stopped for a comfort break and
change of horses at one of the posting stations just after noon.

'I didn't get a chance to ask you, Corvinus,' he said, voice lowered. 'Did Vesca call round?' Vesca, if you remember, was the friend with the convenient empty room and the provider of his alibi for the day of the murder.

'Yeah, she did, as it happens,' I said; she'd put in an appearance at the Residence the previous afternoon. 'You got your confirmation.'

'So I'm off the hook, am I?'

'More or less.'

'Excellent!' He looked relieved.

If he wanted to take the qualification as a straight 'yes', which it wasn't – there was still the possibility that Titus, his girlfriend Aia, and Vesca had cooked up the tale between them – then that was OK with me, for the present. He turned to go.

'Incidentally,' I said, 'I had an interesting talk with your colleague Julius Vindus. About a wolf.'

He turned back. The relieved look had disappeared. 'Ah,' he said.

'"Ah" is right.' I grinned. 'Don't worry, pal, it won't go any further. Investigating the clandestine dumping of dead wolves in market squares isn't part of my remit, and if you and your frat pals want to play silly buggers on your own time then it's no business of mine. However, I just wanted to check something before I left it.'

'Yes?' He was looking wary again.

'Your brother Publius. He knew, didn't he?'

His eyes widened. 'How on earth did you know that?'

'Just a guess, putting two and two together. When I last talked to him and your name came up he got pretty jumpy, for no particular reason that I could see, but he obviously had something to hide. Then when Vindus told me about the wolf I remembered what your Uncle Quintus had said, about Publius walking around town on his own at night. Two and two, like I say. He saw you?'

Titus nodded. 'I'd just pulled the wolf out of the cart and was carrying it to the middle of the square when Publius came round the corner. He swore not to tell.'

'Yeah, I suspect he's good at keeping secrets, is young Publius,' I said drily.

'He's a good brother. Odd, sure, but I can take odd.' The

relieved look was back. 'So. I'm glad we've got that cleared up as well.' He glanced over his shoulder. 'They're harnessing the new horses. I think we're about ready to start off again.'

'Oh, whoopee.' I moved back to our coach, where Perilla and Crinas were already ensconced with the Robbers board between them. Oh, the joys. 'Incidentally, who's your friend Vercingetorix?'

'Who?'

'Sorry. Private joke.' I'd noticed that the big Gaul from the bath-house was one of the merchant party. 'The guy who looks like a fugitive from the Battle for Alesia. Over there, collecting his mule from the horse trough. You were chatting to him when I saw you at the town baths.'

'Oh. I think his name's Segus. Segomarus. But he's not a friend, we just got talking. Why do you ask?'

'No reason, pal. It's just that you don't see many Gauls with that marked an aversion to barbers. At least, I haven't so far.'

He grinned. 'You'll see more in future, Corvinus. We're out in the sticks now, or pretty close to them, and this part wasn't called Hairy Gaul for nothing. Segus is from Burdigala, and you don't get much more backwoods than that.'

'Where's Burdigala?'

'The other side of the country. Down in the south-west.'

'He's a long way from home, then, isn't he? What's he doing over here?'

'I've no idea. You'd have to ask him yourself, although you'd have your work cut out because I don't think he speaks much Latin. Now if you'll excuse me I'll have to be getting back to my troop.'

'Yeah. Sure. I'll see you around.'

He gave me another grin. 'Not much doubt about that. For the next ten days, anyway.'

I was frowning as I walked back to the coach. Backwoods Gaul, eh? So what was a backwoods Gaul who probably washed in a basin and put soap in his hair while he was at it doing in a Roman bath-house?

Ah, leave it; the guy had probably just taken the opportunity to soak up a little of the local culture. No pun intended.

Ten days, right? And with practically no wine and Smarmer

taking up a third of our coach space all the way. Life could not be better, could it?

Bugger.

Ten days it was. The sun was well into its final quarter when we passed through Augusta's Narbonensian Gate.

If I'd needed further proof that we were well out in the sticks then Augusta was it. Lugdunum had been a pleasant enough place, sure, but imperial patronage or not, capital of the province or not, and *pace* the emperor, it was a long way from being hub-of-the-universe material; still, it was Rome, Athens and Alexandria all rolled into one beside Augusta. Even Perilla was moved to comment.

'Is this it, Marcus?' she said staring out at the sparse little wooden houses, the open gutters-cum-sewers that flanked the road, and the yards full of livestock that were rapidly establishing Augusta's prevalent odour through the open carriage window. 'I thought it was a veterans' colony.'

'Yeah, well, it is,' I said. 'Still, you wanted to come, lady. Don't grizzle.'

'But it's so *primitive!*'

'If it's any consolation, Perilla,' Crinas said, 'I think there's a lot of development going on at present. The emperor's very keen on civic improvements in the major Gallic communities; witness my own assignment.'

'Oh, marvellous.'

'And remember, Augusta is only the province's second town. The governor is based at Durocortorum.'

She stared at him wide-eyed. 'I thought we were staying at the residence!' she said.

'We are. Or at least at the place where the governor – and of course the procurator – stay when they come through.' He smiled. 'Don't worry, I'm sure it'll be very nice. And there's plenty for you to see, too, while you're here. I understand there's quite a famous sanctuary of Lenus Mars on the other side of the river which should be well worth a visit.'

Perilla murmured what sounded very like 'Fuck Lenus Mars' under her breath, but I must've misheard, because the lady most definitely does not do the f-word, and the phrase 'famous sanctuary' pushes her culture-button every time. Even so, she was clearly far from a happy bunny. Crinas having beaten her the last three games running at Robbers didn't help, either: she's not the world's most gracious loser, is Perilla.

Ah, well, like I said, she'd only herself to blame; she'd insisted on coming. And we weren't here for fun, after all.

'Perhaps it'll get better when we reach the centre,' Crinas said diplomatically.

It didn't. By the time we came in sight of the residence – which, to be fair, although small was reassuringly substantial, and stone-built – you could've used her expression to pickle radishes.

We'd gradually lost the unofficial members of the company along the way, so it was only us and Laco's team. When we finally rolled to a stop in the residence's courtyard, there was the usual reception committee waiting, headed by a smart-looking young guy in a tribune's uniform.

Laco disembarked from his own carriage.

'Quintus,' he said. 'Delighted to see you again.'

'And I you, Procurator.' The guy smiled. 'Did you have a pleasant journey?'

'Not too bad, not too bad.' I'd got down myself. Laco turned. 'Corvinus, this is Governor Hister's aide, Saenius Balbinus, who will be liaising with you. You had word that Valerius Corvinus would be coming, Quintus?'

'Of course.' Balbinus held out his hand, and we shook. 'A pleasure to meet you, sir. And you, madam.' Perilla had got down behind me, with Smarmer in attendance. 'Everything's arranged. It's not exactly the Palatine, as I'm sure the procurator would be the first to admit, but I hope you'll be comfortable.'

'I'm sure we will, Saenius Balbinus.' Perilla smiled sweetly: the lady can be diplomatic, too, when she likes, and at least it appeared we wouldn't be dossing down on Laco's floor. 'This is Domitius Crinas, by the way.'

'Ah, doctor!' Balbinus positively beamed. 'A real pleasure! I happened on a copy of your treatise on the saline baths in Alexandria a while back. Excellent, simply excellent!'

'You're interested in medicine?' Crinas sounded surprised, as well he might: Balbinus, being the governor's aide, would come from a broad-striper family, and an upper-class Roman who read medical treatises for fun was as rare as a goat with feathers. Unless, of course – which was more likely – he was just buttering Smarmer up and had boned up on him in advance, but if so then he was doing a first-class job. Crinas beamed back.

'Only as a layman. And only certain aspects of it. But I fully endorse the emperor's wish to develop the northern spas for the use of the Rhine garrisons. We must have a long talk about that while you're here.' Well, I was all in favour of that; anything that kept the bastard away from Perilla had my full approval. Political animal or not, I was beginning to like Saenius Balbinus. 'Now. You'll want to freshen up after your journey. The town baths are quite adequate, but the residence does have a small suite of its own which I'm sure the procurator would be happy for you to use.' He glanced at Laco.

'Of course,' Laco said.

'I gave the order two hours ago, so they should be hot. Meanwhile, I'll have you shown to your rooms, and if everything is satisfactory we'll meet again at dinner.'

'That sounds great,' I said. 'Thanks, pal.'

Maybe Augusta wouldn't be so bad after all. And I noticed that Perilla was looking happier.

Score one for the politicians.

THIRTEEN

I got down to business first thing the next morning, while Perilla and Crinas investigated what the town had to offer in the way of shrines and temples: it seemed that we would be having the pleasure of Smarmer's company for a few days yet while arrangements were made for his onward trip, although fortunately it transpired that the local medical network had come up trumps again re accommodation and we wouldn't have the pleasure of watching him munching his groats at mealtimes.

Balbinus had got Diligenta's sister Quadrunia and her husband's address for me before we arrived, although he hadn't, he told me, made any preliminary contact. As a matter of fact, they lived practically next door, in the north-east quarter between the residence complex and the Moguntiacum Gate.

Top of the local property market – which it was, seemingly – or not, the place was no great shakes: wooden-built, like most of the town, two-storeyed, in a plot of land of its own front, sides and back, surrounded by a waist-high wall. Most of the plot was taken up by practical stuff – an orchard plus a vegetable patch with cabbages, beans, carrots, leeks and salad leaves – but the bit at the front, facing the road, boasted a well-kept lawn, a small statue of the Goddess Diana, and a topiary cockerel: evidently, the family had some pretensions and wanted passers-by to take note of the fact.

I unlatched the gate and went up the garden path. The door was open, but I knocked, and a few moments later a young girl appeared, drying her hands on a towel.

'Yes?' she said, her eyes straying to the purple stripe on my tunic. 'Can I help you?'

'Hi,' I said. 'My name's Valerius Corvinus. I was wondering if I could talk to the mistress; Quadrunia, isn't it? She in at present?'

'She is, sir. What was it about?'

'It's a bit complicated. And personal. You mind just asking her if she'll see me?'

'All right. If you'll just wait there.' She disappeared back inside.

Well, so far so good: there had always been the chance, after twenty years, that the family had moved away, or even that Quadrunia was dead; Diligenta, of course, by her own showing had had no contact with her in all that time, and although Quintus had been back and forward there wasn't any reason for him to get in touch off his own bat; quite the contrary, from all indications. At least the journey was proving not to be a washout from the start.

The girl came back. 'The mistress will see you, sir,' she said. 'This way.'

We went inside. Nothing grand here, either: a simple lobby, with the wooden beams and rafters showing through the white-painted plasterwork, and a wooden floor. Clean and neat as a pin, mind: the floorboards were oak, and polished to show the grain, as was the staircase leading up to the second storey. No decoration except for a small table with a vase of flowers on it.

'In here.' The girl opened a door and stepped back.

It was a largish sitting room, obviously the main room of the house: low-ceilinged, and like the lobby with the beams and rafters showing. There was a woman about Diligenta's age sitting in one of the wickerwork chairs. I could see the family resemblance at once.

'Quadrunia, yes?' I said.

'Indeed. And you're Valerius Corvinus, Escena tells me. We don't have many Roman visitors, especially ones with a purple stripe on their tunics. Also, Escena said your business was personal, which is mystifying in itself. Have a seat, please.'

I pulled up another chair facing her and sat. 'I've just come from Lugdunum,' I said. 'From your sister.'

She looked blank. 'My *sister*?' she said.

'Ah . . . Diligenta?'

'Yes, of course.' The blank look disappeared, but now her lips formed a hard line. 'I'm sorry; I didn't—' She stopped. 'You may not be aware of this yourself, Valerius Corvinus, but I haven't seen Diligenta or heard from her in years, half a lifetime, in fact. Which' – and there was ice in her tone – 'neither surprises nor concerns me. Why on earth should she want to get in touch now?'

'She doesn't; she just gave me your name. I'm here on my own account. Your brother-in-law died three months back.'

'Really? I'm most sorry to hear that.' She didn't sound it, and there wasn't a smidgeon either of regret or even of interest in her voice. 'But it still doesn't explain why you came.'

'Actually, his death wasn't natural. He was murdered.' I was watching her face closely; surprise, yes, and faint disgust, but still no concern or interest. 'The emperor asked me to look into it.'

'Did he, now?' Not a trace of emotion, and almost a sniff. A tough cookie, evidently, this Quadrunia. It must run in the family. 'The emperor himself, in person? Well, well, that's nice. What it is to have friends in high places. However, this isn't Lugdunum, is it? And my husband and I have had no contact with Claudius Cabirus these twenty years either, so I'm still at a loss as to what you're doing here. Not simply to bring me the news, obviously.'

'No.' I shifted in my chair and mentally crossed my fingers;

here came the crunch. 'I was hoping you might fill in a few blank areas for me. Tell me why Cabirus and your sister moved to Lugdunum in the first place.'

'Surely the best person to ask about that would be Diligenta herself.'

'True. According to her, it was so Cabirus could be more in the centre of things, business-wise; but—'

'Then I'm afraid I can't add anything further. I'm sorry you've had a wasted journey, but there it is. It was nice to meet you.' She half-rose. 'Goodbye.'

Damn. Not that I was going to give up quite that easily, though, not after a four-hundred-mile trip with Smarmer for company. I didn't move.

'Me, I was wondering if it had anything to do with the Florus revolt,' I said.

She sat down again. 'I beg your pardon?'

'It's just that the timing was too neat to be completely coincidental. At least, that was the idea. And, as I say, it could be relevant to Cabirus's death.'

'I see no reason why it should be. The revolt is ancient history now.'

'True again. But still—'

'Valerius Corvinus. You're a Roman. No offence, but you don't understand these things.' Yeah, I'd been told that before, several times by various people, Diligenta included. 'The Florus revolt was a catastrophe for this part of Gaul, in all sorts of ways. I said it was ancient history, but that's not quite true; we all lived through it, people of my age, anyway, and many of the memories are not pleasant ones. To a certain extent, the problems it caused are still very much with us. All we can do is forget what we can and move on. Which is what I, and most Augustans, have done.' She got to her feet. 'Now I really cannot help you. Diligenta said that she and her husband moved to Lugdunum for reasons of business, which is, as far as I'm aware, perfectly correct. I'm afraid that you will have to be satisfied with that. Good day.'

There was no more to be said; she was hiding something, that was sure, but I couldn't force it out of her. We were still stymied.

I got up and left.

Hell!

So what now?

It wasn't exactly the end of the world; at least we were in Augusta. There must be lots of people who'd been around twenty years ago and known the Cabirus family, and who wouldn't be as tight-mouthed as Quadrunia. It was just a question of finding one. Balbinus might help, or point me in the right direction, at any rate.

I went back to the residence and buttonholed the first skivvy I came across, filling the lamps in the entrance hall.

'Excuse me, pal,' I said, 'you know where I can find Saenius Balbinus at this hour?'

'Oh, yes, sir. He's waiting for you in the atrium.'

'Uh . . . right. Right. Thanks.'

I went through. Odd. There wasn't any reason that I knew of why Balbinus would be keeping in such close touch: he had his own work to do, and I'd made it pretty clear when we'd discussed things over dinner the previous evening that I didn't need squiring around and was perfectly happy left to my own devices. Still, if he was here already then it simplified matters.

He'd been sitting on one of the couches. Now, he got up.

'How did it go, Corvinus?' he said. 'Did you talk to Quadrunia?'

'Yeah. Not that I'm any further forward as a result, unfortunately.' I waved him back into his seat and sat down myself. 'I'll need some help on this one, pal.'

'Certainly. What kind of help?'

'An introduction to someone local who was around at the time of the Florus revolt and knew the Cabiri. Preferably someone with a penchant for gossip-mongering. Possible?'

He frowned. 'I can't think of anyone offhand,' he said. 'But then I'm normally based with the governor in Durocortorum. I don't know Augusta all that well.'

'Damn!'

'Oh, it's no great problem. I can easily make enquiries, and I'm sure I can come up with something.' He hesitated. 'Meanwhile, I have an enormous favour to ask of you.'

'Yeah? What's that?'

'It's just we seem to have had a murder ourselves.'

I stared. 'You *what*?'

He was looking embarrassed as hell. 'Two of them, in fact.

They happened last night. Or that's the assumption, anyway. I thought that since this is your area of expertise—'

'Hang on, Balbinus. What about the local Watch? There is one, presumably.'

'No. No, there isn't, or not as such. You're not in Rome now, or even Lugdunum. Oh, there are a number of town wardens, but they're just that, most of their job involves rounding up escaped livestock and returning it to its owners. Barring the occasional tavern brawl we don't have much trouble here at all, no crime as such and certainly not murder. They wouldn't know where to start, and nor would I.'

'Uh-huh.' Shit; this I could do without. I could see why he'd approached me, mind. And that he'd find doing so embarrassing. The lad must be desperate, right enough. 'Two murders, you said. They're connected, presumably.'

'Oh, yes, definitely. A merchant from Durocortorum and his servant. Actually, I knew them both personally, myself.'

I sighed. 'Fine. So let's have the details.'

'The merchant's name was Drutus. He trades in hides, mostly with the garrison at Moguntiacum. His servant's name was Anda. They were found early this morning by a goat-herd half a mile outside the Moguntiacum Gate.'

'*Outside* the gate? What were they doing there?'

'I've no idea. It's pretty wild country beyond the cemetery, nothing much but hills and scrub. And, like I said, the murder almost definitely happened during the night, which makes it even stranger.'

'How do you know that? If it's all that wild, then the pair of them could've lain there for days.'

'They'd put up at a local tavern. The owner served them a meal about an hour before sunset.'

'Right. Right.' Fair enough; as a *terminus post quem* you couldn't get better than that. 'And he didn't see them afterwards?'

'No. They were bunking down in the hay-loft above his stable, or at least Anda was. He assumed that when they left they'd gone straight to bed as usual.'

I noticed the qualification, but I let it pass for the moment. 'They couldn't have killed each other, could they?' I said. 'Had some sort of disagreement?'

Balbinus shook his head. 'No. Absolutely not. I said: I knew them, both Drutus and the servant. Drutus was the quiet, steady sort, and a good master. Anda had been with him for years, and they were more friends or family than master and man. Besides, Anda seems to have drawn his knife – the goat-herd found it by the body – but Drutus's was still in his belt.'

'OK. Usual question. Motive. Who might have done it, and why?'

'I haven't the slightest idea. As I say, Drutus was just your ordinary merchant who knew his business and kept himself to it. He certainly had no enemies as far as I'm aware, and I'd be very surprised to be proved wrong. His purse was still attached to his belt, so whatever the reason was, it wasn't robbery; although again I'd be surprised if it had been, because like I told you crime here is practically unknown. In any case what would a robber be doing outside the gate at that hour? What would anyone?'

Yeah; that was the queerest thing about the whole affair, to my mind. Oh, sure, the implication was obvious – some kind of clandestine meeting, definitely of the shady variety – but from Balbinus's description of him this Drutus didn't seem the type for that at all. Balbinus could be wrong, mark you, in fact given the circumstances he probably was. Still, that was for me to find out.

'Anyone able to shed light on the matter?' I said. 'Friend, close colleague, that sort of thing.'

Balbinus hesitated. 'There is a local woman. Drutus . . . visits her when he comes through to Augusta.' Uh-huh; that explained the qualification about sleeping arrangements. 'A widow by the name of Severa.'

'Where can I find her?'

'Where she lives I don't know. But she has a vegetable stall in the market.'

'And where's that?'

'On the river side of Market Square.'

Fair enough. 'I'll need to talk to the guy who found the bodies,' I said. 'Preferably take a look at the place where they were found.'

'That's no problem. I'll arrange it and let you know.'

'Also, I'll want to see the bodies themselves. Where would they be at present?'

'At the undertaker's establishment beside the Moguntiacum Gate.' He frowned. 'But why on earth would you want to do that?'

'It can't do any harm. And I might learn something.' I was thinking of my doctor son-in-law Clarus; he'd definitely have been useful at this point. Which triggered another thought. 'Incidentally. Domitius Crinas. You happen to know where he is this morning?'

'Actually, you've just missed him. He and your wife went out just before you arrived. He said they were going to take a look at the Temple of Victory, then cross the river to the Lenus Mars sanctuary.'

Bugger; Smarmer didn't waste much time, did he? Still, it wasn't unexpected, and the first thing the lady does when she goes anywhere is check out the local monuments. 'Where's the Temple of Victory?' I said.

'Not far. In the corner of the market square.'

Great! If I hurried I could catch them mid-jaunt. Perilla would moan like hell, mind, but this was work; she could just do without her prospective boyfriend for an hour or so. I doubted if the guy would be in Clarus's league where reading evidence from dead bodies was concerned – he was more of the diagnose-and-prescribe type of doctor, and it'd need more than a slice of Clarus's morbid interest in forensics for that – but he'd be a lot better than nothing. Or so I hoped.

Besides, I reckoned the bastard owed me for putting up with his company all the way from Ostia. He could just make himself useful for a change.

I set out for the market square.

I ran them down as they were coming out of the temple.

'Corvinus! This is a pleasant surprise.' Crinas smiled his best five-candelabra smile. 'Done what you wanted to do already, or are you on your way somewhere?'

'I've got a job for you, pal,' I said. 'If you aren't too busy, that is.' He had his hand on Perilla's arm, supporting her down the temple steps. I gave it a significant glare, and he removed it. 'Inspecting a couple of dead bodies.'

That got me a blank look. 'I beg your pardon?'

'Marcus!' Perilla snapped; as predicted, she looked distinctly unchuffed. 'If that's one of your jokes then it's in extremely bad taste!'

'No joke, lady. Bodies – murdered – courtesy of Saenius Balbinus. He's just told me about them.'

'Do they have anything to do with your case?' That was Smarmer; a definite sharpening of interest.

'Not that I know of. A merchant from Durocortorum and his servant, found early this morning half a mile outside town. Balbinus has asked me to look into it as a favour.'

Perilla sniffed. 'I would have thought you had enough on your plate already, dear, without taking on anything else,' she said.

'Yeah, well, I saw Quadrunia and she won't play. Balbinus is investigating other possibilities for me, so meanwhile I'm at a loose end. Also, one hand washes the other.' I looked at Crinas. 'So how about it? Willing to give it a whirl?'

'I suppose so,' he said doubtfully. 'If you insist. All the same, I'm not sure what you expect me to do. The men are dead, after all. A bit late to call in a doctor, don't you think?'

Humour, now, or what passed for it. I didn't smile; no point in encouraging him. 'My son-in-law would disagree,' I said.

'Oh, yes. Cornelius Clarus. You mentioned him, didn't you, Perilla? Interesting chap, from the sound of him. Most unusual; I'd like to meet him one day.' Crinas smiled. 'Well, on those terms I don't at all mind "giving it a whirl", as you put it, although Perilla and I had planned to visit the sanctuary of Lenus Mars this morning.'

'So Balbinus said.' I kept my voice neutral. 'But it shouldn't take all that long. They're at the undertaker's up by the Moguntiacum Gate; we can walk there inside of ten minutes.'

'Very well.' He turned to Perilla. 'Perhaps it'd be easier if you went back to the residence. We could start out again from there when Corvinus and I have finished.'

'Lovely,' Perilla said. 'Let's just do that.' I could just *hear* the clenched teeth. 'Marcus, dear, can I have a word with you in private? You'll forgive us for a moment, Crinas.'

'Yes, of course. I'll walk on ahead slowly, Corvinus, and you can catch me up.'

He moved off. Perilla rounded on me.

'You did that deliberately, didn't you?' she hissed. 'You don't need him at all! Marcus Valerius Bloody Corvinus, sometimes I think you are the most—!'

'Look, give me a break, OK?' I said. 'I didn't ask for two extra murders, and it makes sense to use all the help I can get. I'd've had Clarus if he'd been here.'

'Clarus would be a completely different matter; he's family, and yes, he is a little odd in certain ways. But going the lengths of asking a total stranger to—'

'Jupiter, Perilla, he's hardly that, is he? We've had the bastard cheek-by-jowl with us for the past month!'

'And very pleasant it's been. It's nice to have someone around for a change who knows what entasis means.'

'Come on, lady! I'm not that thick!'

'All right. So what *does* it mean?'

'Ah—'

'Exactly. I think I've made my point. Now listen to me, Marcus. I have had your sniping and silly jealousy up to here, so I'll say this just once more and once only: I am not, and never will be, having an affair with Domitius Crinas. That is "affair" of any kind, model, or description you care to name, from light flirtation upwards. Is that perfectly clear?'

'Uh, yeah, but—'

'Good. Please bear that fact in mind during the four or five days Crinas has left with us before he travels on to Moguntiacum.'

Four or five days? Bugger! I'd been expecting two, at the outside!

'Now go and see your bodies. I'll probably be out until dinner.'

She marched off in the direction of the residence.

Ah, well, that'd gone down like a slug in a salad, hadn't it? I sighed and went after Smarmer.

We found the undertaker's place, down an alleyway off the main drag just short of the gate. The two corpses were laid out on tables in the back room, both middle-aged men in their forties.

'OK, pal,' I said to Crinas. 'All yours. What do you think?'

'They're definitely both dead.'

Oh, ha. 'And?'

He lifted the nearer corpse's arm. Or tried to. It didn't move.

'The bodies are a little discomposed,' he said.

'*What?*'

'I mean they're not lying straight, flat on their backs with their arms decently crossed, as a corpse in a funeral parlour would normally be.'

'Yeah, right; I can see that for myself, thanks. So?'

'So rigor was well established when the undertaker's men got to them, which, from the information you gave me on the way, would probably have been at least a couple of hours after sunrise. Do you know the time exactly?'

'No, Balbinus wasn't that specific. He just said the guy who found them found them first thing.'

'No matter. Timing can vary, in any case.' Carefully, he lifted the hem of the corpse's tunic where the thigh touched the table and peered beneath it. I suppressed a shudder. 'Discolouration seems to match the pressure point. That would indicate that the man fell originally in this position. In other words, that he was not moved before rigor set in.'

'Uh-huh. In plain Latin again, please.'

'The body wasn't dumped where it was found; it had lain there for several hours before the muscles began to stiffen. The implication being that the place it was lying was also the site of the murder, and that the murder itself happened at some time between late evening and the early hours of the morning. Relevant?'

'Uh, yeah.' I was impressed, despite myself: Clarus couldn't've done better. 'You're pretty good, pal.'

'I told you, I did my training in Alexandria. They know all about bodies there, and they teach you to look, observe, and interpret, not make unsubstantiated guesses.'

Ouch. That was me told. 'Fair enough,' I said. 'Anything else? How did they die?'

'Oh, that's quite obvious.' He indicated the corpse he'd been examining. 'This one – the servant, from the quality of his tunic – was stabbed through the heart. You can see the bloodstains and the rent in the material. The other' – he moved to the second corpse – 'yes. Throat cut.' He peered closely at the guy's neck. 'Very clean, a single slash, probably made from behind if the killer was right-handed. You can see for yourself that the wound is deeper on the left side of the throat than it is on the right.'

'I'll take your word for it, friend.' I was feeling distinctly queasy; bodies I don't mind, but I'd rather not go into the whys and wherefores, thank you. I had the same problem with Clarus. Still, I'd asked. 'That it?'

'More or less. Isn't it enough?'

'Yeah. Thanks. Very helpful.' It had been, too. Surprisingly so, particularly since my only real reason, originally, for having the guy along was to detach him from Perilla.

'Glad to be of service.' He smiled. 'Now, if you've finished with me I'll get back to the residence and collect your wife for our sightseeing trip. Unless you'd care to tag along yourself?'

'No, I'm fine.' Damn. 'Things to do, people to see.'

'Very well, then. I'll see you at dinner, if not before.'

He left.

FOURTEEN

So. To the vegetable market, and Drutus's girlfriend; what was her name? Severa.

I took a slightly different route this time, down one of the roads parallel to the main drag, although 'parallel' was an overstatement. Being a colony, Augusta had been laid out in the usual grid system, but because the place had existed before the army surveyors had got busy the grid was pretty haphazard, with buildings plonked down any old where and the streets making detours around them. Mind you, like Crinas had said, there was a lot of new development going on; at times it was like walking through a building site.

I'd chosen well, though; the street I was on led me straight to the market. This late in the morning – it was about an hour shy of noon – most of the local housewives would've done their shopping and be at home cooking the midday meal, so it was relatively quiet. I asked the first stallholder I came to for directions, and he pointed out a small, dumpy, middle-aged woman selling root vegetables and cabbage.

Bugger; this I wasn't looking forward to. Perilla was the tactful one, and she was a woman into the bargain.

I went over.

'Uh . . . excuse me,' I said. 'Is your name Severa?'

'That's right, sir.' She glanced at my purple stripe and frowned. 'What can I do for you?'

'You're, ah, friendly with a guy named Drutus, aren't you?'

She set down the bunch of carrots she'd been rearranging like they were red hot.

'He's all right, isn't he?' she said. 'Only I've been so worried.'

Oh, shit; she didn't know. Hardly surprising, mind, since the bodies hadn't been found until a few hours previously. And Balbinus wouldn't have thought to send anyone to break the news to her, either; she wasn't family, after all. So like it or not, I'd landed the job. Where the hell was Perilla when I needed her? Out gallivanting with bloody Smarmer, that was where.

I hated it when this happened.

'No,' I said. 'No, I'm afraid he isn't. You might want to sit down.'

There was a folding stool to one side. She pulled it up and sat on it.

'He's not dead, is he?' she said. I didn't answer, which was answer enough. 'Oh, sweet Mothers, no!'

She hid her face in her hands. I looked around. There was a woman on the stall behind me, watching us with interest.

'You think you could help out a minute here?' I called to her. 'The lady's just had some bad news.'

She came over quickly; obviously she'd just been waiting for the invitation. I breathed a mental sigh of relief as she went into patting-and-there-there-dear mode. Thank the gods for female solidarity.

'I need to talk to her,' I murmured to the back of the woman's head. 'It's important. I'll give it ten minutes, OK?'

She nodded without turning. I walked off and did a slow circuit of the other stalls.

When I came back Severa's face was puffy and tear-stained, but she seemed fairly composed. I nodded my thanks to the other woman, and she went back to her stall. Not, I knew, that her ears wouldn't be pricked throughout the conversation, but that was fair enough under the circumstances.

'Just tell me what happened,' Severa said.

'He and his servant were found dead this morning outside the Moguntiacum Gate,' I said. 'I'm sorry, but it seems it was deliberate.'

She nodded, slowly, her face expressionless. She could still be in shock, of course, but I had a suspicion the news hadn't come as a complete surprise.

'And you are, sir?' she said.

'Valerius Corvinus. I'm, ah, just visiting. The governor's aide asked me to look into the deaths.' I waited, then said gently, 'You were expecting it? Or something like it?'

She raised her face. 'No! Oh, no! It's only that—' She stopped.

I gave her another few moments. Then I said, 'It's only that what?'

'I wasn't expecting it; I'd no reason to. Why should I? Sextus was just a very nice, very quiet, ordinary man who got on with things and minded his own business.'

'But?' I prompted.

'It's just . . .' She frowned. 'This'll sound stupid.'

'Never mind. Say it anyway.'

'We've known each other since before my husband died ten years back, but I've never really *known* him. Even when we took up together, sometimes there was a distance. You understand?'

'Uh-huh.' I didn't, not completely, but at least she was talking. 'Did he have any enemies? Anyone who'd want him dead?'

She shook her head. 'Not one. Everyone liked Sextus. I don't know much about his life in Durocortorum, and I was careful not to ask in case there was a wife, but he'd nothing but friends here. I don't even know anyone who had a bad word for him, let alone kill him.'

'Fair enough. Now what about yesterday evening? Did you see him at all?'

'Yes, I did. But only for a moment, just before sunset. He called in to say he wouldn't be staying the night after all. He'd some urgent business to take care of, and it wouldn't be finished until the small hours. He didn't want to disturb me coming in, so he'd doss down with Anda above the stable.'

'He say what the business was, at all? Give any kind of indication?'

'No. Not a word more. But then that was Sextus for you; like

I said, sometimes he could be really close-mouthed. And I never pried. It wasn't my concern.'

Hell! Still, it confirmed that he and Anda had some sort of clandestine meeting arranged. And although again from Severa's description he hadn't come across as the criminal type a moonlight assignation beyond the city gates stank like a barrel of oysters in a heat wave.

'There's nothing else you can tell me that may be of use to find out who did it?' I said. 'Nothing at all?'

She hesitated, then reached into her belt-pouch and brought something out. 'There's this,' she said, handing it over. 'He gave me it before he left. For safe keeping, he said.'

I turned the thing over in the palm of my hand. It was a gold piece, but not a Roman one; on one side there was a stylized head with the letters COMI, and on the other a prancing horse and a wheel.

'Yeah, well,' I said. 'That's not surprising, is it? Gold coins aren't too common here, from what I've been told. He wouldn't have wanted to carry it around with him, especially if he was going out after dark.'

'No.' She shook her head decisively. 'That wasn't the reason. At least, I don't think it was. Sextus was well-to-do, he was used to carrying a lot of money about. He wasn't afraid of being robbed, either.'

Uh-huh; fair point. And Balbinus had said there wasn't much crime in Augusta to begin with. It was an oddity, however you sliced it. 'You think I could hang on to this for a while? You'll get it back, I promise.'

Another hesitation. Then she nodded. 'All right. If you think it'll help.'

'It might. I don't know. Thank you.' I slipped it into my own belt-pouch. 'Incidentally, where do you live?'

'Up near the Temple of Rosmerta, on the river side of the Moguntiacum Gate.'

'Right. Thanks, Severa. And again I'm sorry for your loss.' I turned to go.

'Where is he?' she said. 'The body, I mean?'

Yeah, she'd want to know that, of course. 'At the undertaker's just off the market square. I don't know the name, I'm afraid.'

'The name doesn't matter; there's only the one. Thank you, sir.'

'You're welcome. Anything else I can do, you'll find me at the residence. Valerius Corvinus, remember.'

'I'll remember,' she said. 'But please. Find the man who did it for me. You'll do that?'

'I'll try.'

There was no more to be said. I left.

Back to the residence, then, to see if by any chance Balbinus had arranged for me to meet the man who'd found the bodies and see the place for myself.

I was crossing the market square towards the main drag when someone shouted my name. I turned. Quintus Cabirus. I waited until he'd joined me.

'What on earth are you doing in Augusta?' he said.

Yeah, well, he wouldn't't've known I was coming, or even that I might be, would he? It was a last-minute decision, and he'd left Lugdunum before I'd set out.

'Seeing your sister-in-law, as a matter of fact,' I said.

His eyes flickered. 'Really? Why should you want to do that?'

'Just an idea.'

'It's a long way to come, for just an idea.' He tried a smile that didn't quite work.

'Maybe.' I wasn't going to elucidate; absolutely no way. Brother Quintus wasn't out of the frame by any means, and whatever reason the Cabiri had had for leaving Augusta, if it wasn't the purely commercial one he and Diligenta had claimed it was, it applied to him as well.

'So,' he said, 'did you see her?' Obviously, from the too-casual way he asked the question, the answer was important.

'Yeah, I did.'

'And?'

'You don't keep in touch yourself, being through so often?'

'No. I told you when we talked last that the two halves of the family have nothing to do with each other. I haven't seen Quadrunia or her husband for twenty years, out of choice on both sides. I don't even know where she lives.'

'It's a shame when you get these family rows,' I said. 'Particularly when they fester. What was it about, originally?'

'I told you before. That's none of your business. And it has nothing whatsoever to do with my brother's death. Doubtless my sister-in-law told you the same, or you wouldn't be asking me now.'

'What've you done to your hand?'

'What? What has that . . .?' He looked blank, then glanced down at the long scratch or cut that ran across the back of his left hand below the knuckles. It wasn't still bleeding, but it looked pretty recent to me. 'Oh. I brushed against the point of a nail at our warehouse. We're having some rebuilding work done, and there's a lot of exposed timber.'

Uh-huh. 'It's quite nasty. You should get it seen to.'

'I've had worse. And I've got too much to do at present. So; you'll be getting back to Lugdunum soon, will you?'

'No, I think I'll hang on for a bit. No need to go dashing off almost as soon as we've arrived. Besides, Governor Hister's aide Saenius Balbinus, who's taking care of me while I'm here, has asked me to look into a couple of murders.'

'Murders?' His eyes narrowed. 'In Augusta? That's impossible! They don't have murders up here.'

'Yeah; I remember being told the same thing about Lugdunum. But there you are. A trader by the name of Sextus Drutus and his servant. You know him?'

'*Drutus*! Who would want to kill Drutus?'

'You tell me, pal. It'd save me a lot of time and effort.'

'Yes, I know him. Not well, but yes. He trades in hides, doesn't he? With the garrison at Moguntiacum?'

'That's him.'

'What happened?'

'That's what I'm still finding out. But it seems that the two of them – Drutus and the servant – were out beyond the Moguntiacum Gate for some reason after sunset yesterday and someone used a knife on them. The bodies were found early this morning.'

I was watching him closely, but there wasn't a reaction other than shock and surprise.

'But that's dreadful!' he said.

'Yeah, isn't it? Where are you staying, by the way?'

Again the momentary blank look. 'Oh. I've got a room fitted

up in our warehouse. Near the town baths not far from the bridge. It's pretty basic, no more than a shakedown with a bed and mattress, but it does me for the short time I'm here.'

'You're on your own, then?'

He smiled. 'I'm a bachelor, Corvinus. I'm used to fending for myself. And I've never been one for seeking out temporary female company when I'm away from home.'

'You're going back soon?'

'Within the next couple of days. I've done most of what I came for, seen our agent and everything, so there's no need to put off.'

'I might see you around, then. Or not.'

'Or, as you say, not. If the latter then good luck with your additional investigations while you're here. Now, I still have a couple of people to talk to, so if you'll forgive me . . .?'

'Sure. No problem.'

I watched as he headed off through the square's southern exit. Hmm. Interesting.

Who should be waiting for me in the residence lobby but Bathyllus, wearing a broad smirk.

This did not bode well. Smirks, broad or otherwise, did not figure prominently in our major-domo's range of facial expressions.

'Hi, little guy,' I said. 'Don't tell me; another palace coup, yes?'

'Not at all, sir. I wouldn't presume to disrupt the running of Procurator Laco's household. But I did ask if where the mistress and yourself were concerned as individuals I could fulfil my usual functions. The staff were quite amenable, particularly when I hinted that you might have some unusual requirements which I was accustomed to fulfilling and they, perhaps, were not.'

I goggled. 'You *what*? What sort of "unusual requirements"?'

'I didn't go into details, sir, because I did not consider it necessary, and they agreed not to press me for them.'

Jupiter and all the gods!

'Bloody hell, Bathyllus, if you've given the residence staff the idea that I'm some sort of pervert with a thing for small bald-headed butlers I'll—!'

'Not at all, sir. Or not intentionally. But I was telling the simple truth. You *do* have some special requirements which only I am aware of.'

'And what the fuck requirements are these, may I ask?'

He stepped aside. On the low table behind him was a tray with a wine-cup on it. A *full* wine-cup.

'Standing orders, sir,' he said. 'A cup of wine to be ready for you whenever you come in.'

I had to grin. 'Yeah, OK, Bathyllus,' I said. 'Nicely done, I admit it. Very clever, and the bribery ploy works a treat. But just the one cup, and the mistress mustn't know, right?'

'Never a word will pass my lips, sir. The God Mercury hear me so swear.'

'Plus if I get a single sideways glance – a *single* one – from any of Laco's skivvies while we're here then you, pal, are cat's meat. Understood?'

'I'll explain the situation fully to them straight away, sir, now that the bargain has been struck.'

I reached past him, picked up the wine-cup and sipped. Nectar! A good Massilian, from the taste of it, and only normally watered.

'Oh, one more thing, sir,' Bathyllus said. 'I was to tell you that you have a message from Saenius Balbinus.'

'Hmm?' I took another sip of the wine.

'He's arranged for the man who found the bodies to meet you just beyond the cemetery on the Moguntiacum road. Any time today will be convenient; it seems the man pastures his goats there in any case, and he'll be looking out for you. His name is Coisis.'

'Great. Thanks, Bathyllus. I'll just let this wine trickle down my throat first and then I'll be off.'

I took it slow. Marvellous. There was a lot to be said for having a devious, position-conscious major-domo, and murder and the goats could wait.

Once I was past the cemetery that flanked the Moguntiacum road for a quarter of a mile or so the countryside got pretty wild pretty quickly: low hills covered with rough grass and scrub, cut up in places with gorges down which small streamlets trickled. I could see why this Coisis, if he pastured his animals here, had chosen goats rather than cattle or sheep: any self-respecting cow would've handed in its milk pail on the first day.

I spotted the guy straight off. Forget your country swains beloved of pastoral poets warbling rustic lays on their oaten pipes as they while away the hour of noonday heat beneath the holm-oak's shade; my informant – presumably my informant, since he was the only person I'd seen all the way from town, and there was a bunch of goats browsing among the thistles on either side of the road – had his back to me and was pissing in the ditch.

'You Coisis, pal?' I said when I'd come up to him.

'I am that, sir, indeed I am.' He finished, shook himself, adjusted his tunic, and turned round. All at a speed that would've disgraced an arthritic tortoise. Clearly not a guy to hurry himself. 'And you'll be Valerius Corvinus, would you? Just so, isn't it?'

'That's me.' The breeze shifted slightly in my direction, and I caught his scent. Jupiter! Essence of goat in its most concentrated form; I'd bet even the animals themselves practised better personal hygiene.

'From Lugdunum, too, they said you were. Fancy. Never did have a hankering for foreign parts, myself. I was in Ricciacus once, when the wife was alive, gods rest her, she had a cousin there getting wed, and that's all of thirty-five miles, but 'tweren't much cop. They talked funny, they ate funny, and they smelled funny. I was glad to be home.'

Yeah, well; to each his own. Mark you, the mind boggled at what the 'smelled funny' bit entailed: any odour that could fight its way through what this guy was generating far enough to register had to be quite something. Probably just cleanliness. 'So,' I said, 'where are we going, here?'

'Just a step, sir, just a step.' He pointed across the ditch, away from the road. 'There's a rise and a hollow, no more nor a dozen yards off. You follow me and I'll show you.'

'Will the goats be all right?'

'Oh, those lazy buggers won't stir more than they can help. They'll be fine left until we get back.'

'That wasn't exactly what I meant, friend.' Once I was over the ditch I'd have to push my way through them, and I was already getting some pointed stares, particularly from one evil-eyed bastard with a fine spread of horns; evidently the boss of the whole caprine gang, and who given half a chance was willing and ready to prove it.

Coisis chuckled. 'Not a country man, are you, sir?' he said. 'Bless you, the lassies won't do you no harm. Just keep your distance from old Rufus there, is all. He can be a bit frisky at times with strangers.'

No prizes for guessing which one old Rufus was. I moved to where there were several of his harem between him and me and jumped the ditch. The goats scattered.

'That's the ticket.' Coisis did the same, and set off at a slow amble, while I followed. 'It'd be a big place, that. Lugdunum.'

'Yeah, big enough,' I said. 'Although actually I'm from Rome.'

He clicked his tongue. 'Now there's a thing! Rome, eh? Aye, well, I suppose you would be, thinking about it. That'd be just a bit further off, now, wouldn't it?'

'Just a tad.'

'Aye, I thought so. Well, it takes all sorts, as they say. Here we are.' He stopped. 'I told you it weren't more nor a step. Found the poor buggers here, I did, both together, like.'

I looked; sure enough, the grass was flattened and there was a great splash of dried blood on one side of it. That'd been where Drutus had had his throat cut, no doubt. There was nothing else as far as the eye could see but Gallic countryside.

Well, I'd seen it, for what it was worth.

'When did you find them, exactly?' I said.

'Ah, that'd be scarce an hour past dawn. Gave me a right turn, you may guess. My young grandson, he was here with me and I sends him to the town officer's house straight off. Then I waited until the undertaker's men came. That's about it, sir, all I can tell you.'

'Thanks, pal.' I reached into my belt-pouch, fished out a couple of silver pieces, and handed them over. 'Really helpful. Oh . . . you ever see anyone up this way? Strangers, maybe?'

He chuckled. 'No. Not off the road, like. What's here for anyone to bother with? And me and the lasses and Rufus there, we've our own home to go to in town when the sun sets.'

Right. So much for that. I left the guy to his goats and went back home.

FIFTEEN

There was no sign of Perilla at the residence – she was clearly still out gallivanting amid the fleshpots of the Lenus Mars sanctuary – but Balbinus was waiting in the atrium.

'Well, Corvinus?' he said. 'What's the news?'

There was a flask of wine and four cups on the side table, but I steeled myself and sat down on the couch without touching them.

'Not much,' I said. 'It's early stages yet. I saw his girlfriend – woman friend, rather – but she couldn't shed any light, apart from telling me that he'd told her he had some important business that'd keep him until the small hours of the morning. Presumably that's what he was engaged in when he and the servant were killed, but she couldn't elaborate any.'

Balbinus frowned. 'That's a bit odd, isn't it?' he said. 'I mean, he obviously had to have some reason for being out there at that time of night, but if it was business then what kind could it have been? And who with?'

I shrugged. 'The natural assumption is that it was something he didn't want people to know about,' I said. 'With whoever else was involved being his killer. A shady deal that went wrong. Some sort of disagreement. A double-cross. Your guess is as good as mine, at this stage. The problem is, Drutus doesn't exactly come across as your typical crook.'

'It isn't something I'd have believed for a moment, knowing the man. Still, judging by the evidence that is the most logical conclusion.' Balbinus sighed. 'It's a mystery, right enough.'

'Oh. Severa did give me this,' I said. 'It belonged to Drutus, and he left it with her. For safe keeping, he said.' I took the gold coin out of my belt-pouch and handed it to him. 'Any thoughts?'

He examined it. 'It's not Gaulish, at least not like any that I've ever seen before,' he said. 'Celtic, certainly, from the decoration. It could be British, I suppose, but what would Drutus be doing with a British gold piece?'

'I don't know.'

'Leave it with me. I'll ask around.' Then, when I opened my mouth: 'Don't worry, Corvinus, she'll get it back. Drutus wasn't married and he'd no family, so I suppose it makes the lady the closest thing he has to an heir. Besides, if he gave it to her, albeit temporarily, then she has a right to it in any case. It's queer, though; why should he give her it "for safe keeping"? Drutus wasn't wealthy, but he had far more than a copper or two to rub together. He wouldn't've worried unduly about losing a single gold piece, wherever it came from. And he wasn't the nervous kind, to be frightened of muggers.'

'Right.' More or less what Severa had said. 'It's a puzzle.'

'Certainly it is. Anyway, I've sent a report – such as it is – to the governor in Durocortorum by my fastest courier, so he should have it inside of three days. Hister will be sorry to hear about the death, too; personally sorry, I mean. Drutus was a popular member of the Durocortorum community. He'll be missed.'

'Incidentally, have you had any luck with my side of things?'

'Hmm? Oh, yes, you wanted me to find you an informant about the Cabiri family's doings at the time of the Florus revolt. Actually, that's proving a lot trickier than I thought it would.'

'Yeah? Why's that? It's twenty years ago now, granted, but there must still be dozens of people still around who'd fit the bill.'

He tugged at his ear in embarrassment. 'That's true,' he said. 'There are. But only locals.'

'So?'

'Corvinus, you've only been here since yesterday; you don't know the place or the people yet. Nowhere near. They aren't Romans, or no more than skin-deep ones. At root, they're Gauls, and not even the sort of Gauls you'll have met in Lugdunum, let alone Massilia, either. Don't forget that it's less than a century since old Julius brought the Treveri under Roman control.'

'Yeah, I know that, but—'

'Listen. They're a clannish lot: they protect their own, and whatever they pretend most of them have very little time for us. The Treveri especially, as a tribe, and you always have to

remember that that's still how most Gauls see themselves, first
and foremost; as members of a tribe, not as Gauls per se, and
least of all as Roman provincials. It's why Julius Florus managed
to whip up enough support here to stage his revolt, because he
was from the local ruling family and had clout in spades. Which
brings me to the point.'

Uh-huh; I was there already. What Balbinus was telling me
was exactly what I'd been getting all along, from Diligenta, her
sister Quadrunia, Quintus Cabirus and practically everyone else
I'd talked to. Bugger! 'You're saying they don't blab, right?' I
said. 'Not to a Roman, not when one of their own's involved.'

He shook his head. 'No. Or rather, yes, but it's more complicated than that. The Florus revolt tore this region apart. It tore
families apart. Some people – ordinary people – chose one side,
some another, whether they did it actively or not. After the revolt
was put down, the two sides were left looking at each other. The
pieces had to be picked up, life had to be got on with, normal
relations had to be restored. The only way they could do that
was to forgive and forget. Which is what they did, consciously
and deliberately, and what they're still doing twenty years on.
I'm afraid that that means you'll have an uphill struggle getting
anyone to talk, whether they have a personal interest or not.
Especially with you being a Roman.'

Fuck. Even so, I had to keep trying, didn't I? I might strike
lucky eventually somehow.

'OK,' I said. 'So let's at least make sure I have the background
straight here. Tell me about the Florus revolt, in detail. Can you
do that?'

He frowned. 'Yes, of course. It's required knowledge for any
diplomat posted to this part of Gaul. But why should you need
that information?'

'I don't know. Perhaps I don't. But it's figuring so strongly in
this case that I may as well get the facts straight in my head
once and for all. OK?'

'If you like.' He stood up and moved over to the table where
the wine flask and cups were. 'But I'll have a cup of wine while
I'm talking, if I may. You want one yourself?'

Hell; this went above and beyond the call of duty. 'No,' I said
between gritted teeth. 'You go ahead.'

'Thank you.' He poured the wine and took it back to the couch. 'So what do you know already?'

'Assume zilch.'

'Very well.' He took a sip. 'Julius Florus, as I said, was a Treveran noble who also commanded a wing of native auxiliary cavalry. Some twenty years ago, twenty-one to be exact, because of some slight, real or imagined, on our part he decided to use his social position coupled with the widespread discontent over tax arrears and debt repayment to stage a revolt. He gained considerable support locally, but not enough for the revolt to succeed, the crucial factor being his failure to win over a majority of his cavalry wing for a projected massacre of the Augustan merchant community. He and his army – more of a rabble, at this point, largely poorly armed civilians – retreated east hoping to regroup under the cover of the Arduennan Forest, but they were cut off by troops sent down from the Rhine and particularly by a group of loyal local auxiliaries commanded by Florus's main political rival, Julius Indus. The rebel army was destroyed and scattered, but Florus escaped. He committed suicide shortly afterwards. End of revolt, but only the beginning of the town's troubles.' Balbinus took a long swallow of wine. 'That do you?'

'Yeah, thanks.' I was frowning. 'Florus was planning to massacre the merchant community here, yes?'

'Probably only the actual Roman, or at least non-Gaulish, part of it – remember that Augusta is a colony – but yes, that's right. Presumably, though, that would include any Gaulish merchants who were considered too hand-in-glove with the Roman authorities.'

'Such as the Cabiri, for example? Who owed their citizenship directly to the imperial family and had their explicit patronage?'

'Ah . . . yes. Yes, I suppose so. If you put it like that. You think it's relevant?'

'I don't know. Maybe. It's an angle to think about, anyway. And if you—'

'Oh, hello, Marcus. You're back too, then?'

I turned; Perilla was coming in from the lobby, still in her outdoor things. She looked bright, breezy and definitely chipper.

'Yeah, so it would seem,' I said a bit stiffly. 'Have a good time?'

'Marvellous, thank you.' Bathyllus, as usual, had materialized out of the ether to take her cloak. 'A barley water and honey, Bathyllus, if you will. I'm parched. Saenius Balbinus. Lovely to see you again.'

'And you, Lady Rufia.' He finished the last of his wine and stood up. 'I was just about to go, actually. We'd done, I think, Corvinus, hadn't we?'

'More or less,' I said: I wondered if, being the diplomat he was, Balbinus had sensed a slight Atmosphere and was making himself scarce before the crockery started flying. 'Let me know, though, if you find anyone who can help.'

'I'll do that. And, of course, you will keep me abreast of the Drutus side of things? I'm not forgetting the coin, naturally.'

'Sure. No problem.' Not that I'd got any more leads there, either. Still. 'I'll see you around.'

He left.

'Well, dear,' Perilla said. 'How was your day? Profitable?'

'Frustrating, if anything. Unlike yours, from what I can see.'

'Hmm.' She gave me a long, slow look. 'Still sulking, are we?'

'I haven't the slightest idea what you mean.'

'Very well. Never mind.' She sat down on the couch Balbinus had vacated. 'No, my day was far from frustrating. The sanctuary of Lenus Mars was fascinating. An interesting mixture of the primitive and the civilized. And of course there were the healing springs. Crinas was especially interested in those, naturally.'

'So he turned up, then?'

'Yes, he did. As promised, and only shortly after I got there, so you can't have kept him long.'

'He probably ran all the way. Jogged.'

'Perhaps he did. I didn't ask.' Bathyllus came in with the barley water and honey. 'Thank you, Bathyllus.' She glanced at the table in front of her, where Balbinus had set down his empty cup. It was the only one there, of course. 'Oh, go on, Marcus, for heaven's sake, don't be silly! Have a cup of wine, if you want it.'

'Yeah, but—'

'I'm not completely heartless. I only thought it would be good for you to cut down a little in your own interests, which you seem to have done. Particularly on the way here from Lugdunum; you always seem to view a long coach journey simply as an opportunity to get drunk.'

'I don't get drunk. At least, not very often.'

'You do; you just don't show it. It doesn't mean you have to abstain altogether or even keep to the four-cup rule, provided that you're sensible. I never for a moment imagined you'd manage that as long as you have, anyway. Well done. Well done, indeed.'

I didn't believe this; I just did *not* believe it! 'Jupiter bloody God Almighty, woman! You mean I've been—?'

'You feel all the better for it, don't you? Admit it.'

Yeah, well, I supposed she had a point; maybe I should cut down a little in future. I got up, went over to the wine flask, poured myself a whopper, and carried it back to the couch, stopping to kiss her on the way.

'That's more like it,' she said. 'Now. Tell me about your day.'

I told her.

'So the Cabirus side of things is definitely hanging fire for the present,' I finished. 'Although there may be some mileage in what Balbinus was just telling me when you arrived, about Florus planning to massacre Augusta's mercantile community. At least, the Roman part of it plus the obvious sympathizers.'

'How so?' Perilla said. 'I could see that there might be if the family had got wind of the revolt in advance and fled to Lugdunum beforehand for safety, but that's not right; at least from what you've already told me I don't think it can be. They left Augusta after the revolt, not before, and, unless I've misunderstood completely there wasn't anything particularly fly-by-night about the move. While if everything was forgive-and-forget after the crisis was over it wouldn't have mattered which side they were on. If any.'

'Yeah.' I frowned; she was right, of course, but there was something there that was important. 'Don't forget, though, that Diligenta's – and Quadrunia's – brother supported the rebels.'

'The same argument applies, surely. He may have done, but that was water under the bridge.'

'Agreed. Still, I'd like to know what happened to the guy. At present all we have is that he disappeared into the sunset and none of the family know where to. Or say they don't, rather,

which is a different thing entirely.' I took a morose swallow of
wine. 'Hell. Leave it. It'll come, with luck, if it's important.'

'How about the other thing? Balbinus's two murders?'

'Yeah; that's a real poser. Drutus had to be crooked in some
way for the whole assignation scenario to fit, only from all
accounts – and accounts by people who knew him well, including
his lady friend – he wasn't. He didn't seem to have any enemies,
either; he was just an ordinary merchant. So why the hell should
he end up with his throat slit at an ungodly hour in the middle
of nowhere? And presumably have arranged to go there off his
own bat? It just doesn't make sense.'

'What about the coin?'

'Perilla, I don't know, right? Balbinus was pretty definite about
it not being Gaulish. He did think it might be British, sure, but
that doesn't mean much: Drutus was a merchant, and gold's gold,
whatever the markings. It travels, changes hands. He could've
got it as part of a payment, from anyone, at any time.'

'So why should he give it to his woman friend for safe
keeping?' She was twisting her lock of hair. 'Of course, it could
have had some significance apart from its monetary value.'

'I thought of that.' I took another sip of the wine: gods, but
that was good! 'Of course I did. Still, what sort of significance
could it have?'

'A token? Like the half coins that are passed down families
as proof of inherited guest-friendship?'

I could see what she was getting at: splitting a coin is a good
old Roman custom whereby someone on a journey can turn up
at a stranger's door, show his half of the coin as proof of his
bona fides, and claim a night's board and lodging: useful if you
don't want to pick up a cargo of fleas or a dose of gut-rot by
spending the night at a roadside inn. And there isn't any time
limit on the deal either: some of those coins are passed down
the generations, and the deal is still valid even if neither party
has claimed their right in living memory.

'It's a possibility,' I said. 'But you hit the same problem: the
guy was no one special, a merchant from Durocortorum, less
than two hundred miles from here. Say for the sake of argument
the coin was British, and by extension, if it was a token, there
was a British connection. If we'd been on the other side of the

country, near the Gallic Strait, and Drutus had trading interests with the tribes on the British side, then I could understand it. But as far as I know his trade was all with the legionary bases on the Rhine. He was a local, more or less. He didn't go anywhere near Britain.'

'That's only as far as you know, dear. It's something to check, certainly. Balbinus will be able to tell you.'

'Yeah. Even so, I can be pretty certain what his answer will be. If that were the case he would've mentioned it straight off when I showed him the coin in the first place. No, the whole thing's a dog's breakfast.'

'So what do you do now?'

I shrugged. 'The priority's the Cabirus side of things. If Balbinus can't help with that, at least at present, then I'll just have to do what I always do, muddle along and hope something turns up.'

'Never mind, Marcus. No doubt it'll all make sense eventually.'

'You think so?' I said sourly. 'Read my lips: we are definitely floundering here.'

'It can't be that bad, surely.'

'Believe it.'

Hell.

SIXTEEN

The situation wasn't completely black, mind. Stymied we might be, but when a case hits the buffers I've always gone for two courses of action to get things moving again: a) rattle the cages of whatever bastards you think are in the running and see whether they jump, and b) find a wineshop with a barman or bar fly who's more than delighted to dig the dirt and keep your ears open. The first, unfortunately, wasn't an option this time because our list of possible perps was zilch. That – now that I was officially if not off the wagon at least perched on the tail-gate, and thank the gods for small mercies – left the second . . .

Or at least it would've done anywhere other than bloody Augusta Treverorum. Tight-mouthed and clannish was right: after four days of trying and a dozen cups of wine – I'd conscientiously limited my intake to a single cupful per establishment – all I'd got was a succession of stony silences and looks that were the equivalent of the straight finger.

Let's hear it for Gaulish solidarity. Everyone hates the Roman.

So there I was, late morning four days down the road, trying my luck in the thirteenth wineshop and getting nowhere fast, when Vercingetorix walks in, does a double-take, hesitates, then comes on over to join me at the bar.

'Valerius Corvinus, isn't it?' he said. 'We travelled up from Lugdunum together.'

'Ah . . . yeah. Yeah, that's me. And yes, we did.' I moved my stool along so he could pull his closer to the counter. 'You're, uh . . .'

'Segomarus. Segus, for short.' He was looking up at the wine board. 'What would you recommend?'

'Pass.' I was staring at him. 'It's my first time in here and I've only had the one. The Cabellian. From just outside Massilia, I think. It's not that bad.'

'Fine.' He ignored the stare and turned to the barman. 'Make it a cup of the Cabellian, please.'

'Ah . . . excuse me, pal, and no offence,' I said. 'But you speak good Latin.'

'Shouldn't I?'

'Not according to Titus Cabirus.'

'Who?'

'The young officer who was in charge of Procurator Laco's guard on the way here.'

He laughed. 'Oh. Yes, of course, I'm sorry. Then it's a misunderstanding on his part. We happened to share a bench at the Lugdunum baths, he spoke to me in Celtic, and I answered in the same. Of course; you were there yourself that day, weren't you?'

'Yeah, I was. If I recall correctly, you gave me a look that would curdle milk and stalked off.'

'Did I? Then it absolutely wasn't intentional, and nothing to do with you. My stomach was playing up, and I was probably dashing off to the latrine. If I offended you then I apologize.'

'No need. Maybe it was preoccupation rather than a scowl at that.'

'Anyway, on the few occasions the lad and I happened to exchange words on the journey up here from Lugdunum we spoke Celtic. To tell you the truth, I encouraged it, which might explain things; it's getting so as you hardly hear Celtic spoken any more outside the country districts, or not in this part of the country, particularly by the youngsters. A sign of the times, I'm afraid.' The barman set the wine-cup down in front of him. He paid and took a cautious sip. 'You're right, this isn't bad at all. A bit on the tart side for Cabellian, mind.'

Bloody hell, first the guy spoke Latin better than I did and now he turned out to be a fellow wine aficionado. It just showed you couldn't go by appearances.

'You're from, ah . . .' I couldn't remember the name of the place. 'Over in the west.'

'Burdigala. That's right. But I travel around a lot.'

'On business?'

'I don't do it for fun, Corvinus. I'm a merchant. Of course, on business.'

'So what kind of business?'

He held up the wine-cup. 'Wine, as a matter of fact. A family firm. My father started it fifty years back. He's long dead now, but my brothers and I keep it on.'

'You produce your own wine over there?'

'Oh, no. Not at present, but trust me that's going to change. The climate's perfect for vines, and the soil's good, too. Once we have the vineyards planted and established we'll be off and running, producing wine that's good enough to match Massilia's, at least. Say ten or fifteen years, at most.'

'Is that so?'

'That's indeed so. It's why I'm here, on this side of the country where the vineyards are. Studying methods, assessing the markets for the future, while my brothers keep the import–export side of things going back home.'

'You do any trade with Britain?'

He'd been lifting the cup to his mouth. Now he set it down again.

'Why do you ask that?' he said.

'No particular reason. It's just that Britain happens to be in the front of my mind at present.'

'No, none at all. Burdigala's a long way from the Gallic Strait, and all the exports – imports, too – go through Itius and Gesoriacum. Our market's mostly local, or south towards the Spanish border. Mind you, if the rumours are right and the emperor intends to add Britain to the empire then that could well change.'

'I wouldn't've thought you'd be holding your breath on that one, pal. He has to take the place first, and it'd be years before any sort of market built up.'

'We're thinking in terms of years. And if things work out then within a decade Burdigala will have the only stretch of quality commercial vineyard in western Gaul. That's something to aim at, isn't it?'

'It is, indeed. Good luck to you.'

'So.' He took a swallow of wine. 'Why are you here, yourself?'

'You mean you don't know?'

'Why should I?'

'No reason. But if you don't then given the way news spreads over here you're probably the only person in Augusta who doesn't.'

He laughed. 'Believe me, I've better things to occupy my time than listen to wineshop gossip. Oh, I know you're official, you have to be, but what kind of official exactly I've no idea.'

I told him. He nodded.

'Interesting,' he said. 'This Tiberius Claudius Cabirus. He'd be a relative of the young guards officer?'

'Yeah. His father, as a matter of fact.'

'There's a Quintus Cabirus, too. Or am I wrong?'

'That's the brother. You know him?'

'No, we haven't met. But I have heard the name, here and in Lugdunum; naturally, I have, since we're in the same business. I didn't make the connection with our young tribune, though. That was dense of me, although to be fair he probably only gave me his name once.' He drained the last of his wine and signalled to the barman. 'You want another?'

'No, I'm fine,' I said. Bugger.

'It still doesn't explain why you're here in Augusta, though, does it? I mean, if the murder happened in Lugdunum.'

'Yeah, well, it's complicated,' I said. 'Basically, I need to know more about a bit of family history. The Cabiri moved from here to Lugdunum twenty years back, immediately after the Florus revolt. Me, I think they were pushed, for some reason. Or maybe they thought themselves that a move south would be healthier. It's all guesswork, sure, and the whole thing may be a mare's nest to begin with, but even so. It's important, I can feel that in my gut.'

He'd raised his eyebrows. 'Can't you just ask around?' he said. 'I'm assuming, naturally, that the family won't tell you themselves. Someone must know the details.'

'You're not Roman, pal. One look at the nose and the purple stripe and the locals zip up. I've met more talkative clams.'

'Yes, I can appreciate the problem. Tricky.'

'Bet your sandal straps it is. Only from where I'm standing the right word's "impossible".' I finished off the last of my own wine at a gulp and stood up. 'Anyway, it was nice talking to you. I'll see you around.'

I was turning to go when he said: 'Do you want any help?'

I stopped, and turned back.

'How do you mean?' I said.

'You said yourself. I'm not Roman. And I'm not particularly busy at present. Nothing that can't wait a few days, certainly. Maybe I'd have better luck.'

'You serious?'

'Of course I am. I told you; I'm interested. I don't come cheap, mind.' He touched the full cup the barman had put in front of him. 'Buy me this and it's a deal.'

'Fair enough.' I grinned and reached for my belt-pouch. 'You want the jug?'

'No, I'm not greedy. Just that second cup will do fine, for the present. We'll leave standing me the whole jug until the job's done. If it ever is.'

'Fair enough. It's a bargain.' I put the coins on the counter. 'Only forget wineshops. I've probably queered the pitch where those are concerned over the past three days.'

'Oh, I think I can manage. Just leave it with me. You're staying at the residence, right?'

'Yeah.'

'Then if and when I find out anything, I'll let you know.'
'That's great.' It was, too. I felt happier than I had for days.
'Thanks, friend.'
   'Don't mention it.'
I went home.
Score one for the wineshop ploy, after all.

Not that, as it turned out, I could put my feet up quite yet. When
I got back there was a message waiting from Balbinus, asking
me to meet him ASAP in the provincial admin building across
the road from the residence itself.
   Hey! ASAP, right? Maybe things were moving after all. I went
straight over.
   The clerk on duty took me through to Balbinus's office. He
was sitting at his desk reading, and when the clerk showed me
in he looked up.
   'Corvinus.' He laid the wax tablet to one side, on top of two
or three others. 'Good of you to come so promptly. Pull up a
stool, if you would.' Then, to the clerk: 'Thank you, Sextus.
That's all. Close the door behind you, please, and make sure
we're not disturbed.'
   Shit; this did not look good, after all. And whatever else he
was, Balbinus was currently not a happy bunny.
   I sat. Balbinus waited until the door was closed.
   'There've been developments,' he said.
   'Yeah?'
   'Nothing to do with you. Or at least, I hope not. But I don't
like coincidences, myself, and this is a little too coincidental for
comfort, which is why I thought you'd better know about it
straight away.' He indicated the message tablets. 'We have prob-
lems. Or at least I think we have.'
   'What kind of problems?'
   'Someone's trying to stir up trouble among the locals.' He
glanced at me. 'You're not surprised?'
   'Actually, no,' I said. 'Or not too surprised, anyway. Licinius
Nerva, the governor's aide in Lugdunum, said something might
be happening along those lines.'
   'Really?' Balbinus frowned. 'Then he knew more than I did
before now. Or perhaps his governor keeps him better informed

than mine does, which may well be the case.' Hmm. Well, every provincial governor had his own way of doing things, and after all Balbinus would normally be based at Durocortorum, two hundred miles away. Still, I could tell that it rankled. 'Oh, it's nothing definite, let alone anyone in particular we can point the finger at. In fact, I'd be happier if there was, because then at least we could nail him before he does any real harm. Just a rumour. Or rumours, rather, and strong ones, because we're hearing them from more than one source. I might discount them myself – you always get a degree of grumbling with provincials, and the chances are it won't come to anything – but under the present circumstances as Governor Hister's current rep I can't take risks, either way.'

Right; the up-and-coming British campaign. I knew enough about political and military affairs to know that mounting an invasion while leaving civil unrest at your back – even if it didn't amount to a full-scale revolt – was a bad, bad idea. 'You've told the governor?' I said.

'Of course I have. I sent a messenger as soon as I knew myself. Fortunately, although it's still bad enough, the trouble seems to be fairly localized at present, which isn't surprising.'

'Why's that?'

He gave a quick smile. 'You want a history lesson, Corvinus? I told you before: this part of Gaul has always been particularly difficult; it was no coincidence that the Treveri were one of the only two tribes that rose twenty years back. And it predates us. The Treveri and the Remi – that's the tribe around Durocortorum – had been at daggers drawn for centuries. If the Remi went one way, which they did by taking our side from the start, the Treveri automatically went the other, and that's still the case, in principle. The reason Florus failed was that he couldn't win over his auxiliaries; as far as the ordinary locals were concerned, he'd all the support he needed. And of course after the revolt was put down the Treveri as a tribe were severely penalized – reparations, loss of their free status, higher taxes, and just plain distrust – so that didn't help matters any. Only twenty years back, mind, and that's nothing to a Gaul. So the consequence is that there's a lot of hatred under the surface, and they only reason they don't show it much is that they can't, not publicly. If anyone did want to stir up trouble for any reason then here's the perfect place. Added to which, there's something even more worrying.'

'Yeah?'

'Some of the rumours mention a druid.'

Oh, shit; again, particularly after that conversation with Nerva, I could see why *worrying* was an understatement. 'You're sure?'

'Like I say, the information comes from rumours, not factual reports, let alone records of sightings. But just the thought it might be true makes my skin crawl. Those bastards are pure poison, they're attracted to trouble like vultures to rotten meat, and if you want to whip up support for a revolt among the local peasantry then bringing in a druid is the best way to do it. They're almost impossible to find, too, let alone catch and kill, even if you know for certain they're there, because no Gallic peasant is going to risk a druid's curse by giving him away, even these days.'

'They're that uncivilized round about here?'

'Corvinus, you go ten miles off the main road – less – into the sticks and most of the people you meet won't have changed the way they live since old Julius's day. Which means, in effect, more than nine-tenths of the tribe.' Yeah, right: I remembered my goat-herder pal. 'The only time they come into town, any town, not even a city like Augusta – if they ever do – is once every two or three months, to sell their produce or get what they need. And even then they do it through barter, not purchase. Oh, there's been a clampdown on druids since the Divine Augustus's day, of course there has, but there are plenty still around in the wilder parts of the country. And of course Britain is heaving with them. That's another reason Claudius is so keen to invade, to stamp the buggers out at source. And, naturally, why they in turn have a vested interest in stopping him.'

'You think it's a concerted plan, then?'

'I'm certain it is. Clever, too. The emperor will need at least four legions for the campaign plus the equivalent number of auxiliaries, they'll all have to come from the Rhine force, which means almost half its strength, and even if he tries to plug the gaps by recruiting or bringing in troops from elsewhere it leaves us spread very thinly. Too thinly to spare the men needed to put

the revolt down, as happened in Florus's day. Claudius couldn't
risk leaving that much danger behind him. At best, he'd have to
make do with a smaller force, which would jeopardize the invasion's success, or delay things until the Rhine garrisons were
more up to strength; at worst, he'd have to cancel the campaign
altogether.'

I sat back. Jupiter and all the holy gods! No wonder the guy
was chewing his nails!

'So how does this affect me?' I said.

'I told you; it doesn't, not as far as I know. But that isn't
much, and like I said I don't trust coincidences. We don't have
murders in Augusta, and although I can't see why the Drutus
business should be connected it's just possible that it is. So keep
what I've told you in mind, all right? And don't spread it around,
either, because that'll only make matters worse. For your ears
only, remember.'

'You've got it.'

'So. How are things going otherwise?'

'Not well. The Drutus part of things . . . well, I'm not exactly
played out there at present, although the options are fairly limited.
The girlfriend wasn't a great deal of help, as you know, but I
might have a word with the owner of the tavern where the guy's
servant put up, see if he let slip anything useful. It's a long shot,
I know, but it's all I have for now.'

'Oh, that reminds me.' Balbinus reached into his belt-pouch.
'The coin Severa gave you.' He took it out and handed it to me.
'It's definitely British, minted by a King Commius of the
Atrebates tribe about forty years back. Or so one of my extremely
knowledgeable clerks tells me.'

'British, right?' I looked at the coin again. 'Significant, you
think, in the light of events?'

'That was my thought. It could be, of course, though in what
way I'm not sure.'

'Hmm.' I slipped the coin into my own pouch. 'I'll see that
Severa gets it back. If that's OK with you?'

'Perfectly. It's your case, handle it as you please. The other
side of things, the Cabirus business. No joy there either, I assume?
I'm afraid I can't report any success in finding you an informant
myself.'

'Yeah.' I shifted on the stool. 'That doesn't surprise me; you'd have the same trouble I did. Comes of being Roman. Still, that's not a total washout. I've had an offer of help from one of the native merchants. A guy called Segus. Segomarus.'

'Segomarus?' Balbinus frowned. 'I don't think I know him.'

'No, you wouldn't. He arrived with us, but he's not a regular. First time here, seemingly. He's from Burdigala.'

'Is he, by Jove? That's right the other side of the country. What's he doing in Augusta?'

'Boning up on wine production and marketing with a view to developing Burdigala as the wine centre of the west. Or so he says. He comes from a family of wine shippers.'

'And he's offered off his own bat to help you get information about the Cabiri?' Balbinus was still frowning. 'Corvinus, you know your business best, of course, but if it were me I'd be asking what his motivation is. Altruism isn't a very highly developed trait among Gaulish merchants, particularly when it's shown towards Romans.'

I grinned. 'Don't teach your grandmother to suck eggs, pal,' I said. 'The thought had crossed my mind. Still, like I say it's all I've got at present, and I'll take it and be grateful, thank you.'

'Fine.' He shrugged. 'Oh, one more thing before I let you get on. Nothing whatsoever to do with either of the cases.'

'Yeah?'

'It occurred to me that I'd been very remiss in my duty where your wife was concerned. It can't be much fun for the poor lady to be stuck here without any women friends. And of course it's not quite right for her to be going around the city unchaperoned apart from her maid, either.'

Well, I'd agree with him there, particularly with Smarmer dancing attendance at every available opportunity. Not that, the good doctor aside, Perilla would think in those terms, mind: she kept a careful distance from the usual society bubbleheads back home, and given the choice between having one foisted on her to keep her entertained out here and going her own way she'd choose the latter every time.

'So what do you suggest?' I said.

'Well, I was talking to Julius Secundus yesterday. He's a

member of the local senate, bit of a dry old stick – he's sixty, if he's a day – and it occurred to me that his wife might be willing to take Rufia Perilla under her wing, as it were, while she's here.'

'Ah . . . right,' I said cautiously.

He must've noticed the tone, and no doubt the look on my face, because he laughed. 'Oh, don't worry, Corvinus,' he said. 'Secundus may be a dry old stick but Julia Optima most certainly is not. She's a good twenty-five years younger than he is, and distinctly, ah' – he paused – 'feisty. It's no secret who rules the roost in that household, and it isn't poor Secundus, bless him. Still, having met your wife I think the two would get along splendidly. What do you think yourself?'

That sounded better. Mark you, if the lady was as feisty as Balbinus said she was then there was always the risk of a major personality clash. If she set her mind to it, Perilla could be hell on wheels to get on with. Still . . .

'OK,' I said. 'We'll give it a try.'

'Splendid! If Julia Optima agrees then I'll ask her to call in at the residence after breakfast tomorrow morning, if that'd be suitable.'

'Great. I'm sure it would be.' I stood up. 'Thanks, Balbinus.'

'Don't mention it. I'm just sorry I didn't think of it before.'

'Oh.' I paused on my way to the door. 'One last thing. The address of the tavern that Drutus and the servant were staying in.'

'Yes, of course, you'll need that, won't you? It's easy to find. Just by the amphitheatre, hard by the gate in the wall. You can't miss it, it's the only one in that part of town.'

'Fine,' I said. 'Thanks again.'

I left.

SEVENTEEN

As per our new bargain, Bathyllus was waiting in the residence's lobby with the welcome-home cup of wine. I took off my cloak, handed it to him, and carried the wine-cup through to the atrium.

Perilla was lying on one of the couches, reading a book roll. She looked up, saw the wine, and said: 'Hmm.'

'Cut it out, lady!' I stretched out on the couch opposite her and set the cup on the table beside me. 'I've had one cup of wine today. One! And that was hours ago.' A slight exaggeration, but still.

'I wasn't criticizing, dear, only observing.'

'Yeah. Right.'

'And congratulations, by the way. You're doing excellently. Very abstemious.' I grinned and took a sip. 'So. How was your day? Any luck?'

'In a way.' I told her about Segomarus's offer.

She frowned. 'Are you sure that's such a very good idea? You don't know the man at all, do you? How do you know he's reliable? Or even honest?'

I told her exactly what I'd told Balbinus. 'I don't. Far from it. But I'm getting nowhere fast on my own, and it's likely to stay that way. Beggars can't be choosers, and I need all the help I can get.'

'If you say so, Marcus. Still, I do wonder if he has some sort of ulterior motive for volunteering.'

'He might well have. In fact, I think it's more than likely. But I'm not going to find out what that is unless I play along, am I? And if he is on the level then what have I got to lose?'

'Hmm.' A different *hmm* this time, contemplative rather than disapproving. 'Very well. But be careful.'

'Aren't I always?' She sniffed. 'Anyway, the Cabirus problem is taking a back seat at the moment.' I told her what Balbinus had said about the *agent provocateur* and the druid; he'd told me not to spread it around, but I reckoned Perilla was safe enough.

Her eyes widened.

'But that's dreadful!' she said. 'He really thinks there might be trouble?'

'It's a definite possibility, yes.'

'And that there could be a connection with the Drutus murder?'

'Again, it's possible. Murders just don't happen here, seemingly, and it's too much of a coincidence to dismiss out of hand, particularly since there doesn't seem to be a reason for this one. Apropos of which, the implication is that the perp wasn't a local. Not a real local, I mean.'

'Who, then?'

I shrugged and took a sip of the wine. 'Could be anyone,' I said. 'There're enough outsiders around. Our pal Segomarus, for one, since we're obviously having doubts about him already. Motive aside, I could make some sort of a case.'

'Namely?'

'If he was the perp then it'd be sensible by his lights to make contact – friendly contact – because he'd know I was looking into the business. That was curious enough in itself, if you like. The only other time we'd met, if you can call it meeting, at the baths in Lugdunum, he made it clear by the way he acted that he wanted nothing to do with me. Oh, sure, he explained it away by saying he was rushing off to the latrine to answer a sudden call of nature, but that could easily be pure hogwash. And on the trip through from Lugdunum young Titus Cabirus said he didn't speak Latin, which was complete garbage.' I frowned. 'That was another curious thing. Either Titus was lying for reasons I can't fathom or it was an impression the guy wanted to create himself. Only then, of course, he had to back-track if he wanted to get pally with me. He had a pretty lame excuse for that side of it, as well.'

'That's as may be, dear, but your Segomarus couldn't possibly be the murderer.'

'Yeah? How do you make that out?'

Perilla sighed. 'Marcus, he arrived with us. That was the previous afternoon, only hours before the murders. And he's a complete stranger; you said this was his first visit to the province.' I hadn't, and to be fair he hadn't, in so many words, either, but it was a reasonable assumption: even if he'd been fudging, Balbinus hadn't heard of the guy, and he'd know the regular merchants both here and in Durocortorum, if not personally then at least by name or reputation. 'He wouldn't have had either the time or the knowledge to set things up. Besides, how could he have had any connection at all with Drutus, which he'd need if he wanted an excuse for decoying him outside the city walls after dark? Let alone to furnish a reason for killing the man in the first place? Assuming he's telling the truth about Burdigala and the wine-growing side of things – and you've no reason to disbelieve him there, because there's nothing to suggest he isn't, quite the contrary – he would have come the southern route across Gaul to Massilia. Nowhere near Durocortorum, where Drutus was based. And Drutus, according to Balbinus, confined his trading to this north-east corner. I'm sorry, there are just too many objections for the theory to make sense.'

Bugger; she was right. Even so . . .

'Fine,' I said. 'Leave all that for the moment. Let's take it from the other end, Drutus himself. The more that you think about the guy, the more of a puzzle he is.'

'How do you mean?'

'On the face of it, he's an ordinary merchant, right? We've got Balbinus's personal assurance on that. Nothing special; trades in hides between Durocortorum and here, then up to the Rhine border and the garrison at Moguntiacum.'

'Yes. So?'

'So out of the blue he tells his long-term woman friend, on very short notice, that he's got a piece of business to take care of, nature unspecified, who with unspecified, but transacted after dark. Obviously there's something dodgy about it, even more obviously because he's found with his throat cut next morning half a mile outside the city limits. Not exactly what you'd expect of an ordinary merchant, yes?'

'Marcus, I know all that already. And I agree completely. Of course it's suspicious; what else could it be?'

'Yeah, but that's not all. He has in his possession an unusual gold coin.' She had her mouth open to say something, but I held up my hand and she shut it. 'OK. Today I find out from Balbinus for certain that it's British, and also that someone is currently playing silly buggers stirring up trouble among the locals. Probably at the instigation of the powers-that-be across the Gallic Strait who'd rather not be invaded at present, thank you very much, and want to create a diversion to take the pressure off. Also that there's a bastard of a druid, sent no doubt by said powers-that-be, skulking around somewhere out in the sticks doing his best to work up the peasants into a killing frenzy. You with me so far?'

She sighed. 'Of course I am, dear. You don't have to make such a meal of it. You're saying that Drutus is Balbinus's *agent provocateur*, the business he had was with this druid, and that the coin was his means of proving his *bona fides*.'

'That's about it, yeah.'

'Nonsense.'

'What?'

'It's complete and utter rubbish from beginning to end.'

'Is that so? And just how do you come to that conclusion, clever-clogs?'

She pulled back her thumb. 'First, it goes completely against what we know of Drutus from Balbinus.'

'Balbinus could be wrong.'

'You think so? Has he given any indication of being either stupid, or unobservant, or a poor judge of character?'

'Uh, no, not exactly, but—'

'So what you're saying is that Drutus had a deep-seated and long-standing hatred of Romans, deep-seated and long-standing enough to cause him to want to play the traitor and foment a revolt against them, and that neither Balbinus nor his governor – who also knew the man personally – never for one moment suspected it?'

'Well, if you put it that way—'

'I do. Two.' She held down the index finger. 'How would he go about it?'

'How do you mean?'

'Marcus, you don't just go around buttonholing people in wine-shops and telling them it might be a good idea to rise up against the Roman oppressors. Not unless you're a complete idiot. Drutus might be well known and liked in Augusta, but he was still an outsider and he'd have no real influence, which would be what he'd need to get anywhere at all; remember, here in Gaul the tribal factor is still very important, and he wasn't a Treveran, he'd no protection of the sort that, evidently, from your own experience, the Cabiri family have. The best he could expect would be indifference, and the worst, if he talked to the wrong person, betrayal to the authorities and an appointment with the public executioner.'

'Jupiter, Perilla, I never even mentioned wineshops! Allow the guy a little subtlety, for the gods' sakes!'

'Very well. None the less.' Middle finger. 'Three. Drutus hasn't been anywhere near Britain, and has no connection with it. He's a native of Durocortorum, and all his business is in this part of the province, hundreds of miles from the Gallic Strait.'

'Come on! Who's free-wheeling here now? We don't know that for sure. He could have—'

She ignored me. Ring finger. 'Four. If he needed the coin to prove his credentials to the druid, then why deliberately leave it with his woman friend before he went to the meeting?'

'Ah, now that is a problem, I admit, but maybe he—'

'Five.' She bent down the last finger. 'If he and the person he was meeting were on the same side then why did he and his servant end up dead? No, dear, I'm afraid it just won't do.'

Fuck. She was right again, though; like with Segomarus, there were too many objections.

There was something there, mind. I could feel it.

'Fair enough,' I said. 'Let's call a truce, shall we?'

'Certainly. Although you did start it.'

'Balbinus has found a pal for you. A female pal.'

'Really?' She didn't sound exactly thrilled. 'Who's that?'

'Her name's Julia Optima. She's the wife of one of the local senators, quite a lively lady, according to Balbinus. He's sending her round after breakfast tomorrow.'

'That'll be nice.'

'Yeah, I thought you'd be pleased.' I smiled. 'It'll make a pleasant change from going around with your friend Smarmer.'

'For your information, I haven't seen Domitius Crinas for two days,' she snapped. Definite points of colour high on the cheekbones.

'Had a bust-up, have you?'

'Don't be childish. As a matter of fact, he's busy in connection with his work, at the spa in the Lenus Mars sanctuary.'

I indicated the book she'd been reading when I came in and had set down on the table. 'That why you've turned to literature?' I said.

'Certainly not! I've discovered a collection of works in what amounts to a small library upstairs. One of them was the part of Posidonius of Apamea's *Histories* dealing with the Gauls, which I'm ashamed to say I've never read. Having nothing better to do, I was simply rectifying the omission.'

I grinned. 'That so, now?'

'That is so. Did you realize . . .? No, better still, I'll read it to you.' She picked the roll up, opened it and scanned the contents.

'Ah. Here we are. "When the Gauls leave the battlefield, they hang the heads of the enemies they have killed from their horses' necks. On returning home, they nail the heads to the doorposts and lintels of their houses. I have seen these grisly trophies myself, on many occasions, and although they made me shudder at first have become quite inured to the spectacle over time, and now find it quite natural."'

'Strong stuff.'

'Isn't it? Of course, Posidonius was writing about the situation a hundred years ago. No doubt things have improved since then.'

'You can't stop progress, lady. Still, it's a shame those quaint old customs are dying out. You'll have to ask Julia Optima what she does with her spare heads when you see her.'

'Marcus, that's not fair. You haven't even met the woman.'

'Yeah, well, from Balbinus's description of her – or rather reading between the lines of it – she's a proper character. It should be interesting.'

Bathyllus shimmered in. 'Excuse me, sir. Madam,' he said, 'the chef was wondering that since you seem both to be at home now you'd like to eat early.'

We'd obviously got our Perfect Butler back, in spades. And a chef who actually consulted you about mealtimes was a welcome change from Meton. Back home, you had to be on the dining-room couches with bib tucked in and spoon in hand when the sun touched the horizon, no earlier and certainly no later, or risk some very cutting comments. Particularly when it was fish.

'Tell him that'd be great, Bathyllus,' I said. 'Procurator Laco isn't eating tonight?'

'No, sir. He's dining with a business colleague, and since the conversation is liable to be mainly of a financial nature he thought that you and the mistress would prefer not to be included in the invitation.'

'Very considerate,' I said. It was; me, I'd rather not have to sit through a couple of hours of fiscal chit-chat, thank you very much.

So, it was just us for the moment again.

We could draw a line under the case for today. We'd see what tomorrow brought.

EIGHTEEN

I wasn't in a tearing hurry to get started next day, mainly because the only item on a skeleton-thin agenda was a talk with the keeper of the tavern where Drutus's servant Anda had put up, in the hopes that the guy had mentioned something useful before he handed in his lunch pail. Besides, after Balbinus's rather tongue-in-cheek encomium of her I was interested in hanging around and seeing how this Julia Optima turned out.

She breezed in as promised just after breakfast. *Just* after breakfast, which was Disquieting Feature number one, or rather one and two combined if you count the 'breezed'. Perilla definitely isn't your chirpy morning person, she doesn't usually start to wake up until halfway through her second omelette, and even then she generally likes to take things at her own pace until midday at least. Breezing is definitely out. The lady, to put it mildly, was not amused.

Disquieting Feature number three . . .

Yeah, well, in retrospect, if I'd been Balbinus I definitely wouldn't've used the word 'feisty', which, translated into male terms, has overtones of jolly wizard romps in the junior officers' mess followed by a wholesome, bracing cold plunge in the local icy torrent. Maybe 'Amazonian' came closest; certainly I hadn't been all that far out with my severed heads crack, because total stunner or not – which she also was – I could just see this lady going in for that kind of DIY home improvement in a big way. Being good at it, too. She was just under six feet and built to match, with flaming red hair, and she trailed Bathyllus into the dining room behind her like an apologetic afterthought.

'The Lady Julia Optima, sir. Madam,' he said, and exited like he'd been greased.

'Pleased to meet you.' Add a voice that a senior centurion would've given his vine-stick for. Although he'd have to be a very unusual First Spear indeed, mind; I'd bet that, once you got down to cases, there was nothing butch about Julia Optima. 'Saenius Balbinus told you I'd be coming?'

'Uh, yeah. Yeah.' I indicated one of the wicker chairs. 'Have a seat, Julia Optima. You've breakfasted?'

'Hours ago.' She pulled the chair over and sat. It creaked. 'Call me Optima, please. And you're Perilla,' she said to Perilla.

'Evidently I am.' I glanced at the lady: expression you could've used to pickle cabbage and a tone straight off the sharp end of a Riphaean blizzard. 'Delighted.'

If Optima had noticed either the expression or the tone she didn't show it. Which, I suspected, was par for the course, because I'd lay odds, even on this brief acquaintance, that she had an ego the size of the Capitol.

As, indeed, had Perilla; *pace* Balbinus, this did *not* look promising. Fortunately, though, it was none of my concern. Time, I thought, for a rapid strategic withdrawal before the plaster started flaking off the walls.

I stood up.

'Well, ladies,' I said, 'if you'll forgive me I'll leave you to it. Things to do, I'm afraid.'

'Connected with the murders of that merchant and his servant,' Optima said. 'Yes, I'd heard about that. A dreadful business, simply dreadful. You've no idea yet why it happened?'

'Uh-uh; not at present. I'm working on it.' I leaned down and gave Perilla a chaste kiss on the cheek. 'See you later, lady. Have a good day.'

'Thank you, dear. I shall at least endeavour to do so.'

Sarky as hell; thank the gods I was out of it before the sarcasm really started to bite. I grinned and left.

OK. So. The Anda angle. For what it was worth.

The tavern in question, over by the city's east gate, was easy to find. Like Balbinus had said, it was the only one on offer, a two-storey wooden building with a thatched roof and stables to the side from which came a strong smell of horse manure. There were a couple of locals sitting on the bench beside the door, drinking what was probably beer from leather mugs. They stopped chatting when they saw me coming and favoured me with a couple of silent stares that didn't look remotely this side of

friendly. I remembered what Balbinus had told me about tolera-
tion for Romans only being skin deep around these parts;
evidently where Gaulish taverns – as opposed to wineshops –
went the depth of skin concerned wasn't all that much. I gave
them a cheerful nod, got a grunt from one of them in reply, and
pushed open the door.

We'd definitely gone downmarket here with a vengeance. There
was a counter, sure, like you'd find in any ordinary decent-sized
wineshop, but there the similarities ended. Instead of the flasks
of wine in their rests behind the bar there were two or three hefty
wooden barrels with spigots, and a shelf of the leather mugs.
The floor was beaten earth covered with rushes, not fresh ones
at that, and what punters there were at this early hour were
standing around with mugs of their own. The chatter gradually
died away to nothing as they turned to face me. In the corner to
my right, a dog scratched for fleas.

Chichi Eighth District wine bar in Rome it most definitely
wasn't.

I walked over to the bar where the landlord – presumably –
was rinsing used beer mugs in a basin. The water in it didn't
look all that fresh, either.

'Morning,' I said. 'You serve wine at all?'

He set the mug he was holding down, reached under the
counter, brought up a jug and poured in some of the contents,
all without a word. I tried a sip. One was enough; wine it may
have been, technically, but if so it was pushing the definition to
its limits. Ah, well; Perilla would be pleased I wasn't using the
investigation as an excuse to soak up some extra booze on this
occasion.

'The name's Valerius Corvinus,' I said. 'I'm looking into the
deaths of a guy called Drutus and his servant Anda. I understand
they were staying here. Or at least Anda was.'

'True enough.' The man reached for another dirty mug, plunged
it into the basin, and set it down on the counter. 'So?'

'So I was hoping you might be able to help with some information.' Silence. 'Come on, friend! They were Gauls! And I was
told they were pretty popular locally. Where I come from, that'd
mean something.'

'Last time I looked, this wasn't Rome.'

'Yeah. So I'd noticed. Me, I wouldn't be too proud of the difference.' My four-day tour of the wineshops re the Cabiri family mystery all over again. Ah, the hell with it; at least I'd tried, and it'd been a long shot to begin with. I took two or three coppers from my belt-pouch, tossed them on the counter, and turned to go. 'Thanks a lot. Enjoy your day.'

I'd got halfway to the door when he said:

'Wait a minute.'

I turned round. He'd set the last of the mugs on the counter and was drying his hands with a cloth.

'OK,' he said. 'What do you want to know?'

Hey! 'Anything and everything. I'm getting pretty desperate here.'

He grunted; it could even have been a chuckle. 'You could've fooled me. We've never had a Roman in this place before, not one who ordered a drink, anyway, and I'll bet it'll be long enough until we see another one. That right, lads?'

There was a murmur of agreement and a few muttered comments that I suspect I was lucky not to catch, accompanied by sniggers. Even so, I could feel the mood in the room ease, and the background noise started up again. I walked back to the counter.

'Now,' the landlord said. 'What sort of information?'

'I told you. I don't know; anything that might be relevant. All I know is that they ate here – both of them – early that evening and then went out. They didn't say where they were going, or why?'

'Nah. Drutus – well, he had a fancy woman, with a stall in the market, so I had a fair notion where he was bound. I hardly ever saw the man all the time he'd been coming here, and that was fifteen years, at least, 'cept when he dropped by to pay for stabling his horses and for Anda's shake-down in the hay loft.'

'So the fact that they had a meal together was unusual?'

'First time I remember it happening, ever, at least since he found himself a lady friend about ten years back. Oh, Anda on his own, sure, he was practically one of the family. He always ate upstairs with the wife and me when I shut up shop at sundown.'

'Not this time, though.'

'Nah.'

'Whose idea was it?'

'How do you mean?'

'Well, somebody must've told you about the changed arrangements. Was it Drutus or Anda?'

'Oh. Right. It was Anda. Came in here mid-afternoon, in a proper taking. Said he needed a favour; that he and Drutus were going out that night on business, they needed to talk something over in private beforehand, and could they have the use of the room upstairs while they did it.'

'Hang on, pal,' I said. 'Anda told you they were going out on business somewhere after dark?'

'Yeah. That's right.'

'That's not what you told the authorities.'

'No.' His eyes challenged me. 'Can't say that it is.'

Fair enough, and I could sympathize in retrospect; like I'd said to Perilla, honest merchants and their servants didn't do business in the small hours, and he'd just told me that Anda was practically family. You didn't peach on family, whatever the reason.

'OK,' I said. 'He say where, or why? Or business with who?'

'No, that was all. Luckily the wife had arranged to go and see a friend that afternoon, so she'd cooked the dinner in advance; it was just beans and vegetables, served cold, and a loaf of bread, so it was easy to stretch it four ways instead of two. I was busy here myself until sundown, naturally, so letting them use the room and giving them something to eat while they talked was no skin off my nose. Drutus paid me well for it, too, cash up front.'

I felt a slight prickle of excitement: maybe we were getting somewhere after all, although I couldn't in all honesty see that being very far. Still, it looked as if the servant was the one who'd made the running here, not his master, and that was unusual in itself where a business deal was concerned. The big question was, what did the running involve? Presumably, setting the fatal meeting up without having either the time or the opportunity to contact Drutus. And it had been important, that was sure, vitally important: our tavern-keeper friend here had said Anda had been 'in a proper taking' when he'd asked for the favour. Excited? Worried? Frightened? It could be any of them, but if so the implications were different . . .

Shit! I was close to something, I could feel it!

'So what happened then?' I said.

'Nothing. They came as arranged and went straight upstairs. I brought the food up a few minutes later when I had the chance and left them to it. They were gone by sunset, and that was the last I saw of them.' He was frowning. 'Look. Anda was a good man, a good friend, and good company; well-travelled, been all over before he settled down with Drutus these twenty years back, so he'd got a lot of stories to tell. I'll miss him, me and the wife both. You get the bastard who killed him, right?'

Uh-huh; twenty years, right? It was interesting how often the phrase *twenty years* kept on cropping up in this case. More than interesting.

'I'll do my best,' I said. 'Thanks, pal.'

'You're welcome.' He was still frowning. 'One more thing. I don't know if it'll help or not, but talking about it I've just remembered.'

'Yeah?'

'When I took the stew up and opened the door they were sitting at the table with their heads together, talking, or Anda was. He clammed up straight off when I came in, but I just caught the last few words. "He's lying. He's never been there."'

'What?'

The guy repeated it. 'Mean anything to you?' he said.

I was thinking furiously. 'Maybe,' I said. 'Maybe it does, at that. Thanks again, friend.'

I left.

Hmm.

I was crossing the market square on my way back when someone called my name. I looked round: an elderly guy, very well-dressed, standing a few feet away and chatting to a much younger man.

'I'm right, aren't I?' he said. 'You are Valerius Corvinus?'

'As ever is.' I went over to join them.

'Julius Secundus. I think my wife called on yours earlier today. At the suggestion of Saenius Balbinus.'

Right; the local senator. I could see what Balbinus meant about him being a dry old stick: sixty-plus, and not a very well-preserved sixty, at that. Mummies came to mind. His friend, on the other hand, was mid-forties, max, and built along the lines of Perilla's pal the good doctor.

'Yeah,' I said. 'In fact, I left them planning their day.' Or not, as the case might be; I might find blood on the walls when I got back. 'Very kind of her to take an interest.'

'Oh, nonsense, my dear fellow. I'm sure Optima will be absolutely delighted to help entertain a visitor to our city. Our pleasure entirely. I thought when I saw you passing that I'd just introduce myself, tell you that if there's anything else we can do to help then by all means just let us know.'

'That's very good of you, sir,' I said.

'Not at all, not at all.' He glanced at the man he'd been talking to. 'This is Sulinus, by the way.' No family name; not a Roman citizen, then. 'He's one of our more prominent merchants.'

We nodded to each other. 'Pleased to meet you,' I said. 'What line are you in?'

'Antiques, mostly.' Strong, confident voice. 'The quality end of the market. But I specialize in silver- and goldware.'

'Nice. Must be lucrative.'

'I get by.'

Secundus chuckled. 'Rather better than that,' he said. 'Sulinus has been a regular supplier of mine for years. It's my hobby, you know, my one vice. I'm interested in antique Gallic silverware, in fact quite passionate about it, and I have quite a collection. You and your wife must come round for dinner and inspect it while you're in Augusta.'

'That'd be great,' I said politely. Bugger, we'd got another Priscus here; my stepfather's bag was semantics and early local Italian antiquities, particularly Etruscan ones, and he regularly bored the pants off us at dinner parties round at Mother's lecturing us about them. I'd bet that this guy was the same. Well, at least he didn't bleat or drool, and the chances were Perilla would get through the dinner without having sauce spilled all over her mantle. Plus the fact that our social calendar wasn't exactly straining at the seams at present. 'We'll look forward to it.'

'Good. I'll have Optima arrange things. She does so enjoy her social life, the poor dear, but we don't have many guests ourselves. Well, I mustn't keep you; you obviously have things to do, and as I said I only wanted to introduce myself while you were passing.'

'Nice to have met you. Sulinus.'

'Valerius Corvinus.' He gave me another nod. 'My pleasure. Enjoy your stay.'

I carried on to the residence. Not that, again, I was destined to stay there for long. Bathyllus met me as usual in the atrium.

'A message from Saenius Balbinus, sir,' he said. 'He'd like to talk to you in his office as soon as you're able.'

What, again? This was the second time in two days. Still, it had to be important.

It was. And, it transpired, a total gobsmacker.

'Drutus was one of our agents,' he said as soon as the door closed behind the outgoing clerk.

'*What?*' I stared at him.

'It's true. He has been for years. I've just had the reply to my message to the governor saying he'd been murdered. The courier made the journey from Durocortorum in record time, on Hister's instructions, and he almost killed five horses and broke his own neck doing it.'

Jupiter in heaven! I sat down on the stool beside the desk. 'You didn't know?'

'No, I didn't. The information was classified top secret, for the governor only. Now, of course, under the circumstances, as Hister's representative I have to. You, too, naturally; I have his specific clearance for that.' He ran a hand across his face. 'What a mess. What a gods'-awful pig-swill of a mess.'

'Yeah. Right.' My brain had gone numb. 'So there's a definite connection with the political side of things after all?'

'Oh, yes, that's beyond any doubt. Not just that, but a definite connection with Britain.'

'How so?'

'I said Drutus was our agent, which in a way he was. More accurately, he was Verica's.'

'Who the hell is Verica?'

'King of the Atrebates tribe. Or to be exact ex-king, king in exile as of two or three years back, when Caratacus threw him out.'

'Pal, you're just giving me names here. Remember you're talking to a political ignoramus. You'll have to explain.'

He sighed. 'Very well. A brief social and political history of Britain over the past twenty years, all right? You're sitting comfortably?'

'Bugger that, chum. Go ahead.'

'Caratacus is the son of the Catuvellaunan king Cunobelinus; the Catuvellauni being one of the major tribes in the south-east part of the island and neighbours of the Atrebates, ditto only a bit further down. You're with me?'

'Sure.'

'Twenty or so years back, Cunobelinus dies and his brother Epaticcus becomes king. Epaticcus is a completely different kettle of fish altogether; he's overtly aggressive, and unlike his brother fervently anti-Rome. He mounts a campaign against the Atrebates and takes most of their kingdom, helped by his nephew Caratacus, who is very much out of the same mould and, in our terms, an even more dangerous piece of work. Epaticcus then goes and dies himself – this is five years ago – and Caratacus takes over. He completes the conquest of the Atrebates and drives their king, Verica, into exile. Verica goes to Rome and puts his expertise at the service of the Emperor Gaius, who is thinking of invading the island and in the process will get Verica his kingdom back. Still OK?'

'Cut it out, Balbinus, I'm not that much of an idiot.'

He grinned. 'I'm sorry. Of course not. Anyway, Gaius's plans came to nothing, but now Claudius is preparing to do things properly, still with Verica's help and goodwill. Which is where we are at the moment.'

'Hang on,' I said. 'We're talking about the situation the other side of the Gallic Strait. Where does this agent business come in? Agenting for what?'

'Yes, well, you need to remember that the Strait is only a geographical barrier. Essentially Gaul and Britain are the same country, the only real difference being that we took the former from the locals a hundred years back and changed things about a bit to suit ourselves. The people are still the same, they've the same language and customs, more or less, even some of the tribes are the same; there's an Atrebates tribe to the west of here, for

example, up around Nemetocenna near the Lower Germany
border, and a tribe of Belgae to match ours over in Britain. So
to a lot of Gauls what is happening across the Strait, or is about
to happen, is relevant, because the British are kin. And you've
been here long enough now to know how important that can be.'
    Yeah, right. 'So they take sides?'
    'Indeed they do. Or they would, given the chance. Which, of
course, both the pro- and anti-Roman camps among the British
themselves – Verica's and Caratacus's, in effect – know perfectly
well and are trying to exploit. Essentially the war – call it that
– has already started and been running for the past three years,
only it's Celt against Celt, a propaganda war beneath the surface.
We can help and hinder at need, sure, we've plenty of actual
muscle, but at root most of the time using direct force isn't the
answer, and it may even make things worse; while for the same
reason the anti-Roman party can't cause real trouble too overtly
because they know at the first signs it'll be stamped flat and the
country stitched up tighter than a gnat's sphincter. Hence the
agents, ours and the *agents provocateurs.*'
    'Only now things have changed.'
    'Yes, indeed. The closer the actual invasion comes the more
desperate the anti-Roman party – Caratacus, because he's effectively the British leader – will be. We've talked about this before.
If Caratacus can persuade the Treveri, at least, to revolt within
the next few months then the campaign will be seriously jeopard-
ized. It's an all-or-nothing throw, but if it comes off then at the
very least he'll have bought himself some breathing space. So
you see how important getting to the root of this business is?'
    Gods! I shifted on my stool. 'Drutus was on to something,
right?' I said. 'Something specific?'
    'He must have been. It makes perfect sense, with hindsight.
Probably he'd identified our *agent provocateur.*' He was frowning.
'But in that case why the hell didn't he just come to me, tell me
the whole story, and let me take things from there? I could've
had the bastard arrested within the hour.'
    'Perhaps he wasn't sure himself. Or more likely he wanted
more names – the agent's local contacts, say – before he took
things any further. That'd make sense, wouldn't it? Coming
directly to you might've blown his cover too prematurely.'

'I suppose so.' Balbinus ran a hand over his chin, and I noticed he hadn't shaved that morning. 'Even so, some sort of formal indication of what he was up to wouldn't have been difficult. A private message. He could've managed that easily.'

'I don't think he had the time or the opportunity. He didn't have the information himself until the evening he was killed.' I told him what the tavern-keeper had told me. 'My bet is that the servant Anda, who must've been in on his secret, had just discovered something off his own bat and the two of them decided to play a lone game. For the time being, at least.'

'Yes. Yes, that's fair enough. Still—'

'You want the theory? For what it's worth?'

'Corvinus, I'm grasping at straws at present. Of course I want your theory, if you think it's valid.'

'All right.' I settled back on the stool. 'Me, like I say, I think the whole thing was a bolt out of the blue. Anda finds out, how I don't know yet, but it doesn't matter, that X is our villain, and also that he's got some sort of secret rendezvous arranged for that night. He tells Drutus, and they meet to talk things over and do the planning in the room above the tavern. Drutus takes the time between then and when things start moving to go round to his lady friend's, to say he won't be staying the night after all and leave her his coin for safe keeping. Then—'

'Hold on. Why should he do that? If he had time to play with then why not use it in contacting me?'

I sighed. 'Balbinus, pal. You married, at all? Any significant other, here or back in Rome?'

'No. What does that have to do with it?'

'Leaving aside the concrete proof aspect of the thing, the guy might not have known he was going to his death, but he sure as hell must have realized what he was about was pretty risky. He may've been a professional agent, but he was human like the rest of us; he couldn't just disappear for the night without warning and leave her to worry. Besides, there was the coin. You said it was British, right? Atrebatan?'

'Yes. Struck by Verica's father Commius.'

'OK. So now with hindsight we know why he was carrying it; it was a sign, if he ever needed to use it, that would prove his *bona fides* to any other undercover Verican sympathizer he came into contact with. Only it'd go the other way, too; if he was caught with it on him then anyone on the other side would know he was an enemy. Oh, sure, the chances were that if he and Anda *were* caught snooping under suspicious circumstances it probably wouldn't make all that much difference, but at least they could try bluffing their way out of trouble. So he had to leave it behind, somewhere safe.'

'All right. I'll accept that; certainly it seems to fit. Carry on, Corvinus.'

'The rest's pretty straightforward, except that before I'm sure of the details I'll have to have another look at the place where the bodies were found. Basically, though, they follow X to the rendezvous point outside town; only they've been spotted themselves, and either X or his co-conspirator kills them. End of story.'

Balbinus pulled at his ear. 'So who's our X?' he said. 'Let alone the person or persons he was meeting? That's the crucial factor here.'

I shrugged. 'Your guess is as good as mine. We've got one clue, though. Before I left the tavern, the owner told me he'd caught the last few words of what Anda had been saying to Drutus when he interrupted them with the bean stew. Quote: "He's lying. He's never been there."'

'Who was lying? Where had he never been?'

'Yeah, right; those are the questions. If we had the answers we'd have our murderer and so your British agent. But we don't. Not yet, anyway.'

'You must have some thoughts on the matter, surely.'

'Just one obvious one. The trouble is, it can't be right because it's completely impossible.'

'Tell me in any case.'

'That Burdigalan wine merchant I mentioned to you. The one who volunteered to help with the Cabirus business. You remember?'

'Yes. Segomarus, wasn't it?'

'That's right.'

'You think it's him?'

I hesitated. 'Under normal circumstances he'd be among my front runners, sure. There's something not quite straight about him for a start, and he's from well out of town, the other side of the country, in fact, as far away from here as you can get. Or claims he is, at any rate, which is just the point: my tavern-owner friend said that Anda had travelled pretty extensively when he was younger, so it's a fair bet that, whoever X is, Anda had caught him out in a lie about where he originated and taken things from there.'

'Sounds good to me.' Balbinus had perked up. 'Good enough to pull him in for questioning, at least.'

'Hold your horses, pal. I said: Segomarus is a non-starter. Whoever X is, he absolutely isn't it.'

'You care to explain why not?'

'Because he arrived with us, in Laco's party. Quite definitely; I can vouch for that myself. He was with us all the way, too, so there's no question of him having ridden on ahead and then come back for some reason.'

'Why should that—?' Balbinus stopped. 'Oh, yes. Yes, of course, stupid of me. You didn't arrive until late in the afternoon, did you?'

'No. And by that time Anda had already made his discovery, whatever it was. So as much as I'd fancy the guy otherwise, he's definitely out.'

'Bugger.'

'As you say, bugger. Still, he can't be the only game in town, can he?'

'Far from it, I'm afraid. That's the trouble: Augusta may not be as big a place as Durocortorum, but it is on the main route to Moguntiacum and the Rhineland. There are plenty of non-locals about. Mostly merchants, but others too. And Anda didn't specify a merchant in any case. Without something else to go on we're looking for a needle in a haystack.'

'Yeah.' I stood up. 'Well, maybe something will come. We just have to hope.'

'It'll have to come damned quickly, then. We're running out of time.'

So, what next? I'd told Balbinus that I needed to have another look at the spot where the bodies had been found, and that was true: as I remembered it, there had been no real cover, none at all. That wouldn't have mattered much in the case of the original theory, sure, – that Drutus and Anda had been engaged in a clandestine meeting on their own account – but it was crucial now. I had to check. I set out for the Moguntiacum Gate and the road beyond.

There was no sign of my goat-herder friend this time; presumably he was pasturing his charges elsewhere. I found the exact spot where the bodies had lain, but his time I went further into the hinterland.

Or started to, rather. The ground rose sharply for twenty-odd paces, then suddenly fell away in a steep scree that was practically a full-blown cliff. The broadish hollow at the bottom, eight or ten feet below, would be accessible on its other three sides but – as I'd just discovered by accidentally almost falling into the bloody thing and breaking a leg – tucked neatly out of sight and completely invisible from the direction of the road.

OK; so far, so good: if someone were to go carefully through the underbrush – crawling, even – to the top of the rise they'd be able to look down into the hollow and see and hear what was going on, without themselves being seen from below, even on a brightly moonlit night like the night of the murder had been.

Only they had been seen, hadn't they? Or possibly whoever was in the hollow had known they were there all the time. Like I'd said to Balbinus, that side of things didn't really matter; whatever the ins and outs of it, the killer had managed to sneak up behind them, take them by surprise, and do the business . . .

Which, come to think of it, was interesting in itself. There must've been something to watch, otherwise they'd've smelt a rat and been on their guard, and that meant there had to be more than two villains involved: two of them down below, to keep the conversation – and so the watchers' attention – going while the third took care of the killing. Chances were, then, that the second theory – that it was a set-up – was the one to go for; that Drutus and Anda hadn't known there *was* a third person involved, probably because they were being followed in their turn. Oh, sure, if they'd turned round to look they might've seen him, granted, but they weren't likely to do that, were they? All their attention would be fixed on the guy ahead, to make sure he didn't leave the road unexpectedly and mess things up for them while staying far enough back not to get themselves spotted. And the third man, if he was being equally careful to keep out of sight as no doubt he was, could well at a pinch have used the cover of the ditch, which was a good three feet deep and bone dry at this time of year.

Yeah. I'd go for that. It would work, and it made sense.

Getting down into the hollow from up top clearly wasn't an option: another argument, if I'd needed one, for a third member of the party and an ambush, since if the guys down below had just happened to spot Drutus and Anda eavesdropping then climbing up to get them wasn't a viable proposition; while by the time any would-be killer had come the long way round the pair would either be ready for him when he arrived – they both had their knives, after all – or would have legged it back to the road long before he got there.

I retraced my steps and went round the side.

Someone had been standing there, right enough: the long grass that covered the hollow's base still showed signs of having been trampled flat.

Check.

So, that was about all I could manage at present. I set off back to town.

There was no sign of Perilla when I got back to the residence; scarcely surprising, mind, because we were still a good couple of hours shy of dinner time. I consulted Bathyllus when he brought a well-earned cup of wine through to me in the atrium.

'The mistress went out, sir, shortly after you did yourself,' he said. 'With the Lady Julia Optima.'

Right; so the girls had patched up their differences after all, had they? Or just declared a diplomatic truce. Absolutely fine by me.

'They say where they were going?' I asked.

'The shrine of Arduinna was mentioned.'

'Who's Arduinna when she's at home?'

He sniffed. 'I'm afraid I haven't the slightest idea, sir. But she has a shrine in the hills, seemingly, about a mile outside of town on the Durocortorum road.'

I nearly swallowed the wine-cup. 'Perilla's gone out *riding*?' I said.

'So it would appear.'

Gods! Next thing was, the sky would fall on our heads. The lady could ride, sure, but she didn't do it for pleasure, any more than I did. Horses did not feature all that prominently in the Corvinus household.

'Fair enough, Bathyllus,' I said. 'We'll just have to possess ourselves with patience.'

She arrived back about an hour later, looking wind-blown and flushed.

'Oh, you're here, Marcus,' she said. 'Good day?'

'Complicated.' She bent down and kissed me. 'I'll tell you later. How about yours?'

'Simply splendid.' She undid her cloak and handed it to Bathyllus, who'd oiled in behind her. 'Yes, please, Bathyllus. I'm absolutely parched.'

'Certainly, madam.' He looked at me and hesitated. 'Sir?'

'Ah . . .'

'Oh, go on, Bathyllus, bring him another cupful of wine.' Bathyllus exited. 'I must say, dear, Julia Optima isn't at all the dragon I expected to begin with. We had a lovely time.'

'Yeah?' Well, the lady certainly seemed in a surprisingly good mood. 'The shrine of Arduinna, Bathyllus said. And riding.'

'That's right. Oh, I don't do it often, I know, but Optima suggested it and I thought, why not? It wasn't all that far, and it was a beautiful day, not too hot. I must say that when she arrived I thought she was going to drag me about on visits to the local society, but it turns out she's more into old shrines and temples and local history. Surprisingly knowledgeable, too. I learned a lot.'

'So who's Arduinna, then?'

'A forest goddess, more or less equivalent to Diana. The shrine was really quite quaint, very old and tucked away in a fold of the hills. I'd never have found it without her help.' She lay down on the other couch. 'So tell me. Anything exciting happen with you?'

'Yeah, you could say that.' I gave her the rundown.

'But, Marcus, this is serious!' she said when I'd finished.

'You're not kidding. No pressure, mind; Balbinus was pretty clear about that. So long as the case is solved before whoever zeroed Drutus and his servant has the chance to persuade the Treveri to throw off the hated Roman yoke and the emperor's plans for Britain go down the tube, we're home and dry. All we've got to do is find him, or them, before it's too late, and there can only be a couple of dozen or so possible suspects to work our way through. Oh, of course there's the Cabirus side of things as well, but since I haven't the faintest fucking idea what's going on there either that doesn't matter all that much.'

'Gently, dear.'

'Yeah, I know.' I sighed. 'But it's frustrating as hell. All we know is who it isn't, and it damn well ought to be.'

'Who's that?'

'My Burdigalan pal. Oh, sure, he was plausible enough, and what he said about himself and his plans makes perfect sense, as far as I can see, but the timing aside he's just begging to be a prime suspect.'

'Look, Marcus, just leave it, will you? There's no use fretting. If you're stuck for the present then you're stuck, and that's all there is to it. Something may turn up, you never know.'

'Yeah, right. Fair enough. Of course it will. Along with the pink giraffe and the herd of flying pigs.' I took a hefty swallow of wine. 'Oh, by the way, I bumped into Optima's husband in the market square earlier. Or rather, he bumped into me and introduced himself. Not a bad old guy, but he's a bit of a Priscus.'

'A bit of a what?'

'A Priscus. Only in his case it's antique Gallic silverware. He wants us to go round for dinner some evening and have a look at his collection. Optima will arrange things with you, seemingly.'

'Oh, that's fine. We're meeting up again tomorrow. I can talk to her then.'

'Another shrine, is it? You're—' Bathyllus oozed in with the tray, but also with his 'I have news to impart' expression. 'Hi, sunshine. That dinner, is it?'

'Actually no, sir, not yet. You have a visitor. Saenius Balbinus.'

I looked behind him. Balbinus was coming through from the lobby. If anything, the guy looked even more worried than he had before

'I'm sorry to barge in like this, Corvinus,' he said. 'Lady Rufia.

But I thought you'd better know right away. There's been another murder.'

I stared at him.

Shit.

NINETEEN

The victim, it transpired, was another merchant, by the name of Trebonius Tarbeisus.

'Sit down and tell us what happened, pal,' I said. 'Bathyllus, a cup of wine, please, a large one. Make it neat, OK? And hurry, I think the man needs it.'

'Damn right I do.' Balbinus sat.

'Just take your time and start at the beginning.'

'Very well.' He took a deep breath. 'He was found stabbed a couple of hours ago, in the commercial quarter – that's the southwest part of town. The body was hidden in a disused warehouse, under a pile of old sacking. It could've been there for days, and it was a pure fluke that anyone stumbled on it at all.'

'And no one missed him?'

'Not that I know of. Certainly there'd been no report. Mind you, from the little information I've managed to glean so far he was in town on his own. Not even a slave or a servant.'

'No reason for the death, presumably? I mean, he wasn't another of Verica's agents, was he?'

'Not that I'm aware of, which isn't saying much. He could have been, but if so then Hister didn't mention him. He could even have been our friend X.'

'Yeah?' I looked at him sharply. 'What makes you say that?'

'Absolutely nothing. Look, Corvinus, I just don't know what's going on any more, right? I'm completely out of my depth here.'

Bathyllus came in with the wine. Balbinus downed it in a oner.

'So what information *do* you have on him?' I said.

'He was a merchant, like I say, from Caesarodunum – that's a town in the west part of the Lugdunensian province – dealing in high-quality jewellery. As far as I can tell, this was his first visit to Augusta; certainly I'd never seen him here before, and neither had any of the few regular merchants I managed to talk to.'

'But did they know who he was? From this time round, I mean?'

'Two or three of them, yes. He was boarding at the inn just opposite the baths; that's your accommodation of choice for the mercantile contingent, and even the ones who aren't staying there use it as a place to network. He was a pretty sociable chap, seemingly, good company and not averse to pulling his weight where buying drinks was concerned.'

'Even so, no one noticed he'd gone missing?'

'Merchants follow their own schedules, Corvinus; they're here today, gone tomorrow, most of them, sometimes without warning. He'd paid in advance up to yesterday for the room – the land-lord's been caught too many times by fly-by-nights to leave settling the bill until the last minute – and any meals and drinks were strictly cash up front. Oh, sure, the landlord knew he hadn't been around for a few days, but that does happen on occasion.' He glanced sideways at Perilla. 'You can guess the circumstances for yourself. His belongings were still in the room, including his samples, and more to the point his mule was in the stables, so the innkeeper wasn't too concerned.'

'A few days, you say. How many would that be, exactly?'

'Four or five. Maybe six. The landlord wasn't absolutely sure.'

Jupiter! Score one for the guy's powers of observation! Still, he'd know his money was safe, so if it turned out that Tarbeisus had been spending a bit of quality time tomcatting he wouldn't be complaining. 'So,' I said, 'that would take us back to shortly after the other murders, Drutus's and Anda's, yes?'

'I suppose it would. You think there's a connection?'

'It seems a fair assumption, doesn't it?'

'Yes, I suppose so. But like I said I can't see what that might be.'

Right; me neither, especially if this Tarbeisus was clean as far as background went. But that was for Balbinus to check on, as far as he could. 'OK,' I said, 'I'll need names.'

'Names?'

'Anyone he'd been in contact with before he disappeared and might be able to shed some light. His drinking cronies, for preference.'

'I hadn't got that far. The best you can do on that score is to go round to the inn yourself around the middle of the afternoon. That's when most of the traders – locals and out-of-towners – get together to make deals among themselves and catch up on the latest news. Like I said, the place is near the western gate, opposite the baths.'

'Fine. I'll do that tomorrow.'

Well, it might be bad luck for the newly deceased, but at least it meant we might possibly be off and rolling again. There's a lot to be said during a case for a fresh murder.

The inn, when I got there just after the ninth hour the following afternoon, was pretty crowded; the downstairs part of it, anyway, where Augusta's trading fraternity obviously did a large slice of their all-merchants-together dickering and insider-info swapping. Drinking, too: when I pushed open the door it narrowly missed a waiter with a loaded tray of beer mugs and wine-cups, and the place was going like a Circus wineshop on a race day. I pushed my way through the crowd to the bar counter and waited to be served.

'Yes, sir, what'll it be?' the barman said eventually.

'Surprise me, friend. A cup of anything you'd recommend that's good.'

'We've a nice Nemausan, just in. It's just as good as most of the top names, and half the price. That do you?'

'Sure.' I took some coins out of my pouch and laid them down while he unlimbered the appropriate flask and poured.

'You're the gentleman from Lugdunum, right?' he said as he set the cup down in front of me. 'Looking into the Drutus affair?'

'That's me. More or less.'

'Terrible thing, that.' He took a few of the coins. 'It came as a real shock, I can tell you; murder's not a thing that ever happens in Augusta. Then of course there's this other one now. It makes you think what the world is coming to, doesn't it?'

'It does indeed.' I took a sip of the wine. Not bad; not bad at all.

'Three killings inside of a few days, all merchants from outside town. It couldn't be worse for business, that. I mean, who's going to want to do their trading in Augusta, or spend more time here than they need to, if they think there's a chance that some crazy bastard is likely to up and stiff them?'

'Ah . . . are you the owner of this place, by any chance?' I said.

'I am indeed. Fifteen years, come the Winter Festival.'

Well, that made sense from what Balbinus had told me about the guy's concern for his customers' welfare. My heart bled. 'Actually, that's why I dropped in,' I said. 'The third murder. I understand the victim – Tarbeisus, wasn't that the name? – had a room here.'

That got me a cautious look. 'He did. What's that got to do with anything?'

'No sweat. It's just that I'm interested in his movements up to the time he disappeared. Who he mixed with, whether he was involved in any particular business deals, that sort of thing. Any help I can get, really.'

'Oh.' The cautious look vanished. 'Not much I can do for you there, sir. As you can see, we're packed out and short-staffed, and it's always like this. I haven't got the time to think what I'm doing myself, if you catch my meaning, let alone watch the customers.'

'Right. Right. Maybe someone else, then? One of his merchant cronies?'

'You could try Frontus over there in the corner. The man with the eye-patch.' He nodded in the direction of a middle-aged guy sitting at one of the tables chatting to another two punters with their backs to me. 'He's one of the big local retailers, in most days to check on who's new in town and what they're selling. He'd be your best bet. Yes, sir.' He turned to another customer who'd come up beside me. 'Same again, was it?'

I slipped the remaining coins into my pouch, picked up my cup and took it over to the one-eyed man's table. He looked up.

'Excuse me for butting in,' I said. 'You have a moment or two to spare?'

'Of course.' He smiled. 'More, if you like. Pull up a stool, if you can find one.'

'That's OK.' One of the other two punters stood up. 'The gentleman can have mine; I was just leaving anyway. We've a firm deal on that consignment of Samian?'

'We do. Delivery by the first of next month, yes? I'll see you later, Tertius.' The man left. 'Now, sir, what can I do for you?'

I sat. 'The name's Marcus Corvinus,' I said. 'I'm looking into—'

'Yes, I know. Poor Drutus. Anda, too. They'll be sadly missed, both of them. They were well-liked, and they'd both been coming here for years. Mind you, I'm afraid if that's what you wanted to talk to me about I know no more than anyone else.'

'Actually, it was about the other guy. The one whose body was found yesterday morning down in the commercial quarter. Trebonius Tarbeisus.'

'Ah. In that case, I can tell you even less. This was his first time in Augusta, and I barely knew him.'

'You talked to him, though? Before he disappeared?'

'Certainly I did. Made a point of it, in fact, as I do with every new face. But then a lot of other people did as well, Ruber here for one. That's so, Ruber, is it not?'

'Aye, that's so.' The other man – a few years younger, built like a wrestler but running to fat – took a pull at his beer mug. 'He was good company, was Tarbeisus. His samples were good, too, what I saw of them, better than what I sell at present, and that shifts pretty smartly to begin with. We could've done a lot of business, him and me. Pity he got stiffed.'

Right. Well, there spoke the voice of healthy commercial enterprise. It was no wonder that trade was the life-blood of the empire and merchants its bone and sinew. 'He wasn't from anywhere near here, as I understand?' I said.

'No. Somewhere down south, I think,' Frontus said. 'I can't recall exactly.'

'So what *do* you know about him?'

'Precious little, like I say.' Frontus was drinking wine. He took another mouthful from the cup. 'He arrived eight or nine days back, from Durocortorum, and he was on his way up north to Moguntiacum, or so he said. Travelling light, sussing out the local markets on the way for future use, the usual kind of thing, so he spent a lot of time in here chatting to various people, showing his samples, getting orders or promises of them. That's about it, really.'

'He'd no connections with Britain, at all, had he?'

That got me a sharp, monocular look. 'Not that he mentioned in my hearing, no. What made you think he might have?'

'No reason. Just a thought.'

Frontus chuckled. 'Then it wasn't a very intelligent one, if you don't mind me saying so. You're in the wrong part of Gaul for that, Corvinus. Oh, over in the west of the province near the Lower German border, certainly, but the traders you'll meet around these parts, the ones who travel, anyway, mostly work the north–south route between Massilia and the Upper Rhine. Durocortorum's about as far west as they go. Certainly things might change if the British market opens up in future, but that's a long way off.'

'He have much to do with any of the merchants here in particular? I mean, anyone who stands out?'

'No. None more than any other. Like I told you, he did the rounds, professionally speaking, as any trader new to an area would. And he was a sociable sort in himself, fond of a drink and willing to put his hand in his money-pouch when his turn came to do the buying.'

'So you can't think of anything, well, out of the ordinary about the guy? Nothing he said or did that you noticed that was in any way unusual?'

'Not a thing. He was just your ordinary out-of-town merchant, drumming up custom and doing a little useful networking before he moved on.'

Bugger. Well, I hadn't really expected anything else, had I? Still, there had to be some reason why the guy had been killed. Drutus and Anda, fair enough, given that now I knew they'd been more than they seemed. But Tarbeisus? If he was as squeaky-clean and innocent as he was beginning to sound, then why the hell should anyone want to take him out?

Anda . . .

The tavern-keeper – his landlord – had said that what seemed to have excited the guy, and led eventually to his and Drutus's deaths, was that someone was lying because 'he'd never been there'. Assuming – and it was a fair assumption, given that Anda was well-travelled – that 'there' referred to a town or city . . .

'One more question, pal,' I said. 'Anda. Drutus's servant. Did he come in here much, by any chance?'

'Anda?' Frontus looked puzzled. 'Of course he did, with or without Drutus. I told you, they'd both been coming here for years. He dropped in most days when the two of them were through from Durocortorum.'

'So he'd've been in the bar when Tarbeisus was doing his networking?'

'Possibly. That depends. It's perfectly likely, though.'

'Can you give me a for instance?'

The guy was frowning. 'How do you mean?'

'Any occasion when they were both in here at the same time. That you noticed.'

'The afternoon of the day he was killed, as a matter of fact. Anda, I mean.'

And Tarbeisus himself had been murdered – probably – two days later.

Bullseye!

'OK,' I said. 'This is important, so I want you to think carefully and take it slow. They were both here, right? Anda and Tarbeisus.'

'Yes.'

'Together?'

'No. Tarbeisus was standing by the counter, Anda was sitting with friends at one of the tables.'

'Which one would that be?' He pointed, and I followed his finger. Uh-huh; practically slap-bang next to the bar counter itself. 'And who was Tarbeisus with? You remember?'

'I'm afraid not. The place was full to bursting. There were half a dozen people standing there who couldn't get seats, and he was just one of the group. Besides, I wasn't paying any attention; I'd business of my own to discuss with a customer. Ruber, you were there, weren't you? Do you remember?'

'Nah, you're wrong, I wasn't in at all that day. I'd the stock-taking to finish.'

Hell! I could have wept! So near, and yet so far: the odds were that whoever Tarbeisus had been talking to, Anda had noticed something screwy going on in the conversation. Screwy enough for him to cut things short and make a bee-line for his master to give him the news. I could ask my friend the barman, of course – at least he'd've been behind the counter, serving the drinks – and I would, before I left, but I'd bet now I'd be on a hiding to nothing in that direction.

'You can't give me any names?' I said to Frontus. 'None at all?'

'One of them could've been Verus. He came in late that day, and he was round looking for a seat. I'm only guessing, mind.'

Hey! Great! 'Who's Verus? He here at present?'

Frontus looked round. 'No. But he's a regular; you shouldn't have any problems checking with him yourself.'

'Local man?'

'No again; he's based in Divodurum. Footwear.'

'You wouldn't know where he lodges?'

'I'm sorry, that I can't tell you. But as I say, he'll be around. Is it that urgent?'

'Pretty much so.' Damn! We were on to something here, I was certain of that. 'Could you give him a message for me, do you think? Next time you see him?'

'Of course.'

'Just ask him to call in at the residence as soon as he can. I'll either be there myself, or he can arrange a time and a place to meet. OK?'

'Perfectly.'

'Thanks.' I stood up. 'Much obliged for the help.'

'You're very welcome.'

I checked with our Argus-eyed owner/barman on the way out, but sure enough he hadn't any thoughts on the matter.

Ah, well, we were a little further forward, anyway. And maybe this Verus, when I finally got to see him, would come up trumps.

TWENTY

Perilla was waiting for me in the atrium when I got back. Impatiently, and dressed to the nines.

'Marcus,' she said. 'You need to get changed. Now.'

'Ah . . . run that past me again?'

'We're going out for dinner. To Optima and Secundus's.'

'*What?* Gods, lady . . .!'

'Yes, well, I know it's short notice, but she asked, and I said we weren't doing anything particular this evening. It's nothing formal, not a full-scale dinner party, just a family meal. Only the four of us.'

'Right. Which is why you're wearing your best mantle, gold-piece-a-bottle scent, and the family jewels. Why the hell couldn't she make the invite for two or three days down the line like a proper civilized person? Or is this some kind of weird Gallic custom? Disconcert the Roman?'

'I suspect it's just her, dear. You've met her yourself. She is rather impulsive.'

Well, that was one word for her. Not the one I would've chosen, mind, but at least it was polite. I sighed.

'OK, party mantle and slippers it is,' I said. 'I just hope the woman's impulsiveness doesn't extend to serving up any local delicacies. An evening of Julia Optima I can stand, but not if it involves roast bear in a cream-cheese sauce washed down with a pot of Gaulish beer.'

'Don't be tiresome, Marcus.'

'Just watch your mantle when old Secundus gets excited and starts splashing the gravy around, that's all.'

'Hah!'

I made for the stairs.

Actually, I needn't have worried; the meal was perfectly normal and absolutely delicious. The wine wasn't bad, either – Massilian, and top of the range. By the time we'd got to the fruit and nuts stage, I was relaxed and pretty mellow.

I'd obviously done Julius Secundus an injustice, too, in comparing him with my stepfather Priscus. Oh, sure, a certain amount of Priscan geekery crept into the conversation now and again, but it was clear he was keeping his hobby-horse on a tight rein, and unlike Priscus he had other interests that didn't teeter on the spinning edge of monomania. Like how the racing teams in Rome were shaping at present. Me, I don't follow the cars all that closely, but you can't go down to the Square for a morning shave without picking up a certain amount of current gossip, and at least it made a pleasant change from a rundown of the uses of the dative in Ancient Oscan. There was no shop talk, either: I'd been expecting to be grilled on how the case was going but it wasn't even mentioned, which came as another pleasant surprise.

Perilla was enjoying herself as well. She'd been right when she'd said that Optima was interested in – and knew a lot about – local traditions, customs and history; despite the fact that the lady was looking a complete and total stunner in a mantle that did for her figure what any self-respecting sculptor given a commission for Venus Clothed would've hocked his chisel for, she was absolutely no bimbo. Far from it. Yeah, well, to each his own; having been thoroughly Perilla'd over the years myself, I had more than a little sympathy for old Secundus. Mind you, being married to a honey like Julia Optima would make up for a hell of a lot.

So all in all when the lads came in to clear away we were having a very unexpectedly pleasant evening.

'Now, Corvinus,' Secundus said, picking up his wine-cup. 'I promised to show you my silverware collection, or some of it, anyway. Only if you're agreeable, of course.'

'Yeah,' I said. 'That'd be great.'

'Then we'll go through to the study. Optima? Perilla? You'll join us?'

'Certainly,' Perilla said.

'This way, then.'

'Study' was the wrong word; oh, sure, there was a reading-couch and table, plus a book cubby on one of the walls, but most of the room was given over to the silverware, everything from what looked like a big mixing-bowl for wine that stood apart on a low plinth to a set of spoons in an angled wooden display frame. I reckoned there was getting on for a hundredweight of the stuff, all in prime condition and gleaming like it'd been freshly polished. Which, probably, it had been: whoever on Secundus's staff had landed that particular job, slave or free, I didn't envy the poor bugger. Even Bathyllus would've blanched, and the little bald-head is never happier than when he's buffing away at the bronzes.

'Oh, my!' Perilla breathed.

'Yes, I'm quite proud of it,' Secundus said. 'All Gaulish made, or Celtic, rather, because I'm not sure myself about the provenance of some of the pieces. This drinking horn, for example.' He picked it up from the table beside him. 'I bought that from a merchant who said he'd had it from a seller in Rhaetia. It may have been made there, or it may simply have travelled; I don't know. In any case, it's a beautiful piece of work.'

'It certainly is,' Perilla said. 'May I see, please?'

'Of course.' He handed it over.

'How old would it be?' I said.

'Again, I'm not sure. Certainly more than three hundred years, possibly older.' He smiled. 'Say about the time we Gauls were sacking Rome.'

I winced. Oh, ha; they couldn't resist a dig, could they? Not even the most Romanized of them.

'This part of the decoration,' Perilla said. 'A . . . ram with a serpent's tail, isn't it?'

'The god Cernunnos,' Optima said. 'Protector of animals. The ram is especially sacred to him, and he's sometimes shown that way.'

'Oh, yes. I remember you mentioning that.' She set the horn down again. 'He's the Gaulish equivalent of Apollo, isn't he?'

'In a way. But our gods are rather more generalized than yours. They don't specialize nearly so much, so it's difficult to put them into compartments.'

Secundus chuckled. 'Optima knows far more about that side of things than I do,' he said. 'For me, these are simply beautiful pieces of craftsmanship. I'm not so interested in the symbolism, or the underlying story.'

'How long have you been collecting?' I said.

'Most of my life. And my father started the collection before me, in a small way.' He picked up a cloak-brooch that lay beside the drinking horn and handed it to me. 'This was the first piece he ever bought, a gift for my mother when they were betrothed. Look at the intricacy of the patternwork! Absolutely flawless! Whoever produced that was not only a consummate artist but a first-class draughtsman.'

Yeah, I'd have to agree. The guy had had first-class eyesight, too, because the amount of detail – pinpoint-accurate detail – he'd managed to squeeze in to a space the length and width of two of my fingers was incredible. It knocked any equivalent bit of jewellery I'd ever seen back home into a cocked hat.

Well, if Secundus was a bit obsessive at least there were worse things to get obsessive about. I was impressed. More than impressed. I laid it back down.

'What about the big one over there?' I said. 'The wine-mixing bowl.'

'Ah. I was saving that for last, because it's the gem of the collection. Still, now that you've asked . . .' He went over to it, and we followed. 'It's not a wine bowl; the old Celts didn't drink wine. It was probably used for holding beer or mead at a religious ceremony. Isn't it magnificent?' It certainly was: a good two feet wide by eighteen inches deep, silver picked out in gold and decorated all over, inside and out. 'I've no idea of age; I think more or less contemporary with the drinking horn, although that's only a guess because the designs may be Celtic but the actual silver-working technique is much more advanced, possibly Thracian. As to the designs themselves, Optima will be able to tell you more about them than I could.'

'That's Cernunnos again, isn't it?' Perilla pointed to the seated figure on the bowl's inside face, crowned with antlers, surrounded by animals and holding a snake.

'Yes, it is,' Optima said. 'The serpent is wisdom. The thing in his other hand is a torque, the sign of a chief's power to rule. So the god is wisdom combined with power, or power to rule through wisdom. At least, that's what I think the meaning is.'

'What about the scene on the other side? A human sacrifice?'

Yeah, I'd noticed that already myself. The scene was made up of a line of armed men led by three guys blowing what I assumed were war horns, and next to them a larger figure holding a smaller one by the ankles and lowering him head-down into a king-size stew-pot. Nice.

'It's the most likely explanation, yes; the old Celts certainly practised ritual drowning. But there might be another explanation, a kinder one. You've heard of the Cauldron of Rebirth?'

'No.'

'It's one of the Three Magical Treasures that the druids talk about. Talked about. Dead men – those killed in battle, especially – who were put into the Cauldron came alive again, to fight another day. That may be what's shown here.' Optima smiled. 'But that's just a guess, I'm afraid. Wishful thinking.'

'Useful if you could make it work,' I said.

'Yes, it would be, Valerius Corvinus. Very useful. And rebirth – whether literal or metaphorical – is an important concept to a Gaul.'

'Well, have you seen enough?' Secundus said. 'I wouldn't want to bore you. And I could, very easily, believe me.'

I grinned. 'Yeah, I think that'll do me,' I said. 'Even so, it's been fascinating. Right, Perilla?'

'Indeed it has,' the lady said. 'Thank you, Julius Secundus. And of course you too, Optima.'

We went back out.

'So it's an ongoing process, is it?' I said to Secundus as he closed the study door behind us. 'The collecting, I mean?'

'Oh, very much so. Not a cheap hobby, I know, but we live quite simply otherwise, and suitable pieces don't come up for sale all that often.' Secundus led the way back along the corridor towards the dining room. 'Of course, I have my network of suppliers who keep their eyes peeled for anything I might find interesting, particularly if it fills a gap somewhere or other. You met Sulinus, didn't you? The man I was with in the market square when we first talked?'

'Yeah, I did.'

'He is especially useful, coming as he does from Caesarodunum. That's more or less the geographical centre of—' He stared at me. 'Are you all right, Corvinus? You look unwell.'

'Uh . . . no. No, I'm fine, thanks. Maybe just your good wine catching up on me all at once,' I said.

Jupiter! Sweet Jupiter and all the gods!

'Perhaps a breath of fresh air?' Optima said. 'If you'd like to have a turn round the garden the back door's this way.'

She turned.

'Uh-uh. Honestly. Even so, perhaps we should be getting back. Thank you for a splendid meal.'

'Indeed.' Perilla was giving me a very suspicious look. 'I'm sure Procurator Laco would be happy to allow us to reciprocate in a few days' time. Isn't that so, Marcus?'

'Yeah. Yeah, definitely.' I managed a weak grin. 'The ladies can arrange it between them, Secundus, if that's all right with you.'

'Certainly it is.' He took my empty wine-cup from me. 'We'll look forward to it.'

'Good night, then. And thanks again.'

'Now, Marcus,' Perilla said when we were settled in the carriage and trundling our way back to the residence. 'Will you *please* explain the meaning of that little farce? We couldn't have left any faster if we'd been greased. I was totally embarrassed.'

'Secundus's merchant pal Sulinus is our perp,' I said.

'*What?* How on earth do you know that?'

'Because he's from Caesarodunum. Or claims he is, rather, which is just the point. According to Nerva, the dead merchant – Tarbeisus – came from there too.'

'So?'

'Gods, lady! It explains everything! One of them must've been lying, and it can't've been Tarbeisus, because he was the one who got stiffed. So it must be Sulinus. And if he's the liar then *ipso facto* he's also the man we want.'

'I'm sorry, dear, you've lost me. Why should either of them be lying in the first place?'

'Because Anda caught one of them out.'

'And when would that have been?'

Oh, yeah; we'd left in such a hurry for the impromptu dinner appointment that I hadn't had time to bring the lady up to date on the case. I did now.

'So one of the punters standing at the bar with Tarbeisus – the crucial punter – must've been Sulinus,' I finished. 'Whatever was said, it showed Anda – who *had* been to Caesarodunum – that he didn't know the place at all. Oh, sure, it was pure bad luck on Sulinus's part. Doubly bad luck, in fact: he'd chosen a town that it was most unlikely any of the merchants frequenting Augusta would know, because it was well off the beaten track where they were concerned, only to find himself talking to someone who actually came from there. Plus his gaffe had been noticed by one of the only two men in town who'd know what it meant. You see? It explains all of the murders together: Drutus and Anda had to die, because they could've fingered him to the authorities, and Tarbeisus had to go as well in case he blew the guy's cover, innocently or otherwise, later on.'

'Yes.' She was twisting her lock of hair. 'Yes, that makes sense. Of course it does. But why should Sulinus need to invent a bogus background for himself in the first place? After all, there are plenty of places in Gaul that he might have been to that he could've used instead. Why choose somewhere he'd never been before? It was simply asking for trouble.'

'Gods, Perilla, use your brain, please.'

'*Marcus!*'

'Well, even so. He couldn't've used anywhere all that big or well-known, because that would've increased the chances of what actually did happen happening: that sooner or later he'd run up against someone who should've recognized him as a fellow townsman but didn't. While if he was fronting for the Brits, which he was and is, choosing a place on that side of the country would've been too much of a risk if he did come under suspicion. Somewhere reasonably small, in the far south or south-west, comparatively out in the sticks and a good few hundred miles from the Gallic Strait, would've been perfect.'

'So what are you going to do now?'

'See Balbinus, first thing tomorrow morning. Shop the bastard. That side of things isn't my concern, or not directly: it's political. Let Balbinus handle it.'

Which wasn't, in the event, how things turned out. But then, I wasn't to know that at the time, was I?

TWENTY-ONE

'First thing' was a bit of an overstatement: there wasn't much point in making too early a visit to the government offices, because civil provincial admin in a relatively laid-back town like Augusta didn't kick in until the start of the second hour, and Balbinus himself, conscientious though he was, probably wouldn't turn up until the sun was a little further along its curve; while things being as hush-hush as they were I couldn't blow the whistle on Sulinus to anyone barring the guy in person. So I had a leisurely breakfast and set out on the short walk to the government admin building just shy of the third.

'Saenius Balbinus, pal,' I said to the clerk on the desk. 'He in yet?'

'No, sir. Nor likely to be, I'm afraid, not immediately. He had some business outside town to look after. Was it urgent?'

Damn. 'Yeah, it was, as a matter of fact,' I said. 'You know when he'll be back? Or where I can find him?'

'I'm afraid not, Valerius Corvinus. He didn't say. He won't be in this morning, certainly, although you can try again in the afternoon. Was there a message I could give? Or perhaps I can help you myself?'

'No, that's fine. And no message as such. Just say that I have to see him urgently.' I was turning to go before I thought again. 'Scratch that. Tell him I know now who X is.'

The clerk's brow furrowed. 'X, sir?'

'Yeah. He'll understand. Exactly those words, right?' And if I wanted to stress the importance of the meeting, then they would do the trick in spades. 'I'll call again after midday.'

'Very good, sir.'

So. Not back to the residence; I didn't fancy sitting twiddling my thumbs for another three or four hours, and Perilla would no doubt be out gallivanting somewhere or other. Maybe the market square and a second shave, just to say I'd tried the Gaulish version. Or maybe even, given the lady was a bit more relaxed now on the subject, a cup of wine in one of the wineshops I hadn't had the opportunity of trying.

I set off down the main drag.

I'd almost reached the square when I spotted a familiar figure ahead. Segomarus.

'Valerius Corvinus!' he said when we'd closed the gap. 'Just the man! I was on my way to see you.'

'Yeah?' I was cautious. 'What about?'

'Come on! We had a deal, remember? The Cabiri family background? You owe me a jug of wine.'

Oh. Right. Gods, this business of the three local murders, not to mention saving Claudius's invasion plans for Britain, had practically put the original case out of my head.

'You've found someone who knew them before they left Augusta for Lugdunum and who's willing to talk?' I said.

'As ever is. A guy by the name of Publius Auctionus. He's not a local, as it happens, which is probably why; retired auxiliary from one of the Tungrian cohorts, been settled here since the God Augustus was in rompers. He looks as old as Tithonus and he's half gaga, but there's nothing wrong with his memory. I said you'd trade him a gold piece for the information. That OK?'

'No problem.' I was frowning. It all sounded plausible, right enough, and we'd ruled Segomarus out of the running for a potential bad-'un, but I still didn't quite trust the guy. There was something there, all right; I just couldn't quite put my finger on it, let alone justify the feeling in the first place. I'd have to play along, sure – the chance of clearing up the Cabirus side of things was much too good to miss, and it looked like this Auctionus was the best shot I'd get at it – but I'd go cautious. 'Look, Segus, I'm pretty busy at the moment. We can see him tomorrow.'

Segomarus grinned. 'The state he's in, he could be dead by then. Besides, he's practically in the next street from here. Come on! It shouldn't take all that long, and you can't be that busy.'

'Fair enough,' I said. 'Lead on.'

He did.

'Next street' was pushing things a bit, although not by much; it wasn't any more than a couple of hundred yards, albeit two hundred yards off the main drag. Augusta doesn't do slum tenements – there's too much open space within the town limits unbuilt on for that – but the house we eventually stopped at was the one-storey equivalent, put together, by the look of it, from whatever the original builders had to hand, which wasn't, in constructional terms, very much; the place looked like one good puff of wind would return it to its basic components. I knocked at the door.

'No point in that, Corvinus,' Segomarus said. 'The old boy's bedridden, in the room at the back. Just go straight in. He's expecting us.'

I did. After the sunlight of the street, the hallway was dark as hell. I waited for my eyes to get accustomed to the dimness . . .
. . . at which point something smacked me hard behind the ear, and what light there was went out altogether.

When I woke up, I was securely tied to a chair by my wrists and ankles, and my head felt twice its size, with Vulcan using it for an anvil. Segomarus was leaning against the far wall, watching me.

'What the hell's going on?' I said. Slurred.

'You'll see in a moment.' He walked towards the open door and put his head round the jamb. 'That's him awake now.'

Sulinus came in. Followed by Julia Optima.

I goggled. 'What the fuck—!'

Sulinus tutted. 'Now, now. Ladies present.' Optima smiled and took his arm. 'You're surprised? Don't be; Optima and I have been lovers practically since I began coming here. And in case you're wondering the choice to begin an affair was hers, as indeed was her choice of sides, made practically at the same time. So don't form any conclusions involving the innocent little woman led astray by the wicked seducer, will you?'

'We're not Romans, Corvinus,' Optima said. 'There are women on the other side of the Gallic Strait who rule their tribes just as efficiently as men, and are equally respected for it. They lead them in battle, too.' She smiled. 'Not that I've any intention of doing that, you understand. It's far too dangerous.'

I ignored her.

'Look,' I said to Sulinus. 'You're not a Roman citizen, right? So when the authorities get you for this, which they will, they will literally nail you to a fucking plank and leave you to hang. Just so we're clear on that point.'

He chuckled. 'Oh, I don't think you'll be in any position to arrange my execution, Corvinus. You're a dead man walking yourself. Or sitting, rather, to be accurate. And you're perfectly right; if you were found too obviously murdered like the others – a Roman purple-striper and the emperor's personally accredited representative – there would be hell to pay. One of the two reasons that you're still alive now – and it's purely temporary – is that we want to make your death look like an accident.'

A cold ball of ice was forming in my stomach. 'Yeah? And how do you propose to do that?'

'Remember the place Drutus and his servant were killed? If a person was very unlucky, a tumble there, down from the high ground, might well result in a broken neck. You, of course, would be very unlucky.'

'Why the hell should I be going back there?'

'I don't know. To search for more clues, possibly. It's a long way from being the perfect solution, I admit, but frankly it was the best we could think of at such short notice, it will at least cloud the issue, and of course you do have to die, by one means or another. Not that you'll be going there alive, naturally; your neck will already have been broken by then. Segomarus will be taking care of that shortly.'

Oh, shit. 'So why this chat?' I said. 'Why not have done it while I was out cold?'

'That's the second reason. Please believe me, I'm not a cruel man by nature, and I'm only doing my duty as I see it. I don't begrudge you an explanation before you go. It's the least I can do, apart from making sure that your death will be relatively painless.'

'My wife—' I stopped, just in time. Jupiter, that had been close! What I'd been going to say was that Perilla knew he was the perp, so all the cover-ups in the world wouldn't do him any good. Only I couldn't say that, could I? Not with Optima standing there. They were friends, and Perilla trusted her; she wouldn't last five minutes. 'My wife'll be wondering where I am. She'll contact the authorities.'

'No doubt,' Sulinus said blandly. 'She already knows that I was involved somewhere along the line, so perhaps trying to falsify your cause of death is pointless after all.' Shit! Evidently, I could add mind-reading to the bastard's accomplishments. 'Never mind; the decision's been taken, and this way involves very little extra trouble. She does know about me, doesn't she?' I didn't reply. 'Oh, come on, Corvinus, I'm not stupid! You must have told her on the way home from Optima's dinner party, when you put two and two together. Which, of course, is why you're here now, because Optima is no fool either, and she notices these things. Actually, that isn't all that important. My part in this is

over, so by the time they come looking for me I'll be gone. And
with you dead there's no way to link me with Optima, which is
the crucial thing. No, please don't be concerned about your wife.
I said: I'm neither needlessly cruel nor a villain. As long as she's
no threat she's quite safe, believe me.'

Well, that was something, at least. Not that it left me bubbling
with cheer altogether, mind: there was still that broken neck to
look forward to, and I'd try to put that off as long as possible in
the hope that something turned up. Not that there was any chance
of that.

'OK,' I said. 'You want to explain to me exactly what's been
going on? Just for information.'

'Naturally. I told you; that's the other reason why you're still
alive. What have you got so far?'

'That you're working for the tribes on the other side of the
Gallic Strait, what's-his-name in particular—'

'King Caratacus, yes.'

'—and that you're fomenting some sort of local revolt in an
attempt to get the emperor's campaign cancelled, or at least
postponed. How exactly are you setting about that, incidentally?'

'With money, first of all, quite a lot of it; gold, supplied by
Caratacus and brought in by me over the past few years from
Britain. I've been stockpiling it since just before the Emperor
Gaius's abortive attempt to invade, and by now we have a war
chest of several thousand gold pieces. Crude, yes, but you'd be
surprised how much money can buy in Gaul, and who it buys.
Not only locals, either; you Romans are a very venal race.
However, money's not the only way, far from it. Some people
– idealists, patriots, fanatics if you like – can't be bought, at any
price.' He put an arm around Optima's shoulders and gave her
a squeeze. 'That's where my darling girl comes in. She's one of
them herself, you see, so she knows how to talk to them.'

Optima's chin lifted. 'My ancestors were chiefs of the Treveri
for half a thousand years,' she said. 'Julius Florus was my
mother's uncle. People here – influential people – have long
memories; they don't forget their blood or their loyalties, and
they're proud; too proud, given a choice, to knuckle down to you
Romans altogether.'

'And then, last but not least, there's our druid friend,' Sulinus said. 'You never met him, of course, and weren't likely to, but he's more important than the two of us combined. He'll give us the rank and file, the peasants. Weaponless, for the most part, barring a few hunting spears and bows, but there will be a lot of them. Hundreds. And with a druid urging them on they'll fight to the death.'

I just didn't believe this. 'Jupiter!' I said. 'That's all you're basing your revolt on? A handful of misguided aristocratic malcontents, maybe a few mercenaries in it for the cash, and a mob of yokels who wouldn't know one end of a sword from the other? They won't last five minutes when the regulars arrive. You haven't the faintest chance of winning, not in a million years, any more than Florus had.'

'Oh, we know that perfectly well,' Sulinus said calmly.

I stared at him. 'Then why the hell—!'

'We don't expect to win; we never have. But the threat will be enough. If we can force the Roman authorities to divert sufficient troops to deal with it then the British tribes will at least have a breathing space. Caratacus is already treating with the tribes nearest to his own kingdom, persuading them to send armies of their own; a few months – more, if winter intervenes – may make all the difference.'

'You know how many people will die before you're finished?' I said. 'Not to mention the misery when the troops arrive and your so-called revolt is stamped flat. Which it will be before you can fucking sneeze.'

'That's a shame, but it can't be helped. And it's in a good cause.'

Said without a smidgeon of emotion. My initial reaction, obviously, was that despite the matter-of-fact delivery the guy was stark raving mad; that all three of them were. Only that didn't quite cover things, did it? Sulinus was absolutely right; Rome just couldn't take any risks where Gaul was concerned, not this close to the Rhine with the hostile German tribes on the far bank itching to exploit any weakness, and Balbinus himself had admitted that any distraction could put the kybosh on the emperor's campaign plans, at least for the time being. Plus the fact that, yes, I had to admit it, we had a clash of genuine principles here: traitors in Roman terms Sulinus and Optima might be, but not by their own reckoning; they had their own loyalties, and alien as they were they were as valid as ours.

Bugger.

'So Drutus and Anda had to be got rid of before they blew the whistle prematurely?' I said.

'Yes.' Sulinus frowned. 'We knew – we've known for months – that they were spying for Claudius's lapdog Verica, and so for Governor Hister, but we also knew they were getting nowhere, or nowhere important, anyway. Certainly they didn't suspect me, not to mention Optima. That all changed when Tarbeisus arrived. I have to admit that it was my own stupid fault; I'm not sure what slip I made exactly that afternoon when we were chatting in the wineshop, but I could see that he'd noticed and it puzzled him. Plus, of course – and far worse – that Drutus's man Anda had overheard and noticed in his turn. By chance I was already planning to meet with our druid friend that evening outside town. It wasn't difficult to arrange things so the pair of them followed me – secretly, or so they thought – to the rendezvous, and Segomarus here was already in place, lying hidden in the bushes. He was able to catch them almost completely unawares while they eavesdropped, and that was that. Then naturally we got rid of Tarbeisus as well. Just in case.'

'Right,' I said. 'I was wondering how our Burdigalan pal came into it.' Segomarus grinned at me, but said nothing. 'You two had met before, yes?'

'Actually no, we hadn't. Oh, we knew of each other's existence; he was in Augusta for a purpose, as I was, and he'd been instructed to make contact as soon as he got here.'

'Instructed by your British friends?'

'Yes, indeed. By Caratacus personally, in fact. But he's no Burdigalan; he's never been to Burdigala, no more than I've been to Caesarodunum. He came here by a very roundabout route, of course, for reasons of security, but he's spent most of the past twenty years at King Caratacus's court.'

I turned my attention to Segomarus. 'Is that so, now?' I said.

'That, Corvinus, is so,' he said. 'I'm sorry, but there you are. I'm more British than Gaulish nowadays, I'm afraid.'

'Uh-huh. So why exactly did you come? Or were sent, rather?'

'To Augusta? Because I still had friends here. Old

comrades-in-arms, people who knew and trusted me from the time of the Florus revolt, that I could put Sulinus in touch with and the other way round. Save him a lot of time and trouble, not to mention minimizing the risk of sounding out the wrong ones and so maybe putting the whole conspiracy in jeopardy. A twenty years' absence is a long time, sure, I look a lot different from how I did before, intentionally so, and naturally I had a different name, but like Optima told you people here have long memories. Some things they don't forget.' He was watching me, still smiling. 'Come on, Corvinus, you're being thick! I'd expected better! You haven't got there yet?'

'How do you mean?'

'I promised you I'd help you solve the Cabirus family side of things, and I always keep my promises. I reckon you owe me a jug of wine. Not that you'll be in any position to honour your side of the bargain, mind, but under the circumstances we'll let it go.'

Oh, shit: the penny finally dropped. 'You're Licnus,' I said. 'Diligenta's brother.'

'Congratulations. Give the man the nuts.'

Sweet gods! 'Does she know? Your sister?'

'Of course she does. Why do you think I went back to Lugdunum before I came on here? I had to see her while I was in Gaul. We were always close, her and me.'

'You're saying she knew all the time?' I was still trying to take it in. 'Right from the start?'

'No. For all she knew – for all any of them knew – I was dead and gone. The last Diligenta saw of me was here, the time of the revolt, and precious little then. I had to run to save my skin, and bloody fast, at that. I ran all the way to Britain, where you Romans couldn't get me, and I've been there ever since. Wife, family, the lot. I said: nowadays I'm far more a Catuvellaunan than I am a Gaul. Only I couldn't let the opportunity slip, could I? Even if it did take me a bit out of my way.'

Things were beginning to add up. 'Titus,' I said. 'He knew too.'

'I told him myself, right after I told Diligenta. Made a point of it. He's a good lad, my nephew. Pity he's chosen the wrong side, but I bear him no ill-will for that; he's sound enough at

heart, and young enough to change his mind. He'll see Rome
for what she is, in the end.'

'What about the other boy? Publius?'

'No, Publius doesn't know who I am. Or I assume he doesn't,
unless either Diligenta or Titus let it out. I'm afraid I don't have
much time for young Publius. The lad's a milksop.'

'All this – telling your sister and your nephew, I mean –
would've been before your brother-in-law's death, would it?'

That got me a bland look. 'Shortly before, yes. As it
happens.'

'And there would be a connection?'

'There might be. But I've said all I'm saying.' He glanced at
Sulinus, who'd been watching the exchange with a smile on his
lips. 'He's had enough time. Let's get it over with.'

'Fair enough,' Sulinus said. My blood ran cold. 'Optima and
I will leave you to it. The wagon's round the back. We can take
the body out of town as soon as it gets dark.' He hesitated, then
turned to me. 'Goodbye, Valerius Corvinus. You won't believe
me, I know, but I am truly sorry about this, and about the other
deaths. I wish none of it had been necessary. However, there
really is too much at stake. It has to be done.'

'Yeah. Right.' I felt sick.

They left. Optima didn't even give me a backward glance.

'For what it's worth, I'm sorry too,' Segomarus – Licnus – said.
'You were good company, Corvinus, and I'm not a killer either
by nature. Even so—'

He moved towards me. I tugged desperately on the ropes, but
I was tied securely, wrists and ankles. If I could just overbalance
the chair, maybe, head-butt the bastard in the chest—

I almost made it; near enough, anyway, for him to take a
cautious step back. Which was when fate in its most unlikely
and unexpected guise took a hand . . .

He'd obviously been waiting, hidden, outside somewhere until
Sulinus and Optima had gone. Now he edged in and came up
on Licnus from behind. There was no messing, either; whatever
he was holding – it might've been a table leg – came down on
the other guy's head with a solid thump. Licnus folded up and
lay at my feet like a wrung-out dishrag.

*   *   *

'So,' I said to Crinas when he'd untied me and used the ropes to tie up the still-unconscious and seriously damaged Segomarus/ Licnus. 'What the hell are you doing here? I thought you were on your way to Moguntiacum.'

He grinned. 'Yes, well, I'm afraid I have a small admission to make.'

'Yeah?' Gods, today was just chock-full of surprises, wasn't it? 'And what's that, now? Believe me, if it can explain how the fuck you knew I'd be in a crumbling Gallic shack tied to a chair and about to have my neck broken, let alone why you should be on hand to help in the first place, then "small" isn't the word I'd use for it, pal. Not that I'm not grateful, mind.'

'The first bit's easy. I followed you.'

'Fine. That I might've guessed, given time and several goes at it. Now what about the second?'

'That's the admission.' He cleared his throat. 'Yes, as I told you and Perilla, I am a doctor charged with reporting on the local hot springs for possible exploitation by the Rhine garrisons. However, my other purpose – less, ah, overt – is information gathering of a different kind.'

Uh-huh. Click. 'In other words, you're a spy,' I said. Bugger; the woods were full of them. It would seem you couldn't move a yard in Gaul without tripping over one of the bastards.

'More or less.' He was looking, for Smarmer, unaccustomedly sheepish. 'Specifically, though, I had the task – given to me by the emperor personally, I hasten to add – of watching your back. Should you need it.'

I stared at him; that I hadn't been expecting. 'Why in the gods' name should Claudius think I needed my back watching?' I said. 'He sent me out on a straightforward murder investigation. All this cloak-and-dagger stuff was incidental. Not to say accidental.'

He shrugged. 'I don't know. But he's a very clever man; very clever indeed, and very cautious. Perhaps he was just making doubly sure of your safety while you were engaged on his private business, no more than that. Even so, I had my instructions, and they were quite clear and unequivocal.'

'What was all this business of squiring my wife around the sites? How does that square?'

'You seemed in no particular danger for the present,' he said.

'It was a good way of checking up on your movements at second hand, without making you suspicious.'

'Yeah? Very laudable and sneaky. You sure that was your only reason, friend?'

He actually blushed. 'Well, you must admit that your wife is extremely charming and personable. Plus, we shared a genuine interest in local curiosities. In my own defence, when it transpired that your case was taking a more sinister turn I put my duty first straight away. I haven't seen Perilla for days.'

Hmm. Well, no doubt even government spies got these lecherous urges, and the smoothie bastard had just saved my life, after all. I was prepared to give him the benefit of the doubt, this time round.

'OK,' I said. 'So how did you know about the political side of things to begin with? That was supposed to be top secret.'

'Oh, that was Balbinus, naturally. He told me.'

I stared at him. 'Balbinus knew who you were? Or what you were, rather?'

'Of course. From the very start. I showed him my official credentials almost as soon as I got here. Signed, as I say, by the emperor personally. Licinius Nerva knew, too.'

Fuck; wheels within wheels. I'll never understand what makes these political bastards tick, or emperors, for that matter; I'm not sure I want to, either. 'They might have let me in on the secret,' I said. 'I am a sodding imperial procurator, after all, for what it's worth.' Evidently that wasn't very much, at the end of the day. 'You'd've thought I rated. As well as having a personal interest.'

'That would have defeated the purpose. Or at least confused the issue. Both they and I decided it would be better for you not to know, and for me to preserve my anonymity.'

Yeah, well, I supposed he had a point, and it had paid off in the end. Still. 'So,' I said. 'What happens now?'

'We hand the whole thing over to the people in charge.' He touched Segomarus/Licnus with his toe. 'Including this fellow here. I'm sure they'll deal with it to everyone's satisfaction.'

I shuddered, remembering what had happened a couple of years previously: yeah, I'd had experience before of traitors, or would-be traitors, being 'dealt with', in the bowels of the imperial palace when Gaius was emperor. It wasn't a memory, unfortunately, that I was ever likely to lose. Things like that had to be done, no doubt, if the state was to be kept safe, but they turned my stomach.

'Fair enough,' I said. 'There's a cart out the back, seemingly. I'll give you a hand to load chummie here onto it and you can deliver him to Balbinus. Or whoever. Tell him about Sulinus and Optima while you're at it; no doubt he can pick them up no bother and add them to the bag.'

He frowned. 'And you? What are you going to do?'

The hell, for once, with moderation. Besides, I reckon I deserved it, because the case was solved. Or at least if my assumptions were right it was. Those I'd have to check, but not today: today, I'd had enough.

'I, pal,' I said, 'am going to find the nearest decent wineshop and get stewed.'

TWENTY-TWO

So that just about wrapped it up, both for the Cabirus side of things – barring one small but important detail – and the Treveran conspiracy. That was dead meat, too, if that wasn't an unfortunate phrase in the circumstances, particularly after Balbinus managed to nail Sulinus's druid friend, which he did in double-quick time. Me, I was careful not to ask how, but thinking back two years to the question-and-answer session I'd attended *chez* Gaius I had my sick-making suspicions: Optima was a Roman citizen, sure, so she'd be exempt from torture (not that that had weighed with our former emperor, of course), and she could at least expect a clean death. Sulinus and Segomarus/ Licnus were another matter. All I could do – and it didn't help much – was to tell myself that the result of putting them away had been the saving of hundreds, maybe thousands, of lives and a fresh round of human misery; plus, of course, potentially at least, a new province added to the empire. Lucky Britain.

Yeah, well, not a bad few months' work, all told. Claudius would be pleased. I'd be glad to get back home, though.

There was still that one small important detail I mentioned, mind, and *that* I wasn't looking forward to at all.

We were just about to leave for Lugdunum a couple of days later, Perilla and I, with Perilla upstairs supervising the last of the packing, when Titus Cabirus came into the atrium.

'I'm sorry to disturb you, Corvinus,' he said. 'But I wondered if I might have a word before you go.'

'Sure, pal, sit down. We're in no hurry.' Bathyllus was hovering. 'Some wine?'

'No, thank you. And this won't take long, so I won't sit; I'm on duty today, only here by Procurator Laco's permission.' He hesitated. 'I only wanted to make it clear that where my uncle was concerned I knew absolutely nothing about the treason side of things. Or even suspected it.'

'I never thought you did,' I said mildly. 'You're no traitor. If you had you'd've reported it straight off, uncle or not.'

He gave a stiff nod. 'Good. That's got that off my chest. I'll leave you to get on. Have a safe journey home.'

He turned.

'Hang on,' I said. 'You still have some explaining to do, if you don't mind. On the Lugdunum side.'

He turned back. 'What needs explaining?' he said, and for the first time there was an edge to his voice. 'The case is over. My – Balbinus has told me that Licnus freely confessed to murdering my father. So that's that; you have your killer. Problem solved.'

I let that one go for the present. The tone, too; although he'd never known him, according to what Brother Quintus had told me back in Lugdunum, thanks to his mother young Titus had idolized his missing uncle all his life. It would've come as a shock to discover at one and the same time that the guy had not only been a traitor to Rome but was his father's murderer into the bargain. He was doing pretty well in keeping his feelings in check, sure, but there was no reason to push things unnecessarily.

Even so.

'He didn't say why he did it,' I said. 'Not to me, at any rate. You happen to know, by any chance?'

'Yes, of course.' Stiff as hell. 'Or at least I can guess. He did it out of revenge.'

Uh-huh. Revenge. Well, that much was true enough. 'Care to tell me the details?' I said.

'Why should you bother? It can't matter now. He's—' He frowned, and cleared his throat. 'Once they're finished questioning him my uncle will be dead anyway, won't he? They can't execute him twice, for treason and murder both.'

Yeah; that was how I read it, too. Just as he had, himself. Still, I waited. Finally, Titus said: 'The time of the Florus revolt, or just after it, rather. My father . . .' He stopped, swallowed, then began again, carefully and deliberately, his eyes never leaving mine. 'It seems that my father was secretly passing information to the authorities on who'd been involved and how. Names, details, anything they didn't already know and might not even suspect. One of the names was Uncle Licnus's; they'd never got on, even before my father married my mother. Oh, he'd been involved in the revolt, sure, but not to the extent Father told the authorities he was, and that made all the difference between them turning a blind eye and pulling him in. He was lucky; he escaped in time and managed to get clean away. A lot of the men – and women – my father put the finger on weren't so fortunate.'

'Right,' I said. 'Which explains why, when things began to settle, your family had to move to Lugdunum.'

He nodded, his face still completely devoid of expression. 'People here aren't stupid; they could put two and two together. Letting bygones be bygones for the sake of peace and harmony was one thing, but knowing someone had actively gone out of their way after the event to betray their own kind stuck in a lot of throats. Where my father was concerned, Augusta wouldn't have been a very comfortable place to live in future.'

'And no one in the family knew what he'd done at the time?'

'No. Like I said, he'd kept it secret. Uncle Licnus didn't get the chance to tell them, either; he suspected it, yes, but he only knew himself for sure some time later, when he was already on the run.'

Check. I frowned; this next bit was going to be difficult, and I'd far rather have avoided it altogether – would have, if the lad hadn't come round to see me. Still, what was done was done; he was here, he had a right to know the truth, and I couldn't very well in all conscience shirk my responsibilities.

'Maybe you'd best sit down after all,' I said.

He looked at me blankly. 'I beg your pardon?'

'Just do it.' I waited until he was perched uneasily on the other couch. 'Your uncle might be a traitor and a killer three times over, but he didn't murder your father.'

'*What?* Then who did?'

I told him.

We got back to Lugdunum twelve days later, too quick a trip this time round for my liking.

Walking past the summer house where Claudius Cabirus had been killed, I glanced up at the house's second storey. Sure enough, young Publius Cabirus was looking down at me through the window from his seat at the table where, no doubt, he was working on his models. I gave him a wave, but for all the response I got he might not have noticed me.

He had, though. That was the point.

I knocked at the door, and the maid I'd seen last time opened it.

'Ah . . . Cotuinda, isn't it?' I said.

'That's right, sir.' She gave me a guarded look.

'The mistress at home?'

No answer, but she opened the door wider and stepped back. I went in and followed her through to the living room.

Diligenta was sitting next to the open window, stitching what looked like a piece of embroidery.

'Valerius Corvinus!' She set the embroidery aside. 'You're back!'

'Yeah.' I glanced at the wickerwork chair opposite. 'You mind if I sit down?'

'Not at all. Something to drink?'

'No, I'm fine, thanks.' I lowered myself into the chair.

'Very well. Thank you, Cotuinda. That's all.' The servant went out. 'Now. What can I do for you this time?'

'Nothing at all, as a matter of fact,' I said. 'I know now who killed your husband, and why.'

Things went very still. 'Really?' she said. 'You found that out in Augusta?'

'Not exactly.' Bugger; I hated this. 'But I did talk to your brother there, and it cleared things up for me.'

She stared at me. 'My *brother*?'

'Licnus. Or Segomarus, as he was calling himself. He admitted he was responsible, which in a way he was. Not that that matters much.'

'I'm sorry, I'm not with you.' She'd gone pale as a ghost. 'And *Licnus*? I told you: Licnus has been missing these twenty years. He's probably dead.'

'Yeah, well, I hope that's the case by now. Certainly for his sake.'

'Corvinus, you're not making sense.'

'I'm afraid I am,' I said gently. 'He'd've been executed for treason.'

'*Treason*?'

I told her, the whole boiling. Or the treason part of it, anyway. She sat and listened without saying a word, her face expressionless.

'The thing is,' I finished, 'traitor or not, whatever he claimed to the contrary he couldn't have done your husband's murder. Oh, sure, he had good reason to, your son Titus explained all that. He had the opportunity, too, because he was in Lugdunum at the time. And like I say he admitted to the killing of his own free will. Even so, he couldn't have been the killer. It's just not possible.'

'How do you know that?'

'Because he may have told you and your son Titus who he was, but he didn't tell Publius.'

She shook her head. 'Valerius Corvinus, I'm sorry to have to repeat myself, but you really are not making any sense. Why should that matter?'

I sighed; we were at the heart of it now, and I couldn't put things off any longer. Much although I would've liked to.

'It's crucial,' I said. 'When I talked to him Publius insisted that he hadn't seen anyone go into the summer house that afternoon. Me, I'm certain that it wasn't because he was resting with the shutters closed, like you and he claimed; he'd been at his table working all the time, with a good view of the garden, just as he is now. If he'd seen Licnus – Segomarus – then he would've said. Oh, if it'd been anyone else – one of the family, his brother or his Uncle Quintus, for example – then he might have kept his mouth shut to protect them. But as far as he was concerned Segomarus was a stranger; he had no reason *not* to peach on him. So the logical assumption was that he was telling the absolute truth: he didn't see anyone, no one at all.' I paused. 'That is, not until you went in yourself, to wake your husband up, and found the body. Which of course can mean only one thing.' She hadn't moved; she could've been a statue, for all the reaction I was getting. 'You want to call him down, let me ask him again? Just to make certain?'

'No,' she whispered. 'No, that won't be necessary.'

'So,' I said gently. 'There was no early business appointment that your husband had forgotten about and that you had to wake him up to remind him of. When you went into the summer house he was still asleep, and alive. Which is when you stabbed him.'

'Yes.' I could barely hear the word.

'You want to tell me why, exactly? I mean, I can understand your basic reasons, but after all you had been married to the guy for twenty-odd years. That must've weighed, surely.'

She lowered her head. When she lifted it again, she looked me straight in the eye.

'I told you before,' she said. 'You're a Roman. You don't understand these things.'

'Try me,' I said.

'I loved my brother. I still do. It pulled the heart out of me twenty years ago when he disappeared so suddenly, and there hasn't been a day since that I haven't thought about him, wondering if he was alive somewhere. Then, three months ago, Tiberius was away on business, I was sitting here as I am now, and he walked in. I recognized him at once, despite the long hair and moustache; I'd have recognized him anywhere. He told me the whole thing, how after the revolt Tiberius had lied about him so that he'd be arrested, possibly even executed. And that he hadn't been the only one my husband betrayed.'

'You believed him? Just like that?'

'I'd had my suspicions. Oh, not where Licnus himself was concerned; I'd never have believed Tiberius was that rotten, or I'd have left him long ago. But the rest of it, the betrayals . . .' She stopped. 'The final months, before we left Augusta, were quite bad. Nothing was said as such, not directly, but the atmosphere was poisonous. I found I had no friends any more, not even acquaintances, and enough hints were dropped to show we weren't welcome and to suggest why. Quintus noticed it too. I faced Tiberius, asked him straight out whether there was any truth behind it, and he swore that there wasn't. He *swore*. He was my husband; what else was I to think but that he was telling the truth, and it was all a misunderstanding?'

I said nothing.

'So eventually we gave up and moved away, down here to Lugdunum. Oh, we kept the wine business on, or rather Quintus did: they'd nothing against Quintus as such, quite the reverse. He'd been no supporter of Florus, and made no secret of it at the time, but afterwards he'd spoken up in defence of those who were to the Roman authorities, even although it made him a suspect himself. That had got noticed. They're not bad people, the Augustans; they can make allowances.'

'But not in your husband's case.'

'No, and I agree with them. Some things you can't forgive and forget, ever: time makes no difference. I found out from Licnus that Tiberius wasn't the man I thought I'd married, not the kind of man I'd ever have contemplated marrying for one moment if I'd known what he was; he'd lied to me from the start, and the fact that we'd been together for over twenty years since then only made matters worse. I killed him, and I've no regrets. I'd do it again, gladly.' She took a deep breath. 'So. What happens to me now?'

'I don't know,' I said.

She frowned. 'What do you mean, you don't know? Valerius Corvinus, I killed my husband, I've admitted it, and you have the authority, as the emperor's representative, to do whatever you like with me. How can you not know?'

I'd been thinking about this ever since we'd left Augusta, and it seemed the best way to go about things. 'Just that,' I said. 'The decision's not mine to make. Like you say, I'm only the emperor's rep, not any sort of judge in my own right. My job, which I've done, is to find out the truth and report back to him. The rest's not my concern.'

She was staring at me. 'You're letting me go?'

'No, not at all. What happens to you, one way or another, is up to Claudius. After all, we already have a self-confessed killer, so as far as that side of things goes the case is technically closed. And you can't get a higher authority than the emperor himself. Me, all I can do is go back to Rome, give him the facts – all the facts, with no fudging – and let him decide where to take it from there. Which is what I'm going to do.'

She sat very still for a long time. 'Does Titus know?' she said, finally. 'That I killed his father?'

'Yes.'

'Did he say anything when you told him?'

'Only that he understood your reasons.'

'Not that he sympathized?'

'No. He said nothing else at all. You'd have to ask him that yourself.'

She nodded. 'Very well. Publius knows too, I think, although he hasn't said anything, or even hinted.'

Yeah. If I was right about the whole looking-through-the-window bit – and I was – then he'd have to know; would've known all along, from the very beginning. He was far from stupid, young Publius. And he was used to keeping secrets. 'You'll tell him?' I said. 'Straight out?'

'Yes, I will. I'll do it now; you have my word.' She stood up; I did, too. 'Thank you, Valerius Corvinus. You've been very . . . understanding. For a Roman.'

Well, I'd take that as a compliment, back-handed though it was. And I was glad, now, that I could go home with a clear conscience.

I still had a fair slice of sightseeing to look forward to, mind, particularly where Massilia was concerned: having been balked of what she viewed as her basic holiday ration of temples, public monuments, and antiquities on the way out, Perilla would no doubt insist on a double helping during the return journey. Even so, we'd be doing it without Smarmer in attendance this time around, and I was sure I could trade it off against a protracted tour of the wine-shops. After all, when Claudius and I did get round the table he'd expect a preliminary chat about the merits of the different local vintages. I was looking forward to trying more of the seafood, too.

We didn't go abroad much, the lady and I, and certainly not as pampered guests of the empire. We might as well enjoy ourselves.

AUTHOR'S NOTE

The revolt strand

The projected revolt of AD 42 is a complete invention of my own; however, the rationale behind it is, I hope, tenable. First of all, the Treveri were, even for Gauls, a problematic tribe right from the start: they put up a stiff fight against Caesar at the original conquest, staged a revolt a generation later, a second, together with the Aedui, in AD 21 (this was the Florus revolt) as a result of which they lost their free-tribe status, and a third in AD 70. Evidently, happy with their lot as provincials they weren't, during the first century, at least.

Second, the months preceding Claudius's invasion of Britain (which took place in AD 43, the year after the story closes) would have been the ideal time for a rebellion, particularly, as I suggest, if there were British agents around to foment it: as Balbinus says in the story, Gauls and Britons were basically one people, separated only artificially by history and politics, and Gauls already disillusioned with life as part of the empire would not – at least in their hearts – view its expansion across the Channel with any favour. A revolt at this point, however minor, might well have serious consequences where the invasion was concerned, particularly if it spread to other areas or if the German tribes across the Rhine chose to seize the opportunity to break the always-uneasy truce: the British campaign needed four legions (together with the auxiliary troops, about forty thousand men in all) with a fifth in reserve, and three of these came from the Rhine garrisons, which had a total strength of only eight. Safety margins, therefore, would have been extremely slim.

Towns in Gaul

Roman Gaul, although it corresponds in general to modern France, was a little larger: since its northern border was the

Rhine, it included what is now Belgium (hence the name of its
northernmost province, Gallia Belgica; the other two were
Lugdunensis, in the middle, and Narbonensis to the south) and
a slice of Germany. I've kept the original Roman names for the
towns (except for Vienne, whose Latin name Vienna might have
caused confusion), but you may be interested to know their
modern equivalents.

    Acunum – Anconne
    Aquae Sextiae – Aix
    Arausio – Orange
    Arelate – Arles
    Augusta Treverorum – Trier
    Burdigala – Bordeaux
    Caesarodunum – Tours
    Durocortorum – Rheims
    Gesoriacum – Boulogne
    Itius – exact site disputed (possibly Wissant), but another
        Channel port
    Lugdunum – Lyon
    Massilia – Marseille
    Moguntiacum – Mainz
    Valentia – Valence

Julius

Readers may find it odd – and perhaps annoying! – that a large
number of the Gallic characters in *Foreign Bodies* have Julius/
Julia as part of their name. Not my fault: because most Gauls
– at this point in time, at least – would have had their citizenship
(individual, or as one of a community) granted through, originally,
Julius Caesar, and after him the Julian emperors Augustus,
Tiberius (by adoption), and Gaius, by Roman custom their new
'family' name would be Julius as well. I'm afraid I rebelled
myself when I got to the merchant Tarbeisus: his citizen name,
Trebonius, was taken (totally spuriously, and without any logical
justification whatsoever) from Gaius Trebonius, one of Caesar's
lieutenants. Any Roman names buffs who got hot under the collar
about this will have to forgive me.

    One last (brief) note on Secundus's Gallic bowl. I've based

this on the famous Gundestrup Cauldron, found in a Danish peat bog at the end of the nineteenth century, which – although, as Secundus says, it is more typically Thracian in terms of technique than Celtic – remains one of the finest examples of ancient Celtic silverware in existence. I chose this because the ambiguity of the subject matter (is the scene I've described a human sacrifice, made for military reasons, or as Optima suggests connected with renewal/rebirth?) seemed to fit very well with the theme of the planned revolt.

I hope you enjoyed the book. Please, if you want to make any comments or ask a question, or if you simply have nothing better to do with your time, don't hesitate to get in touch through the website. Always a pleasure to hear from readers (well, usually, anyway . . .)

My very best wishes to you.
David Wishart

Lightning Source UK Ltd.
Milton Keynes UK
UKOW08f1600270417
300054UK00002B/31/P